MW01382694

AMANDA ROMINE
ANABEL UNRAVELED

To Rhonda -

ANABEL UNRAVELED

AMANDA ROMINE LYNCH

Thank you for all your love and support!

Amanda Romine Lynch

Anabel Unraveled

By Amanda Romine Lynch

Cover Design by Jesse S. Greever and Chad Thomas Johnston

ISBN: 1482392445

ISBN-13: 978-1482392449

For Carly

CONTENTS

Acknowledgements

I have been so blessed with the love and support of my family and friends. Without them, this book wouldn't exist.

To Jon, who didn't blink an eye when I informed him I wanted to quit my job and write a book, I appreciate your love and faith in me more than I can say.

To Carly Leotti, who has been with me for pretty much every step of the writing process—thank you. I love you.

To my parents, brother, and sister—thank you for always believing in me.

To Nicholas and Noah—thank you for sleeping so Mommy could work on her book.

To Chad Thomas Johnston—your enthusiasm for my writing and total willingness to help me means so much to me. You are a great friend, and Becki and Evie are lucky to have you.

To Jennifer Harris Dault, my fantastic editor—you are a rock star.

To Ian Makay—thank you for being a shoulder I could lean on, cry on, and take out my frustrations on.

And to the rest of the Dessert Islanders—Landra Graf, Jacqueline Wilson, Jennifer Luitweiler, and Liza Hawkins—thank you for your consistent love and support.

Chapter 1—Anabel

My name is Anabel Martin, and I am an orphan.

I can't say that. I shook my head and sighed, pivoting slowly in front of the mirror, taking in my hair, my legs, my dress. My blue eyes looked sullen in the mirror, and I wondered if nineteen was too old to be considered an orphan. Does it count if you've never known your mother, and your father was emotionally unavailable for your whole life?

"Stand up straight," I heard a voice say from behind me. I closed my eyes, ready for the lecture.

I turned and grimaced at my brother, Sam, who is more than twice my age. He studied me, taking in everything about my appearance. Being next to him, all stylish in his suit with his well-groomed hair, made me and my obnoxious curls feel wild and savage. "Standing up straight isn't going to hide it, Sam."

"No, but it's the best we can do for now." He came and kissed my forehead, and pulled me into a hug. "It will be okay, sweetie." Then he turned and said, "Meet me downstairs in five minutes, okay?"

He paused at the door. "You know, there are ways around this, Anabel. It's not too late."

I rounded on him. "If you suggest that ever again, I'll tell everyone. Those will be the first words out of my mouth, Sam. I promise you."

"Take it easy," he soothed. "I just wanted to remind you..."

I gave him a stiff nod, and he exited the room.

My name is Anabel Martin, and I ruined my brother's life.

The fact that Sam is treating me with such tenderness is wreaking havoc on my sense of right and wrong, and truthfully, if I were in his position, I don't think I would be behaving as wonderfully to him as he is me.

But then again, my brother is almost a saint, whereas I have a dark spot on my soul.

I sat down on my bed that wasn't really mine and stared at my shoes. They were some designer, Steve Madden, I guess. I had never bought my own clothes and proved to be a horror to my sister-in-law, who had been forced to spend time with me and fix me up with a wardrobe. Taking me shopping was the only thing that we had done together since I moved in with her and Sam, and I hadn't impressed her when I informed her that I did not know the difference between Calvin Klein and Ralph Lauren. When we had finally settled on the Gap, she had thrown her hands up in disgust and waited outside until I called her, needing the credit card.

She doesn't like me. I haven't been allowed outside much because nobody likes me due to the fact that I am the sole reason that my brother resigned from office. So far, my social interactions have included him, my sister-in-law, and the rotating bodyguards who all look the same and barely acknowledge me. Sometimes I see my doctor, but he has to make house calls, so those times are rare.

My name is Anabel Martin, and I am very much alone.

Alexis barged in. She's beautiful—gorgeous, really—and like my brother, also twice my age. She stared at me, judging, and then said, "You look okay, but you need some makeup."

"I don't know how to put it on," I mumbled.

She let out a frustrated noise which was a cross between a groan and a wail, and immediately attacked me with powder and eye shadow. I tolerated this invasion as best I could, but when she tried to assault me with an eyelash curler I pushed her away. "It's too much."

"Everyone does this, Anabel," she snapped. "You're ready. Grab your coat and go with Sam."

I glared back at her. "I think it's ridiculous you are making me wear a trench coat in September."

"Deal with it," she sniffed, and turned on her heel and headed toward the door. She paused to look at me and say, "Watch what you say, and whatever you do—"

"Do not talk to Jared Sorensen," I chorused with her. "As if I'd forgotten."

She nodded. "You don't want to hurt your brother any more than you already have, do you?"

"No, Alexis." I pulled the green coat around me.

"Have a good day then," she said crisply.

"Yes, Alexis." I wondered if she caught the edge of sarcasm, but she nodded her blonde head and left.

My name is Anabel Martin, and I hate my life.

I made my way down the stairs and Sam shot me a warm smile of approval. "You look lovely."

"Alexis fixed me," I announced. Flanked by Nate and Henry and their earpieces, we walked down the steps and got into the Lincoln Town Car.

The ride to the Capitol Building was a blur. It consisted of me staring at my shoes and my brother clearing his throat. Finally he began, "Look, Annie—"

"I know what you're going to say," I closed my eyes.

"I'm your brother, I have to."

"I wish you wouldn't." Maybe if I keep my eyes closed, this will go away.

"Try not to talk to him," he cautioned. "Nobody has gotten wind of what happened with you two yet, and I want to keep that under wraps as long as we can."

I opened my eyes and nodded, trying to keep my face as impassive as possible, even though my brother was lying. There were all sorts of rumors flying about the two of us. I stared out the window and swore to myself that I was not going to cry, because crying would probably result in Sam causing some sort of physical harm to Jared, and with his temper, that could include anything from punching him to disemboweling him. While that would be slightly entertaining to watch, it probably wouldn't be good for PR.

My name is Anabel Martin, and I am very bad for PR.

"So what are you going to say?" he asked, pulling me from my thoughts.

I managed a thin smile. "It's all I've been thinking about this morning. I guess it will just come."

The car sidled up in front of the Capitol Building. There were a million people there, with their eyes, cameras, and microphones all trained on our car. I looked at Sam, stricken. "You promised we would have a quiet entrance."

He sighed. "I'm sorry. I didn't want you to worry. We'll do this quick, okay? I just need you to put in an appearance and look normal. Look Annie, the rumors are that you aren't okay, and I just need you to smile at the cameras and play the game for me a little, please?"

I stared at him. Sam was the consummate politician: he always had a smile and a wave for the crowds, despite any inner turmoil. I was not similarly gifted. Still, I'd do just about anything for him—so I composed my face and nodded.

Sam looked at Nate, who muttered something into his mouthpiece and opened the door. I stepped out into the bright sunlight and immediately was mobbed. Desperately clutching Sam's arm, we walked through the masses of press people and TV cameras, and I smiled like a doll and ignored the barrage of questions bombarding us from every direction. I had no idea what anyone said to me, I merely gave the big plastic grin and stared straight ahead. I had to give Nate and Henry credit; somehow they navigated us through the mob in one piece. The hearing was thankfully closed to the press, and when the doors were shut behind us, I stared at my brother in disbelief. "Do you have to deal with this every day?"

He smiled at me, and it was genuine. "Well, one of the perks of resigning from office is not as many people are interested in me anymore."

"I disagree," I rejoined, mirroring his smile.

My name is Anabel Martin, and I am a phony.

"Excuse me for one second, okay?" I nodded at him, and he moved to talk to some guy in the back of the room. It was pretty much like the hearing rooms I had seen on TV: an empty table above all the others for the members of Congress, benches much like in a courtroom, and two tables in the front for testimony. I meandered down the aisle, looking at the chairs, the random people, until my eyes fell upon a familiar face, one that I hadn't seen in a long time.

She was sitting at a table in the front of the room, her long purple skirt falling demurely around her ankles. Her red hair was starting to go gray, I noticed. She looked soft, womanly, motherly, and I wanted nothing more than to throw my head onto her lap and cry my eyes out.

She was Marilyn Jessamyn, my nanny, governess, babysitter, and the closest thing to a mother that I had ever had. Her hazel eyes smiled up at me. "Anabel?"

"Miss Marilyn!" I shrieked, causing everyone else in the room to turn their heads and stare. But I didn't care. As she stood up, I sprang into her arms. "I'm so happy to see you!"

"Sweetheart, you don't need to call me 'Miss Marilyn' anymore." There were tears welling in her eyes. "You look gorgeous."

I smiled. "You're just saying that. It's very kind of you to lie."

"No, I'm serious. You're practically glowing, you look so lovely!" Although I stood a bit taller than she, she reached up and smoothed my hair. "I guess DC life is suiting you, huh?"

"I'm sorry I haven't been in contact with you," I lamented. "I haven't been allowed to talk to anyone. Sam and Alexis and all of their legal team are petrified I am going to say something wrong."

She frowned. "What could you possibly say?"

A lot, actually, but I feigned innocence. "I don't know, but every word that does come out of my mouth makes Alexis glare at Sam and hurl angry French curse words at me."

"Oh, my," she said, with laughter in her eyes.

"I wish I was making that up, I really do." I beamed at her. "It's incredible to see you! I'm surprised you are here though, they weren't letting in anyone but those of us testifying and immediate family—" And then it dawned on me. "You're here with Charlie, aren't you?"

"Oh honey, I wanted to tell you." She extended her hand, and I saw the thin gold band. "We got married!"

"That's wonderful," I managed, hugging her again. "Where is Charlie?"

"Right here," he said, coming up next to her. "Hello, Anabel."

"Hi Charlie," I said, feeling shy. "It's been a long time?" It came out as a question. I hadn't meant it to.

He pulled me to him, but I still felt awkward. I stepped back and offered, "I'm sorry, I don't know what's wrong with me. I'm really, really happy for the two of you."

They both grinned lovingly at each other, and I was then spared from further discomfort by one of Sam's many lawyers touching my elbow. "Miss Martin? They want you to sit over here."

I smiled at the two of them, hoping it didn't look as fake as it felt, and followed Mr. Benson over to one of the tables in the front. He seated me next to Sam, who touched my arm. "Are you okay?"

"Marilyn and Charlie got married," I told him.

"How do you feel about that?"

"Are you my shrink now? I feel great about it. Fantastic. My father just died, why don't we talk about that next?"

Sam looked hurt, and I instantly regretted it. "I'm sorry. I'm just on edge." I slumped back into my chair. "Please tell me that we're not sitting anywhere near that vile Jared Sorensen."

"I missed you too, Anabel."

Open mouth, insert foot.

"Get away from her, Sorensen," snapped Sam, rising from his chair.

"Back off, Sam," he said silkily. "I have no interest in upsetting your little sister." He backed away and took a seat at the farthest end of the table. I tried to not look at him, but through many furtive glances I couldn't help but take in his perfectly styled blonde hair, cool manner, and the suit that made him even better-looking than normal. My heart skipped a beat, and I scowled inwardly at myself. Now was not the time to lose my head. I'd lost enough to this man already. From then on, I kept my eyes focused on the floor, trying to calm the unsettling rage that was burning in my stomach.

My name is Anabel Martin, and I want Jared Sorensen to die.

A few more strangers wandered in, and then the members of Congress filed into their seats. Forgetting my resolve, I shot a sidelong glance at Jared, which he seemed to notice as he turned straightaway to focus on me. I averted my eyes and pretended to be concentrating on the table when Congresswoman Fischer brought the hearing to order.

There was a moment of tenuous silence, and then she began, "Ladies and gentlemen, welcome. So that we are all clear, these hearings are to discuss the murder of Jonathan Martin on April 27th on the Caereon

Storage Facility."

Oh no. DO NOT CRY. I took a steadying breath, and Sam put his arm around me.

"I do not know," Ms. Fischer went on, "what happened that night, but I am convinced that all of you have valuable information to present to the Committee. As the storage facility in Caereon is a government-run facility, the murder is a federal crime. While no charges have been filed against anyone here, it should be noted that anything you say in these hearings can and will be used against you in a court of law if the need arises. The testimony that all of you will be providing should take us back to your experiences on the island of Caereon. Leave out no relevant information."

She took off her glasses. "Anabel Martin, where are you?"

I raised my hand. Ms. Fischer glanced at me. "Your brother has requested we let you go first due to some health issues?"

I nodded. Jared cleared his throat and stared rather pointedly, but I looked up, glassy-eyed, at Ms. Fischer.

"Miss Martin. Please give your account of the events leading up to when Mr. Sorensen arrived on the island."

I took a deep breath. This was it. I caught Sam's eye, and he gave me a slight, encouraging nod. So I began, and I said the first thing that came to my mind: "My name is Anabel Martin, and it is a confirmed fact that I am a b—."

"Anabel!" gasped my brother. But the spattering of laughter around the hearing room gave me the courage to go on, and even Ms. Fischer looked amused. I slipped back into my former life, and thought about who I was back in April. I became that Anabel and was glad I could poke fun at myself now. I couldn't then, you see. I used to take myself way too seriously. I closed my eyes as I spoke, and was home, back on the island.

So here I am, living with my father, who—nine months prior—fired my nanny. She wasn't really my nanny anymore and rather had become a mother to me. I loved her, and my father took her away—and I hated him for it. Without Marilyn's influence, I have become cold. Heartless. I am alone and carry around a quiet anger that burns steadily and refuses to subside.

Don't get me wrong. Here, I have my uses. After all, I am the only female to traipse around Caereon Storage Facility, aside from Ida, who weighs 250 pounds, and Evelyn, who is old enough to be my grandmother, so I provide excellent eye candy to the hundred or so males who work here. Even though I consider the lower half of my body entirely too fleshy, and my bosom not ample enough, and I downright hate my hair, all of this was lost on the lonely men who probably while their nights away jacking off to pornographic magazines, or—and I shudder at this thought—images of me. It might seem that I'd be in a precarious situation here, knowing that the quantities of women are rather scarce, but all of them know better. You see, my father, Jonathan Martin, basically owns their souls during their stays on Caereon. One false move and they answer to my dad—which makes me wonder what he's doing to Kevin Miller right now.

Kevin had the misfortune of actually talking to me. For the record, I warned him it wasn't a good idea, so I take no responsibility for it. But—to my surprise—we became friends. Earlier this evening my father found the two of us curled up on a couch. Again, I refuse to accept any fault for this; rather, I blame it on my father, as I wouldn't be hanging out with Kevin if my father hadn't allowed him free time on the grounds for good behavior. But I digress. The point is that Jonathan was not happy about this at all. In between many vulgarities and columns of spit (my father has a lisp and stutters when he screams), he informed Kevin that he would in no way, shape, or form support his daughter's fornication with a convicted felon, and despite my many protestations of innocence, my father grabbed Kevin by the ear and hauled him into his office. They've been in there ever since. I've been waiting anxiously on a bench outside the rather massive (and, unfortunately, soundproof) heavy oak door, straining my ears, but I hear nothing. These circumstances are unfortunate, because as I sit here, I'm starting to realize that I was growing very fond of Kevin. He was the only companion I had who was near my age, was literate, and didn't stare at my chest all the time. I sat up straight. I had been deluding myself with Kevin's friendship for a while, but the problem lay much deeper. The fact was, I was sick of being here, and I needed out.

I suppose now is as good a time as any to explain what Caereon is and why I detest it so much.

You won't find Caereon on a map, but you wouldn't want to visit anyway. It's a tiny little island in the South Pacific that is often overlooked by any seamen who happen to pass by. From all appearances, it looks like a deserted island, overgrown by trees, brambles, and marsh.

But those of us who live here know better. The deserted island facade is the perfect hiding place for an extremely technologically-advanced socie—

No. Definitely NOT a society.

Caereon is a vault. We protect the most important assets that belong to the United States. On this small little island there is an enormous vault that is more highly protected than the Pentagon, the White House, or Fort Knox.

I made a sardonic smile at that. Much more so than Fort Knox.

Without Caereon, the United States as you know it would cease to exist. Your money would be valueless. You would be in debt with no shot at ever getting out. Consumerism and capitalism as they now are would be obliterated. I just think it's funny that a place so integral, so key to the very existence of that nation houses roughly 100 convicts, a situation that arose after the closing of several prisons. Before, we were just a vault; now, we're a vault and jail. Don't worry, the irony of the situation does not escape me.

I will give the cons credit, however. Many of them are quite brilliant. You see, when you commit a crime, there are three options. They can release you, they can kill you, or, if you're of the particularly twisted-yet-brilliant criminal variety, they ship you here.

Come to think of it, I'm really not sure why they sent Kevin here. He's smart, but not stellar. He's got a wry sense of humor but he lacks a certain quickness and clarity that marks the other fallen members of society who live here. Moreover, he's a decent person, and his crime was neither murderous nor cunning. He's just a doctor who euthanized a celebrity out of pity for her intense suffering. She was dying of a plethora of diseases and had begged him not to prolong her pain. He wasn't even her doctor; he was a gynecologist who struck up a friendship with the poor woman. Despite what I thought about assisted suicide, I couldn't help admiring Kevin. He put everything on the line—his job, his freedom, his life—for this woman.

Truth be told, Kevin's probably the best person I know.

The door to my father's office swung open and Kevin stepped out, his face ashen. He closed the door, shaking his head. His eyes fell on me. Neither of us spoke for a minute.

"I've gotten you in trouble, haven't I?"

He came and sat beside me. "That's not it at all."

"It is," I alleged. "My father cannot stand the idea of me actually enjoying myself."

"Stop it, Anabel. Besides, you knew that this would probably happen anyway. I shouldn't be here."

I looked at him, horrified. "They're not kicking you out!"

His face was grim. "Jonathan is recommending that I be placed into a secure facility."

"Kevin, no," I protested. "They can't. They wouldn't—"

"They can and they will," he said. His hand reached up and brushed a tear away from my eye. I hadn't realized it had fallen.

"I'll get you out," I vowed. "I'll get you to stay here. I'll arrange it—"

"There's no way Jonathan would go for that, first off. Secondly, how would you do it?"

"I have connections," I pointed out. I then looked at him, anxious. "You do want to stay with me, don't you?"

He grinned. "Of course I do, silly. Among other things, you're the best friend I've ever had." He kissed my forehead.

The moment was broken by someone clearing her throat. I looked up and saw Evelyn, the vile woman who ran our household affairs, glaring at me. "Yer father is wantin' to speak with you, Miss Anabel."

Kevin stood up. "I should be heading back to my bunk anyway. I'll see you later, Anabel. Goodnight, Mrs. Evelyn." He turned and slowly walked down the hallway, a defeated man.

I glared right back at Evelyn, the old bat. She turned away from me and bustled down the hallway, muttering in Polish. I slid off of the bench, squared my shoulders, and prepared for confrontation. My steps were bold, and I pushed past the door and marched over to my father's desk.

My father's office, like my father, was large, imposing, and just a tinge menacing. Gigantic bookcases lined the walls, filled with long-forgotten literature and lore. A picture window at the far end of the room provided light, and in front of that sat my father's desk. I stared at the back of a leather chair, which was turned to face the window.

"Hello, Daddy," I murmured.

The chair slowly swung around, an act that I somehow always felt was rehearsed, and I came face-to-face with Jonathan Martin. His hair had turned a deep silver, and his dark brown eyes peered at me over horn-rimmed spectacles. "Anabel." He gestured with his arm. "Have a seat."

I sat down and stared him in the eye. "What you're doing to Kevin is ridiculous, cold-hearted, and just plain mean."

He sighed. "I don't expect you to understand."

"Understand what? Kevin and I are just friends, Daddy. There was no 'fornication,' as you called it." I glared at him.

"Precisely my point. My daughter, friends with a convicted felon?"

I threw my hands up in the air. "Kevin is a doctor. He did what all doctors do, he helped a patient." I crossed my arms. "Besides, who else is there on this blasted island to be friends with besides convicts? You took Miss Marilyn away from me, isn't that enough?"

"You were too old for a governess. There was no sense in keeping her." He waved an impatient hand. "We're straying from the subject here."

I jumped up. "No, I think we're precisely on subject. Any time there is someone I can actually tolerate, you get rid of them!"

"Your social needs are adequately met," Jonathan intoned.

I scoffed. "By whom? I only see you when you're angry. Evelyn only speaks to me to scold or chastise, Ida disgusts me, and you barely let me see Charlie anymore. The men who work at the control tower are a nuisance, and you won't let me talk to the soldiers or the other workers." I flipped my hair in disdain. "So who is it that I socialize with? This I really must hear."

Before he could reply, there was a knock at the door and in stepped another man. While he was close to my father's age, the difference in the two men was striking. Unlike my father, this man was none too tall, and his face was not purple with rage. "Good evening, Jonathan," he stated, his voice calm. He then sent a smile my way. "Hi Annie."

I dashed to his side. "Charlie! Oh, Charlie, you've got to do something, my father has gone off the deep end once again—"

"Anabel," Charlie cut in, "will you let me have a few words with your father? Step out into the hall, I have something I wish to say to you afterward."

Only for Charlie would I comply. I bid my father a cool goodnight and then slid out of the room, leaving the door open a tiny crack so I could attempt to hear what was going on.

I made out a few mumbled formalities, and then Charlie began, "You can imagine why I came, Jonathan."

"Yes, my old friend," my father sneered, "I know you've come to criticize me, so I eagerly await it."

"Kevin Miller did nothing that deserves you throwing him off this island. He will waste away in a regular prison, you know that." Charlie's voice was sharp. "You're the one who insisted on bringing him here in the first place. You gave him a false sense of security, when the fact of the matter is you wanted him here for some pretty twisted reasons of your own."

He had brought Kevin here? That was interesting. I strained my ears to hear more.

"And what if Anabel had realized who she was dealing with? What then?" hissed my father.

"Anabel supports what Kevin did," Charlie remarked.

"Oh, does she now? You know, it's a good thing I got rid of Marilyn, before she instilled any more faulty morals in that girl!" he roared.

"That's not why you kicked Marilyn out, and you know it. Besides, Anabel's not exactly a girl anymore," retorted Charlie.

Oh good. Someone had finally noticed that, as I approached twenty years of age, I wasn't interested in dolls anymore.

A short pause ensued after Charlie's statement, and then I heard my father say in a voice that encouraged caution, "I don't know what you're talking about."

Charlie sighed. "You know exactly what I'm talking about, but that really doesn't matter now. The point is, something's got to be done in regards to your daughter, or you can be certain that Sam will get involved. Kevin was a distraction for her. What's going to occupy her mind now?"

"Forget Kevin. What does S-Sam have to do with anything?" he spat, losing his cool.

"He and Anabel are close, despite your wishes, and you know he will pull her out of here if he sees fit. She'd go, too." There was a pause, and then: "I don't have to remind you that his authority supersedes your own," finished Charlie.

"What exactly have I done that's so wrong? She is my daughter—I've taken care of her."

"All the same, news travels fast. When Sam found out about Kevin arriving here in the first place he mentioned to me that he had decided to send out Jared Sorensen, to evaluate the situation on the island. If you're kicking him off, I can only imagine the visit will be moved up. I don't even know if Sorensen knows he's going yet."

"S-Sorensen is a filthy, s-slimy—"

"Nonetheless, he is Sam's choice, and Sorensen will report back, and—"

"I see." Jonathan was curt. "I expect you to work on damage control. I will see you in the morning."

There was a shuffle of papers, and then Charlie walked out of my father's office. I caught his arm. "Charlie! What on earth—"

"Annie, I'm sorry," he apologized, sounding weary, "but there's a lot going on that you don't understand." He kissed my cheek. "I'll see you tomorrow."

"But what did you want to say to me?"

"It doesn't matter now."

"What on—"

He stopped me. "I can't help you, love." After staring at me long and hard, he moved briskly down the hall.

Then I made up my mind. I didn't care if I would be waking him up at an ungodly hour. He loved me. I needed some answers.

So, I called my brother.

Chapter 2—Jared

"Jared, I have something I need you to do for me," Sam announced over the telephone.

"I gathered that," I muttered, rubbing my eyes. "It's 4 a.m., Sam. Somebody better be dead."

"If it makes you feel any better, I've been up for over an hour," he said with aplomb. "I need you to come down here, now."

"Fine," I grumbled. Last Night's Girl stirred in bed next to me. I guessed she was not going to be happy when I told her she had to leave. "Will you at least tell me what this is about?"

"My sister," he said. Then he hung up.

"You don't have a sister," I said to the dial tone. Then I slammed the phone down. "Great," I moaned.

The blonde next to me stirred. "Is everything okay, baby?" she simpered.

"No. You have to go. I'll call you a taxi."

She sat up. "You're kidding me, right?"

"I have to go to work," I got out of bed. "Now, I can call you a taxi or you can leave on your own. I don't care which one, but either way, I want you gone by the time I get out of the shower."

She stared at me, and then started getting dressed. I watched her, somewhat concerned she might do something violent, but she picked up her heels and then slammed the door so loudly that it shook in its hinges.

Somehow I didn't think we would be getting together again. I couldn't even remember her name. Cathy? Caroline? Something with a C. I locked the door behind her and jumped into the shower, trying to shake the fog I was in. It was all a blur as I showered, dressed, went downstairs, and hopped in the car.

"Morning, Jared," called Daniel, the driver, cheerful as ever.

I stared at him. "Why am I up right now, Daniel?"

"I would guess that's something between you and the President."

"I would guess it is," I sighed.

I had a great job. I did. I worked when I wanted, most of the time, and was very, very good at it. The problem was that I worked for my best friend. It had been great when he had been Speaker of the House. He was high profile, sure; but not to where he was calling me at all hours of the night. He did his thing, and I cleaned up the messes that always arose along the way. Every politician, I assured myself, had someone who did that for them. The ones who didn't weren't re-elected.

Then, two years ago, Air Force One had crashed, killing the president. A day later, as they were about to swear him into office, the Vice President suffered a fatal heart attack. As a consequence, Sam Sallinger had reluctantly stepped into the role. I doubted he had ever wanted to be president—despite the aspirations of his wife—and it was now an election year. He hadn't been elected, and his opponent was trying to play this. Still, Sam had maintained a high approval rating and was looked on as a national hero for guiding the country through a tragedy.

I had no doubt he would win. He also kept his nose clean, and I was there to get rid of the times that he didn't.

All the same, I felt disturbed about being called in at this hour.

I went into the Oval Office, and Sam didn't even look up. "Good morning," he said, staring down at a file.

I seated myself. "So what is it this time?"

He pushed a photograph toward me, and I picked it up. The girl in it smiled widely for me. She had brown hair, a nice enough face, and she looked really, really...young.

"So what, is someone saying that this is your kid? What do you want me to do?" I grinned at him. "Don't tell me that Sam Sallinger actually has a blemish on his squeaky clean past?"

"No, not as bad as that, but not good. She's my sister," he confided.

"She looks sixteen! Your mom is way too old to have a kid this age."

"She's nineteen," he replied. "And you've never met my mom."

"Yes, I have," I retorted. "That's how we met, in case you forgot. My dad worked for your parents. Kristin loves me."

"Kristin's not my mother," he admitted, keeping his eyes downcast.

"Look, I don't have time for this. I'm adopted."

I almost fell out of my chair. "You're serious?"

He nodded.

"How did this never come out before now? I can't believe you never told me. Sam, we've known each other since I was five!"

"I wasn't supposed to tell anyone," he replied. "My mom—my real mom—died a few years ago, and she charged me with taking care of my sister, whose picture you're staring at."

"She doesn't look a thing like you, except for the hair. She looks like—"

"It doesn't matter," he cut me off. "Here's the deal. Anabel—my half-sister—is Jonathan Martin's daughter."

"That scumbag has a daughter?" I asked. "I get it. You're sending me to Caereon?"

He nodded. "There's a situation with my sister. You see, Anabel used to have a babysitter, whose name was Marilyn Jessmyn. Marilyn kept her perpetually busy, but her father fired the woman."

"Why?"

"From what my sister tells me, her father was in love with Marilyn, and Marilyn was in love with Jonathan's second-in-command. Apparently Jonathan became overcome with his feelings and had decided to tell Marilyn that he'd been in love with her for years and years...and he walked in on her and Charlie."

"Oof."

"Yes. And let's face it, Jonathan's not known for having a good temper. So Marilyn was sacked. Anabel tried to stow away on the helicopter, to no avail."

"Got to give her credit," I acknowledged. "But Jonathan's not your father. He's much too young." I studied the picture again. Sam and Anabel had a similar smile.

"No, he isn't," Sam affirmed. "Let's keep the focus on her, okay? She just called me about an hour ago. She's miserable and lonely, and I've been trying to get her out of there for years, but it's very complicated."

"I can see that. So you want a report?"

"Yes, detailing everything you see. Check up on Jonathan, too. I like to keep him on his toes, even though he does a fantastic job running the place." He glanced at his watch. "Look, we don't have a lot of time. I need you to leave tomorrow."

"I have Caps tickets, Sam."

"Not anymore, you don't," he ordered. "We'll fly you to Los Angeles, and you will go from there to Maui. From Maui you will be leaving on a freighter, and from the freighter, a helicopter will take you to the island."

"I guess I better go pack," I stood up.

"You should also know that Anabel is not in a good mood right now. She had made a friend with an inmate, and he has been banned from the island."

"From what I understand about the people housed there, I can't believe she was allowed to talk to one of them."

Sam took off his glasses and looked at me. "She wasn't. It was a very unfortunate circumstance. Anyway, you should know my sister's temper rivals Jonathan's."

"I look forward to meeting her then," I noted, walking toward the door.

"One last thing," he called.

I turned.

"She's my sister. You know better." He didn't look up, but I knew what he meant.

"She's a kid, Sam. I definitely know better."

***

Ms. Fischer turned to me. "Tell us about when you first got to Caereon."

So it begins. "Well, I left right after that conversation with President Sallinger, and when I arrived on Caereon, Anabel and I were thrust together a lot, mostly as a ploy by her father to prevent me from doing a proper investigation of the premises. I do not think he was aware, at the time, that I had been sent there to investigate her."

Ms. Fischer leaned forward. "Why don't you start off by describing your relationship with Miss Martin?"

Anabel squirmed in her seat. Sam watched her, concerned. He hated me, and every glance he sent my way was filled with a cold fury that I had never seen on his face before. I was doing really well. The girl who used to adore me and my former best friend both could care less whether I lived or died. Still, I smiled and said something that I knew would make both of them even more uncomfortable.

"I didn't know what to say to Anabel sometimes. The truth is, I didn't know what to say to her the majority of the time, especially when she thought that she loved me," I revealed, making eye contact with her. She shrank back in her seat, and the damage was done.

Sam looked hard at her. "He's not serious, right? That was for show, to throw off your father. You didn't really love him?" It was more of a statement than a question.

Anabel sat there motionless, her face devoid of emotion. I had never seen her like this, not even right before we were rescued. The Anabel Martin I knew was always warm and engaging. I wanted to shake her and bring her out of it. But I knew better. I had ruined her life and she would never trust me again. Not that I faulted her for it. We'd been in the same room for only a few hours, and every word out of my mouth was hurting her.

I was a jerk. That was what they paid me for, right?

***

The first time I saw Anabel was that day I stepped off the helicopter and onto Caereon. It had been a long journey, but I had reanimated at the prospect of meeting her. It had been hard for me to stomach that Sam had a sister—especially one that was more than twenty years younger than he was. She was there on the helipad, standing next to Jonathan. She was a sight, though. It was windy, so her hair was blowing all over the place and her skirt was climbing to dangerous levels above her knees. My eyes flicked from her (still no glimpse of the face, hidden by all of her hair) to Jonathan, who was approaching me. You would have thought that he was nearly seventy by his way of walking, but I knew better. Jonathan wasn't much past fifty, and his daughter...well as I'd said to Sam, was a kid—a kid who I was supposed to babysit and at the same time keep my distance from.

It was the most nonsensical assignment I'd ever had.

At dinner I got a good look at her. She didn't look anything like

Jonathan. Her bright blue eyes were inquisitive, her smile alluring, and (from what I could tell) her figure wasn't too bad either. You couldn't help but feel bad for her, as she looked out of place in the odd grouping that consisted of her father, the head of security, Jonathan's assistant, and a couple of older ladies. Doing some quick calculations, there was at least a fifteen year age gap between her and anyone else in the room. Studying her further, I still didn't see any resemblance to Sam—who was it she looked like? That was driving me crazy—and it wasn't until she started talking that I realized she shared the same shrewd intelligence that characterized her brother.

"Miss Martin," I began, "I'm curious. It must be a boring existence for you on this island. What do you do all day?"

Anabel stared into my eyes. She had a very disconcerting gaze. "I study a fair amount," she replied. "When I leave the island—" and here was a pointed look at her father—"I would like to study English literature and maybe go into library science. I was on a rigorous course of study until my father fired my instructor." The bitterness in her voice was overpowering, and it almost made me chuckle. She wasn't one for subtlety. "When I'm not doing that, there's always something to do around here. Sometimes I help Charlie with the data and information, and—"

"Our Annie is quite the bookworm," interjected Charlie, his hand lingering on Anabel's shoulder. "If you are ever at want for reading material, Mr. Sorensen, you should see Miss Anabel's library." Anabel did not look pleased at this suggestion, which I took some twisted pleasure in. Still, I was incredulous.

"She has a library?"

She nodded. "My personal one. My father has a much larger one, but I have a small one with my book collection adjacent to my bedroom."

"You must show me later, Miss Martin," I smiled at her.

She looked uninterested, but nodded. "I'm getting tired of this 'Miss Martin' routine. My name is Anabel. Understood, Jared?"

That was when I decided that I liked her. Here was someone who I could at least count on to give her real opinion. It was a refreshing change from Washington. I answered her question with a curt nod, but thought to myself, All right, Anabel. You and I are going to be friends.

***

After dinner I asked her to show me around. Jonathan Martin's place is practically a castle, and since we were on an island in the South Pacific, I figured I might get some time on the beach. That particular evening, however, Anabel wanted to stick to the house, which was fine with me—as it was, I had a long trip over there. She didn't seem to want to walk next to me, keeping her pace just above mine, no matter how much I increased my step. Watching her move, a slight wiggle in her hips, caused me to lose focus and stare at her.

"What do you like to read?" she asked, shaking me from my thoughts.

"Why do you ask?"

She turned and rolled her eyes. "You asked to see my library. I was merely curious as to what you liked to read." She quickened her pace again.

I decided to give her a surprising answer. "Byron," I called.

Her steps came to a halt. She turned to me with an amused glance. "You read poetry?"

"Stranger things have happened," I offered.

She still looked unimpressed. "Are you a fan of the Romantics then?"

"They were much less depressing than the Victorians," I replied.

She smirked, and I could tell she was trying not to laugh. Then she flung open a door. "This is my library," she proclaimed.

I was floored. Never before had I seen such a collection of books. Bookcases were wall to wall, with patterned rugs over the stone floor. Two armchairs sat in front of a blazing fire.

"Anything you don't find in here, well...you'll find in my dad's library, but it's all the way on the other side of the building and I don't feel like walking over there."

"Have you read all of these?"

She grimaced. "One gets bored." She flipped her hair over her shoulder. "Surely you don't expect me to hang around with Jonathan all day?"

I laughed, letting my guard down. That left me unprepared for when she pushed a strand of hair out of her eyes and glared at me. "Why are you here, Jared?"

"What do you mean?"

Again, she smirked at me. "Come off it. I know you're here for some other reason than to pay a visit to the island." She flopped into a chair. "It's not exactly the most happening place. Did my brother send you?"

I wasn't going to lie to her. "Yes, Sam sent me. He's concerned about you."

"He must be," she remarked. "He doesn't normally share the fact that we're related, but you knew it, didn't you?" She tilted her head. "I was a bit of a shock to my sister-in-law, I can assure you."

She had trapped me. I improvised. "Well, he brought me into his confidence two days ago. He sent me here because he thought I was the one to get the job done."

"Oh?" queried Anabel. "And what job is that, exactly? I mean, my father thinks you're a snake, and Charlie spent the first part of my day warning me to watch my tongue around you. I'm not even kidding," she continued, taking in my stark surprise. "Jonathan went on and on about what a horrible person you were, and I think if he had the resources, he would have had me fitted for a chastity belt then and there. So what's the deal, Sorensen? Why does everyone think that you're the big bad wolf?"

I cleared my throat. "I don't have the best reputation in DC."

"And why is that?"

"I have a lot of girlfriends." There was no point in evading her.

"I bet you do." She uncrossed and recrossed her legs, and I really needed to not watch her do that. Your best friend's *sister*, I scolded myself. Anabel was only nineteen, and I had to remind myself that she was still practically a girl.

But looking didn't hurt, right? "So will we be spending more time together?" I asked her.

She sighed. "Probably not. I don't care much for other people. I'm fairly self-absorbed."

At least she was honest. She was smiling at me, though, with the bright eyes, so I took it that she might deign to tolerate my presence.

Anyway, the conversation ended well. I think Anabel was starting to like me, despite her cool demeanor. We agreed to meet the next morning after breakfast and take a tour of the facility. She suggested that I should bring my walking shoes, and I looked forward to my time alone with Miss Martin.

How could I have known things would have turned out the way that they did?

"Alright, that's enough for today," Ms. Fischer announced. "This hearing will reconvene next Monday." She banged her gavel and they filed out of the room.

I looked at the floor, figuring that I would just wait for everyone else to leave. I had hoped to avoid the two people at the end of the table the most and I was certain that Sam would not allow Anabel to talk to me.

But somehow she eluded her brother's grasp and came to stand before me, scowling. "Looking didn't hurt, right? You're such a pig." She let out a brittle laugh. "But hey, at least I'm honest, right? I love this revisionist history, Jared. It's classic."

I met her eyes, but what could I do? She had every right to be mad.

"Is there anything I can say?" I asked her.

"No," she pronounced, and then Sam was at her side.

"What are you doing?" he hissed at her.

"Leaving. With you," she responded. As they left I heard her say to him, "So what exactly do these Congress-people have to do that's more important than solving Jonathan's murder? I can't believe we have a whole week before we come back. I mean, seriously! This is why people whine about government, Sam!"

I almost smiled. At least she still called it like she saw it.

Chapter 3—Anabel

The week passed by in relative tranquility. I spent the bulk of my time reading and taking walks when nobody was looking. I was getting lazy and fat, not being on the island where I had to walk everywhere. I felt restless and had a fair amount of wanderlust. Nearly every day I proposed an excursion; I had been here for over four months and had never ventured into a single Smithsonian Institution. My brother protested he was too busy; Alexis was constantly gone at some charity function or on the phone with her nanny about the children, who had been removed to Martha's Vineyard while we dealt with the fallout of, well, me existing. So in vain I begged the bodyguards, but they refused to go anywhere not authorized by Sam.

Sam at least acted like he felt bad.

"I'm sorry, Annie," he offered in an attempt to console me. "But the press wants to talk to you, and we're in a delicate place right now. You don't have the coaching to handle this sort of situation."

"What if I wore a disguise?" I whined. "Sam, this is so unfair. I have a case of cabin fever so severe that...that..." I trailed off.

He raised an eyebrow, and I knew he was getting annoyed at me. "You can't tell me this is worse than where you were before. All you did was complain and swear up and down that if I got you off of the island, you'd never ask me for anything again. I held up my end of the bargain."

"I just didn't think I would be going from one prison to another," I lamented.

"This will soon be over, and you can do whatever you please," he snapped. He turned away, but over his shoulder came, "I expected better of you, Anabel."

After that I felt so terrible I maintained an aura of obedience for the rest of the week.

Before I knew it, it was Monday again and I was in the car with Sam. "You're quiet today, Anabel," he remarked.

I stared out the window. "I'm just not looking forward to this, that's all."

He cleared his throat. "I'm sorry about the other day; I know you are probably a little stir-crazy."

I cracked a grin. "Oh Sam, I know you're just trying to protect me." When he answered in the affirmative, I said, "Just remember that Jonathan also said he was trying to protect me."

He colored, and we finished our car ride in silence.

When we got into the hearing room, I took my seat at the front and waited impatiently for the members of Congress to arrive. When they did, and Ms. Fischer had called us to order, I raised my hand.

"Miss Martin?" she acknowledged.

"Ma'am, I really would like to take charge in handling any of your questions about my relationship with Mr. Sorensen. I feel that he is imagining things that I may have said, and he is extremely misguided in purporting that I had any supposed regard for him."

"Objection, your honor," Jared interrupted. "She was completely in love with me."

I let out a dramatic sigh. "Yes, Jared, of course I was. By the way, this isn't a courtroom." The room filled with laughter, and Jared looked almost embarrassed. I stood up. "Ms. Fischer, here's what really happened."

"So, Jared and I met up the next morning at seven. I had spent the night unable to sleep, visions of Kevin haunting me. I hoped nothing terrible had befallen him, but the fact was, I had watched a lot of specials on maximum security prisons. I had overheard Charlie mention to Evelyn that Kevin was sent to ADX Florence, and a quick perusal on the internet made me horrified. I knew what happened there, and the anxiety caused me to toss and turn for hours.

"What did I think of Jared? Well, I wasn't impressed at our initial encounter, but Sam had sent him, and I trusted my brother's judgment. I know that I haven't exactly been a huge presence in my brother's life, but we had become close—despite the thousands of miles that separated us. After the death of our mother, Sam had gone out of his way to make sure that I was tolerably happy on the island, and I appreciated it a great deal. After all, I'm a lot younger than he is, and Sam had never let me down before. Therefore, I had every reason to believe that Sorensen's presence on the island was a sign that things were going to improve for me. I did not think that things could get any worse.

"Anyway, so Jared and I met up in the front hall, and we went outside. It was a bright, sunny day, and we walked along the outer wall of the storage facility. It's beautiful there, you can really see the ocean, and a lot of conversation is drowned out by the crashing of waves against the shore. To be honest, I had wanted that—I was starting to realize that I was uncomfortable talking to Jared. I couldn't explain why to myself, exactly. I think part of it was he was so unlike everyone else around me. We walked for about an hour and a half, neither of us saying much. He turned to face me at several points, but I avoided his eyes. It was starting to get hot, and a few beads of sweat exploded onto his forehead. I had taken care to wear plenty of sunscreen and a hat, and wasn't all that bothered, but I felt a twinge and thought I shouldn't make him suffer.

"Do you want to go back?" I yelled.

He shook his head. "Why? Would you talk to me then?"

I stared at him. "It's too loud to talk out here!"

"Then why did you bring me?"

I shrugged. "You wanted to see the place?"

He then grabbed my arm and leaned into my ear. "I wanted to get to know you, Anabel."

You see, this put me in an awkward position. I had been, up to that moment, extremely sheltered in terms of my sexuality. Miss Marilyn had taught me the facts of life, but, living on an island like that, well...there wasn't much opportunity for me to...explore it, per se. I had never been attracted to any of the convicts on the island. I mean, the closest thing would have been Kevin, and I thought of him much like I did my own brother. Which was why, when Jared drew me close to him, I felt something that I had only felt when lusting after movie stars. His husky voice set my hair standing on end, and his breath tickled at my throat. I pulled away from him, but the truth was, I wanted to feel that way again.

It felt good, for lack of a better word.

I faced him, staring into his eyes. He couldn't see mine, as they were hidden by my sunglasses. I reached out and grabbed his hand, and led him away from the roaring surf. We walked for about fifteen minutes until we came to one of the small cottages along the coastline. Sometimes when we had visitors, we let them stay in one of the cottages if they felt uncomfortable staying in the fort.

I couldn't blame them. It was full of criminals and, on top of that, my father was there.

I should point out that I loved my father, but ever since I turned eighteen his obsession with me had grown fanatical. He had done everything he could to prevent me from leaving. However, we barely spoke anymore, and if we did we just screamed at each other. The loss of Miss Marilyn had hit me hard, and I pined for her daily. It should also be understood that I knew I was taking a risk showing Jared the cottage, as it would probably send Jonathan into another rant about my chastity. Going there alone? With a man? I could hear the impending tirade already. I was feeling reckless, however; and with all sorts of new sensations coursing through my body, I decided to be bold.

Typing in the passcode, I unlocked the door and led Jared in to the sitting room. I sat down on the nearest chair, took off my sunglasses, and stared hard at him. "So. What do you want to know about me?"

I've always had a way of filling people with unease, a skill which I attribute to years of living in relative isolation. For his part, Jared seemed uncomfortable as he lowered himself onto the chair. "Anabel," he began.

"Jared," I replied.

"I shouldn't have grabbed you like that back there, I'm sorry." But the way he said it, he didn't seem sorry.

"It's okay. I'm a big girl. I can handle it." I hoped to sound coy, but it rang false in my ears, and it caused him to look even more uncomfortable.

There was silence, and then, "You're just a kid."

I looked at him for a moment. "I'm assuming that you came to that clever deduction on your own." I took off my hat. "I thought that there was something that I could help you with."

He attempted a grin. "You must know why I am here."

"I would guess that it's because I woke up my brother in the middle of the night to whine about how rough my life is and how Daddy never lets me go out with the boys," I lamented. "What time was it over there when I called Sam? 2 a.m.?"

Jared snorted, and I continued. "I'm surprised that my father let me go show you around. But I have some theories on why he did it."

"Oh really?" Jared looked entertained. "What are those?"

I leaned forward and lowered my voice conspiratorially. "Well, Jonathan hates me, so it can't be because he wants me to have any fun. So, Option Number One is that he's doing something terrible in the facility, and he doesn't want you to find out, so he sent me to distract you while he covers up whatever it is. However, he's just not like that. He's pretty straight when it comes to how he runs his ship, which leads me to Option Number Two." I sat back and continued, "He wants me to distract you from looking into everything that happened with Miss Marilyn, and why he won't let me leave."

Jared looked puzzled. "What did that have to do with anything?"

"Miss Marilyn was my babysitter / teacher, although Jonathan liked to call her my 'governess.' Anyway, she wanted me to go to college in the States, which made perfect sense to everyone involved—except for Jonathan. I took the appropriate standardized tests, I applied to several schools, and then my dear father decided he didn't want Marilyn here anymore, and so he fired her. She was the closest thing that I had to a friend here, and she really loved me. She had sacrificed any sort of a normal life to take care of me, something that I appreciate much more now that she is gone. After Jonathan got rid of her, he pulled me into his office and explained that he didn't want me leaving because I wouldn't do well in an 'alien environment,' as he called it. He said that I didn't have the social skills necessary to survive in a co-ed school, and I would probably wind up raped and murdered in a gutter," I finished with gusto. "My father has a peculiar obsession with my sexual morality. This is why he got rid of Kevin. He said that he wouldn't allow his daughter to 'fornicate' with a convict, even though what we were doing was the furthest possible thing from fornication. Unless that word means something different in that 'alien environment' that I've never been exposed to."

Jared started laughing. "You're pretty funny."

"It keeps me sane," I replied.

"So there was nothing going on with you and this Kevin guy? I don't mean to pry, but Sam did mention he didn't have the whole back story." He leaned forward, and I couldn't help but notice how nice his smile was.

I shook my head. "No. I mean, he was interested in me, I guess, but I really just viewed him as my friend. I cared about him very much, but like all people I care about, Jonathan took him away. As a consequence," I continued, "if you decide that you want to be friends with me, I suggest you tell me so I can pretend to be uninterested so my dear father doesn't decide to ship you off to a maximum security prison."

Jared shuddered. "Is that what happened to Kevin?"

I nodded.

He leaned back in his chair. "So what are you saying? Do you want to be my friend?"

I laughed. "Well, I don't have a lot of options, and you'll at least amuse me until you leave." I stretched my legs out onto the ottoman. "How long are you planning to stay?"

"Until the job is done," he declared.

It occurred to me that my hair must look incredibly disheveled. I grabbed my bag and began fishing through it for a comb. "What is it that you do for Sam, anyway?"

"I'm a lawyer," he began, easing back into his chair, "but really what I do is damage control for Sam. I handle the press a lot of the time, or I go and investigate situations before they become too questionable—that sort of thing."

My fingers clasped around the comb, and I drew it out and went to work. "Doesn't his press secretary do that?"

"Yes, but my job is to take on jobs that the press secretary shouldn't be seen at."

I smiled. "Like me?" I paused and met his eyes. I was getting that weird feeling again, and I tried to push it out of my head. "Don't answer that. I know that I'm a deep, dark secret. Would you like something to drink?" I stood up and brushed my skirt out. "Usually there's something down here, Jonathan makes sure to keep it stocked in case we have visitors." I moved toward the kitchen. "So are you and Sam friends?"

"I consider him my best friend," he admitted, sounding rather genuine.

"Tell me about his wife. I've only spoken to her on the phone a couple of times, and she doesn't really seem all that friendly."

"She isn't," he replied. "If it's all the same to you, I'd rather not discuss her."

Startled, I stammered, "Okay." I was rummaging through the fridge when I heard Jared mutter something.

"I'm sorry, I didn't catch that," I turned so I could look at his face.

"You can't expect me to do this."

"Come again?"

"Look, Anabel, you're nice and all, but I can't do this cat and mouse thing with you."

"Excuse me?"

"Whatever the game you're trying to play with me is, I suggest you knock it off."

I stared at him, defiant. "What do you want, Jared? You know, I'm getting ready to call my brother and ask him why on earth he sent you here." I lowered my voice. "I Googled you, you know."

He looked amused, which annoyed me. "You did? And what exactly did you find?"

"I read about how you're the defense attorney from hell, how nobody wants to go up against you—and you've kept a lot of vile people on the streets instead of behind bars where they belong."

"So what?" he asked.

"So," I continued, my temper rising, "I think you're slime, and I don't know why my brother would associate with you, anyway."

He raised his eyebrows. "Okay."

"Now that we're straight," I said coldly, "I'm still unclear as to what you want from *me*. Care to share?"

He laughed. "I'm here to make sure nothing bad happens to you, Anabel. Your brother doesn't like how possessive Jonathan's gotten over you, and he wanted me to assess the situation. If necessary, we'll pull you out of here. If you make me mad, I'll recommend you stay."

I glared at him. "You would really do that out of spite?"

"Those are the breaks, babe." He stood up. "I have seen plenty of spoiled brat children much like you who expect the world to be handed to them. Just because you're Sam Sallinger's sister, don't think that everyone is going to bow down and worship you."

Is that so? "I think we're done here."

"Retract your claws, Princess," he replied. "I see no reason why you and I can't get along."

"Why is that?"

"You're not a bad looking girl. At least my trip won't be a total waste."

Chapter 4—Jared

Anabel was interrupted by her brother's scoffing. "You've got to be kidding me," he said, glaring at me. "If I had any idea that you would have been trying to flirt with my barely legal sister that early in the game, I would've yanked you out of there and you would have been careerless faster than—"

Anabel cleared her throat. "Enough, Sam. What's done is done."

I had actually gotten to the courthouse early that morning so I could wait and watch Anabel get here. I hadn't seen her in almost five months, and I wondered how she was holding up, if she was spending her days pulling out her hair (a nasty habit she had), if she was getting on with Alexis (who I was sure hated her), and how someone like her, who had lived in such utter seclusion, was adjusting to life in these United States…

If nothing else, it should be noted that I do care about her. I adore her, truth be told.

I did something most regrettable to her, and I doubt that she will ever forgive me. Again, I don't blame her, especially with how terrible I was to her on the first day of these hearings.

She's talking again, relaying our flirtation in the beach house. She calmed down, got me some ginger ale, and we chatted some more. And then I started to back off. I shouldn't have lost my cool earlier, but there was something about her that aroused my temper. In her artless manner she began to open up to me and verify the things that Sam suspected. She was miserable and lonely. She had absolutely nothing to do during the day. Jonathan ignored her, and Anabel was suffering from his neglect. I noticed the desperation that filled her voice, which she tried to cover up with jokes. More and more, I vowed to get her out of this situation. She was endearing, and you couldn't not care about her—I was trying really hard not to do so, but she was tearing away at my resolve.

"Can I ask you something?"

"You already did," she replied. "But you can ask me another question if you so desire." Her eyes brightened.

"How are you and Sam related? Because I know Jonathan's not his father, he's much too young."

"Ahhhh," she said, "you want to know *that* story—but wait." She looked at me, eyes beginning to fill with distrust. "I thought you already knew about all that."

"I've heard bits and pieces," I replied. "But I'll level with you, Anabel. Sam has always been known to me as Kristin Sallinger's son. It's embarrassing to not know the particulars of your closest friend's life."

She raised her eyebrows. "Fair enough," she acknowledged with a smirk. "At least you're honest. Okay, so Sam and I share the same mother, the actress Cassidy Carmichael."

That's why she looked so familiar. Anabel and Cassidy shared the same eyes and the same hair color. Unlike Cassidy, however, Anabel was much taller, her figure much slighter—Cassidy had been rather voluptuous in her day. "But Sam's a Sallinger, not a Carmichael—are they the same family?"

She stared at me again.

"Please? I can't go back to your father so ill-prepared. What if he realizes, as you so cleverly have, that I am a fraud?"

She laughed then. "Flattery will get you everywhere, Mr. Sorensen. Well, Cassidy became pregnant with Sam at a young age—I think she was only fifteen. However, she was a cousin of Kristin Sallinger, and Kristin had found out that she couldn't have any children." The Sallingers were a wealthy oil family, and had risen to power in politics. "So, Kristin, who was happily married, agreed to adopt the baby and allow Cassidy visitation. From what I understand she loved Sam very much, and when she became famous and wealthy as an actress she tried to get him back—only to have Kristin guilt trip her, and then she realized it would fare better for Sam if he was a Sallinger, and an heir to the fortune and good name."

"You're nineteen. How old is Sam, again? Forty-two or forty-three?"

"He's forty-three, now," she replied, "the youngest president in office." She looked away. "So Cassidy got married to Jonathan when she was in her early thirties. She had me a few years later, and Jonathan's a bit younger than she was."

"They seem like such an unlikely pair," I commented, rubbing my forehead. "In all of Cassidy's movies she's so vibrant and funny; Jonathan just walks around like an old man."

Anabel nodded. "Well, he's been under a great deal of stress. He's only been like this in the past few months. I guess though, she was attracted to him because he provided stability. You know, a government worker with a level head. Especially since she never saw Sam's father again. From what I understand, mostly from what Sam has told me, she and my father were very happy together—at first. Of course, after she had me she got bored—he bullied her into quitting her acting career and being a stay-at-home mother, which was very hard for her. It's hard to go from being constantly in the spotlight to living in some place named Mclean, which I guess is outside of the District of Columbia?" I nodded, and she continued, "So this is the part where the story gets sad. One night, Jonathan came home and found her in bed with another man...so he took me and left. I was maybe two, at that point. Anyway, the Caereon position was open, and Jonathan just wanted to get as far away from my mom as he could, so we have been here ever since." She tucked her legs under herself, and sighed wistfully. "I never saw my mom growing up, and of course you know that she passed away about two years ago."

"I read the headlines—I couldn't believe it," I commented, trying to not give anything that I knew about that affair away. "They didn't disclose too much about the particulars. Do you know what happened to that doctor?"

She shook her head. "No, my dad kept me out of most of that. I'm just sorry that I never really got the chance to meet or talk to her." She stood up. "Let's go back, I'm not really in the mood to be out here anymore." She grabbed her hat and led the way back toward the fortress.

Chapter 5—Anabel

Ms. Fischer looked at us over her glasses. "Yes, the doctor, the one who got the pardon..."

Jared hesitated. "Well, while she didn't know it then, it was, of course, Kevin Miller."

"Excuse me, Ms. Fischer? I'm not a moron. I knew it was Kevin," I glared at Jared. "I just did not trust Mr. Sorensen at that time, and now I know I was right to trust my instincts."

"You know, you need to grow up, Anabel." He sounded exasperated.

Sam shook his head. "I think we need a break, Ms. Fischer."

"Very well," she said. "Fifteen minutes."

Sam was still looking at me. I was studying my nails.

"How long have you known?" he asked in an undertone.

"Kevin told me. I figured it out right before they shipped him off." I sighed. "Look, Jared did something right for once. We couldn't go on pretending anymore, anyway." I stretched a bit. "I have to use the little girls' room, excuse me."

"Anabel—"

"Let's not do this." I turned from him and walked away, feeling guilty. It was unfair of me to take out my temper on him, but it was also profoundly obtuse of Sam to think that I wouldn't put two and two together.

As I left the hearing room, I noticed the guy who Sam had been talking to on the first day followed me out. I shook my head at my own paranoia. "The world," I told myself, "does not revolve around you." So I made my way to the ladies' room, locked myself in a stall, and vomited until it didn't hurt anymore. Sighing heavily, I sat back against the wall, feeling the same pain I had when Jared had first asked me about my mom's death.

Kevin had approached me one day when I was sitting at the public library, reading. I had convinced myself on that particular occasion it would do me some good to have a change of scenery. The loss of Miss Marilyn had hit me very hard, and I was lonely. I was struggling through a European History book when I looked up and saw Kevin standing there.

"Hi," he drawled.

A Southern accent? Really? I ignored him and stared at my book. I was not supposed to talk to inmates; they were not supposed to talk to me. Those were the rules.

"It's Anabel, right?"

"Yes." I didn't look up.

"I'm sorry to bother you, it's just I couldn't help but notice that you look just like your mother."

That made me drop my book. "What did you say?"

"I said you look just like your mother. I used to love to watch her movies." Kevin sat down next to me. "Is it okay if I sit here?"

And thus began our star-crossed friendship, which was doomed from the start. Nobody, not even Marilyn, dared speak to me about my mother. I think they were forbidden by Jonathan. Of course I was curious about her, but all I had to go on were her movies and an occasional search on the internet. When I found out the details of her death, I was horrified. My father and brother had let me live in happy ignorance as to her lifestyle, and it all came as a shock the day that my brother told me she was dead. I hadn't even known she'd been ill.

Cassidy had realized that she had made a horrible mistake in cheating on my father and losing her precious baby girl. She tried for years to get Jonathan to reconcile with her, but he refused to take her calls, let her talk to me, or let her near the island. So, she started doing drugs. Cocaine, mostly. And she started going around with the wrong sorts of people. As a consequence, about two and a half years ago, she was in a hospital bed, dying.

She was in a lot of pain, from what I understand. She could barely move, and her digestive tract no longer functioned of its own accord. She kept a picture by her bed of a beautiful baby girl, which caused her eyes to fill with tears every time she looked at it. She had sores all over her body that could barely stand the touch of her hospital gown.

What follows next is a sore subject with all of us. You see, my mother begged and pleaded with a doctor to put her out of her misery. That doctor knew she would be spending months and perhaps years in this state, with no possible cure, and so he overdosed her on morphine and let her pass quietly into the night.

My brother called me crying that night. I had never heard him cry before.

How did my dad take this? I can only surmise that he was still in love with her and perhaps felt guilty for how her life turned out. However, Jonathan was never the type to accept responsibility, and he would never admit that he did something wrong. Therefore, he decided his best course of action would be to punish the doctor. After pulling some strings, Kevin was brought to Caereon so Jonathan could keep an eye on him. I think he thought that if he had Kevin here, he could penalize him for his misdeeds. Even though he and Cassidy weren't together anymore, I believe he still thought that she belonged to him. So in his mind, Kevin took her away from him. And seeing me with Kevin, especially with how much I look like her, pushed him over the edge.

As for me, I could not hate Kevin. I was simply glad that he had been there for my mother in her last moments. Having my only memories of my mom being a pocket of warmth in the back of my mind, I sincerely hoped that she was at peace.

I took a few deep breaths, pulling myself together, and rinsed my mouth out in the sink. I had a suspicion that my fifteen minutes were almost up. I wiped off my face, opened the door and practically raced out of it—only to almost collide with the man from the hearing.

"Oh, goodness, I'm so sorry," I gasped. He caught my arm and helped me steady myself, and I found myself staring into two very kind brown eyes.

"Are you okay?" He seemed concerned.

"I'm fine, just glad I didn't barrel you over," I smiled at him. "I'm Anabel Martin."

"I know," he stated, looking away.

"I suppose everybody does, I stand out a bit," I attempted to joke.

"I'm Matt, Anabel. I work for your brother," he revealed. "Look, you'd better get back in there—just do me a favor."

I was surprised. Nobody ever asked me to do anything. "What's that?"

"Watch your back with Jared Sorensen. He isn't to be trusted."

I laughed mirthlessly. "Thank you for telling me that. Maybe I'll actually listen to you, as I haven't done so with anyone else." I flipped my hair a little and looked up at him.

He studied me, and then he nodded. "I'm sure you hear it a lot, but believe me, you should stay away from him."

"Matt, I won't have any problems with that." He held the door for me, and I retook my place next to Sam. I turned back to smile at him, but he wasn't looking my way. Oh well. At least it was my turn to talk again.

***

A few days after the whole cottage fiasco, I was furious at Jared and was about to call my brother—but Sam beat me to it.

"And how is my favorite baby sister?"

"Don't you sweet talk me, mister. What's going on with this Jared guy? Why is he here? And why aren't you? You promised me two months ago you would come visit me soon," I whined into the telephone. Normally I would have slammed Sam for the "baby sister" comment, but too much was going on.

Sam sighed. "Is he that intolerable?"

I paused. "Well, no," I replied. "It's just I'm used to you giving me a heads up over what goes on here. The only reason I knew that Jared was coming at all was because I was eavesdropping outside of Jonathan's study."

I heard him laugh. "That's a terrible habit, Annie. Impressive though. I may have to have you work for me. I think the Director of the CIA wants to retire within the next year."

"Oh please do. I'm so sick of it here. I hate everything." The words were out of my mouth before I really thought about them.

"Is it really that horrible, Anabel?" he asked gently.

My eyes welled up. "Yes, it is. Do you realize how dysfunctional I am? Jared's the first person close to my own age who I've met in years! I've spent my entire life around adults, and now that I am one I feel awkward and ill-equipped to deal with—well Jared, for instance. I don't know what to say to him, and Jonathan keeps making me babysit him."

"Interesting," noted Sam. "Go on."

"Well," I warmed to the task, "the other day I barely got any time to myself, I had to schlep Jared around the island and all we did was talk. Then I took him back and it was time for dinner, and then after that Jared insisted on hanging out in my library while I scoured Daddy's CD collection for some song Jared mentioned, but when I came back he was going through my desk, so I threw him out and I haven't spoken to him since," I finished with a flourish.

"Did he say why he was going through your desk?" he mused.

"Well, no," I admitted, "I really didn't give him time, I just screamed at him to get out, which he did while trying to give me excuses. Sam, it's my desk! I mean, all of my personal effects are in there, including my diary, and I don't want some strange guy looking at that!"

"Anabel, I sent Sorensen over to the island so he could keep an eye on you."

"What do you mean? I thought—"

"Well honey, you've been calling me in the middle of the night more and more, and I'm worried about you. You're right; your social life is dysfunctional. So yes, I've sent Jared to give me a report on you firsthand. Your father knew that I wanted everything with Dr. Miller investigated. I figured Jonathan would think I sent Sorensen to the island to spy on him, which is what I wanted him to think—so he would push him off on the one person who Jonathan knew had nothing to hide—you."

"Oh," I managed. "Well, that explains it, then."

"I'm sorry, I didn't have time to contact you before I sent out Jared. I don't recall telling him to go through your desk, but in spite of the fact that he is somewhat of a slimeball, he usually has a good reason for what he does. The good news is I will be there in about three weeks to make my routine visit to the island, so I will confer with Jared and talk to you, and perhaps get you to come stay with me."

"Are you serious? Because toying with my emotions is a really evil thing to do, Sam."

He laughed. "Yes, I'm serious. You're an adult now, Anabel. He can't tell you what to do forever, and if I bring you back with me, I won't have to go through massive red tape in appropriations." Sam had previously tried to get me off the island, but it was a tricky endeavor.

"So you're saying I have to put up with this guy for at least three more weeks?"

"I'm afraid so."

"Is he really your best friend? Because that's what he told me."

"Yes, Anabel. He is."

"Why?" I needed to understand this. "He's so...arrogant, and sure of himself. He's got a terrible reputation, Sam. Not only did I look him up on the internet, but Jonathan basically told me that I needed to dress like a nun around him. I just can't believe you would associate yourself with someone like that."

"I've known Jared since he was five. His father used to work for my mother, and when he got older and finished college, I was in the House, so he started working for me. When he got his law degree, he became one of my top advisors. I trust him with my life, Anabel, and I trust him with you, which—believe me—says a lot."

I sighed. "Fine. I'll go and try to make amends with Jared. But you really should've told me."

"Hang on a second, Anabel. There's one more thing."

"What's that?"

"Has he hit on you?" The question came out of nowhere.

I tried to laugh. "Sam, I told you, I looked him up online. I've seen pictures of some of these girls he's been with. I doubt I'm his type."

"You're avoiding the question." I could hear the anger building in his voice. "Has he done anything to you?"

So my thoughts flashed to Jared grabbing me on the beach, Jared telling me I was good looking, Jared smiling at me as I cracked jokes at him...and then I surprised myself. I told my brother a boldfaced lie. "No, Sam, he hasn't."

He let out a sigh of relief. "Okay good. I have total confidence in him, but…"

"…but you also know what he's like," I finished. "I understand. But I can assure you, I'm the last girl in the world he'd have any interest in." I started to pull at my hair, shocked that I had lied to my brother—and lied so easily.

"Good-bye, Annie. We'll talk soon. Love you"

"I love you, too," I said, hanging up the phone. I was mad at Jared, yes...but I didn't want him to go. Looking back, I regret not telling my brother the truth, but I knew that if I had Jared would be gone—and through my anger, I knew that wasn't what I wanted. What I wanted was revenge. Payback. And I thought I knew exactly how to handle it.

***

At this juncture, Congresswoman Fischer started asking questions of Charlie about how Caereon was run. As I twirled a curl, I wondered how it was being run in the absence of Jonathan. I then realized that it must be someone completely new, as Charlie would have been banned from working there until the murder investigation was over.

It was very odd for me to think that my father was dead. He and I had never had a good relationship, but it still hurt when I thought that I would never see him again. In spite of everything, he was my father, and I did love him. I really was an orphan.

Charlie started talking, and then it was five o'clock and the session was adjourned. I don't even remember what he said. We were to reconvene on Thursday, a note that made me shoot another dirty look at my brother. He had the fortitude to ignore my childishness.

I was feeling sick again. Every morning for the past month I had awakened and thrown up. Still, I reflected, as long as I could make it out of the room without speaking to Jared I might have a chance at getting through—

"So, do you want to grab some dinner?"

He was hovering over me. How had he gotten there? How had my brother left me, unprotected? I looked frantically around and saw that Sam was talking to a lawyer. This was not what we had agreed on.

"I have to go home," I began, but then I choked up. I didn't have a home.

I lived with my brother and his wife who hated me. I had nothing. "Why are you even talking to me? Sam's going to flip out on you."

"I don't want to do this...verbal sparring...with you every day. You could talk to me about it, you know."

"I have nothing to say to you."

"Well, what if I have something to say to you?" His voice rose, but then he calmed. "I could buy you a drink? It would just take a few minutes."

I glared at him. "I'm not twenty-one, remember?" Not like I could drink anyway.

"Ah. Look, Anabel, I feel terrible, and I've been incredibly rude to you. Why don't you let me treat you to some dinner?"

"You really don't get it, do you?" I stood up. "I want nothing to do with you. I don't want you to buy me dinner. I don't want you to buy me anything. I will not go anywhere with you, Jared. What I want most in the world is for you to crawl back into the hole you live in and die. How's that?"

He swallowed. "I understand." He turned around and walked off. A pang hit me, but I couldn't keep doing this. As I watched him leave, I caught Matt's eye. He nodded at me, and I sensed that I had gained his approval. I also made a mental note that I really needed to find out who he was.

Sam and I walked out of the room about ten minutes later. They had actually arranged for us to leave a back way, and when we got into the Town Car I heaved a huge sigh of relief.

"What a nightmare," he groaned, rubbing his temples as we slid into the car. "I just don't understand why everyone needs a photo of you."

"It's because we're trying to hide it," I pointed out.

"Murphy's law and all that?"

I managed some sort of grunt in reply.

"It wasn't really too terrible today, was it?" he asked, concerned.

I slumped back in my seat. "I just can't believe they haven't figured out who killed Jonathan."

"All we can really surmise at this point is that it was someone who knew

Caereon well. I had no idea that there were rooms in the fort that didn't have video surveillance, and of course someone knocked out the feed in your father's office." He smiled tiredly. "What do you want to do for dinner?"

"The wifey isn't cooking for us?" I asked. That was silly, of course. Alexis was not exactly the domestic type. Briefly I thought of how her attitude toward me had not warmed as we had gotten better acquainted. At least I knew it wasn't just me; Jared obviously did not like her. The uneasy truce between me and Alexis had gotten more and more tenuous during our cohabitation. As soon as Jonathan's will gets straightened out, I vowed, I'm leaving this place.

"Alex had a meeting, so I thought you and I could get some carryout or order in," he suggested.

I started to laugh, which felt really good. "The prospect of eating with you is much more appealing than dining with Jared. Shall we stay up all night watching cheesy movies?"

"If you like," he replied. "I wouldn't mind some Back to the Future."

Oh, how I loved my brother. "You can't do that again though, Sam."

"Do what?"

"Let Jared near me. You left me alone and he just swooped in."

"That's a bit dramatic, Anabel. I don't think he's the swooping type."

Now he was making fun of me. "We talked about how I wouldn't have to talk to him, and you left me! I am extremely uncomfortable with him there," I fumed.

My brother rubbed my arm. "I know. As soon as these hearings are over, you'll never have to see him again."

"I disagree," I warned. "I have a nasty suspicion I'm going to have to see him more."

Sam ignored me. "Also," he lectured, "your doctor has informed you that it would be best if you kept your stress levels low, and he's coming tomorrow morning to look at you. The best thing right now is to just forget Jared and focus on enjoying yourself for once. Okay?"

I grinned at him. "Twist my arm. But none of this Marty McFly crap. I want to watch Indiana Jones."

Chapter 6—Anabel

The following Thursday brought us together once more. As I took my seat, I was comforted by the fact that we would probably not be reconvening on Friday, and I would have another whole weekend pass in which I could avoid Jared.

A gray-haired woman, Ms. Halsey, cleared her throat. "Mr. Sorensen, I have a question about your relationship with Miss Martin." I liked how she just cut to the chase. She stared straight at him in a rather unsettling matter. I was impressed by the gutsiness of her glare, and resolved to learn how to give that exact look. It was scary.

"What's that, ma'am?" asked Jared. He, of course, was cool as ever.

"To what extent were you two romantically involved?"

"I don't really see what that has to do with anything," Sam interjected.

"Sam," I interjected, "you don't need to protect me." I stood up. "Ms. Halsey, I would like, if I may, to answer any questions you have about us." I smiled at her. "Besides, he's a guy; he'd probably muck up all the details."

Ms. Fischer gave me a small grin back, and there were a few laughs around the room. Ms. Halsey continued, "Are you sure you're up to it, Miss Martin? You've been through an ordeal and—"

Jared interrupted with, "You know, I'd like to present my point of view as well."

"Okay," I replied, "but ladies first." He stared at me like he was trying to figure me out, and I smiled sweetly back at him, trying to hold back tears. I knew—I knew—that it would do me absolutely no good to cry. Crying would betray me to Sam, which I did not want to deal with, and much more distressing, it would betray me to Jared.

Moreover, I could not let Jared know how I still had strong feelings for him—and I also knew I had to keep my other secret. I still couldn't understand my attraction to Jared, how it managed to persist after everything that had happened, but it made me angry at myself—and at him. So, when the Congresswomen brought up our relationship, I knew that I had to be the one to talk about it—otherwise, I would blow my cover. Besides, in terms of the blossoming of the saga of Jared and Anabel, I knew the perfect story to illustrate what had happened.

***

After I caught Jared going through my stuff, I was more than a little mad at him. I didn't care what Sam had said, I felt wronged. He had no right to go through my desk. I was also angry that his actions had forced me to lie to my brother, and so, I thought about how to punish him...until it came to me. Brushing aside any moral scruples, I told myself the ends of this one would justify the means. So I avoided him for a couple days, and when I could take it no more, I decided to put my feminine wiles to work.

Okay, so I might not have had much experience using said wiles, but I'd seen enough movies to know what to do to get a guy excited. At dinner the night before, I had sneaked glances at him—and then I realized that Jared was looking at me in a way that reminded me of how my father used to look at Miss Marilyn.

I kept turning over in my mind what he had said to me—the flimsy excuses, how he was growing to care about me, and all that other absolute garbage. What drove me the most crazy was how Sam had said Jared was his best friend. If Jared was indeed his best friend, why was he hitting on me, his best friend's sister? Now, I may not have had a lot of experience with relationships, but I knew what was wrong when I saw it. If he cared about Sam, he wouldn't try to put the moves on me. And as for caring about me, well…I kept coming back to the same thing. The reality was Jared didn't care one bit about me. He just wanted some.

"That's all men really want, anyway," I told myself, smoothing my favorite white dress as I stood in front of the mirror. Oh, my white dress. I wish I still had it. It's a gorgeous number. My father had ordered it for me as a gift, and had not realized how immodest it was until the first time I wore it and he screamed at me to put on a sweater and not run around half-naked. As an insurance policy (it would ruin my resolve if I ran into Jonathan), I draped a powder blue sweater around my shoulders to bring out the color of my eyes. Jared Sorensen was not interested in me, I repeated to myself. Of course, my knowledge of relationships had, up until this point, been a result of what I had learned from movies and television. Until I was about sixteen, I had thought all couples were like

Buttercup and Westley in The Princess Bride: sweet, romantic, and while sometimes dangerous, they always wound up happily ever after.

Then I discovered Sex in the City and concluded that all men were swine. It was a lot easier to watch these things that my father didn't want me to see with my babysitter out of the way.

And for those reasons, I had made up my mind not to care about Jared.

Even if I had wanted to. Which—and I had to firmly remind myself of this—I didn't.

On top of our fortress is a piazza-type area that I had seen Jared admiring. It has an incredible view, overlooking the forest on one side and the vast expanse of the Pacific on the other. I had caught him eying the site and had a hunch—call it women's intuition—I would find him up there.

As I came up the stairs I saw him leaning over the rail. I approached him, letting my sweater fall from my shoulders. I leaned over the rail. "Beautiful view, huh?"

He started. "Anabel!"

"Yes, that would be me," I said in my most offhand manner.

"Listen, I wanted to tell you—"

"Jared, I really—" I said at the same time. We looked at each other and laughed, and I could not deny that I liked the look on his face.

"I said some things I shouldn't," he began.

"Like what?" I asked innocently.

He opened his mouth, but then he paused, and took me in. "That's some dress."

"You ignored my question." It was all a game to me, and my heart was racing.

"I have other things on my mind," he muttered, leaning in toward me.

"Like what?" I asked, breathless.

He turned and looked at me. I gazed straight back into his eyes, and before I knew it he pulled me close to him and firmly pressed his lips to mine. I was so startled, I lost my balance, but he tightened his grip around me and I gave in to him. My arms weren't my own as I wrapped them around his neck, and that only made him kiss me more urgently, more deeply. It was like we were suspended in time, and for a moment, all that mattered was me and Jared. I was reeling for an instant, but then I pulled myself apart from him and turned away, horrified. I was already losing this. I struggled to clear my head and take control of the situation.

"You kissed me," I gazed into the ocean, trying to conceal my shock. Feeling calmer, I ventured a glance at him.

He looked shamefaced. "Yeah, I did."

I tossed my hair. I could work with this. "You seem upset," I observed, in what I hoped was a cool and detached manner.

He looked away, keeping his arms crossed over the rail. "Well, I didn't...that is...Anabel."

"Jared," I returned.

"I didn't—that is, I shouldn't have kissed you. If your brother, let alone your father knew...I apologize," he said, staring into my eyes.

I shifted my gaze to the waves. The sun was beating down, and I thought about how wonderful ice-cold water would feel right now. My heart still thudding, I contemplated shimmying out of my dress and jumping into the water right then. I would probably die on impact, but it would solve a lot of problems.

"Anabel?"

"Yes?" I turned back to him.

"I apologized." There was a bit of an edge to his voice.

"I heard you. And I have to admit, I'm quite offended." I picked up my sweater and threw it onto a chair. "Is it hot out here?"

He swallowed. "Quite. Why are you offended?"

I crossed my arms and glared at him. "Did you not like kissing me? Am I not a good kisser?" I leaned backwards against the rail, making sure to thrust my chest out a bit. "Not that I've had a lot of practice, but really, I didn't think I was half bad."

Jared looked taken aback. I almost lost my composure and laughed at the look on his face. Then he slowly said, "No, that wasn't it."

"What then? You find me repulsive?"

"Anabel, for crying out loud! You're not a bad kisser, and no, I do not find you repulsive."

I beamed at him. "Oh, so you want to give it another go?" I then proceeded to invade his personal space.

He looked at me, incredulous. "What the devil has gotten into you?"

"Oh, come on, Jared," I moved toward him. "I've seen the way you look at me. At the same time I can't sit here and pretend like I'm not attracted to you." I pressed my body against his and whispered in his ear, "It doesn't have to mean anything, you know. We can have sex just to have sex…and you'll leave, and that will be that."

I felt his breathing change, as he murmured, "But Anabel, what about Sam…"

I looked around. "I don't see him here."

"This isn't right…"

"Shh," I whispered, "isn't this what you want, Jared?" I slowly ran my finger down his chest.

I heard a sharp intake of breath, and then he uttered, "Yes—"

I broke away and smiled at him. "Well, today doesn't work for me, but maybe some other time then." I picked up my sweater, turned on my heel, and marched off, trying to hold back the giggles as a slew of profanities erupted from Jared's mouth.

It's not easy to get Anabel Martin's panties in a twist. Jared would do well to remember that. Or so I thought, anyway.

***

Sam looked appalled. "You made that up. Please tell me you made that up."

I looked down, ashamed. "I'm sorry, Sam."

The council members all exchanged glances, but I was pretty sure any image they had of me as the poor innocent victim had flown out the window. I turned around and ventured a glance at Matt, but he wouldn't catch my eye.

I still didn't know what he did. Sam had been very elusive on that point.

So I sneaked a glance at Jared, who looked smug. He sat back in his chair, his arms folded, smirking at me. "You shut up," I admonished him.

"I did not say a thing, babe," he grinned, self-satisfied.

"I think now is a good time for lunch," proclaimed Ms. Fischer. "Mr. Sorensen, we will hear from you after the break." They filed out, and Sam was still staring at me like he had never seen me before.

"I just thought it would be a way to put him in his place. I felt like he was wronging the both of us, treating me like that. And I thought it would be a way to get him back. You know, tell him I'll put out and then take it away." I shrugged my shoulders. "I just figured he wasn't used to rejection."

"I can't even look at you right now," he stated. "Behaving like that..."

I touched his arm. "Please don't be mad at me. I wasn't thinking. I just wanted to get back at him, you know? I didn't know any better!"

"You didn't know any better?" He repeated. "You know what? It's no wonder what happened with you happened. I am at a loss, Anabel." He stood up and walked away. I crossed my arms and put my head down on the table. I had broken my brother's heart, and he had cut me down. I could not go any lower.

And then, of course, he was there. "Hey."

I looked at him through the pile of my hair. "What?"

"I heard what Sam said. You didn't deserve that." Jared stopped, and then asserted, "You definitely didn't deserve what happened."

"I don't want your pity."

"Still, it was uncalled for. Anabel…"

"What?"

Jared was smirking at me. Again. "I can't believe you told them that."

I turned my head back so it faced the table. "I had to tell the truth, right?"

"You just didn't show yourself in the best light, is all. I'm surprised that you would do that for me."

"I didn't do it for you. I did it because it was the right thing to do," I muttered.

"Well it was nice of you. Made me look a little less awful. Made you look a little less pure."

I sat up and looked at him. "Jared, I was behaving like a horny schoolgirl, I don't think there was any way to portray myself so I looked good."

"You could give your own revisionist history." He was smiling at me now. I smacked his arm.

"Stop that," I ordered. "It doesn't work on me anymore."

"I doubt that very much, love."

"Leave her alone, Sorensen," came a voice. I smiled hopefully at Matt. He didn't smile back. "Anabel, I've been instructed to take you to eat."

"I'm not hungry," I grumbled, but I got up anyway and left Jared there, staring at the both of us openmouthed.

Which was what he deserved, after all.

I had to almost run to keep up with Matt. His legs were longer than mine. "Thank you for getting me out of that. I was uncomfortable."

"I bet," he agreed. "What do you think you can keep down?"

"Um, there's a smoothie place around the corner, I usually—wait," I stopped, realizing that he knew. "Did Sam tell you?"

He gave me a curt nod, and I wasn't quite sure why, but I felt a sense of disappointment. Even though I couldn't quite explain it to myself, for some reason, I didn't want him to know. I looked down at my shoes, suddenly unsure. "How long have you known?"

"I knew it the moment I saw you," he admitted. He leaned in a little closer, and in an undertone said, "I don't think this is the best place to be discussing this, Anabel."

I agreed. So I let him buy me a strawberry banana smoothie, and I sipped it in silence as he walked me back. I kept looking at him, puzzled. "What do you do for my brother again?"

He caught my eye briefly, and then looked straight ahead. "I'm a bodyguard."

"Are you Secret Service?"

Matt looked down. "I was. Now I'm private." He gently slipped his arm around my shoulders to guide me away from an oncoming mob. "We should get you back into the hearing. There aren't quite so many onlookers in there."

"Thank goodness for that," I proclaimed. "A much smaller audience to see me make an idiot of myself."

He raised an eyebrow. I continued, "It's bad enough that I'm making poor Sam relive this again, but—"

"Sam can take care of himself. Just tell the truth, Anabel. It will be fine."

I nodded, and then smiled at him. "Thanks. It's nice to have a friend. Even one that my brother has to pay for."

He laughed then, and I was pleased as I sat back down next to Sam, whose color had returned. "I'm sorry I left you like that," he told me.

"I'm sorry I pained you like that," I offered.

"It's because I care about you," he said.

"I know," I returned. "But this is going to get a whole lot worse before it gets better, and you know that."

He nodded, and we both looked up as Jared stood to tell his side of the story.

Chapter 7—Jared

After Anabel left me, I nearly lost control. Watching her retreating figure, I kicked a chair in frustration. I was incredibly mad at her display of...well, what was that? I turned and leaned against the rail, breathing heavily, until I had pulled myself together.

Sam had totally underestimated her. If he knew what she was doing, he'd lose it. "Who does she think she is?" I muttered aloud. If she thought she could get away with that, she was gravely mistaken. How dare she pretend she was this sweet, innocent, little girl, and then turn around and behave like that?

I'm not going to sit here and claim to be an expert on morality, but I've never pretended to be something I'm not. Anabel knew what I was, she'd said it herself.

She, on the other hand, had fooled me, and for that matter, her brother. It's no wonder her dad wanted to lock her up. In my mind, she was as bad as I was. Worse.

But even as I decided that, I also felt furious at myself, and all sorts of recollections of how Sam had explicitly told me how much he trusted me with his sister's welfare were running through my head. I could just imagine explaining the whole thing to him. I did not do this. She did this. I just came here to do a job, and she got mad because I was going through her desk to make sure her father hadn't bugged her room. Sam hadn't been kidding about her temper. She had screamed at me and thrown me out of there before I knew what was going on.

That wasn't what bothered me though. The worst part was she had gotten under my skin, and I had never allowed that to happen before. She wasn't even the sort of girl I would normally go after—if I had seen Anabel on the street, I would've just kept walking. No. I knew it then. She was off limits, and that's what this was about. Nothing more than a reaction to her brother telling me to leave her alone. It's not like she was special. She was pretty, and rather smart, but there were ten million other girls like that in the DC area alone. It was obvious that I wanted her because my every instinct was to stay away.

There would be no more of this, I told myself. Just do your job.

Needless to say, I immediately took a very cold shower.

I avoided Anabel for the rest of the afternoon. When I arrived to dinner that night she had put away the sexy white dress in favor of something much more puritan. Part of her hair was pulled back and the rest flowed around her face, making her look softer and sweeter than she had earlier. I thought I had my temper under control, but I got annoyed when she refused to make eye contact with me and only said, "Good evening, Jared," by way of greeting.

"So Mr. Sorensen," began Jonathan Martin, deigning to notice me, "have you found any useful information for Sam? Or has my stepson sent you here to merely make me uncomfortable?"

"Daddy, Sam's what, ten years younger than you? I don't really know if you can call him your stepson," pointed out Anabel, dabbing at her mouth with her napkin.

"That's enough, Anabel."

"I'm just saying," she continued, "it's not even like you were ever really his parent, he never lived with you."

"I said that's enough." The cold rage behind those words seemed to intimidate everyone at the table but Anabel, who looked like she was about to retort. However, last thing I needed was Jonathan and Anabel starting an argument at the dinner table, so I jumped in. "Mr. Martin, I'm not here to cause any trouble. I have my orders, and it looks like I'll be leaving here even sooner than anticipated."

"What? Why?" asked Anabel, dropping her fork. Then she froze. I think that question had escaped her lips before she could think, and she tried to cover it by saying, "When I talked to Sam, he said you'd be here for at least three weeks. I mean, you're here on behalf of the United States Government. Shouldn't you do a thorough job?"

"I think I've seen everything that I need to," I told her, and she blushed a bit. She looked uncomfortable—and upset. Excellent.

"Have you come to any conclusions?" Her voice trembled a little, and her eyes gave away everything. I knew she was scared I would tell her brother what she'd done. And I had no interest in putting her mind at ease—I wanted to torment her a little. Like she had done to me.

"Well, I'll call Sam in the morning, report to him what I've found, and we can go from there." I smiled cordially at Jonathan Martin. "I really appreciate how kind you were to me during my stay, sir. Your daughter is lovely, and she has provided me with wonderful company. I do not regret the amount of time I spent with such a charming hostess, but I wish I had seen more of the business side of the facility. Perhaps tomorrow morning you could give me a tour?"

"I could come with you," Anabel offered.

"That won't be necessary, Miss Martin," I cajoled. "I believe I'm familiar with your opinions on everything, but I would like to get to know your father a little better."

Jonathan had been watching this discourse with interest. When she slumped back in her chair, defeated, he frowned and said, "I hope Anabel hasn't been too much of a bother for you, Mr. Sorensen. She's a good girl, and she means well, but sometimes she forgets her place."

Ouch. That was cold. Anabel was fighting tears, so I relented.

"I think very highly of your daughter, sir," I acknowledged. "I regret that I won't be spending more time with her. Nonetheless, business is business."

She looked at me through her teary eyes, unsure of whether or not she should believe me.

"On second thought, perhaps you should come with us, Anabel," I suggested. "You may be able to lend your own unique perspective to our discussion tomorrow."

"I'll be there as well," added Charlie. The look he gave me let me know that he intended to keep an eye on my interactions with her, and I shot him a glance, trying to communicate to him that I was not the problem where Anabel was concerned.

Of course, now I know that I was only the start of her problems, and I completely regret the way that I treated Anabel Martin. I would like for the record to state that I, Jared Sorensen, completely failed this girl—this woman—who I was supposed to help out of a terrible situation, one that was destructive to her sense of well-being and mental health. I regret even more that the night after that conversation, I became intoxicated and forced myself on her, an act which is reprehensible and also one for which I know she will never forgive me.

Chapter 8—Anabel

Of course, the room exploded with Jared's statement. Sam jumped out of his chair and began shouting at him, Charlie and Marilyn appeared out of nowhere and tried to put their arms around me, there were cops who had to keep people from rushing us, Ms. Fischer was banging her gavel...while I sat in my chair and mulled over Jared's words.

He was sorry he raped me, huh? I wasn't expecting that. I didn't know he could feel sorrow, that he actually cared that he had hurt another person.

The thing is...well, let me back up. In order to get to that part of the story, we need to go through what happened in the hallway after dinner and what happened the next day. See, this is what I hated about Jared. He always had to rush to the end and leave out the details. In this case, the details were important. Unlike Jared, I understand that you can't give away too much information at once. Like my big secret. I also haven't even alluded too much to the death of my father, which you know is coming up. So, here's some foreshadowing for you: Jared is about to rape me, my father is about to die, and things are about to fall spectacularly to pieces.

But anyway, back to dinner. I had tears in my eyes and was fuming at Mr. Sorensen. Jared. He hadn't liked the way I had behaved and in spite of swearing up and down that he cared about me, he was going to punish me by telling Sam everything was fine and just leave me in this godforsaken hell-hole. Can you see why I was so upset? I don't even remember what we ate that night; I just remember that I had it in my head that it was necessary to get to the phone before Jared. I had to call my brother and tell him that sending Jared Sorensen had been a huge mistake, that Sam had made a drastic lapse in judgment when hiring a rat bastard like the snake sitting across from me to work for him, and that he had to get me off this island. Or I was going to become crazy. I probably already was crazy.

As soon as I could, I excused myself from the dinner table and made a dash for my room. I wanted to go in there, lock the door, and blast the most depressing music I could find. Maybe watch Bridget Jones' Diary.

I guess I should mention that the end really was in sight for me. Despite my mother's poor choices at the end of her life, she had left me a significant amount of money in a trust fund, which was mine the moment I turned twenty-one. When I had that money I could pay for my own transportation off the island, which my father refused to do. Jonathan was, of course, opposed to me leaving, and I worried that even when I had the funds to leave, he would find a way to keep me there. As I stamped down the hall toward my shelter, all sorts of thoughts ran through my head. Even though I had initiated everything on the top of the piazza, Jared's response to me—and mine to him—frightened me. A lot. It also hurt me the way he had acted at dinner, blowing me off. I shook my head. I couldn't let him get to me; after all, I was the one who was supposed to be using him. But then I reconsidered. What on earth was I doing, making pretend advances at some guy who was more than ten years older than me? I was far too inexperienced with men to be indulging in this insanity. This was the sort of behavior that gave my father justification for preventing me from attending college! This was the sort of behavior that would leave me dead in a gutter!

I then had another horrifying realization. "And now I'm justifying his lunacy?" I started to bang my head into the wall.

"Stop that."

I didn't even turn around. "Hi, Daddy."

"What are you playing at, Anabel?" My father came up next to me. "I saw your exchange with him. I even watched the security tape of you two going into Cottage 4."

"Yes, God forbid I follow your instructions and I do what you tell me to do. You told me to show him around. I did that!" I glared at him with my full fury. "Yes, we went into the cottage. But there are security cameras in there, too, so you saw that nothing went on between us that wasn't perfectly kosher!"

"Perhaps you've forgotten where else there are cameras? Not to mention other people looking around and watching?"

I felt the color drain from my face.

"Anabel! What on earth were you thinking?" The vein was really throbbing now.

I crossed my arms and exhaled, leaning against the door. "You really want to know what I was thinking, DAD?" I pushed open the door to my room. "I'm a girl. Jared likes girls. So, I figured I had a shot, and I was thinking that maybe if I slept with him, he'd get me off this awful island. BECAUSE I HATE IT HERE! I HATE IT, AND I'M SICK OF YOU, AND I WISH YOU WOULD JUST LEAVE ME ALONE!" I started crying. "For once, Daddy, I wish you would think about what your choices do to me every single day. I'm lonely. I'm afraid I will never get away from here, and all I want to do is get as far away from you as possible." I choked back a sob. "I hate being here so much. I'm going to bed. Goodnight." And I walked into my room and closed and locked the door. Then I threw myself on the bed and sobbed hysterically for a few moments. I had visions of myself as a middle-aged spinster who didn't even have a cat, living with my father. I prayed to God that He would find a way to get me out of here.

True to form, about two minutes later he started knocking on the door. "I told you to leave me alone," I called.

"Well it's been awhile since you said that, so I thought maybe you had changed your mind. Women do stuff like that," asserted Jared.

I opened the door and stared at him. "Are you serious?"

And he gave me a wolfish grin. "May I come in?"

Chapter 9—Anabel

I started to feel sick. No, no, this wasn't good. I caught Sam's eye and he nudged our lawyer, as was the signal, and our lawyer asked to take a break.

I hurried down the hall to the bathroom, and threw up three times. When I was through, I walked over to the mirror and stared at myself. Then I slowly unbuttoned my coat and took a look at my belly.

I couldn't hide it for much longer. I was four months pregnant, almost five, and I was definitely showing. The morning sickness had not subsided as the doctor said it would, and any sort of weird smell triggered the nausea. Thinking about Jared coming to my bedroom that night made me sick to my stomach, and without a clear course of action, my desperation was becoming greater. Sam's advice the other day had been to stand up straight to hide it, but the baby was growing. I didn't know who he thought he was kidding. It had sure been easy for Matt to spot it, I reflected. Today the dress that I was wearing clung to my belly and made no effort to hide the fact that there was a baby in there.

So here it was. I was carrying Jared's child. One time, apparently, is all that it takes. Sighing, I studied my reflection. I was so pale. I splashed some water on my face and was drying it off, willing myself to hold it together, when Marilyn barged in. "Annie, are you okay? Sam said to leave you alone, but I saw your face go all white and—oh my goodness!" She gaped at my stomach. "Please tell me that's not what I think it is."

I stared at her. "Go on, ask me."

She swallowed. "Are you...Annie, are you pregnant?"

"No, just super fat." I threw away the paper towel and turned to face her. "You can't tell anyone. Please. I'm not ready yet."

"Well you can't hide it forever...that bump is only going to get bigger," she stated matter-of-factly. "Besides, wearing your coat all day long is going to make you even more uncomfortable. I wondered why you were doing that." She hugged me, but I stood limp in her arms, unwilling to return her embrace. Marilyn knowing caused all sorts of complications that I didn't quite know how to deal with. She smoothed my hair. "Oh sweetheart, you poor thing...is this baby—"

"Yes, it's Jared's. He doesn't know. He doesn't know that his spawn is making my breasts sore and my ankles swell and is the reason I can't keep any food down." Tears pricked at my eyes. "Marilyn, what am I going to do? As much as my brother wants to pretend otherwise, I can't hide this for much longer, and when this comes out things are going to be so much worse for all of us!" I exhaled, reminding myself it was important to breathe.

"So you're going to keep it?"

Being asked this question made me angry. "I'm going to take this opportunity to remind you that my mother kept my brother. Besides, it's a bit late for that."

"I see," she told me, but I could tell she didn't.

"But at some point I have to tell Jared, and Sam already wants to kill him, and who knows how he will react." I ranted in such a fashion for at least a few more minutes, until I stopped crying and while my eyes were very red, I was no longer sniffing.

Marilyn looked at me with loving eyes, the same way she had looked at me when I was a little girl, and she squeezed my hand. "It'll be okay, honey," she promised.

I managed a small smile. "I don't see how," I contended. "You are right though. I am extremely uncomfortable wearing this stupid coat every day."

"You know," she commented, "hiding this isn't going to make it any better. In fact, I think it's making it worse."

"What are you suggesting? That I prance in there and show off the baby bulge for the entire world to see?"

Marilyn attempted to smile at me. "I merely think it would help you to not keep it to yourself any longer."

I looked in the mirror, watching the red start to fade away. I straightened my shoulders and then said, "You know what? You're right," I smiled. "Why should I be afraid of this? He can't hurt me anymore. I may as well tell him right now!" Over Marilyn's protests that perhaps I ought to think this over, I slung my coat over my arm, blocking my stomach, and I marched down the hallway and came into the hearing room.

Matt saw me, and I saw his face change when he noticed I wasn't wearing my jacket. He looked like he might try and stop me, but I glared at him full force and he took a step back. I nodded at him and walked to the front, trying not to lose my nerve.

Jared was talking to his lawyer, and Sam was hovering nearby. I walked up behind Jared and tapped him on the back. He turned around, surprised to see me. "Hey," he got out.

I smiled. I hadn't been sleeping well and was probably delirious. "Hi Jared, how are you?"

"I'm fine," he responded. "Anabel, are you alright?"

"Well, no, I'm not, Jared. I need to tell you something." I was grinning like a fool.

He smiled back cautiously, probably surprised I was making an attempt to be civil. "Well okay, do you want to go somewhere and we can talk, because—"

"No, right here is fine." But then, staring into his eyes, I lost my resolve.

"You know what, I'm sorry, I can't do this," I turned to go, but he caught my arm.

"Now hang on a minute," he demanded. "You and I aren't done here, you know."

"Let go of me!" I shrieked, and as I yanked myself away from him I dropped my coat. And that was when he saw my stomach.

"Anabel," he gasped, his eyes wide, "what is that?"

I giggled, the hysteria in me rising. "What do you think it is, Jared? It's been almost five months since you, well..." I trailed off.

He was staring at me like he'd never seen me before. "Don't play around. Are you saying that—?"

There was nothing to be done now. "Well, now you know. Jared, you knocked me up."

I heard a few gasps and my brother was staring at me, shaking his head. Some of the press people, who had been allowed into the hearing room during the recess, pulled out their cameras and started snapping away. I turned so they could get a full view of my swollen abdomen and beamed at the cameras. My life had turned into a circus; I may as well have a little fun.

That was when Jared grabbed my arm and pulled me back toward him. "I don't believe this."

"Well believe it, sugar dumpling, you are my baby daddy. I think it's a girl." Insanity caused me to start giggling again. The situation really was kind of funny, I thought, and the look of intense horror on Jared's face was giving me a sort of perverse pleasure. Good. He should suffer everything that I did from the moment I realized my period was late to having to ask my sister-in-law to buy me a pregnancy test to all of the physical discomfort that ailed me on a daily basis.

"But Anabel, we only had the one time, and—"

"Let me explain something," I bellowed at him. "My date of conception was April 26—the one and only time in my life that I have had sexual intercourse. So apparently, Jared, taking my virginity was not enough for you, and you just had to leave a memento for me to remember you by!" I was angry now. Sam appeared at my side.

"I think this discussion should continue outside of the hearing," he hissed at the both of us. "Sorensen, you can come to dinner with us tonight. You know that we're staying at Blair House, you may meet us around six and we will discuss this." He yanked my arm and pulled me back to our table. "I don't know what's gotten into you. I really don't, Anabel. I want to kill you right now. We agreed to keep this quiet—"

"Marilyn saw my stomach," I explained. "It was only a matter of time." He looked like he wanted to retort, but we were interrupted by the Committee filing back into the room. "I am tired of lying about things, Sam." I leaned back in my chair. "This whole thing is tearing at my heart, and maybe you can go on with the deception, but I can't."

Ms. Fischer retook her seat. "Where were we?"

"Ma'am?" I stood up.

"Yes, Miss Martin?"

"I just wanted to let everyone know that I'm pregnant." My brother let out an audible groan, and I heard more murmurs throughout the room. I didn't care. My life was spiraling out of control at an alarming rate, and this was my poor effort to at least pretend I was in charge. "Jared

Sorensen is the father, in case there was any doubt, and I predict the baby will be born sometime in January." I retook my seat. "That's all."

She rubbed her eyes. "Is there anything else you wish to share with us, Miss Martin?"

I contemplated this. "No, not today, I don't think," I conceded. I turned to my brother. "Do you have anything, Sam?"

He shook his head and stared at the table. I smiled up at Ms. Fischer. "I think we're all set, ma'am."

"Very good. Mr. Sorensen?"

Chapter 10—Jared

"I'm sorry about the trouble I caused you with your father," I apologized.

Anabel rubbed her eyes. "It's okay. I'm used to it." She grinned. "Don't worry. There aren't any cameras in here."

"No? I'm surprised." And comforted. I didn't want to think about how Jonathan would respond if he found me in his daughter's room.

"My father promised me that he wouldn't put any in, but there are some in the library, so let's stay out of there." She settled back on her bed. "What do you want?"

"Anabel," I sighed, "what's going on with you? One moment you seem fine, and then the next you're kissing me, and then the next moment you're spurning me, and—"

"You broke my trust," she snapped. "I just wanted to put you in your place."

I almost laughed out loud at her, but then I thought better. So I switched tactics. "Alright, so you were mad at me. I get it. But what did I do to offend your delicate sensibilities to the point where you felt the need to shove your tongue down my throat?"

"Why, so you can learn how drive women to these extremes?" she retorted.

Now I did laugh at her. "You're feisty, Anabel. I like that."

She glared at me. "I was angry because I saw you going through my personal effects without my prior consent. How's that?"

"You mean your desk. There's a good reason for that."

"I would love to hear it," she murmured, softening. "Because I'm pretty sure that's a major invasion of my privacy, and you had no need to sneak around. I would have shown you if you had just asked." She pushed some hair out of her eyes.

"I guess...I'm sorry." I sighed. Poor kid, she looked overwhelmed and uncomfortable. I decided to go easy on her, in an attempt to ignore the feeling that was clawing at the pit of my stomach. "I was just treating you like I would treat any other job. It's nothing personal. It never occurred to me to ask you if I could root through your desk."

"Find anything interesting? I don't think I gave you a chance to tell me earlier, when I screamed at you." She grinned flirtatiously.

"Nothing abnormal," I confirmed. This was getting awkward. "Anyway, I just wanted to make sure you were alright." I stood to leave.

"Don't go," she begged. "Please."

"I don't think it's a good idea for us to be alone, Anabel." I didn't look at her.

She stood up. "Look, I'm sorry about everything, I was angry. I spoke to Sam, and he told me that you were just following his orders," she acknowledged. "My dad saw us kissing, but he concluded it was my fault. Which it was," she continued. "I just wanted to get back at you, and that was the best way I could come up with." Now she was next to me, touching my arm and forcing me to look at her. "Please don't go," she appealed, looking like she was about to cry again. "I really don't want to be by myself right now."

"I don't think—"

"Look, otherwise I'm going to be stuck watching chick flicks and crying. Please tell me you're not angry with me," she implored.

"I'm not angry with you." That wasn't it.

"Well what then?" She stared into my eyes. "Did I repulse you that badly?"

"No, Anabel. It's just I don't trust myself with you right now."

She looked surprised, and a little flustered. Her cheeks reddened. "Oh," she stammered. "I see."

"Let me give you a life lesson, Anabel," I warned, "don't start what you can't finish."

Her eyes widened. "You can go now. Forget it." She turned around and slumped back on her bed.

Knowing full well she was probably moments away from waking up her brother in the middle of the night again, I tried a different strategy.

"Anabel," I offered in a much gentler tone, "my half of the species is full of dogs, okay? And you brought out that side in me, and my way of not having your father—let alone your brother—kill me is to push you away."

She was still scowling, so I continued. "I can't sit here and pretend like I don't feel something between us, because I do. And that's why I need to stay as far away from you as possible."

She looked thoughtful. "But...my brother sent you here to look after me." I didn't like her tone. Then, Anabel got up and walked over to me, and soon our faces were inches apart. "You wouldn't want me to give him a bad report, would you? Because if I don't think you do a good job, I will."

"Are you serious?"

"You don't have a choice here, Jared."

"This is blackmail," I swallowed hard. "That's illegal too, you know."

"Maybe it makes up for the invasion of my privacy," she murmured, twining her arms around my neck.

"Anabel, this is not fair—"

"Shut up."

The next thing I knew she and I were kissing in a way that would have appalled her father. Our arms, legs, and tongues became intertwined as we fell back on her bed. I had wanted this—to touch her soft lips, run my fingers through her hair, pull her closer—and then I broke away and stared at her. I should not do this, I should not do this. But Anabel was a sporting sort of gal, and clearly had no intention of stopping. Her cheeks were flushed and her blue eyes sparkled. "Well?" she implored, "What happens next?"

"This is wrong," I murmured, kissing her neck. Then I stopped. "Anabel," I said, "is that your teddy bear?"

She picked up the stuffed animal affectionately. "Yeah, don't laugh, but I still sleep with Theodore. Please don't judge me. It's force of habit."

"I can't make out with you with Theodore staring at me. It feels too weird." Even as I said that, I realized I had no right to be kissing this kid. She still slept with stuffed animals, for crying out loud. I was thirty-two, she was nineteen. She was Jonathan Martin's daughter and Sam Sallinger's sister. All of these reasons to leave were running through my mind over and over again. "Anabel…"

She sighed. "I know, I know. But what do you want me to do? In spite of the fact that you seem to be exactly what I shouldn't want, I do, and—I hope you don't think I'm a tramp," she reflected.

Chapter 11—Anabel

"Oh please, I did not say that," I insisted.

"You said something like that," he replied, staring hard at me over the table.

I raised my hand again. "Excuse me, Ms. Fischer? He's dragging this out. What happened at this point was we kissed a little more, he said we shouldn't, I said I know, then we kissed again. Eventually he left for the evening, and I did wind up watching my chick flick."

"And what night was this, Miss Martin?"

"April 25th," I announced. "The day before the assault on my person, and the subsequent murder of my father." I let out a yawn. "Goodness, I'm sorry. I'm just getting a bit worn out."

"I think this is as good a time as any to stop for the day," indicated Ms. Fischer. "We will resume on Monday." She banged her gavel and my brother turned to me.

"You really were not thinking, were you?"

"I was getting hot, wearing that coat all the time. It is September in DC, you know." As if I was some expert on the climate in our Nation's capital. I placed my hands on my belly. "Besides, I am uncomfortable in here. I think sitting in these chairs is killing my back." Then I paused. "Or did you mean the whole throwing myself at Jared thing? Because in that case, I agree with you. I definitely wasn't thinking."

Sam shook his head. "When you smile like that, you look exactly like our mother."

"Does that make you sad?" I asked.

"No. It makes me worried. For you."

I grinned. "Oh Sam, let's not go down that road."

He rubbed my shoulders. "So you really think it's a girl?"

"Oh yes," I said dreamily. "My precious little Emma. That's what I'm going to name her."

"I hate that name." Jared was hovering. He was really pale, leading me to conclude that my news had really done a number on him. I would feel guilty, except it was his fault I was pregnant in the first place.

"This is neither the time nor the place," growled my brother. "Sorensen, we will see you later." He then put his arm around me and led me through the fray of photographers, all shouting questions at me about my baby.

"Miss Martin," I heard one say, "Anabel, is it a boy or a girl?"

"I think it's a girl!" I called back. "I'm naming her Emma Claire!"

Sam nearly shoved me into the car. "You're hurting!" I whined.

"You are clearly out of your mind, Annie. What is wrong with you?" Now he looked furious. His face was beet red and there was no warmth in his eyes whatsoever.

"I'm tired of all of this. Jared and I had an inappropriate relationship. I don't get what that has to do anything. I mean, really! That doesn't change the fact that my father is dead, Sam." I slumped against the car door. "I don't understand why we have to keep rehashing this. These hearings are preposterous and have accomplished nothing except to mortify me. We haven't even touched on Jonathan's murder yet!"

"Anabel, you need to focus. Jared's in a lot of trouble. Do you not realize that?"

"What do you mean?"

"Well, he's still a chief suspect in Jonathan's murder, for one. Sexual assault, if you decide to press charges—and you should—is also a hefty crime. Not only did he admit it in front of all sorts of witnesses, but now you have decided to make no secret of it." Sam's eyes bored into mine. "You should prepare yourself with the knowledge that he may be going to jail for a very long time."

"He didn't kill Jonathan," I retorted. "He doesn't have it in him. Jared is a lot of things, but not a murderer. And I'm not going to press charges against the father of my child, I'm just not."

"I really think you—"

"I'm not," I interrupted him. "Let it go. Emma deserves to have both of her parents involved in her life, no matter how slimy her dad is and what a basket case her mother is." I attempted to slow my breathing. "Look, Sam, I know you don't understand this, but I did once care for Jared. And there's no way he killed Jonathan, I know."

"And how do you know that, Anabel?"

"Jared was with me," I explained. "The security tapes should show that, and I think you're making up the whole 'chief suspect' thing, because wouldn't he be in custody if he'd done it?" Sam stared at me, and I continued. "Don't look at me like that. I'm not stupid. Besides—and believe me I hate to say this—but you do need to give him the benefit of the doubt. I haven't made any secret of my actions on Caereon with regards to Jared. He's not the only one at fault."

"Listen to me," my brother seized my arms, holding so tightly it hurt. "You didn't deserve that, nobody does. He should have controlled himself with you, for the sake of our friendship, if nothing else."

I saw the pain in Sam's eyes, and I knew Jared's betrayal had run deep. But I also knew there was nothing I could do to comfort him. "Please let go of me."

He released his grip, and I rubbed my arms. Sam sighed and looked out the window. "I know you haven't wanted to talk about that night, and while I don't blame you, you will have to eventually."

"When I'm ready," I replied, and then neither of us spoke until we reached Blair House.

Chapter 12—Anabel

As the driver opened my door, I took a moment to admire the building.

I loved staying at Blair House. It is the official guest house of the President, and our new commander-in-chief had offered us sanctuary there until the hearings were over. It also was a way to make sure that we were watched by the Secret Service at all times.

Alexis was there when we arrived. As she and Sam kissed, I took a moment to study her. She was extremely beautiful, very tall, very thin, very blonde. She's about forty, like my brother, but she doesn't look a day older than thirty. When she was First Lady the cameras loved her, and she always had a big toothy grin for them and a friendly wave. It didn't detract much from what everyone said about her, but it made for some exquisite photos. "Alex," announced my brother, "Jared Sorensen is joining us for dinner tonight."

"I hate that man," she called to him. Extremely straightforward, she was. "Anabel, what do you feel like eating?"

I sank onto a sofa and put my feet up. "Tacos? I don't know why, but that sounds phenomenal right now."

"You know, that sounds really good to me, too," she declared. She turned away as if to go back to the kitchen to tell the cook, but then paused. "So is your doctor boyfriend coming tomorrow?"

I groaned. "He's not my boyfriend. I'm surprised he wants anything to do with me," I admitted. "He's actually coming on Saturday, Emma needs a checkup and I need blood work done. He's concerned I have some sort of gestational issue since I can't keep any food down."

"You don't seem very worried," she remarked.

"No, I don't think there's anything wrong. I've always had a weak stomach." I rubbed my belly. "I do need to figure out a way to get my meals to stay down, though, because she needs some nourishment."

"So do you, Anabel. You look ridiculously skinny for a pregnant woman." In Alexis land, this was nearly a compliment.

"Well it's not for lack of trying," I rejoined. "What can I say? My little girl is probably going to give me as much trouble as I gave all of my caretakers. In fact, I'm still causing all sorts of problems, so I guess all is fair."

She almost smiled at me. "So you think it's a girl?"

"I know," I told her. "We talk. Believe me."

She nodded. "I knew when I was pregnant with Abby that she was a girl, and the same with Caleb. It's just mother's intuition. I think it's a good sign." She even smiled at me.

Surprised at the sweetness she was showing me, I looked up at her. "Can I ask you something?"

"What's up?" she asked, sitting down next to me. Without thinking, I scooted back a bit; I wasn't used to being in such close proximity to Alexis. It's hard to be around someone who you know doesn't like you, and Alexis' dislike of me was blatant.

Still, I should at least try. "It's becoming real to me that I'm going to have a baby," I revealed, "and I'm just worried I'm going to be a terrible mother. I don't know what to do, Alexis. How am I supposed to take care of a child?"

"Oh, Anabel," she sighed. "You will have plenty of support in that corner. Sam and I will help you out, and once the hearings are over you can attend some parenting classes. If you want, I'll get you some books."

I gave her a small smile. "Thank you. I guess I was just afraid about doing this all on my own. You know, since Emma's father is Jared and I have trouble being within five feet of him."

"I loathe Jared Sorensen," she asserted. It was really nice to have an actual conversation with her, especially one in which we had similar opinions. "He really does a number on my nerves. He was always lurking in the shadows or popping out of a door and scaring me. I never understood why Sam counted on him so much." She leaned forward and lowered her voice. "I used to think that he had a crush on me, as he always seemed to find a reason to talk to me alone."

"Well I'm sorry you have to see him tonight, as it's my fault he's coming to dinner. Sam wants to talk to him about what we're going to do once the baby's born."

"What are we going to do?" she asked.

I shrugged. "I have no idea."

That was when the doorbell rang. I looked at my brother, who had re-entered the room. "Now listen, Anabel," he lectured. "You must control yourself. Do not say anything that you will regret. Understood?"

"I think I've done enough of that for one day," I muttered. Alexis raised an eyebrow. "Oh, I may have announced that I'm carrying Jared's child to not only him, but the distinguished members of the press. Please don't lecture me," I continued. "Marilyn came upon me in the bathroom with my jacket off, and she knew."

She stiffened. "Well, you need to watch what you say to them. They're already fascinated that you talk back to Sam."

"He's my brother, not my dad." I looked up at him. "I'm sorry, but I don't care if you were President, you aren't my boss."

The doorbell rang again. "I'm answering that," my brother called to the guard at the door. The guard nodded, and Nate appeared. Sam walked off, his security detail in tow.

Alexis looked like she wanted to say something, but I closed my eyes and she held her tongue.

"Anabel?"

I opened my eyes and saw Sam and Jared. Alexis excused herself, and I managed a half-smile at the two of them. "I'm sorry. I just got really tired all of the sudden."

"If you're not feeling well, we can do this another time—" began my brother.

"No, let's get it over with, shall we?" I looked at him. "Sit down, Jared. Next to me."

His discomfort was evident as he lowered himself onto the sofa. Sam moved to sit down as well, but I ordered, "Leave us."

He stared hard at me. I stared right back. Sam let out an exasperated sigh. "Fine, but call me if you need anything," he muttered as he walked away.

I turned to Jared. "So."

"So," he managed.

Then there was silence. I pulled my ponytail loose and ran my fingers through my messy pre-Raphaelite curls.

Then Jared started to laugh.

"What's so funny?"

"I can't believe you just stared down the former president of the United States."

"I've never had much regard for propriety."

Silence again.

"So…how pregnant are you?" he asked.

"Very pregnant, Jared. I hadn't been aware there was any other kind," I smiled in spite of myself.

"I mean, how far along are you?"

"Almost five months." I reached onto the table and picked up a couple of ultrasounds. "Here she is. Her sex is indistinguishable in this picture, but when they do my next ultrasound, I predict they will say it's a girl."

He looked at the pictures in astonishment. "This is insane. A baby. We're going to be parents," he said, almost in a daze. Amazing, I thought. I had managed to throw off Jared Sorensen.

"Yes, about that," I began.

He looked at me, and I was surprised to see he looked a bit sad. "Anabel, I do want to be in her life," he told me.

"Yes," I acknowledged, "it's just I am unsure as to what extent I want you in mine." I stood up, and began pacing. "A child should have both her father and her mother in her life. I feel very strongly on that point. However, as to the matter of it being you and me as her parents, well...that brings certain complications, and we need to figure out where we stand with each other before we can even begin to contemplate raising this child together."

"Well, I'll be there for you, Anabel. For you and for her," he vowed.

"You're really confusing," I shook my head. "I never thought of you as the paternal type, honestly."

"Well, what do you want? I suppose we could move in together."

"Ugh," I grimaced. "That doesn't sound right to me, Jared. I'm pretty sure my brother would have a fit over that."

"So what, do you want me to marry you or something?"

"Do you want to marry me or something?" I shook my head. "Don't say stuff like that."

"Marrying you wouldn't be the worst thing in the world."

"Don't be ridiculous," I scoffed. "You have no intention of marrying me."

"I'm serious!" And he almost looked it.

So I decided, for his sake and mine, to set the record straight. "I'm not going to press charges, Jared," I assured him.

"What?" he asked, confused.

"I know you're just saying that to cover your bases." I rubbed my still-aching head.

"Wait, honey, you're mistaken."

"Do not call me honey," I snapped.

He ignored that. "Look, I deserve it if you want to prosecute me. However," he continued, "I owe it to you to do the right thing by you. And if that is to marry you and raise our daughter together, then that is what I want to do. If that's what you want."

"I don't—I hadn't considered that," I stumbled over the words. I was starting to get annoyed with him. What business did he have being all moral? I had just assumed we would work out some sort of custody arrangement after the baby was born and I could go on with my very messed-up feelings for Jared tucked securely away in the back of my mind. "Do you love me?" I asked.

He didn't answer, but stared at me.

"Do you love me, Jared?" I asked again. "Because now's the time to tell me."

"I think I do, Anabel," he said.

I stared down at him, pursing my lips. Then I threw my hands up in the air. "Well that's just it. I don't know what I feel for you. Some days I see you as Prince Charming, who came down and taught me how to feel things I had never felt before. Other days I see you, and it's not just the morning sickness making me retch. I see you as the man who took away from me something that I should have been able to give freely." I turned away. "Then there are the days where I remember that, like it or not, you were the one who saved me. I hate feeling like I owe you something," I finished.

"I take it your feelings for me aren't so straightforward," he concluded.

"Yes, thank you, Captain Obvious," I turned and sent him what I hoped was a scathing glare. "I didn't plan to be pregnant, but here I am. I'm tired all of the time. My ankles have started to swell. Supposedly I shouldn't be having as much morning sickness, but every morning I wake up and head straight to the bathroom. My hormones are all over the place, and every day I have to see you, and I don't know whether to laugh or to cry at our predicament. Soon I'm going to have all sorts of responsibilities to a tiny helpless baby, and I have no idea how to take care of one of those. I can barely take care of myself at this point! My brother and his wife have given up their lives, their lives, Jared, to take care of me, and I feel horrible. I can't even offer them any sort of compensation until the mess with my father's will is straightened out. So here I am, mooching off of them for God only knows how long. I can't even get a job at this point, and—ooh," I stopped, and felt my knees give way as the room started getting white.

And he was at my side, supporting me, holding me. "Anabel, are you okay?" He sounded worried. "What's wrong?"

"Dizzy," I managed. He helped me back onto the sofa. I leaned against him and he put his arm around me. We sat there for a few minutes, and my head cleared and the ringing in my ears went away. "Jared?"

"Yes?" He pushed some curls out of my face.

"When I was little and Marilyn first came to live with us, I used to get very angry with her because she wasn't my mom." I shifted my weight a little bit. "I would throw things at her. I was only two, maybe three, but I would tell her I hated her. I'm sure it must have been an awful situation for her, on an island with a crazy toddler and no one to talk to but my dad...well, when I had these tantrums, she would always tell me she forgave me. So I learned that when people wrong you, you forgive them." I paused. "I'm having a lot of trouble forgiving you, though."

"I don't blame you. What I did to you is without excuse."

"Yes, you've said that," I commented, "but you know, we should talk about it."

"I didn't want to rush you into discussing that."

In spite of myself, I started to giggle. "It's been five months; I don't know how much longer I have to wait."

"Anabel, I just—"

I cut him off. "What really bothers me about the whole thing is I just don't understand—why did you do it? It didn't have to be like that, and—"

"Dinner," announced Sam, appearing at the door. Jared stood up and extended me a hand, and I took it. We walked down the hall to the dining room and sat down to eat.

Oh, *that* was an uncomfortable affair. We ate in silence, with Alexis staring at Sam and Sam staring at me and—well, I was going to town on those tacos. I was rarely hungry, but the tacos were amazing. Plus, if I didn't have enough food in my stomach the chances were extremely high of me throwing up my prenatal vitamin. Pregnancy was becoming my personal eating disorder and feeling hungry for once was really bolstering me. Jared cleared his throat a few times, but I was determined not to look at him and instead focused on eating. I loaded each and every taco high with chicken, sour cream, and tomatoes galore. I had consumed about two and a half of my concoctions when my brother finally came out with, "After tonight I think you should stay away from us as much as possible."

"Excuse me?" said Jared, and I opened my mouth to object when my brother continued. "You heard me, Sorensen. I don't want you trying to talk to Anabel at the hearings. I don't want you to implicate her in anyone thinking she had a hand in her father's death. I especially don't want you sending messengers here with notes for her at all hours, and—"

"Wait," I interjected, "he's been sending me notes?"

Sam looked a little guilty. "Annie, it was for your own good—"

"This is exactly the sort of thing Jonathan would do to me, Sam, and I can't believe you would do it too!" I turned to Jared. "I owe you an apology, I just thought you were ignoring the messages I sent you in the beginning."

"You were sending him messages?" I could hear the judgment in Sam's voice.

"Yes, Sam, I was. I wanted to see if he was going to behave responsibly." I really should eat that other taco. I shoved it in my mouth and chewed deliberately, staring all of them down. "That's why I was so angry with him. I thought he didn't care about me, and I wanted to see when I should tell him about the baby." I took a long swig of juice. "Now I'm angrier at you than I am at him." I turned to Sam. "I love you, I do, but I'm not a kid anymore. Jared?" I looked across the table. "You and I are going for a walk."

"Someone will see you," protested Sam. "The last thing we need is pictures of you two gallivanting around town, looking like you're in on this together."

"In on what together? I haven't made any effort to be nice to Jared. I do believe that last week I told that man who called from the Washington Post who called that he deserved to be disbarred!"

Jared looked uncomfortable. "We don't have to go, Anabel."

"Yes we do." I was determined.

"Where are you going?" asked Sam.

"I want ice cream. He's going to buy me some."

Chapter 13—Anabel

Blair House is located on Pennsylvania Avenue, right by the Ellipse and Lafayette Park. I had wanted a walk, but Jared convinced me that since I had nearly fainted before, it would probably be a good idea to take a car. And because we were taking a car, I felt it necessary to head up to Larry's Homemade Ice Cream.

My first week in the District of Columbia, before they had put me under house arrest, Sam had (rather covertly) taken me there. Their ice cream was amazing—they had all the normal flavors, like chocolate and vanilla, but they also had some amazing creations: Key West, Ecstasy, Fred and Ginger...but my favorite was the Oatmeal Cookie Dough ice cream. The base is a cinnamon ice cream, and it contains huge chunks of oatmeal cookie dough and chocolate chips. Of course, now that I knew about the baby, I settled for a chocolate milkshake. Jared, however, got the Oatmeal Cookie Dough, and I saw a look of pure enjoyment pass over his face as we sat down at the table together.

"I know, it's amazing." I slurped a little milkshake. "In spite of the fact that I have a lot of trouble keeping food down, I've gained a lot of weight not being on the island. When I feel like it, I eat everything in sight."

"Aside from the belly, you look the same," he smiled.

"Don't," I said. "I've had a rough couple of months, Jared. I haven't talked to you—really talked to you—in a long time. I barely remember the last time I saw you! My brother, I am pretty sure, is waiting for the opportune moment to draw and quarter you. And just so you know, for your safety, I didn't tell him about what happened with us until I got a positive pregnancy test."

"I imagine that didn't go over well."

"No," I returned. "No, it didn't. When we were summoned for the hearings he ranted and raved and swore up and down that justice would be served and your uppance would come. It also didn't help that Alexis, for whatever reason, thinks that you are in cahoots with the Prince of Darkness and reminds Sam as such on a daily basis." I briefly thought about what Alexis had said earlier, but decided to ignore that. "He sent his kids away, and I feel terrible about that. He resigned from office to take care of me."

"It was a very honorable thing to do," acknowledged Jared. He ran his hand through is blonde hair and then took mine.

We sat there for a moment, him holding my hand. I attempted to smile at him. "You know, this is almost nice."

"Yeah?'

"Yeah." I looked down. "But Jared, about Sam, I just don't know what I'm going to do."

"Do? What do you mean?"

"I feel guilty," I blurted out. "I'm causing a strain in his marriage, I've ruined his political career...and I can't do for him the one thing he wants me to do, which is press charges against you. Plus, I'm pregnant. He's been paying for my doctor, and my wardrobe, and he feeds me, and, well, he's like my parent. And I don't want to be an ungrateful child and disappoint him."

"So this is about Sam," commented Jared.

"Yes." I shivered a little, and drew my sweater around my shoulders. "He's spent years protecting me, Jared. I have to look at this from his perspective. Even if I were to forgive you, it would hurt him very deeply. I don't want to be...well...selfish, and—"

"Anabel," he interjected, "you are not a child. Furthermore, you're not his child. I think you're just using Sam as an excuse."

"An excuse for what?"

"You want to be with me, and you know it." It was just like Jared to go from one minute being almost likeable to downright disgusting in the next. He was so self-satisfied that, had my milkshake not been so heavenly, I would have thrown it in his face.

"Oh yes, Jared, that's it," I said, heavy on the sarcasm. "Have you forgotten what you did to me?"

"Look," he said, his voice heated, "I told you I was sorry. You don't understand what happened that night. Your father got me drunk, and—"

"Oh no," I said, standing up and backing away from him, "you are not—you are not blaming this on my father. He is dead, and he would never have wanted you to touch me. This is why I don't think you and I are a good idea," I snapped. "We really bring out the worst in each other."

"Yes, we do," he agreed. "So you could make the argument we're perfect for each other."

I stared at him, unsure whether to laugh or cry. "I hate when you do that."

"Do what?"

"You disarm me like that. It's not fair. I'm trying to be mad at you here."

He stood up and moved close to me. "But you're having a hard time, aren't you?"

"I told you," I protested, "this doesn't work on me anymore."

"And I told you, I think you're very wrong about that." His face was inches away from mine, and I thought what it would be like to give in to him again...but I couldn't. Taking a deep breath, I stepped back. "I'm not in a place to do this with you, Jared."

I saw something flash in his eyes, but he nodded and stepped back. "I respect that."

"Okay, now I'm convinced that you are not the Jared I used to know," I teased.

But he looked serious as he sat back down. "No, you were right. We have other things we have to deal with. Monday, well, it's pretty inevitable we're going to have to talk about what happened with us."

"I still don't see what that has to do with Jonathan's death. It's not like either you or I killed him. Although," I reflected, "I guess I had as much of a motive as anybody."

"Sit down, Anabel. We have to talk about that."

"Talk about what?" I asked, sitting down and scooting my chair as far away from him as possible.

"They're going to ask me questions, and I don't want to lie, but if I tell the truth...it portrays your father in an extremely negative light," he said, looking away.

"I don't believe that any of us have held back our criticisms of him thus far," I pointed out.

He looked frustrated. "You know, you talk like a book sometimes."

I grinned. "Well, you have to remember that books still are my only friends. I haven't exactly been socializing while I've been here, and the people who I do meet don't know what to say to me."

"Look, the point is," he stopped himself. "What he said to me that night, and what happened..." he leaned in closer to me, "it was a game to him, and he said some horrible things about you. I just want you to be prepared, because I am going to tell the truth, and it may not be easy for you to hear."

I studied his face. He looked a lot older than he had when we first met. There were deep purple bags under his eyes that must have been a result of many sleepless nights. It was apparent to me that, in whatever twisted way it was, he cared about me. The media hadn't exactly been giving him an easy time, they were portraying him as possible murderer—and I was guessing after my outburst, they would start presenting him as a statutory rapist. A wave of compassion ran through me, but I steeled myself. It didn't really matter what I did or did not feel for him, I had to protect myself—and my baby.

Finally, in a matter-of-fact tone, I said, "Well, you have to tell the truth. And the truth hurts sometimes. We just have to accept that."

"Why are you being so nice to me?" he asked, his voice strained. "I don't deserve it."

"No," I agreed, "but I am a pragmatist, Jared. I always have been. I have always been trying to figure out a way to survive, whether it was on the island or here. I have to view the world that way, otherwise I will lose it. I have to take the facts as facts, the past as past, and I can't change it, so I just deal with it. Do you have any idea how horrible I feel?" I looked into his gray eyes. "The last time I saw my father, I screamed at him about how much I hated him. He was what he was, Jared, but that does not mean that I didn't love him. Now I will never have the opportunity to tell him that, and it eats me alive." I took a deep breath. "Then I look at you, the only person who I felt understood me—who I am—and accepted me. You made me feel like a normal person, even though I'm not. Now," I continued, wringing my hands in my lap, "I have to deal with the knowledge that you did something to me so heinous, so unforgivable, that I ought to cut you out of my life entirely. So the very first person who is actually my friend, a friend that I made on my own...the point is, this afternoon, Marilyn came upon me in the bathroom and saw my belly, and something inside of me snapped when she discovered me. I had to take charge of the situation. I had to tell you on my own terms. I didn't want you, much less the press, finding out any other way. Granted, I probably should have thought a little bit before I put on my show, but I wanted to be in charge. Do you understand?"

He looked at me with pity and regret, and I glared at him. "Stop feeling sorry for me," I snapped. "I can't take it. I just need you to understand what is going on with me."

There was silence, and then he asked, "So where does that leave us?"

"That's up to you," I replied. "You won't encounter any legal troubles from me. You are welcome to see Emma at any time."

"But what about you and me?"

I shook my head at him. "I can't answer that right now. I don't know how I feel about this—about everything—and I need time to figure it out. At this moment, though, what I can tell you is that there is not a you and me, and you have to respect that, or I will go completely and utterly insane."

He gave me a sad smile, and I continued. "What I don't want is for you to put your life on hold for me, because it would not be fair for me to ask that of you. I hate to admit this, I really do, but I do care about you a great deal, and I want you to be happy. If that means you find someone who makes you happy, you should be with that person."

"I don't think I can be happy without you," he remarked.

"You know, you didn't know me this time last year."

"I wasn't happy then, either."

We walked outside and down Connecticut Avenue until the car picked us up. On the ride back to Blair House we were both quiet, until he turned to me and said, "I'm not giving up, Anabel."

"No, Jared," I returned. "I wouldn't expect you to." I sighed. "Look, the doctor is going to do another checkup on Saturday, so you may as well come. He's coming around eight. I know it's early for a Saturday, but I would like you to be there."

"Your doctor, huh?"

"Yes," I said cautiously. "Why?"

"I need to ask you something."

I looked at him. He seemed to be concentrating very hard on the seat in front of him. "Are the rumors true?"

Ugh, he knew. Still, I feigned innocence. "About what?" I had hoped to avoid this, but Jared wouldn't let me off that easy.

"About Kevin Miller."

"Sam pardoned him, if that's what you mean," I kept my voice as light as I could. "A bit controversial, really, but again, another reason why I ruined his political career."

"You know that's not what I mean," he said.

"Well, what do you mean, then? I'm tired, Jared, I had a long day." I avoided looking into his eyes.

"Are you seeing him?" He was trying to sound nonchalant, but I knew better.

"Well, he is my doctor," I pointed out. "I see him a lot; he doesn't have a whole bunch of patients at the moment."

Jared sighed in frustration, so I relented. "No, Jared. As much as my brother would like me to, I am not, nor will I ever be, dating Kevin. Sam agreed to take him on as my doctor since he was free to make house calls, and it gives him time to get re-established in his practice. There's nothing going on with us. You're the only person I've ever felt like that about. You were the only one with whom I've even considered what it would be like to have a relationship. So much so that I cannot even countenance the idea of being with someone it actually makes sense to be with. Does that make you feel any better?"

His face relaxed. "Yes."

"I'm glad one of us does."

Chapter 14—Jared

The answering machine clicked on. "It's Meghan. Call me back. You know why."

About two hours later: "I know you're there. Call me, Jared."

And then another hour later: "Honey, it's your mom. I saw the newspapers…thought you might want to talk…"

And finally, Meghan called me again. "Look, if you don't answer, I'm coming over there."

So I picked up. "What?"

"Don't you talk to me that way!" my sister hissed. "I wanted to make sure you hadn't done anything stupid. Well, stupider than get a teenager pregnant."

"I take it you read the papers this morning."

"'I take it you read the papers this morning,'" she mimicked. "Yes, Jared. I did. I read the papers, watched the news, and had several people at work ask me about what my opinion was of your little escapades with Sam Sallinger's sister!"

I rolled back over in my bed. I hadn't gotten up yet. "I appreciate your concern, Meghan, but I am fine, aside from feeling like I just got hit by a truck."

"So you're hung over?" I could hear her disapproval.

"No," I groaned. "I haven't had a drink since that blasted island. That's how this whole mess started."

"I want to see you," she demanded. "Can you meet me tomorrow?"

"In the afternoon, yes. I'm seeing Anabel in the morning."

"Oh, for the love of God," she moaned. "Fine. Do whatever you want. Just call Mom back, she's having a breakdown."

I hung up on her, and pulled a pillow over my eyes. After I left Blair House, I had come home and gotten in my bed and hadn't moved since.

Out of all the things to come out of Anabel's mouth, the last thing in the world I expected her to say was, "You knocked me up, Jared."

Or, "Do you want to marry me?" The scorn that accompanied that question had bothered me. She didn't need to get so defensive. Things were impossible with us, anyway. Still, I couldn't help but wonder...

Did I want to marry Anabel?

I remembered a conversation I'd had with Sam, many years ago. He and I were at some function, and we were both watching my date, a gorgeous redhead, chat up the bartender. He grinned at me. "So what's the deal with this one?"

I had shrugged.

"Are you ever going to settle down?"

"Maybe if I find a girl who's worth it."

"That is the problem," he lamented. "There are girls you sleep with and then there are girls that you marry."

"You lucked out," I said, clapping his shoulder. "You found one who is both. I doubt I will ever make enough effort to find one of those."

But Anabel, well, she was complicated.

It could be worse, I reflected. Considering everything, it was shocking that I hadn't gotten a girl pregnant before now. And the fact that it was her…

I definitely liked Anabel. She was really funny and smart and endearing. She was also oblivious to the fact that she was gorgeous. I normally dated beautiful women—but they always knew how hot they were.

On the other hand, she also antagonized me in a way that no other woman had ever done before—which was why she had made me so angry the first day of the hearings. It was also why half of our conversations on the island had resulted in one of us snapping at the other, which caused the other to fire back. My temper was as bad as hers; worst of all, she knew how to push me. Maybe our problem, I reasoned, is that none of our fights had ever resulted in make-up sex. If we could factor that in…

"What is wrong with you?" I asked myself. "That's more wrong than the rest of this combined."

At least life with Anabel would be a challenge. If she wanted me. And I knew, even if I didn't want to admit it to myself, that I wanted her. More than anything.

The moment she had told me she was pregnant, life made sense. There was no one for me but her.

Screw it. I called Sam.

He answered his phone with, "Why are you calling me?"

"I need to talk to her."

"You can talk to her tomorrow."

"Is that Jared?" I heard her say in the background.

"Put her on, Sam."

"Anabel, no, I'm not—"

"Sam," and Anabel sounded dangerous here, "give me the phone."

Sam sighed. "You have five minutes."

So then she came on. "Hi."

"You okay over there?"

"I guess," she said. Then she continued in a thunderous whisper, "But Sam and Alexis brought over all of these people to coach me on what to say to the press. I've been listening to all sorts of lectures on how inappropriate my behavior was yesterday."

"Did they at least give you a how-to manual on how to handle it next time?" Thinking about her show for the cameras made me smile.

"No, but I was made to feel incredibly guilty for exposing my brother to such negativity." She paused. "So what's up?"

"I need to ask you something. How long has Sam known?"

"How long has Sam known what?"

"You know what I mean. Don't do that. How long has your brother known that you're pregnant?"

"Oh," she stammered. "Well, let's see. They took me from Caereon and brought me here, and I just laid around for a while, and after I had been here for about a month it dawned on me that I couldn't remember the last time I had my period..." She paused. "I thought it was just from stress, you know? But then something didn't seem right, and I started to get all nauseous and one day I threw up my breakfast." She fell quiet again.

"And then, Anabel?" I prompted her.

"And then, Jared," she continued, "two more weeks went by and I asked Alexis what I should do."

"How did she take that?"

"Not well at all," she admitted. "I came up to her and said, 'Hey, Alexis. How do you know if you're pregnant?' But I didn't have anyone else to go to, and she was mortified. So then I took like three pregnancy tests just to make sure. And then I had to tell my brother." She laughed bitterly. "Our conversation started out the way most of our conversations go nowadays: 'Sam, you're not going to like this...'"

"I see," I digested this.

"I hadn't told them about us," she confided. "Not at that point. I mean, Sam resigned pretty much right away, and we were dealing with all of that. So when I told him about us, he did not react well, as I'm sure you can recall."

"I suspect you're alluding to our phone conversation that night."

"I did eavesdrop, a little," she admitted. "But I had implored him not to tell you about the baby, and he did that for me." She sighed. "I just didn't want to upset him, you know? But now all I do upsets him."

"Your brother loves you," I barked. Why was it every time I tried to say something comforting to her it made me sound like more of a jerk?

"I know," she retorted. "Love doesn't have anything to do with it."

"Anabel—"

"Did you want something? My five minutes are almost up."

I sighed. "I was thinking about what you said yesterday."

"Which part?"

"The part where you asked me if I love you."

"Oh," she stammered. "Jared, I don't expect you to—"

"I have an answer for you."

"I oughtn't—I shouldn't have asked," she sputtered.

"What are you scared of?" I asked her.

"I'm scared of what I might do, depending on your answer," she admitted. "Why are you calling me on the phone to tell me this, anyway? Don't I deserve a face to face?"

She seriously made me mad. "Well, forget it then."

"No, wait, I—"

"No, clearly you don't care about what I have to say," I reprimanded her.

"Jared, I didn't mean—"

"Anabel, I don't have time to argue semantics with you." And with that, I hung up on her.

Then I threw my phone down. If there was one thing I'd learned about Anabel and me, it was that together, we could ruin any moment.

Chapter 15—Jared

The next morning I woke up mentally berating myself. I needed to cut her some slack; pregnant women weren't known for their rationality. As I showered, I resolved to be nice to her, no matter what. Getting dressed, I told myself that this was the mother of my child and that I would show her some respect. It was with this mindset that I left my apartment with a spring in my step.

I was mildly entertained when I showed up at Blair House and a scowling Alexis pushed past the Secret Service guy and glared at me. "Good morning, beautiful," I greeted her. "You're looking fantastic, as always. I can only assume that because you're answering the door, you want some alone time with me, but sadly, you have a husband." I made a show of looking over her head. "Where is Samuel, anyway?"

"Nice to know you haven't changed," she spat. "But I don't really understand what you're doing here, Jared." She ran her perfectly manicured fingers through her hair, and then crossed her arms. "Nobody wants you here, you know. Not even her."

I leaned forward and whispered in her ear. "Oh, maybe not her. But there's always you."

"Shut up, you idiot," she hissed. "Do you not realize there are people listening to our every conversation?"

"Unlike you, I have nothing to hide." Nothing like she did, at any rate.

She stared at me, disgusted. "You aren't going to be here long, are you?" She was a beautiful woman, especially when she was angry. Having made a career out of making Alexis angry, I was intimately acquainted with this side of her.

"It depends on what Anabel wants." I watched to see how she took that one.

Her expression did not change. "Anabel wants nothing to do with you. She isn't that dumb."

"Are you sure about that, Lexie?" I said slyly. "Or are you just saying that because you're jealous?"

She banged the door open. "Upstairs. Doctor Miller is with her."

As I walked up the stairs, I heard Anabel talking to Sam. "He should be here any minute," I heard her say. "I didn't expect Kevin to be here so early."

"I can't believe you invited him," he replied.

"Well, I can't change that now," she retorted. "Besides, I need to see more of him so I can figure out what to do about—oh." As I stood in the doorway, her blue eyes focused on me. "It's no wonder Alexis doesn't like you. You shouldn't sneak up like that."

A greeting I probably deserved. "Good morning to you, too," I replied. I looked at her brother. "Sam."

He grunted. "I have things to attend to. I will see you later, Anabel." Ignoring me, he left the room, leaving the two of us to stare awkwardly at each other. She was still in her nightgown, her messy hair spread over the pillow. She indicated a chair close to her. "You can sit there if you like."

"Won't the doctor need to sit there?" I asked.

"No, he usually uses that little stool over there." She pointed to the far corner of the room. Then she grinned. "Don't worry. I know it doesn't look it, but I did brush my teeth this morning."

I sat down next to her. "Hey, I'm sorry about yesterday."

"It's okay. I didn't behave any better than you did." She looked away, and another uncomfortable silence ensued.

"So," I said, attempting to break the tension, "I was talking to my mom this morning."

She looked thoughtful. "I guess it never occurred to me that you might actually have parents. I just assumed you hatched somewhere."

"Ouch." She was smiling, though. I supposed it was no different from most of the other accusatory epithets she flung at me.

"Tell me about your parents," she demanded.

"They're both retired and live in Cape Cod. My mom was an elementary school teacher and my father was an accountant who used to work for Sam's parents. They're both very sweet people—despite having me for a son."

"Do you have any brothers or sisters?" She ignored the self-deprecation.

"Two sisters, actually. They're twins and are eight years younger than me. Crystal is in England right now. She's a Rhodes scholar and is studying at Cambridge. Meghan actually lives in the District. She's a public defender, and we usually get dinner every Wednesday night, during which she repeatedly tells me what a horrible excuse for a brother I am."

"They sound delightful," came the reply. "Are they identical?"

"Yes, but they don't look that much alike. Crystal has long blonde hair that she keeps down to her waist, and she always dresses vaguely medieval. You know, long flowing skirts, etc. Meghan cut her hair short and dyed it red, and I can't remember the last time I didn't see her wearing a pantsuit." I should probably call her and confirm for this afternoon. She had left me two more voicemails the night before, which I hadn't answered as I was too preoccupied with the recent realization I was about to be a father. Also, I was looking forward to her perception of Anabel's disclosure to the media, and I was sure she would lecture me on how irresponsible she thought I was.

There was a tap at the door. "Anabel? May I come in?"

"Hi Kevin!" she called. "Yes you may, I'm dressed."

So Kevin Miller walked in, and I took a moment to size up the competition.

I'm taller than he is, but not by much. He was thin—gaunt, really—and his lab coat hung on him. My best guess was his time in prison did not treat him well.

Anabel was cheerful. "Kevin, this is Jared, the unsuspecting father of the baby. Jared, this is Dr. Kevin Miller, my good friend." We shook hands. Despite the lean appearance, he had a firm grip, and I could tell I was not welcome with him.

"How are you feeling?" he asked her, tenderly. It was obvious he still had a thing for her.

"Dandy," she replied. "I haven't thrown up yet this morning! I think we're making some progress!"

He laughed and then started checking her vitals. "How's your stress level?"

"Gross," she said, making a face. "I lost it at the hearing yesterday."

"So I read," he told her.

Her eyes widened. "Oh no—where?"

"In the *Post*," he replied.

"Really?" she asked, fascinated. "I'm that big of a deal, huh?" She beamed. "Were there pictures?"

"Oh yes," he said, "of you and Mr. Sorensen here."

She let out a hysterical giggle. I didn't like this at all. Her moods were all over the place, and it wasn't just the pregnancy. I wanted to get her away from all of this. Maybe if the two of us could go somewhere, somewhere far from everything and just talk things over, then we could work out all of this insanity.

"Jared?" she asked, and I looked at her. Her face was flushed. "Do you want to see the baby?"

"Oh, uh, yeah, sure," I said.

Her eyes narrowed. "You don't sound that sure," she accused.

I smiled, hoping to placate her. "I am sure. I just was thinking. I'm sorry."

She relaxed. "Ok, show us," she told Kevin.

He looked at me. "Can you turn out the lights?"

I obliged, and he said to her, "You'll feel a little cold. Let's see what's going on here." The next thing I knew, there it was. On the screen. Our baby.

"There's the heart, nice and strong," Kevin showed her. "And it looks like…it's definitely a girl."

Anabel sent me a sideways smile. "I told you."

"I believed you," I said. "This is amazing." I took her hand.

"Well, everything looks good." Kevin began packing up his things. "Call me if you need anything, otherwise I'll see you in two weeks."

"Thank you, Kevin," she smiled. "You're the best."

"I'm just glad you're feeling better. I know it was really rough for you."

She nodded, and I frowned. "What does he mean by that?"

"Oh, well…" Anabel paused. "Well, you see, I got really sick once I hit nine weeks along."

Kevin was packing up his things and he stopped to look at her. "That's almost an understatement. She couldn't keep anything down. She could barely get out of bed—"

"—and," Anabel cut in, "I went through a minor fit of depression. I spent most of my time, lying in bed, alternating between reading and watching reruns of The Golden Girls and old movies." She sighed. "But I just didn't feel like doing anything else. And once I realized how hard eating was, I lost my desire to do it."

There was another uneasy silence, and then she added, "But then I realized that there was a poor, innocent baby who was depending on me for sustenance, I started forcing myself to eat. And I have to admit, I started to feel better."

Kevin nodded again. "She's done a lot better in recent weeks, but we were concerned she might not be well enough to go to the hearings."

"The health issues your brother mentioned," I recalled.

She nodded. "Yeah, nobody wanted to broadcast the pregnancy, for some odd reason." She smiled up at Kevin. "I don't know what I would've done without Kevin."

He smiled at her, grimaced at me, and left.

I looked at her. She looked happy for the first time since I had seen her. "You should probably go, too," she decided. "I can guarantee you it's only a matter of minutes before Sam comes up here and tries to kick you out. He was not happy when I told him that you were coming this morning."

"Do you want me to go?"

"No," she acknowledged, "but my opinions don't really matter too much around here." She flattened herself against the pillows. "Besides, I need some time to myself. I may even bathe, who knows?"

I wanted to talk to her about everything, and she was frustrating me. "You know, you're driving me insane."

"This whole thing is crazy," she agreed. "I am sorry about that, though. I know I can be a bit of a challenge. Still, cheer up. I think I'm in a worse situation than you. I mean, I know darn well that you wouldn't even have any interest in me if I wasn't pregnant. I have to deal with that."

"Anabel—"

"No!" she insisted. "I can't do this with you, this is—"

"I don't want to talk about how absurd this is. We could go around for hours doing that. I just want to tell you I'm on your side, okay? Stop treating me like the enemy. Unless you haven't forgiven me, in which case—"

"I forgave you a long time ago," she cut me off. "So don't do this. We're on the same team right now. We want what's best for the baby, right?"

"Right," I said, confused.

"Well then, I'll see you later." A yawn escaped her lips. "I'm so tired. I was up late last night writing about my hatred for you in haiku form."

I couldn't believe this. "You were not."

"Was too," she countered. "Jared Sorensen / Knocked me up, now I can't sleep / baby hurts my back." She gave me a grin. "It helps that your name is five syllables."

"You are the most ridiculous person I have ever met."

"I have no doubt," she chuckled. "Now go away. You can come over tomorrow if you want. I'm going to read a book today." She picked up a copy of The Historian.

"That's a long book to read in one day, Anabel."

"Well then, I had better get started." She smiled. "Goodbye. Please don't talk to anyone on your way out. It makes my life easier." She looked thoughtful. "Come around two tomorrow. We'll talk shop for Monday." Anabel buried her nose in her book, and I knew I had been dismissed.

When I walked into the hallway I was met with three angry faces: Kevin, Sam, and Alexis. Not wanting to deal with this, I announced, "I'm not allowed to talk to any of you, so I will see you tomorrow afternoon, per

Anabel's request." They all gaped at me, and I let myself out.

I could at least keep my word to her in that respect.

Later, I met Meghan at the Starbucks by the National Gallery of Art. As I had feared, she had a copy of the Post. I sat down, and by way of greeting she thrust it in my face.

"I already saw it."

Meghan stared at me. "You are a nightmare, you know that?" She straightened her glasses. "I'm also more than a little grossed out, Jared. She's nineteen. NINETEEN!"

"She's almost twenty," I offered.

Meghan glared at me frostily.

"You look tired, Meg," I observed, hoping I could steer the conversation away from me.

"Of course I do," she scoffed. "I work eighty hours a week. My weekends are spent preparing for trial. Plus, I'm your sister, God help me, which is a full-time position on its own."

"I don't want to do this with you." This was a mistake.

"Well, too bad!" She sat back in her chair. "Buy me a latte and then we are going to discuss this, mister. Light whip."

When I returned with the drinks, she got right down to business. "So I'm going to be an aunt, huh?"

"Before you even start," I warned, "I've already been dealt several severe blows to my ego not only by our esteemed mother, but Miss Martin herself this morning. Mom felt the need to point out that when Anabel was in diapers, I was going through puberty, and then proceeded to lecture me on the state of my soul. And you and I both know how Mom feels about the state of my soul." Meghan grunted, so I continued. "When I arrived at Blair House I was screamed at by Alexis and nearly jumped by Anabel's doctor—who, in case you were wondering, was that inmate that Sam pardoned—and speaking of Sam, I think that if I hadn't gotten out of there so quickly, he would've slugged me. Now, as for Anabel, she has put her absolute disgust of me into poetry. It wasn't bad, really, but does nothing for the old self-esteem."

"How's Alexis looking?" she asked sharply.

I shrugged. "Same as usual. Gorgeous."

My sister snorted. "You always had a problem with her."

"No, she always had a problem with me. I told you, it wasn't like that. She was my best friend's wife."

"And what was Anabel?"

I ignored this. "She really hates Anabel, though, that's pretty apparent."

"I can't believe you got the little floozy pregnant."

"She is a lot of things, but floozy isn't one of them."

"Oh please," she rolled her eyes, gesticulating toward the paper. "She just busts out with, hey, got a bun in the oven? In front of everyone? Embarrassing not only herself, but you, and her poor brother." Meghan shook her head. "She is clearly unwell. She's kind of pretty, but that's really all she has going for her, except for the damsel in distress complex. You always liked to date those girls who needed rescuing, and this one definitely needs to be saved from herself."

"Meghan," I began, "she's been through a lot. She lost her father, and—"

"And she's a nut job! Who's to say that she didn't kill Jonathan Martin?" Meghan proclaimed. Some of the patrons of the coffee shop were starting to stare.

"Lower your voice," I ordered her. "She didn't kill Jonathan."

Meghan leaned across the table. "Jared, you are my brother, and I love you. So I want you to think long and hard about what you're doing right now."

"What do you mean?" I asked.

She looked at me, her expression softening. "Look, I have friends who are in those hearings. Everyone knows you're hung up on her, and I am sure it makes it much worse for you to know that you got her pregnant. You're concerned about her, but because she's playing hard to get, you're obsessed. I get it! But she's just some kid you had a little fun with. And hey," she continued, ignoring my protests, "I know you, and unlike everyone else, I know that there is—while extremely hidden—a kind, decent side to Jared Sorensen. However, from what I hear, Anabel Martin wants nothing to do with you."

I shook my head. "Well, she told me she wants me in our kid's life," I began.

"But what about hers?"

I looked away. "She doesn't know."

Meghan nodded her head. "Of course she doesn't. Because she's just a kid." She reached across the table and patted my hand. "I just want you to be prepared. She could change her mind. I mean, she's not a normal person. She spent the last seventeen years of her life trapped on an island with no one her own age, a father with some incredible control issues, and she just latched onto you. At some point, though, she's going to discover that there are billions of other people in this world, and—"

"Look, you don't need to tell me all of this," I cut her off. "I know it all. I've been over it in my head again and again. And that was before I even knew she was pregnant. I didn't sleep at all last night because I spent the entire night tossing and turning, wondering what's going to happen in four months when Anabel has that baby."

"Yes, little Emma Claire," my sister mused. "I do like that name."

"I hate it, but she's made it clear I don't have a say," I told her. "I believe it's a nod to Jane Austen. *Emma* is her favorite." I had a flashback to the island, of us escaping, and Anabel clutching a copy of that book.

Now my sister focused on me. "Oh, I see," she frowned. "This complicates things. It's not just an act. You really do care about her."

"I give myself away so easily?"

"Jared, you've dated all sorts of women, and I've never heard you mention a book that they liked. In fact, I sincerely doubt any of them ever read a book."

"Well that's just it with her," I said. "Anabel loves books. She had an incredible library at the island—" I broke off. What had happened to Anabel's books? I wondered if they were still there. She probably missed them more than she missed anything else.

"She had an incredible library," Meghan prompted.

"Right. Sorry. That's where we first became friends. The books were her constant companions, her escapes, her security blankets," I continued. "I think it was the one thing that she and Jonathan agreed on, reading. She loved everything Jane Austen. She also had every single book that Kurt Vonnegut ever wrote, and her biggest guilty pleasure was James Patterson."

"Wow," said Meghan. "Alright, I give her credit for being well-read. Jared, I just want you to understand something."

"And what is that?" This lecture was getting repetitive.

"That you have experienced a whole bunch of things that your Anabel hasn't. You've traveled, you've dated other people, you were in a fraternity—you went to college!" Meghan finished with a flourish. "I just want you to understand that you may not be her number one priority."

"How could I be?" I asked. "Not only did I treat her horribly, and play games with her, I forced myself on her, Meghan. I'm not proud of that."

She pursed her lips. "I wasn't going to bring that up, but since you did, I think it's fair game. Why did you do that, Jared? I mean, what possessed you to—"

"I was drunk," I confided. "Drunker than I've ever been. The worst part? I was drunk under the table by a man twenty years older than me, and to get back at him, I went and raped his daughter."

She looked horrified. "Is that why you did it?"

"More or less. It comes to me in bits and pieces. I would like to think that wasn't my motivation, but it's the best I can come up with."

"Well, I hope you avoid her," declared Meghan, sipping her latte. "I can only imagine what is going to be said about you next."

"I'm supposed to see her tomorrow." I avoided making eye contact. "She summoned me. She's started telling me what to do."

Meghan sighed. "Okay. I'm coming with you. You need someone who is in your corner." The subject was clearly not open for debate.

"I think she'll like you."

"I don't care."

Chapter 16—Anabel

I woke up Sunday around 11 a.m., bleary eyed from finishing The Historian at two that morning. Why no one had looked in on me before now bothered me. Then I checked myself. I didn't like having everyone in my face; why would that bother me? Still, something felt weird. In my underwear, I studied my closet for a moment. Then, yanking a dress over my head, I contemplated brushing my teeth but that thought made my stomach reel. Settling for a vigorous mouth washing, I pulled my hair into a clip and then sidled out of my bedroom. There wasn't anyone except the usual Secret Service detail in the hall.

"Hello?" I called, walking down the steps. "Sam? Alexis?" No one in the living area, dining area, or kitchen. I supposed they must've stepped out; but no note? Then it hit me: they were probably at church. I was not allowed to go to church with them. After all, I was an embarrassment.

"Oh well," I told myself, and began rummaging for food. I grabbed an apple and washed it carefully. As I took a bite out of my apple, it hit me: I was alone.

It was nice.

My life had been five straight months of constant attention, and I had not been used to it. Having a security guard around me at all times—even one who didn't have any interest in making small talk—made me edgy. Before Jared came to Caereon, I had spent most of my time with myself, and it was nice to not be putting on a show for someone, pretending to be happy, pretending to be calm, and pretending to be sane. I spent so much time pretending that I was often unclear as to which emotions of mine were real.

I wandered through the downstairs rooms, marveling at the quiet. Not that Sam and Alexis were loud, but normally one was calling to me, yelling at the other, or screaming into a BlackBerry. I had developed a particular fascination with Sam's BlackBerry and wanted my own. My brother, however, insisted that we wait.

There were so many things I wanted to do. I wanted to learn how to drive (Caereon had had a couple all-terrain vehicles, neither of which I was allowed to go near); I wanted to travel around DC and do all of the touristy things that there were to do, like see the monuments and visit the Smithsonian; but overall, I wanted to meet people.

Not that anyone here had been particularly friendly.

When the Caereon Murder Case (that's what the press was calling it) broke, my face was all over the news, often juxtaposed with images of my late parents. For someone who barely looked in the mirror, it was surreal to see my visage on the television and in various newspapers. Request after request for an interview came to me, and all were turned down. Sam was anxious that I not say anything that would get us in trouble, so I hid from the spotlight. I could not turn on the television or the radio without hearing "the half-sister of President Sallinger" on every news station. I had heard numerous comments and read all sorts of articles commenting on my physique, my hair, my face, and my clothing. My sassy comments to my brother had made headlines; even my attire had been scrutinized. It had not occurred to me that I would be vilified for wearing a "trench coat from the Gap" every day. I made a mental note to confer with Alexis about my wardrobe. I dropped onto the divan, tucking one leg under myself as I took another bite from the apple.

Jared would be here soon, and we needed to come up with a plan of attack for tomorrow. We would be discussing some extremely sensitive, uncomfortable areas for us both, and I knew that no matter what, it would be unpleasant. It would also be all over the newspapers the following day.

At least, I thought to myself, my father wouldn't have to see it. I was stunned to realize a tear was sliding down my face. I wiped my eyes and steeled myself. If nothing else, Jonathan would want me to be brave.

Suddenly the phone was ringing. I glanced around, and it hit me then that I hadn't seen anyone since I came down the stairs. Great. I supposed I would have to answer. Really, I thought, where were my bodyguards? I lifted it off of its receiver and stammered, "Blair House, Anabel speaking."

There was a silence, and then, "It's Jared."

"Hi," I managed.

"Hey, I'm sorry to bother you, but my sister is with me and she wants to meet you." At least he sounded as pained as I did.

"The hippie or the redhead?" I asked.

"The redhead." He sounded like he was fighting a chuckle.

"Oh right. The hippie's in England. Well, bring her over!" I proclaimed as merrily as I could. "I'm alone, and I'm not sure when Sam and Alexis are returning, so please, come over."

As I hung up the phone, I wondered if I should brush my teeth. I decided I would try and eat a piece of toast instead.

By the time Jared and Meghan arrived, I had managed to down not only the toast, but some fruit salad that I had discovered in the fridge. While Jared smiled at me, Meghan did not seem impressed with the crumbs I was wiping off of my skirt or my bare feet. As I led the way into the sitting area I offered drinks and was declined. Meghan took a chair, and Jared took the one next to her, so I wound up sitting on the divan by myself.

"It's nice to meet you," I offered.

"Mm," she said, sizing me up. I knew I should have brushed my teeth, but the thought still evoked nausea. "So where are the Sallingers?"

"I don't know. They abandoned me," I grinned at her. "Too much trouble, I guess."

Her unsmiling face indicated to me that she felt I was too much trouble for her brother. "Indeed," Meghan said. "Listen, Anabel, I am sure that all of this has been overwhelming for you, but I want you to consider what you're doing to my brother."

"What I'm doing to your brother?" I repeated.

"Meghan, I don't—" began Jared, but she cut him off.

"Jared isn't exactly Mr. Popularity here, and you're contributing to the bad press," she went on. "I'm not trying to insinuate that your motive is to make his life miserable, but you're doing a fantastic job of doing just that."

I bristled, and turned to Jared. "I'm sorry. I had no idea that I made your life unbearable."

"I didn't say that," he protested.

"Well she did, and she's your envoy, isn't she?"

"Anabel," he began.

"Save it," I looked back to Meghan. "So what is it you want from me?"

"Well," she said, crossing her legs, "maybe if you came out of hiding from the media and gave an interview and told the world that Jared isn't Satan, they might back off. He can't find a job, you know."

"I didn't." I looked at the floor.

"Your testimony on Monday may make things worse for him," she continued. "He's already told me some disturbing information about what happened, and it will not reflect well on his character."

"What did you tell her?" I frowned at him.

"I told her what happened," he muttered, looking away.

"I don't even know what happened; would you care to enlighten me?" I snapped.

"This is what I'm talking about," sighed Meghan. She looked at me, not unkindly. "You two can't fight like this. I just think it would be a good idea if you got your stories straight."

"Fine," I said, still annoyed at Jared. "I just thought you had come to visit, not give me the Spanish Inquisition." Above his protests, I began.

The next day after we kissed was awkward. Seeing Jared that morning as we waited for my dad and Charlie brought a flush of pleasure to my cheeks. I had taken extra care with my appearance that day. I had gotten up early and showered, and had let my curls air dry so they fell sweetly around my face, and down my back. I had left the white dress behind and had settled for a pink one with cap sleeves that, while it was a little low cut, fell past my knees. Enough so that Jonathan would probably not comment on my attire. Jared had gotten there before any of us, and as I approached him, I felt positively radiant.

"Good morning," he greeted me, not failing to notice my neckline.

"Did you sleep well?" I asked him with a smile. Now that I think about it, I must admit I'm appalled at the way I was throwing myself at him.

"No, I was awake for a while," he lamented.

"I had that problem as well," I admitted, lowering my voice. "I couldn't stop thinking about you."

"You don't want to do this," he told me, his hands in his pockets, looking every which way but at me.

"Not this again," I groaned. "Jared, I'm not about to spend today denying that I feel something for you. I'm also not going to allow you to pretend that you don't feel something for me. I realize that there are millions of complications and at some point you're going to leave me here, but I want to enjoy our time together. Look, I need you to be my friend. I don't have any. If you don't want to kiss me anymore, fine, but at least talk to me," I implored.

He was beginning to relent. I could sense it. "Okay," he gave in. "Okay."

Just then we were interrupted by Charlie. "Good morning. Annie, you look nice today."

Before I could reply, Jonathan showed up. "You should change, Anabel."

"I brought a sweater," I defended, and pulled it around my shoulders.

"I think that's good enough," stated Charlie.

My father looked like he was about to say something, but then stopped himself. "Alright, Sorensen," he said. "Let me take you on the grand tour."

"So how exactly does the vault work?" Jared asked, falling in step next to my father.

"I can explain," I piped up from in front of them, sending my father an anxious glance. He nodded, so I continued as we walked down the stairs. At least if I was talking I wouldn't stand there like an idiot, grinning at Jared. "Well as I'm sure you know, the majority of our nation's gold bullion used to be stored in Fort Knox. The American people are under the impression that it still is stored there."

"How much gold is it?" asked Jared, coming to walk by me as we turned a corner.

"About forty-seven-hundred tons," I told him. "Fort Knox has been around since 1936. It is also used to house precious items, such as the Magna Carta and other key documents. It's designed much like our storage facility: it has a fortress and then below," I commented as I pushed the elevator button, "is the vault. Fort Knox's vault, like ours, is lined with granite and you have to get through several different rooms to get through to where the gold is."

"We're going to take a detour to the prison," announced my father.

"Very well." I caught Jared's eye. "Just below the surface level of Caereon is our prison level. It's divided into solitary confinement and then there are the prisoners who have open cells who get to leer at me when I walk by. Hence the sweater." Jonathan made a grunting noise, and I failed to look up. I was going to get a talking to, I knew it. We got off and walked to the main entrance. The guard let us in, and we continued our tour. "We only housed a few prisoners in the beginning, but as I'm sure you know, when several of the major high-security places were closed, we were one of the few places where taking in extra prisoners was a possibility. My father was not happy about it, I can assure you." Jonathan nodded his assent. "Through this door," I indicated the one on the left, "is solitary. I'm not allowed to go in there."

"Some of the most dangerous men in the world are through that door," Charlie interjected. "Even I don't go in there unless it's absolutely necessary."

"There are cameras everywhere you look," I continued. I moved to Jared's other side. "I don't like to let them see me," I confided.

We walked past about twenty cells. The prisoners all gaped at us but were silent. I turned to Jared. "I'm sure you've heard all of the conspiracy theories about Fort Knox."

He frowned. "I seem to remember hearing that it was empty, and all the gold had been moved to Jerusalem." He was standing so close to me that a thrill went down my spine.

"Yes!" I said. "The gold actually wasn't moved here until the Nixon administration. Conspiracy buffs have a field day with it. The only thing they really have to go on is the audit reports, which only account for about 21 percent of the gold. They actually only have 25 percent."

"And the rest is here?"

"It is," I affirmed. We walked to another door and my father put his finger on the pad. It opened, and we hurried in to another long corridor. "In spite of its image, Fort Knox has been broken into more times than the government wants to admit. Nobody has ever gotten far enough to find anything, but it became increasingly worrisome during the 70s...so President Nixon had our fortress built, and here we are."

"Is there anything besides gold in this vault?"

"Just the Ark of the Covenant." I gave him a flirtatious grin. Jared's face remained impassive. "I'm not allowed in there very often, something to do with my lack of security clearance." Charlie suppressed a laugh, and I caught his eye and winked. "Mostly it's just the gold, but again, occasionally we house special items. I believe that information is on what my father would refer to as a need-to-know basis." I slowed my pace to walk with Jonathan.

He assented. "Absolutely. Sorensen, my daughter has told you much more than I would have, but the information is correct. The main vault is through this way, and I assume," he said, rather archly, "you would like to see the gold. It is the main attraction on the island."

I raised my eyebrows. "Daddy, don't act like you have a sense of humor now! I hardly know what to say."

"That's a shocker," said Jared. I shot him a nasty glance, but my father actually emitted a chuckle. He stepped to do the retina scan, as Charlie turned to Jared. "Don't fall over," he warned.

I nodded in agreement. "It is rather breathtaking, and most people at least experience mild heart palpitations."

Jared smirked. "I think I'll be okay."

"Very well then," said Jonathan, and he turned the door of the vault and opened it. "After you, Sorensen."

Jared walked through and sucked in his breath. Charlie and I exchanged a meaningful glance. Jonathan merely looked bored.

"Wow," Jared gaped. "This is incredible."

Indeed it was. When you first walk into the main vault you're assaulted on all sides by gold. Right in front of you is the mint gold, the bars that are almost entirely pure gold. They shine the brightest, in my opinion. The stack of bars is as tall as me and several feet wide. All along the right wall are the coin bars—the bars of gold that are made of melted gold coin. Further back, past all the bars, are the repositories that hold the gold coins. Some of them are Sacagawea dollars, while others are just standard gold coins.

Jared stood there, his mouth hanging open. I smiled at him. "I'm sure I would be overwhelmed, too, if I wasn't used to it."

He ignored me. "So who has access to the vault?"

"I do," commented my father. "Charlie also can pass a retina scan, Major Briggs in security does as well, but that's it."

Jared nodded. It was really exasperating how he was completely ignoring me while I was basking in his presence. I was infatuated. I had images of me and Jared running down the beach together, of him running his fingers through my mass of tendrils and pulling me close and kissing me, needing me, wanting me. I was delirious in his presence.

Looking back on it, I was being positively ridiculous.

"So you will spend the evening with me, then?" my father was saying, yanking me out of my fantasy.

"That sounds fine, sir. I will join you after dinner," assented Jared.

Wait. I had expected to be spending the after dinner time with Jared.

Charlie turned to me. "So what are you up to today?"

"Oh," I flushed. "I just assumed you would be pawning him off on me." I gestured to Jared.

"We all saw what happened on the piazza, Annie. I imagine Sorensen will be kept as far from you as possible."

Well then.

Deciding to not put off the inevitable any longer, I turned to my father. "Daddy?"

"Yes?" He looked tired.

"What do you want me to do today?" I shifted my weight uncomfortably. Jared was standing a few feet away, oblivious to the fact that I was pining for him as he took notes.

Jonathan put his arm around me, and I leaned into him. It was a surprisingly tender moment for me and my father, and I simply hugged him for a few moments. Then he suggested I spend some time on the beach. "Bring Sorensen if you like," he said, nodding at Jared. "You've been spending too much time indoors. You have no color in your face."

"That's not my fault, it's genetics," I grinned. I walked over to Jared. "Do you want to come to the beach with me?"

He glanced at my father, who nodded. "Go with her, we'll discuss the other matters later." He glanced at Charlie. "We should get out of here."

Charlie nodded, and we made our way out. I walked next to Jared, about five feet behind my father and Charlie. "So?" I asked him.

"What?"

"Are you coming with me to the beach or not?" I tried to contain my excitement, but I think my voice gave me away.

He looked straight ahead. "It's not a good idea. Besides, I have work to do."

"No, you don't," I retorted. "I thought—" but then I stopped, and he glared at me. Jonathan and Charlie weren't supposed to know that I was the reason Jared was on the island. "Fine," I said. "I'll just tell Sam that you are awful." Then I mentally punished myself for my childishness.

He sighed. "Fine. I'll meet you in ten minutes."

I clapped my hands and went to get ready.

Chapter 17—Jared

My sister interrupted Anabel. "So what we're getting at is you had every intention of seducing my brother."

Anabel's eyes widened.

"That's enough, Meghan," I snapped.

Anabel looked at me, and then back at my sister, amazed. "Wow, you really don't like me, do you?"

Meghan adjusted her glasses. "It's just that I don't think you're entirely blameless in this affair."

"I never pretended to be!" cried Anabel. "That's the problem with the whole thing. My brother and I have argued this out over and over again. He wants me to press charges against Jared, and I can't because I would have—I mean, it's just if he hadn't, I would have wanted to...if things had been different, then I..." She paused. "Look, I wasn't thinking, and I was reckless and irresponsible in the way I was behaving. I admit that. I made many poor decisions, and I'm not proud of it at all, and—ooh," she said, her hand going to her stomach.

"What's wrong?" I asked, instantly at her side.

She gave me a small smile. "Emma's moving! I think. Feel," she said, grabbing my hand and putting it to her stomach.

My hand rested there and I felt something tapping against the side of her belly. Anabel's eyes lit up, and she sighed. "I guess she's done."

"Amazing," I told her. I stayed by her, my hand lingering on her stomach.

Meghan cleared her throat. "Okay. So we've established that you weren't thinking."

"Yes," Anabel nodded. "To be fair, Jared was rebuffing my advances at every turn. When he and I went to the beach, he wouldn't speak to me. I thought it was because my legs were so white I was blinding him."

I sighed. It had been uncomfortable from the moment I saw her that morning. I knew she had dressed up for me, and the dress she had chosen was slightly big on her, so it wasn't like the neckline left anything to the imagination. However, I couldn't check her out with her father standing right there, glaring at me every time I even accidentally glanced at Anabel. I will say that she looked beautiful that morning. I knew, though, that if I didn't pretend to be distant, her father and Charlie would probably lock her up and then it would be even more difficult to get her off of Caereon. The previous night, while I lay unable to sleep, I contemplated just taking her with me when I left. She was unstable, for one thing. Her behavior the day before had shown me just that. Hot one moment, cold the other, and now she was fixated on me, and it made me uncomfortable. I had shown unmistakably poor judgment by kissing her; however, I had not expected this show of idolization.

So when we went to the beach, no, I didn't talk to her. Her swimsuit was pretty modest, and she had pulled her hair up on top of her head. She and I laid out towels and sat quietly listening to the surf roar. It took her about twenty minutes to apply sunscreen. She was having trouble getting it on her back when I relented and started rubbing it in.

"Thanks, Jared." She sounded distant.

"Do you really need that much sunblock?"

"Yes," she grew defensive. "Look at me. Do I look like I get out in the sun very often?" It was true. Her skin was milky white. I smoothed the sunscreen over her back as she continued. "The last time I wasn't liberal with my sunscreen, I got burned after about thirty minutes and wound up miserable for a week."

"I don't burn," I replied, moving back to the safety of my own towel.

She smiled over her sunglasses. "I envy you. I got my mother's complexion. It's the one thing of Jonathan's I really wanted." She lay back on her towel. "We can go back to not talking now. I won't disturb you anymore."

She was really not making this easy. "You weren't disturbing me in the first place."

"Whatever." Anabel pulled off her sunglasses and closed her eyes. "We are done."

I should not take the bait, I told myself. I shouldn't start this with her. She was behaving like a spoiled kid. The best thing to do is just let her be angry with you and get her off of the island and safely with her brother. He can take care of her and—

But then I stopped for a moment. How exactly was Sam going to take care of her? Anabel's presence in his life would unearth all sorts of questions. She hadn't been mentioned once during his current campaign. How was he going to explain away a 19-year-old half-sister? I tried to ignore these thoughts. This isn't your problem, I told myself. I'm sure some sort of spin will be put on it, like she had joined the Peace Corps or had been a missionary or something.

The thought nagging at the back of my mind, however, was that Anabel needed someone to really look after her. Helping her interact with the real world would be no easy task. At most, she had dealt with, what, five people at a time? She would feel so out of place in—well, in DC, for example. I envisioned her on the Metro, or in Tyson's Corner Shopping Mall surrounded by all sorts of pushy people, shoving her out of their way. I could, however, see her walking around the Mall and visiting the Smithsonian. Alone. I glanced at her. She had turned onto her stomach and let her hair loose. As the sunlight glinted off of it, my heart softened toward her. She was just a kid, after all. And she had been cheated out of a loving childhood. Everything I had taken for granted—two parents who had loved me and worked hard to ensure I had the best life possible—had not been her experience at all. When Anabel left Caereon, she would need someone to be there for her all of the time.

It couldn't be Sam. He had a country to deal with.

But it couldn't be me, either. I knew the minute we got her off of the island she would tell her brother how horrible I was to her. And she was right. I should have handled the situation differently. It had just been wholly unexpected. When Sam sent me here, it had never occurred to me that Anabel would be anything different than any other job he had me do. I hadn't expected to care about her.

That was it, I reassured myself. I cared about her. I had a brotherly sort of interest in her. It made sense. Her brother was my closest friend, after all. Kissing her had been a mistake, but I was fixing that. Furthermore, she was an unusual case, and one couldn't help but feel pity for her. That was it; nothing more.

Satisfied with my conclusion and ignoring the voice in the back of my head which told me that I was deluding myself, I decided to talk to her.

"Annie?

"We aren't pals. It's Anabel," she muttered.

"Anabel, I'm sorry. Can we be friends again?"

She propped herself up on her elbows. "I suppose this means that we are just going to forget everything that happened yesterday."

"I think that would be the best for both of us."

She nodded, clearly disappointed. "Fine. So since you're not meeting my dad until after dinner, what would you like to do for the rest of the afternoon?" She started to brush sand off of herself. "I unfortunately cannot stay out in the sun much longer, so if you want to hang out with me, we have to do it indoors. If you would rather spend the time by yourself, I understand that too."

Inwardly I groaned. I didn't want to hurt her, but this was best. She needed to become disenchanted with me; she needed to get off the island and forget that I existed. Vague thoughts played in my mind of Anabel at the White House; seeing her when I saw Sam. No—that would be ridiculous. I supposed it would be inevitable that our paths would cross; yet if I kept this up, it would be unpleasant.

She was folding up her towel. She yanked the little dress over her head and sent me an icy glare. "Well, I'm going inside now. You know where to find me."

I watched her walk back. I think she was trying to stomp but the sand wouldn't let her. I chuckled a little to myself. Maybe, I told myself, once I got her off of the island and she saw me as a hero, we would be able to really get to know each other and be friends.

Until then, it would have to be this way. I wanted to get off of Caereon alive, and I had a feeling Jonathan would kill me otherwise. Also, if Sam got wind of me kissing his sister, I would probably get fired.

I sat and watched the waves roll in. Out of nowhere, guilt hit me. I should just talk to her and explain. Anabel was rational, after all. She would understand.

Then, Charlie appeared. "Hi there," he greeted me. "Mind if I join you?"

"Not at all," I lied.

He sat down next to me. For an older man, Charlie seemed remarkably fit and energetic, the opposite of Jonathan. "Are you enjoying your stay?"

I shrugged. "It's fine. It's a job."

"And Anabel?" He was staring at me.

"I think she has a crush on me, and I'm doing my best to dissuade her from it," I assured him.

"Good," Charlie affirmed. "It doesn't do her any good, you know. Gets her hopes up and all, you being here. She thinks her brother will get her off of the island." He offered me a bottle of water.

I took it and swallowed. "You don't think he will?"

Charlie laughed. "He's been promising her he'd get her out of here for a very long time. She just thinks it's a matter of funding; but I know better."

"What do you mean?" I asked.

"It will cause a lot of uproar when she appears. Let me be frank here. It's easy to explain away a lot of things, Jared, but a nineteen-year-old girl?" He squinted into the sun. "Besides, she's been living here for years without a security clearance, and a lot of questions are going to arise."

"Well, surely some story will be invented?"

"Yes, but who's to say she can stick to it? Say she goes to college and winds up at a party. She has a little too much to drink and starts sharing all sorts of details about her life here and what we protect. She's very young and doesn't really understand a lot of the things that go on." Charlie sighed. "Besides, it's not like Jonathan would ever let her go."

"He can't keep her prisoner here forever."

"No," Charlie prodded. "But what if Jonathan gets reassigned?"

I laughed at that thought. "That's doubtful. Sam feels that Jonathan does an excellent job running Caereon."

Charlie considered this. "Yes, but who is he getting this information from?"

"Jonathan, I suppose." I hadn't really thought about it.

"Precisely!" he said. "Jared, most of us are fed up with the way he runs this place. We are required to work ridiculous hours. He enacts severe punishments for anyone who comes within twenty feet of his daughter. I know you heard about Kevin Miller."

"I asked Anabel about it the other day. Do you have any more information on it?"

"I think Jonathan is becoming unhinged," he confided. "He took special pains to get Kevin flown out here so he could keep an eye on him."

"Why was Kevin hanging out with Anabel anyway? I'm surprised Jonathan allowed it in the first place."

"Well, they get good behavior privileges sometimes. Depending on the inmate, of course. We obviously do not allow terrorists on the premises unattended." Charlie frowned. "It was really an oversight on all of our parts. According to Annie, she was reading one day in the public library when Kevin came upon her. She doesn't normally go there, and no one had bothered to follow up on her." He sighed. "You see, she used to have someone who—who watched over her, but her father—"

"Miss Jessmyn," I acknowledged. "I heard about what happened between the two of you."

He nodded angrily. "Yes, Marilyn did an excellent job preventing Anabel from consorting with the inmates, but now there isn't any such oversight. I admit I looked the other way. I thought it would do the poor girl some good to have a friend."

"Do the criminals talk to her often?" That thought bothered me.

"No, the rules are if you see Anabel, you keep walking. They all know it—but Kevin didn't. Or perhaps he did and chose to ignore it. He had only been here a brief amount of time when they met each other, and as I mentioned, none of us said anything to Jonathan at first because we thought the companionship did her good. She's very lonely," he stated, and I knew that was a jab at me.

Ignoring that, I pressed him. "So what happened when Jonathan found out?"

"He went ballistic," Charlie said. "He screamed at the guy, threw him off the island, and made sure he went somewhere—well. Anabel was so angry, and I think she still blames herself."

"Where is he now?"

"ADX Florence."

I narrowed my eyes. "Where they housed the Unabomber? Is he in solitary?"

"Yes." Charlie watched for my reaction.

I shook my head in disgust. "That's ridiculous. ADX is for terrorists and traitors. Why on earth is he there?"

"Because he knows we're here. He was supposed to stay here, Jared. You don't get to just leave. None of the people here are ever going to leave." He put major emphasis on that last statement. "If word gets out about us, well, you can imagine the implications."

"So you're telling me people are sent here to die?"

"Well, you know the kind of people they send here. We have quite a few members of Al-Qaeda. Everyone here is presumed dead. So it really doesn't matter whether they live or die here." He sounded bitter and angry.

"So how did you handle Kevin's return to the States?"

"It was very quiet. No questions have been asked, thank God," he replied. "But that doesn't mean that will happen with Anabel."

"Why are you telling me this, Charlie?"

"I'm telling you this," he stressed, "because you alone have the power to make this okay for her. You can tell her brother she's best off where she is."

"But she's not," I protested.

"I care about Anabel very much, and I don't want to see her hurt," he shared. "You must realize that it would not be easy to assimilate her into society. Think about it. What is she going to do if she winds up in DC? She'd probably get hit by a car because she wouldn't know any better. No one ever taught her to look both ways before crossing the street. So you see, Jared," he continued, "you have to tell Sam that she needs to stay here. You have to do this to protect Anabel. Despite what you say, I can tell that you care about her, and this is best for her."

"I see," I said. I didn't see. I wondered if Jonathan had persuaded Charlie to come and talk to me, and that's what this was all about. Jonathan wished me as far away as possible from his little girl. He didn't want to lose her. While I could appreciate that, the look of desperation in Anabel's eyes haunted me when she talked about how she needed out. It was stifling her; it was killing her. But I didn't want to stir the pot with Charlie. It was best to play his game, at least for now. "I appreciate you talking to me—it sheds a light on things I hadn't even considered."

Charlie nodded. "You and me, Sorensen—we're men of business. We understand how things have to run. Sam will let his emotions cloud his judgment when it comes to her. But we all know that she needs to stay here. I mean, if she came back and it destroyed Sam, you would be out of a job."

"Thanks, Charlie." He clapped his hand on my shoulder and left.

He left me to my thoughts, which were growing more and more turbulent. She needed off of the island, period. It bothered me that Jonathan had sent Charlie to do his dirty work. It bothered me that Anabel was probably locked in her room crying. Despite Charlie's flimsy reasons, I knew she would be fine.

Maybe for once, I wouldn't be the bad guy, the guy lurking in the shadows, the guy doing what needed to be done. Maybe for once I would be the hero.

I just had to lie.

I wanted to tell her. So she wouldn't hate me. Which set me face-to-face with another ugly fact: Anabel's opinion actually mattered to me. For lack of a better word, Anabel...suited me. She was easy to talk to. Her self-deprecating manner and ready sarcasm made me laugh, and she could be laughing and full of vitality in a way that would catch any man's attention.

Except.

Except when she was sharing her fears about being trapped on the island. That transformed her into someone completely different, and her eyes looked haunted.

If I didn't get her out, I would be followed by those eyes for the rest of my life.

I brushed myself off and prepared to tell her everything, when another thought attacked me. What if I told her...and she lost her temper and blabbed it to her father? Or Charlie? That could have dire consequences as well. Charlie did have a point; she was a bit of a risk sometimes, as manifested by her screaming matches with Jonathan.

I wanted her to think well of me. I sighed. That was selfish. I should just keep it to myself, and then when we got off of the island, I could be Knight in Shining Armor.

Perfect.

Chapter 18—Jared

"Stop," Anabel said.

I looked at her. She was shaking her head. "I can't take this. I can't take hearing about you caring about me. I mean," she said, choking back her tears, "you couldn't tell me you loved me the other day, and now you're saying you looked at me like I was your sister, and then when you called me I thought...I thought..."

"What did you think?" I asked her.

She swallowed. "What does it matter? We can't have a sensible conversation without having a fight."

"Maybe it's because we've never tried."

"What's the point?"

"Look, I've been going crazy. I can't stop thinking about you." I may as well be honest.

She rolled her eyes. "I'm sorry. Am I supposed to pity you? Aside from the fact that I'm pregnant with your child, you have no other reason to want to be with me. You don't even love me."

"Of course I do," I protested. "Anabel, don't you see? I was just fighting my feelings. I just didn't want to believe that I felt that way about you. Sort of like how you feel now."

She looked up at me and frowned. Meghan was shaking her head, but I stood up and continued. "You don't want to admit to yourself that you have feelings for me, do you?"

Anabel's cheeks were flushed, her eyes darkened. "This isn't the time or the place."

"I'm done with the games, Anabel. You need to knock this off. Look, I don't blame you. I understand that you're confused, and you're pregnant, for crying out loud. But I know you love me. It was in your every look, every touch, every smile, and every kiss. Even when you look at me now your eyes give you away. So don't act all high and mighty and pretend like there isn't something there, because there is.

I've apologized to you. I've begged for mercy. But you can't keep stringing me along, because I won't tolerate it from you."

She rose and walked over to me, hands on her hips, glaring. "You won't tolerate it from me? So what are you saying? Are you giving me an ultimatum?"

"Yes, I am."

She slapped me then. I didn't know she had it in her. I don't think she knew it, either. She froze and stared at me, shocked at what she'd done. I rubbed my face. "Ouch, woman. If you wanted to play rough, all you had to do was say so."

"I can't take you anymore! You know your sister's sitting right there." She waved her arms toward Meghan, who had her head in her hands.

I paused and stared at her. Anabel was radiant in her anger, with her eyes flashing, her cheeks flushed. She was absolutely beautiful, from her scowling face to her rounded belly. I couldn't help myself, she just looked too good. I wrapped my arms around her and kissed her.

She resisted at first, but then kissed me back passionately. My hands ran through her hair, and she wrapped her arms around my neck. Then she pulled herself away and attempted to glare at me. "What was that?" she asked, half angry, half amused.

"What you wanted."

Meghan cleared her throat. "You guys," she began.

But Anabel was inches away from me again. "I am so sick of you thinking that every woman on the planet wants you."

"No, honey. But I know you do."

"Jared!" hissed Meghan. I looked at her, and she pointed. Sam and Alexis were staring at us, dressed in their Sunday finest. I could tell from their faces that they had seen everything.

"Sam," said Anabel, moving toward her brother "don't get upset. This was my fault."

"You can't keep taking responsibility for his actions, Annie," he seethed.

"Well in this case, it is my fault," she said. She looked from me, to my sister, to her brother and his wife, and then her gaze switched back to me. “I can’t do this here,” she said.

“We can go somewhere. Anywhere,” I told her.

She eyed my sister. “We can’t. We have to go through everything for tomorrow.”

“Hi Sam,” my sister managed. “Remember me?”

“Of course, Meghan,” he said, exasperated. Then he turned to his sister. “Anabel, I need to see you alone.”

“No,” she said, as if in a daze, her eyes locked on mine.

“I’m sorry, did you just say no to me?” Alexis put her hand on his arm.

“I’m not your child, Sam.” She closed her eyes. “Please come in here. Please, let’s just finish this, because otherwise we’ll be going in unrehearsed.”

“What is there to rehearse? You tell the truth, he tells the truth, we’re done.” Sam came and stood next to her. “Stop trying to protect him.”

“It’s my decision, whether you like it or not. It’s not like you want me here anyway,” she spat.

“Anabel, what are you talking about? Where is this coming from?” Sam gestured at me. “Did he say something to you?”

She turned and looked at him, troubled. “What would you have done with me once I was off the island? If Jonathan hadn’t died and everything hadn’t come out?”

He was perplexed. “What do you mean?”

“Jared told me,” she stopped, and frowned. “He told me that Charlie tried to dissuade him from telling you I needed off of Caereon.” She hunched over her belly and crossed her arms as she looked at her brother like she didn’t know who he was. “Charlie said that I would have been a problem.”

He stared at her in disbelief. “Anabel, you would never have been a problem, I don’t know what you’re talking about.”

“Don’t lie to her, Sam,” snapped Alexis. We all turned to look at her. “You know as well as I do that there were all sorts of problems.” She turned to Anabel. “When some Cabinet members found out the connection between you and Sam, we had to admit everything to them, but we had kept you a secret. You were a need-to-know. So we didn't want it to get out, it would have caused a scandal."

"I see," she whispered.

"You need to give your brother credit, though," Alexis continued. "He did fight for you, but we both knew it couldn't be, Anabel! And then, what we all feared happened: you emerged, Caereon's cover was blown, and Sam lost his political career. You can't really do anything else after resigning from the presidency!"

Anabel looked at her brother. "I thought you didn't blame me."

"Sam doesn't. I do," she spat. "Do you think this is the life we wanted? Sam could have been president for at least another term. He was doing wonderful things for this country, and you ruined it!"

"That's enough, Alexis!" Sam turned to her.

"No. No, you know what? Your spoiled brat sister needs to understand the repercussions of her actions!"

"It's not my fault Jonathan was murdered!"

"I disagree," snapped Alexis. Her heels clacked as she walked closer to Anabel. "Now, I have tolerated your presence. I have bent over backwards for you. I understood, Anabel, that it was a shock to have your father murdered and your life in danger—yes, I get it. But don't you dare act like we haven't been there for you. I sent my kids away for you. I have done everything I could for you. What kind of a life do you think I have now?" Her voice was filled with hysteria. "It revolves around you—and for what? Sam and I are young, what are we going to do for the rest of our lives? Play golf?"

"I said that is enough, Alexis!" Sam roared. "How dare you talk to my sister this way?"

"HALF! HALF-SISTER! WHOM YOU BARELY KNOW!" Alexis began striking at Sam. "I supported you! I helped you win your seat in the House! I used my connections to help propel you to the Presidency! And now look at you," she sneered. "You threw it all away—and for what? For her?" She gestured in Anabel's direction. "Do you think she's grateful? She might be at first, but the fact of the matter is, as soon as she gets Jonathan's will money, she'll want nothing to do with her washed up brother!"

"Oh please," scoffed Anabel. "Sam's the only family I have. I would never cut him out. You're just trying to stir up trouble."

She lunged at Anabel, who shrieked and jumped back. "ALEXIS! I am pregnant, for crying out loud!"

"Oh, that's another thing. I'm pretty sure you did that on purpose." She pulled away from Sam and stamped up the stairs. We all heard the door slam.

Anabel and Sam looked at each other. Neither of them spoke for a moment.

Anabel broke the silence. "I'm sorry."

"So am I," he told her.

"I think it would be best if I went somewhere," she suggested.

"Don't be ridiculous."

"Sam, this is your marriage. You two aren't going to resolve anything with me here making it worse."

"We have to talk about this," he insisted. "I need you to understand—I wanted to get you out of there, I really did."

She smiled sadly. "I know you did." She ran her fingers through her hair and looked out the window. She walked over to her brother and slowly put her arms around him.

Then she tilted her chin. "I love you. But I also know that I can't come first in your life. She's your wife, and I am going to respect that."

He didn't meet her in the eye. "I didn't realize she felt that way."

Anabel broke into a rueful grin. "Of course you did, whether you acknowledged it to yourself or not. And of course you miss your kids. I'm so sorry that they were sent away; that is my fault."

"I had to take care of you," he began.

"Yes," she cut him off. "Yes, and that's the problem. You've been doing a wonderful job taking care of me; who's been taking care of her?" She gestured up the stairs.

He was silent.

Anabel nodded. "I thought so." She turned to me. "Can I stay with you for the night?"

"Absolutely not," said Meghan. "That will look horrible, especially if you show up at the hearing together."

"Agreed," seconded Sam.

Anabel contemplated my sister for a moment. "Can I stay with you?"

Meghan didn't really look like she liked this suggestion, but she nodded. "Sure. I can take you to the hearing tomorrow, I actually have business that way."

"That's very kind. Thank you." She turned to me. "Let's go then. You can buy me and your sister dinner, and we'll figure out everything for tomorrow."

"I live in Northwest," said Meghan.

"Sam! What was that fantastic pizza place up there that we went to? Remember, where that crazy woman recognized us? Oh, it was so good!" Anabel's eyes lit up.

Sam looked at Meghan, torn. "Nothing excites her more than good food. It was 2Amys."

"That's actually right by my apartment. I'm a bit surprised you know them." My sister shrugged. "That's fine with me, though."

"I've eaten my way around this city," Anabel was beaming. "Well, before they realized I shouldn't talk to anybody. Come upstairs and help me pack."

Meghan looked a bit unsure at how to deal with how forward Anabel was, but she got up and followed her.

As they headed up the stairs, Sam turned to me.

We had been friends, up until this business with his sister, and it was a friendship I had been sorry to lose. Before, even though he made me do the dirty work, he respected me. Now he could barely look me in the eye.

"Sam," I began, but he stopped me.

"I realize she's my half-sister, I realize that, up until now, I have never spent more than two weeks at a time with her, and yes, I realize that if it were not for her, I would still be in a position of power." He sat down.

"However, I also accept—even if my wife refuses to do so—that if we hadn't lied about her existence in the first place, none of this would have ever happened. There were a million chances we had, all sorts of proactive things we could have done, and we didn't. So, yes, Jared, I know that I brought this on myself."

"I wasn't going to say anything."

"You know I could've handled this better."

"Sam, all of us have things like this happen, where we handle the situation wrong."

"Still, I shouldn't have kept her a secret." He sighed. "Alexis has always insisted she be a need-to-know. I didn't tell her until after we were married, actually." As he rubbed his temples, a trademark move of his, I noticed his hair. He was really starting to go gray.

"Well, I didn't even know about Anabel until right before you sent me to Caereon," I said. I sat down across from him. "And I was your best friend."

He focused on the floor. "I felt guilty for not saving her before. You would have judged me, I know it."

"I'm not in a position to judge anybody. You of all people know that."

"I've seen how you treat your sister. Both of your sisters. You've always been there for them. You would never let what happened to Anabel happen to Meghan or Crystal. Look at her, she's a mess. Alone, both her parents dead...pregnant..."

I couldn't argue with him. "We both betrayed her."

He nodded.

"If I had been thinking, I never would have—"

"Don't bother," he cut me off. "I'm not interested in your excuses."

"Jonathan got me drunk," The words just came out, and relief washed through me. It felt good to tell the truth.

"What?" Sam stared at me.

"Anabel didn't tell you?"

"She refused to go into it."

"He got me wasted. It was the drunkest I've been since college. He challenged me to a drinking game...and then he threatened me."

"He threatened you? With what?" Sam looked annoyed.

"Well, by that point I had kissed her, and he had seen. He threatened me with my job, he threatened to not let me see Anabel—which would have made her think that I wasn't going to try and help her—and then he drank me under the table." I hadn't expected him to have an alcohol tolerance. "I was so drunk, I wound up roaming around the halls of Caereon—and it put me right outside of Anabel's door."

Sam was grim. "And we all know what happened there."

"I don't even remember it that well," I said. "That's the worst part. I don't even know what I did to her, or how badly I hurt her." The image of Anabel sitting in a pool of blood went through my brain.

"You'll understand if I don't wish to discuss this with you," said Sam.

"You'll hear about it tomorrow," Anabel called from the stairs.

We both turned to look at her and Meghan. "That's why we should leave it until then. I'm ready to go," she announced. "Do we need to take a car?"

Chapter 19—Anabel

I loved 2Amys. They made Neapolitan Pizza, and it was amazing. It was much better than the stuff we frequently ordered in. As we placed our takeout order, I noticed some people staring. I wasn't surprised. After my outburst, I was already a familiar face on all the talk circuits. I managed a terse smile and looked at Jared. "We should get out of here. I'm causing a bit of a stir."

He looked at me, anxious. "That should go away at some point."

"At some point," I echoed.

He frowned. "I'm surprised you're in such a good mood, given what just happened."

I shrugged. "Jared, up until now, I was privy to some pretty intense emotional displays by my father. That was nothing."

"Do you miss him?"

"Um, yes and no," I admitted. "He was my father, and I loved him, but the man kind of ruined my life." I caught his eye. "How's that for honesty?"

He nodded. "He didn't make it easy for you."

"No, that wasn't Jonathan's style," I mused. I looked down at the floor as he signed for our order. "But in his own, messed-up way, he did love me, I truly believe that." I paused. "I have to believe that."

"I do, too," he told me, as we walked back to the car.

Meghan lived in a cute apartment building off of Massachusetts Avenue, up by Ward Circle. "This is a really nice neighborhood," I exclaimed.

Meghan sort of grunted at me as we got out of her car. "It works," she stated. "You can sleep in my office. I have a spare bed in there that I can make up."

I smiled at her with gratitude. "Thank you for letting me stay. I'm sorry that I invited myself over."

"No you're not." I rather admired how blunt she was. She caught my eye as she shut her door. "But I don't blame you. I wouldn't want to be in that mess either."

"I've never seen Sam and Alexis like that," I continued. "Granted, I've only been here a couple months, but they don't fight."

"At least, not in front of you," observed Meghan. I paused, and she gave me a patronizing look. "It's no secret that they have a tempestuous marriage. Everyone knows it."

"Oh," I managed. I didn't know what to say. I looked to Jared for guidance.

He was nodding. "You should read more tabloids. Alexis doesn't exactly have a penchant for keeping things to herself, and your brother often hushes her in public."

"Wow." I was at a loss. I struggled with my bag—why I had thought I needed three different pairs of shoes for tomorrow was a mystery, even to me. Jared took it from me and groaned.

"What do you have in here?"

"Rocks," I offered. Meghan snorted. I smiled to myself. I think I was growing on her.

We climbed into the elevator and got off on the fourth floor. Meghan's apartment was small, but cozy: her furniture was mostly all the same shade of brown, but she had some brightly colored rugs and blankets that made the room feel homey. A painting of an elephant hung on one wall; a copy of a Renoir on another.

We all sat down at the table with our pizzas, but I only picked at mine. It looked delicious, but I was losing my appetite. "Eat, Anabel," ordered Meghan. "You're going to feel even worse if you don't."

I took a bite. "Very true."

As I ate, I began to feel a little better. I even got down a rice ball and was on my second slice when Jared cleared his throat. "So what time is Mom coming tomorrow?"

This caught my attention. "Your mom is coming?"

Meghan nodded. "You have to understand, while my mother is not thrilled about all of this, she does like the prospect of a grandchild. If you let Jared see the baby, that is."

I swallowed. "I'm not...I'm not really comfortable around other people," I faltered.

"So we've noticed," agreed Meghan. "It might make you feel better to know that our mother is completely unlike Jared. And me, for that matter. She's really sweet, and is probably knitting something for the baby as we speak. Also," she added, "something came up and she changed her itinerary and isn't coming for another couple weeks, so you have time to get accustomed to the idea."

"Oh." I looked at my plate.

Jared patted my arm. "You don't have to meet her if you don't want to."

"I'm pretty sure that would hurt her feelings," I pointed out.

"Yes, but she would understand," he said.

"It's fine." I was losing my patience. "It's getting late, Jared. Let's just talk about everything already."

Meghan nodded. "Indeed. So you and Jonathan had a drinking contest?" she asked, turning to her brother.

I cut in. "Yeah, Jonathan drank him under the table. It was kind of amusing to watch."

Jared looked startled. "What do you mean?"

"Well, my father had the whole thing planned, Jared. He made sure to do it in a room where I would be able to watch the whole thing. It's not like you were in his office."

"How did you watch it?"

"In my library, there is a video monitoring system. In case of emergency. The parlor where you two were is a room that I could monitor from my bedroom. It's part of how we got out of that place alive." I tucked some hair behind my ears. "So I saw the whole thing."

The atmosphere during dinner was tense. I didn't say much and pretended to be interested in my food, complimenting Evelyn on her masterful cooking. She gave me a rare smile.

"Are you alright, Anabel?" my father asked. "You're quiet tonight."

I managed a thin smile. "I'm fine, just tired. I was up late last night reading." I made a show of yawning and stretching. "I think I may go to bed early, if that's alright with you."

"Of course." Jonathan looked smug. I knew he thought he had won, especially since I wasn't asking to tag along with him and Jared. "Mr. Sorensen and I have a great deal of business to go through this evening. We'll be in the front parlor."

"Mm," I said, trying to sound nonchalant.

"What are you reading, Annie?" Charlie asked me, smiling kindly. He was such a sweet man, always so concerned about me.

"Um...a book on the rise and fall of Tudor England," I lied. I was reading *The Other Boleyn Girl*, but I knew Jonathan wouldn't approve. "It has some really long title to that effect."

I walked over to Jonathan and kissed him on the forehead. Then I turned to the other members of our party. "Goodnight, Charlie. Jared." I didn't even look at him as I stomped off.

When I got to my room, I sighed. I decided to have a lazy night. I changed into my favorite white nightgown. It fell just around my knees, and the top was laced with pink ribbon. It made me feel delicate and feminine, and was just the outfit to read one of my favorite love stories with. I put *The Other Boleyn Girl* aside for now, and stared at my shelf, contemplating. Then I grinned, and I pulled out *Pride and Prejudice* and was settling in one of my armchairs when I heard the knock at my door.

I groaned and searched for my bathrobe. "Just a minute," I called, and pulled it around me. My heart skipped a beat. Was Jared there, ready to apologize and sweep me up in his arms? With gusto I ran to the knocking and flung open the door. "I knew you'd come—oh." I stopped when I saw Charlie's bemused smile. "Hi there."

"Hi Annie," he greeted me. "In your pajamas already?"

I shrugged, trying to hide my sinking heart. "I felt lazy, and I'm not planning on going anywhere. Jonathan is meeting with Jared, and I don't usually get the pleasure of your company."

"May I come in?"

I stepped back and Charlie walked in. "Let's go to your library," he suggested.

"Alright," I agreed, stymied by his presence. "Can I get you something to drink?" I gestured at my little fridge.

"No, I'm fine," he declined. We sat down in the armchairs. He studied me a moment. "Anabel, I can only imagine how hard the past couple of days have been on you."

"It has been a bit awkward," I admitted.

"I know you're not used to...other people. I fear that having Jared Sorensen here has been a difficult experience. He may have gotten your hopes up."

I frowned. "What do you mean?"

"I overheard him telling Jonathan that he is going to recommend that Sam not let you leave Caereon."

"WHAT?" I shrieked. "No, no, Charlie, that can't possibly be right. He's spent this entire time telling me that he's on my side, that he would do anything to get me out of here. I know he doesn't want to admit it, but he does care about me, Charlie, I know he does." But the words rang hollow as I said them, and I drifted into thought. "Or maybe," I mulled it over, "maybe he was just saying that because he didn't want to upset me."

"Your behavior has been most unlike you, Annie," observed Charlie. "I've never seen you like this, and I'm sure that Jonathan has commented to Jared the same. So Jared probably views your erratic behavior as a sign that it would be best if you stayed."

Erratic behavior. That was the phrase everyone kept using. Still, I bristled. "Sam wants me to come and live with him," I claimed, defiant.

"Yes, but there's been red tape that he has been fighting for years, Annie—it hasn't been easy for him," noted Charlie. "I think, however, you need to understand that the people who really care about you are here, honey. As misguided as he is, Jonathan loves you very much. And I—I view you as my own daughter," he declared, his voice filled with emotion.

"Oh Charlie!" I cried, and sprang into his arms as the tears began to fall. He held me for a few moments and stroked my hair, letting me cry it out.

"I know, baby, I know," he murmured. "It's tough to have someone break your trust like Jared has broken yours, and of course it's affecting you. You've never had someone betray you quite like this."

"No," I sniffled. "No, you're right."

"So you see, sweetheart," he continued, "I know you may not think it, but you'll come to understand that this is the place for you, at least for now. There are people who care about you just as much, if not more, than your brother does. And furthermore," he paused and looked at my red face, "Jared Sorensen—he's just the kind that thinks only of himself. It's been wrong of him to use you like this."

"Wh—why do you think he did this to me?" I asked, hiccupping.

"Something you will learn when you do go back to the States is that people like Jared put themselves and their own well-being above everything else. And look at you! You're a beautiful girl, charming, and easy to talk to—of course he wanted to spend time with you. I just also think that he took advantage of how trusting you are. You attached yourself to him, Anabel," he continued, "because you thought he was your rescuer."

"But he's not. I was completely mistaken about him." I managed a small smile at Charlie. "Thank you for coming to talk to me."

"Of course, honey. Now listen, I really think you should just stay in your room tonight, and keep out of the way of your father and that man, okay?"

I nodded. "I have Elizabeth and Mr. Darcy to keep me company." I gestured to my book.

He gave me a gracious smile. "Have a good night, Annie." He made his way to the door.

"Charlie?" I called.

He turned to look at me. "I know I probably should have told you this a long time ago, but...I'm...I'm sorry about Marilyn," I blurted out.

"That's not your fault, Anabel." As he said that, I noticed his jaw clench, and I detected an edge to his voice.

"I know. But still, I feel terrible. I know you cared a great deal for her."

He paused, as if about to say something, but then stopped himself. "That's alright then, Annie, don't blame yourself. Now have a good evening."

I should have locked the door, but I didn't. Instead, I sat on my armchair, lost in thought, attempting to read *Pride and Prejudice*. It was after I realized that I had reread the same sentence five times that I threw the book down in disgust. I couldn't concentrate, and I stared at the floor for a minute, trying to figure out what to do.

It was then that I remembered something.

When my father had moved me into this suite (I had previously lived in adjoining rooms, which were connected to the east end of my library, with Miss Marilyn), he had taken me to a small door in the back of it. "Anabel," he had announced, "I need you to listen to me."

I, of course, was still mad at him for taking away my only friend, so I stared at him in my most defiant way.

"Even though I believe we are safe here, we must allow for the possibility that something could happen to endanger our lives. We live on an island full of convicts, after all."

"Mm," I acknowledged.

"For that reason," he continued, "it never hurts to take some precautions."

"Uh huh."

"Anabel, focus," he snapped. Jonathan flung open the door, and I let out a gasp.

There were monitors in that room, monitors that showed all of the main areas of Caereon. The view from the top of the piazza, the dining room, the front entryway, and all of the sitting rooms. I'd say there were at least fifteen monitors. "If the occasion ever arises that you need to know what's going on, this will be your entryway." He paused. "I suggest you do not mention this to anyone."

"How can I?" I snapped. "It's not like I have anyone to talk to."

"Anabel, I know you don't understand this, but it's for the best."

"I don't want to talk about this with you anymore," I warned. "All we will wind up doing is yelling at each other, and I don't have time for that."

That memory propelled me to the back room to spy on Jared and Jonathan's conversation.

I focused on the screen that held my father and Jared. Neither of them looked pleased to be there. Jared's tie had come loose; his top shirt button was undone and the suit jacket that he had been wearing at dinner was slung over the back of his seat. His face looked redder than normal; it was with annoyance and revulsion that I realized he and my father had been drinking.

At that point I wondered if my father had told me what room they were in on purpose so I would watch it. I'm pretty sure Jared would not have wanted me to hear what transpired.

First off, it's important for you to know that my father can hold his liquor. I've seen him drink glass after glass of whiskey; it doesn't faze him. He was a connoisseur of the spirit: he had a liquor cabinet that housed bottle after bottle of the amber liquid. Having never tried it, I personally cannot tell you a thing about the taste, but I can tell you that Jonathan preferred single malt. He had at least one glass every night after dinner. Focusing the screen, I saw that he had a bottle of what looked like Belvenie on the table. He was sitting on one side, Jared on the other. Quickly calculating the amount of time that had elapsed since dinner, I figured that Jonathan had consumed at least two glasses, and was working on his third.

Jared took a long sip out of his and put it down on the desk with gusto. I thought he looked like he should have stopped after that, but Jonathan refilled his glass.

"So you know, Mr. Sorensen, why I chose the Belvenie for us this evening?"

"Can't imagine," Jared slurred.

"Because, Mr. Sorensen," my father continued in a velvety voice, "it goes down very easy, and I wanted to make sure that you were not in complete control of your faculties before I spoke with you this evening." He topped off Jared's glass. "Let's get down to brass tacks, shall we?"

"I don't understand what that even means," Jared muttered.

"It means we need to discuss why you're here." Jonathan leaned over. "At first I thought you were here to respond to some complaints that I know one of my senior officers has lodged about the treatment of the inmates here. However, when we showed you the prison the only thing you seemed interested in was looking down the front of my daughter's dress, so I concluded that was not the issue."

"I wasn't—it was her," Jared attempted to protest. "She was—throwing—herself at me."

"Be that as it may, I expect you to control yourself around my teenaged daughter." Jonathan took another sip.

"Sh—she's almost twenty," pronounced Jared, nearly sounding proud of himself.

"Indeed," sniffed my father. "The point being, Mr. Sorensen, it was with a growing annoyance that I realized that you were sent here to monitor her. I hadn't thought Sam would stoop that low, but here it is." He sat back. "What I don't think my stepson will like, however, is how much hands-on monitoring you have been doing."

Jared groaned. "Cut the crap, Martin. I know you already sent Charlie to try and talk me out of getting her off the island, but let me," he paused, "let me tell you something, Jonathan Martin. I'm going to tell Sam everything."

"Everything?" My father's eyebrows went up. "Including the fact that you were, as one of the inmates so graciously put it, swapping spit with my daughter on top of the piazza?"

"Now wait just a minute," Jared went a bit cross-eyed. Some dashing hero, I thought. Can't even hold his drink.

"What I am saying, Mr. Sorensen, is that I highly suspect that my stepson will not be pleased with your recent actions, and I would like to offer you a deal," he proposed. I leaned forward with interest.

"What?" Jared asked, sitting up and taking another swig of whiskey.

"I think we can work out an arrangement, the two of us. We're both men, aren't we?" Jonathan swirled his glass in a manner I knew to be dangerous. Jared stared at him. I didn't like where this was going.

"I know that Anabel is nothing to you. You were just looking for a bit of fun with her, weren't you?" Jonathan asked.

Jared looked like he was about to disagree, but then nodded.

I fell back in my chair, feeling my heart deflate.

"I understand, Jared," my father continued. "I remember what it was like to be young, and a pretty girl catches your eye...it's nothing more than a little attraction, that's all. And why not? You're a good-looking man."

Jared was hanging on my father's every word. My disgust was rising.

"The problem, my friend, the problem..." That was the moment that my father's eyes narrowed and he scowled across the table at Jared. "The p-problem is that it was my d-daughter you were toying with, and now there are consequences!"

A smile spread across Jared's face. "You're just scared I'll take her away, aren't you, Jonathan?"

"YOU WILL N-NOT TAKE HER ANYWHERE!" Jonathan roared. "What makes you think that Sam will believe your word over mine, Sorensen?"

"Because he knows you're a nutter," proclaimed Jared.

"Ah, but despite that, if I show Sam pictures of you sexually harassing my daughter—"

"For the record, SHE sexually harassed me!"

"Do you really think Sam is going to believe that, given your reputation?" Jonathan asked, his voice low and dangerous.

Jared sat back in his chair.

I had seen enough. I turned off the monitor and went back into my room.

He couldn't stand up to my father.

Nobody could. I don't know why I thought Jared would be any different.

I was defeated. My father would have his way, of course. It had been silly of me to think that anyone could do anything for me. I was alone. I had always been alone. .

Which was Jonathan's fault.

"Why is he so obsessed with me?" I wondered out loud. But even as I said it, I knew why.

He hadn't been able to control my mother. And Jonathan hated not being in charge, as manifested by the way Caereon was run. Every detail of the operation was meticulously accounted for...but he hadn't been able to do that with Cassidy. So he was refocusing his energies on controlling me.

The fact that I looked a lot like her didn't help. Still, I meditated, he wasn't always terrible. In all fairness, he could be tender to me and quite generous when he chose. I always had lovely birthday gifts. He knew my tastes when it came to books—and clothes for that matter—and had always ordered beautiful things that had been delivered to us from the mainland. But this was just another way of manipulating me. Want to keep Anabel indoors and away from the inmates? Buy her *The Lord of the Rings*. Buy her Jane Austen. With the accompanying movies, of course. I owned all five hours of *Pride and Prejudice* with Colin Firth and had watched it many times. And the clothes! Gorgeous pieces. I loved dresses. I could spend hours in front of my mirror with my wardrobe alone.

And so, I lamented, I had spent day after day, hour after hour, reading this, watching that, studying this, wearing that...I sighed. If I had been smarter, I would have realized this before. He had trapped me, and I really hadn't put up a fight.

"But why is that?" I murmured aloud. Oh, who was I kidding? I knew the answer to that, too. It was because I liked my possessions. I liked them a lot. If I were to leave, it would be sort of ridiculous to pack up my library. Books were heavy, and it would cost all sorts of money—money that I did not have—to ship them anywhere. We only got supplies from the mainland three to four times a year, after all, because of the high costs. We were self-sufficient otherwise. Some of the convicts worked the land, and we also had a small meat plant.

Possessions couldn't make me happy, though. I longed for friendship. I longed for any sort of relationship, really. Maybe even a dog. Perhaps, I thought, resigning myself to the idea that Jonathan wasn't going to let me go, I could get a dog. He wouldn't deny me that, would he?

But staying here—well that meant a lot of things, really. It meant only spending a week or two out of the year with my brother, and our situation dictated that we didn't get to spend any time together in private. He always had Secret Service with him, for one thing; for another, Jonathan did not like it when we talked. Perhaps because Sam always talked about taking me away from the island.

It also meant no Jared. Not that I had even presumed that he would be a part of my life, but we may have seen each other. If I had made the decision to stay in Washington, and he was still working for my brother, the chances were there that our paths would cross. I hated liking him, I really did. No good could come of it, especially if my father had won him over. How could Jared have such a lack of strength of character?

I stood up and tossed my robe aside. I walked over to my desk and sat down, flipping open my laptop. As it booted up, I contemplated what I had decided to do. It was a bit sketchy, but there was a reason everyone thought so poorly of Jared, wasn't there?

So I plugged his name into Google.

Before, I had only read one or two things about Jared. This time, I looked at all the websites that came up with renewed interest. There was an article which told the story of a married woman who he purportedly had an affair with, whose husband confronted Jared in a restaurant. Apparently they came to blows. All these women. Gorgeous women. They came to life on the screen before me: vivacious redheads, blonde bombshells...apparently brunettes were not his style, I thought, tugging at my own chocolate locks. Shaking my head, I began to read more and more suspect articles: more lists of women he had gone through, a minor banking scandal that looked like it had been hushed up, shady deals he had been entangled with that had my brother standing up for him. When he had said he did side jobs, it had never occurred to me that it might be something not quite right. Perhaps Jared was doing dirty work for Sam—but I tossed that thought out the window. In my mind, my brother was perfect, and I could not countenance the idea that Sam would be involved in anything that fell in the "shades of gray" area. Still, I mused, he did have Jared on staff for a reason .

And why, exactly, was Jared here, dealing with me?

My discomfort mounted. Maybe I was a "shady deal." Maybe I was something that Sam wanted kept quiet. That would explain Jared's involvement, I thought, and that made me uneasy.

I picked up my phone, but then stopped. I should probably let Sam get a good night's sleep for once.

Throwing it down in frustration, I climbed onto my bed and tucked my knees under my chin. So much was swirling through my brain at the moment. I felt numb. My heart was hurting me.

Oh, come on, Anabel, I thought. Stop feeling sorry for yourself. This is ridiculous.

"Today," I proclaimed aloud, "is the first day of the rest of my life." I was not going to be lost in a sea of self-pity anymore. All I had to do was act calm, and that would convince Sam I had not gone all crazy. I would just prove to him that I needed to leave. If that did not work, then I had less than a year and a half to tough it out until I could get my hands on Cassidy's money. Then, if I had to, I would charter myself a yacht and get the heck off of the island. Really, I thought, straightening, squaring my shoulders, I did not need anyone but myself to get out of here.

That thought empowered me. I had not been all whiny until Jared came to the island. He was the one who brought on my self-doubt. I did not need him. I took a deep breath and smiled.

That was when my introspection was interrupted by a wild pounding at my door. "ANABEL! AN-A-BEL!"

In my haste, I didn't even bother throwing on my robe. I flung open the door and came face to face with Jared. Sweaty, red-faced, completely inebriated Jared.

"What are you doing here?" I hissed, letting him in lest my father see him.

"Anabel, I need—I need to talk to you," he panted. He leaned over onto my bed.

I stood staring at him, unimpressed. "I don't have anything to say to you."

He stared at me. "Your nightgown..."

...Was definitely not the sort of thing I should be wearing around him. I reached for my robe, but he stopped me. "No," he said, "I like it."

"I don't want you to like it." I was growing angry. Something about this did not feel right. "I need you to go now, please."

"Anabel," he whispered, his voice intense. "Anabel come here, I need to tell you something."

I was growing more and more uneasy, but I came and stood close to him.

He was about two inches taller than me, so I had to look up to see his eyes. He looked so serious, despite his feverish face. We were inches away from each other, and he started to put his arms around me. He drew me close to him, and briefly I thought about how earlier I had longed for him to do this, longed for him to sweep me into an embrace, but this...this did not feel right. It felt very improper when he firmly planted one hand on the small of my back, and one arm around my neck, drawing me into a kiss. I could taste the whiskey on his breath, and I drew back, repulsed. But he continued to kiss me, at first gently, searching, and then harder. And harder, and I tried to pull apart from him. Then he seized me, and the look in his eyes scared me. "Let me go, please let me go," I begged, panicking, but he was intent upon me, and then I realized what was about to happen.

And then it was over, and I felt a strange warmth on my leg as he pulled away from me, and calling me "Natasha," he passed out on the floor. I pulled myself up, unsteady. Then I looked down, and I was shocked to see that blood was streaming down my leg, on my nightgown, and onto my rug.

I had said no. I had said it over and over. I had screamed, even though I had known that no one would ever come to rescue me. I had flailed and tried to pull myself away. In the end, I had been overpowered. Shaking, I looked down at my wrists and noticed bruises were starting to form on them, and on my arms. Something inside of me felt bruised and broken, as well.

I sat there, frozen to the spot, for a long time. I felt like I couldn't move. I could barely breathe. Words would begin to form at my lips, and then disappear. Tears would form in my eyes, but they wouldn't fall. I could not think; I could not feel. My mind was reeling and my heart was pounding and the only thought that was going through my mind was that I had lost my virginity—it had been stolen from me.

And I could never get it back.

I don't know how long I sat there. I began tugging at my hair. Pulling at it. I tucked my knees under my chin and started to rock myself. My hair fell around me. I closed my eyes and thought this is just a nightmare, it did not happen, when I wake up it will all go away, oh please, oh please go away, please.

Then he stirred. He looked at me, blinking. "Anabel?"

I stared at him, unable to say anything, incredulous that he would even presume to speak to me.

His eyes wandered to the stain on the rug. "Oh no," he said.

I found my voice. "I really need you to go now," I croaked.

"Anabel, I—"

"Get. Out. Now," I ordered.

"How did this happen?" he whispered. He took in my mussed hair, my cowering position, and he realized. "I hurt you. Oh Anabel, I hurt you, honey, I'm so sorry—"

I looked at him, unable to believe my ears. "Do not call me honey. Do not pretend like you care. Just get out. Now."

"You must know I never—that is, I—I don't know how this happened." He kept tripping over his words. It was all an act, I knew, which made me burn with rage.

"You don't know how this happened? Are you kidding me? You burst into my bedroom completely drunk and you force yourself up on me, and YOU DON'T KNOW HOW THIS HAPPENED?" I screeched.

He looked at me, abashed.

"You don't even care about me." My voice broke on the end, and I took a deep breath. "I heard you tell Jonathan that you don't. So why would you do this?"

Again, Jared didn't have a response for me.

"Get out now, or I will tell my father." It was the best threat I could come up with, and it was a good one, too—I saw the color drain from Jared's face. "You have until the count of three," I warned, sounding much braver than I felt.

He got up, grabbed his clothing, and walked to the door. "Is there anything I can say?"

I stared at him stonily, trying my hardest to hold it together. After he closed the door I sprang up and locked it behind him. Then I climbed into my bed and then, and only then, was the moment that I began to sob.

Chapter 20—Anabel

I met Meghan's eyes. "I don't think I can talk about this anymore," I told her.

"Anabel?" she ventured.

"Mm?" I looked at her, trying to force away the tears that had appeared.

"I know we don't know each other very well, but I feel like, um, that is..." She gave a frustrated sigh. "I want to hug you. I think you need it. Can I?"

I blinked away my tears and held out my arms. She stood up and walked over to me, and held me, stroking my hair, in a way that was almost maternal. "Thank you for sharing that, it must have been really hard," she said.

Jared had not said a word. I glanced at him through my watery eyes. He looked strained.

"Anabel," he choked a bit on my name.

"You don't need to say anything," I told him.

"I'm so sorry," he whispered.

"Please don't say anything else."

"But Anabel…"

"I can't do this." I pulled apart from Meghan.

She snapped into action and looked at Jared. "You should go home and rest up for tomorrow. I will take the Princess to your hearing, so all you have to do is show up."

I knew he was looking at me, but I couldn't return his gaze. I knew that if I looked at him, I would lose it, and I had to hold it together. That was all I could focus on. I was aware of him saying goodbye to me, to Meghan, and then I heard the door close, but I was lost in my own thoughts. Which is why it took me a few minutes to realize that Meghan was sitting next to me, holding my hand and looking at me, her eyes filled with compassion.

"You know," I broke the silence, "you couldn't stand the sight of me earlier."

"I know, Anabel. I'm sorry. It's just the kind of women Jared finds himself entangled with usually...well they aren't like you." Meghan looked away from me, as if she was searching for how to explain this. "I just have developed a certain cynicism whenever he gets involved with a woman. Mostly they're airheads who want to be connected with his power and prestige. Do you know how hard it is to have all of your friends be in love with your brother? Wait, don't answer that," she said, and I couldn't help but smile. Meghan continued. "Besides, you turned up pregnant, so it caused me to judge you prematurely. Again, I am truly sorry," she apologized, and her voice was sincere.

"You don't have anything to be sorry for," I replied. "We don't even know each other. How could you possibly have any idea who I am, what I'm like? Everyone I have loved is isolated from me or dead, I'm not exactly the most popular girl right now."

"Well, I'd like to be your friend, if I could, Anabel."

"For the love of God, why?"

She started to laugh. "You're funny, for one thing. You're certainly interesting. Also, I wrote my senior thesis on Jane Austen, so I know a kindred spirit when I see one." She smiled. "Besides, it appears my brother actually does care about you, despite what you may think."

I snorted. "One moment I believe he does, the next moment I relive...that." My speaking skills were deteriorating rather rapidly. "What a lucky girl I am, I get to do it again tomorrow." I put my head in my hands. "I wish I knew who Natasha was. I had forgotten he had said that to me. Do you know?" I looked at her through my fingers.

She looked away. "I really think that's something he ought to tell you, not me."

"I understand." And I did, even though I was dying to know.

"I don't really know what to say," she admitted. "So what I think we should do is get you into your pajamas and into bed. Can I make you some hot chocolate?"

I smiled at her. "I would like that."

I had gotten into my pajamas and was letting the air mattress fill when she brought in the cocoa. "It's very hot, so be careful. I'm going to go get your sheets."

"Thank you," I accepted it gratefully. She came back into the room and started making up the bed. I shifted, unsure of what to do or say.

"Why are you fidgeting?" It was like she had eyes in the back of her head.

"I guess, well, I don't know, I invited myself over here, I feel very thankful that you took me in. Is there anything you want to ask me?" I dropped into a chair.

She frowned. "I don't know. I don't know what to say to you, except that I'm so sorry you went through that, and my brother is a jerk sometimes."

"Why did you call me Princess?" I asked.

"I don't know." She turned to look at me. "It just seemed to fit, somehow."

"That's my codename, is all," I leaned back in my chair.

"I guess I'm just psychic then," she laughed. "Who came up with it?"

"Alexis," I almost giggled at the memory. "She was talking to Sam and said, 'I can't believe I have to deal with some spoiled princess, Sam!' And so it stuck. From what I'm told, Sam's head of security turned to the detail and said, 'When Princess arrives...'"

"That Alexis is such a sweetheart. You're all set," she announced, turning down the bed for me. I slid into it, enjoying the feel of the cool, crisp sheets.

"I can't thank you enough." I slipped my arm under the pillow.

She sat down on the floor next to me. "Okay, I do have to ask. How do you feel about him? Honestly?"

"I don't know," I groaned. "I should never have let myself get caught up in the moment with him earlier. I made a complete and utter idiot of myself."

She nodded. "I know I keep saying this, but he really does care about you."

"But only since he found out I was pregnant," I pointed out. "He was such a jerk to me that first day at the hearings, Meghan. All I kept thinking about on the drive over there was that I wanted him to die."

"I'm sure it would make things easier," she noted, a hint of amusement in her voice.

"But he's the father of my child, so he's in my life whether I like it or not," I continued. "It would make things easier if I knew I could count on him, if I could trust him."

"Well, just give yourself time. See how things work out. That's all I can tell you," she offered. "You know, I'm glad you're here. It's better for you to be away from Alexis."

I frowned. "Is there something going on that I don't know about?"

"You mean you don't know?" Meghan looked surprised. "Well, she did an interview the other day and basically called you an ungrateful little...strumpet."

"She did not say strumpet!" I started to giggle.

She laughed along with me. "No, but something along those lines."

"Well, that would explain the nice, tense atmosphere around Blair House. She and I don't get along; I think she took an instant dislike to me."

"My guess is she doesn't like your relationship with your brother."

"Yeah, I suppose." I put my head down.

"I'm serious, Anabel. You know, she would never contradict him. Not in public, which is why all the tabloid stories about them were from dinners, events where they thought that they were alone. But you—you don't seem to care he used to be our President, you know? The media thinks it's delightful that you backtalk Sam, and they've been quoting you left and right."

"Oh, dear," I closed my eyes. "My poor brother. I should go a little easier on him. I guess that's why they put me through those lovely 'how to talk to the press' classes."

"You're kidding."

"Oh yes." I sat up. "Well, it doesn't surprise me. The other night she made an effort, but she's since gone back to being her usual heinous self."

"Well, you don't deserve it."

"You're sweet. I should go to bed though. Goodnight, Meghan."

"Pleasant dreams, Anabel."

Chapter 21—Jared

I didn't sleep that night.

Listening to Anabel talk had been just about the worst experience of my life.

I couldn't deal with it. I couldn't deal with her, and I couldn't deal with myself.

Around four I got up and went for a jog.

Irony of ironies, I found myself in Rock Creek Park. There were a few deer in sight, and I broke into a run. It had been months since I had been down here, and I didn't enjoy it. Too many bad memories.

I ran until my lungs felt like they would burst, and then I paused and bent over, catching my breath. And then, I heard her voice. "What are you doing, Jared?"

I looked up and saw Natasha. "Not you, too."

She approached me, half-smiling, just like she used to. She was dressed for a run, her almost black hair in a high ponytail. She had always looked like this: perfectly put together, flawless in her attire; she could run for miles and never break a sweat. "You can't run away from the little mess you've created this time."

"I don't know what to do." I couldn't lie to her.

She laughed a little. "I know you don't. But you screwed up last night."

"What do you mean?"

"You left her, Jared. You shouldn't have done that. You should have at least attempted to comfort her. And to leave her with Meghan, of all people! Let's face it, your sister—she's not exactly the friendliest, is she?" She came closer. "Listen to me. Anabel Martin...you only get a limited amount of chances with a girl like that. Sort of like with me."

"That was different, Nat." I closed my eyes.

"Was it?"

"We weren't supposed to be together."

"I loved you," came her fierce declaration.

"I know you did. And I messed that up. I can't forgive myself for that."

"You're going to do that with Anabel, too, you know. There's no getting around it, Jared. You're running out of time, and there are things you can't fix."

"You should leave now."

"Why?"

"Because," I said, keeping my eyes closed, "you're not really here."

And when I opened my eyes, she was gone. I took a few deep breaths, and then ran back to my apartment. I had errands to run.

A few hours later, I was standing outside the Capitol Building. Scanning the crowd, I didn't see her mass of brown hair or my sister's neat red bob. I checked my watch again. 9:01. I had to talk to her before we went in.

A few minutes later, I was relieved to see them, walking closely together. Anabel looked relaxed. She was giggling, and Meghan was smiling back at her, but also looking around. I had a feeling she was doing her best to keep their entrance inconspicuous. I was surprised to see Anabel lean in and whisper something in Meghan's ear, and then to see my sister actually laugh. Anabel had won her over.

As they came closer I overheard Meghan say, "Now, when's the last time you talked to your father's attorney?"

Anabel frowned. "You know, I haven't heard from him, I'll ask Sam today."

"Good, because you really need your document—oh," she said, noticing me. The two of them stopped in their tracks.

"Oh, hello," Anabel stammered.

"Hi. Hello Meghan." I stared at my sister.

Meghan smiled. "Well, this is where I leave you. I have to go down to the office." She kissed me on the cheek, and whispered, "Hey, she had a pretty bad nightmare last night, go easy on her." Then she turned to Anabel. "Bye Princess!"

"Good-bye!" she called. She then turned to me. "Your sister is rather lovely."

"Yeah, she's okay," I agreed. "Hey, Anabel—"

"There is a long list of things that I do not feel like talking about right now," she began.

"I know," I cut her off. "Listen, I got you something."

She looked surprised. "Oh?"

"Yes, here," I thrust the package at her.

We had all sorts of people milling about us, but oblivious little Anabel was lost in her own world of unwrapping my gift, blocking the way without noticing. When she got the paper off her eyes widened. "Oh Jared," she whispered.

"Does this mean you like it?"

"I LOVE it!" she practically screamed. "My very own BlackBerry!"

"Well, you insist on clinging to a keyboard," I rolled my eyes. She grinned. "Only I have the number, so I guess I'm the only one who can call you at the moment. It's written on the box," I said, feeling awkward. "But it's all activated and ready to go."

She hugged me, then seemed to regret it in the same instant and stepped away. Then she frowned. "But doesn't this cost money?"

I stared at her.

She quickly recovered. "Okay, dumb question. But, Jared, you don't have a job right now."

"That doesn't mean I don't have money," I told her. "Look, I wanted to do something nice for you, okay? I needed to. Just allow me this."

She looked unsure.

"Please, Anabel. You can ask Meghan, she'll tell you I don't do this sort of thing for just anyone." I tried to smile at her.

She stared at me for a moment, biting her lower lip, but then she nodded. "Okay, but I will pay you back as soon as everything gets straightened out with—"

"Miss Martin?" called a voice through the crowd. Anabel turned from me and beamed at the bespectacled stranger.

"Mr. Holbrook! I was just talking about you!" She turned to me. "Jared, this is Nathaniel Holbrook, he was my father's attorney, and now he's the executor of Jonathan's estate."

"Nice to meet you." I extended a hand.

"Quite," he returned, ignoring the hand. I deduced he probably knew who I was. He was an older man, with thinning hair. He straightened his tie. "Miss Martin, can we meet during your lunch recess? I need to discuss the particulars of Jonathan's will with you."

"Sure! Here, I just got a BlackBerry, let me get your phone number, and I'll call you when we get out..." She grinned at me as they exchanged numbers.

Mr. Holbrook was on his way when she turned to me.

"So, we don't have a lot of time, the hearing is starting in a minute, but I have to say something to you," she informed me. "About today, Jared, I need to tell you that I just want you to tell the truth."

"Can you handle it?" I asked.

She nodded. "Just be honest. That's the best way to handle this whole mess." Then she grinned and took my arm. "You bought me a BLACKBERRY!"

"Does that make you feel better? After last night?"

"Did Meghan say something?"

"Yes, she's sneaky like that."

She frowned. "Yeah, the nightmares are coming back. I haven't had too many in recent months." She fell in step next to me. "They're all about Jonathan's death—I'd rather not talk about it."

"Fair enough."

We walked into the hearing room and were accosted by Sam and Alexis. "Where have you been? It's almost 9:30!" Alexis scowled at me.

"I'm sorry, traffic was really bad on Massachusetts Avenue," sang Anabel. "Look!" She held up her new phone.

Sam blinked. "Where did you get that?"

She pointed at me. Sam did not look happy. "Do not try and buy my sister's affections, Sorensen," he warned.

"Everyone else tries to," she shot back. I snorted.

Alexis took her arm. "Annie, I want to apologize to you for yesterday. I was out of line, and both Sam and I would really like it if you would come home with us this evening."

Anabel smiled at her. "That's very sweet, Alexis, but I think it is time that I moved out. I will come by later to get my things, but after that I am just going to stay away. Besides, you and I both know that you are telling anyone who will listen that I'm a total slut, and staying with you just destroys my credibility."

Both Alexis and Sam looked flabbergasted, and they turned to stare at each other for a long time.

Anabel looked at me and whispered, "I think they're having a telepathic conversation. And I think Alexis is winning."

I choked back a laugh and turned away. Anabel was grinning at me with a conspiratorial smile, and I had a flash of the girl I used to know.

It was Sam who spoke first. "Anabel, you can't be serious."

"Oh, I'm quite serious," she affirmed. "Meghan has offered to let me stay with her until I figure things out. As it happens, I am having a meeting with Jonathan's attorney today, so I can at least see what my options are with regards to his will, and maybe I can get my hands on my trust fund money early."

Sam glared at me. "I assume this is your doing?"

"It's news to me," I replied.

Alexis scoffed. "Anabel, sweetie, you don't know a thing about how to take care of yourself. And this is the District of Columbia!"

"I think I'll be okay," she declared, looking at Sam. He looked at her, long and hard, and then nodded.

But Alexis was getting angry. "You are coming home with us, young lady, and that is that." She glared at Sam, but his eyes were on Anabel.

Who, for the record, looked extremely amused. "You have no right to tell me what to do, Alexis, and I think we need some time apart."

"Is this because of Jared?" Sam asked her.

"Oh no, absolutely not," she told him. With a furtive glance at me, she threw her arms around her brother. "I love and adore you, big brother, but I need to get my life together, and I think it is just best if we make a clean break." She pulled away from him, looking sad. "You miss your children, and I'm sure that the two of you are anxious to find a house, or something. Besides, it's just better if we do it now, before the baby is born."

"You don't know the first thing about taking care of an infant!" Now Alexis was starting to cause a scene.

Anabel shrugged. "No, but as you pointed out, there are books." She frowned. "Alexis, I thought you'd be happy. I mean, yesterday you were proclaiming what a burden I was."

"I changed my mind," she sniffed. I looked at her, trying to figure this out. This was not Alexis. I was well aware of the things she was saying to the media about her sister-in-law, and this change in demeanor bothered me. Had Sam threatened her? Or was there some sort of ulterior motive?

"Anabel, please come home with us this evening," Sam begged.

Her eyes narrowed. "What's wrong?"

Alexis sighed, finally becoming conscious of people looking her way. She gave a tight smile. "You are much better protected with us, Anabel."

"Why do I need protection?"

"Because you are clearly oblivious," she snapped. "The person who killed Jonathan is still out there. Have you forgotten?"

Anabel slumped. "But wouldn't that person still be on Caereon?"

"We just don't know who it is, honey," Sam reminded her. "We sent protection to watch you last night, but it made me really uncomfortable to think that you might be in danger."

"He didn't sleep," Alexis put in.

Anabel nodded, mulling it over. "I will think about it," she said. "I think we ought to go in." She walked in, but Sam caught my arm.

"Listen to me," he growled. "You can't fix this by buying her things, Jared. You and I both know that." He pushed past me and went to stand by his sister, before I could even open my mouth to protest.

So we sat down. As much as it annoyed Anabel, it also really grated on me to be here. It made me severely frustrated that this was the third week of hearings for us, and we hadn't covered any ground. I didn't have too much time to think about that, however, because I was asked to speak.

This is what Anabel missed when she turned off her monitors.

The world was spinning, and Jonathan was glaring at me. I definitely should not have had that fifth glass of whiskey. "So I think we have a deal, Mr. Sorensen? You will tell Sam that Anabel needs to stay here, and to stop meddling in her life?"

"Why won't you just leave her alone?" I asked, point blank. "She's so unhappy, can you not see that?"

Jonathan contemplated me, his eyes cold. "You surprise me."

"Yeah? Whyzzat?" I needed to stop slurring, but my mind and my mouth weren't connected.

"You feel concern for her. Not exactly your style, but I understand. I've seen how my daughter is." He sneered. "She's even more beautiful than her mother was, and she inherited Cassidy's open flirtatiousness." This is bad, I thought. Anabel had warned me that her father never spoke about her mother. "Cassidy had a nasty habit of falling in with the wrong sort of men, and it appears her daughter is doing the same thing."

"She's your daughter, too."

Jonathan ignored me. "I understand, Jared. Let's face facts. I know that Anabel is beautiful, but it goes beyond that. She is engaging, and more than one man has felt more than a curious interest in her." He took off his glasses. "So let's get something straight. I love my daughter. That is not diminished by her recent poor choices. She means the world to me. However, she does not understand what she would be getting into if she were to leave Caereon. The world is not a happy place, Jared, you know that."

I willed the world to hold still for a moment. "What are you saying now?"

"I did not take as much of an interest in her education as I should have, and so she spent sixteen years under the tutelage of a woman who I fear installed faulty morals in the girl."

"Oh please—" I began to protest.

"My fears," he continued, ignoring me, "were confirmed when I saw the two of you together. I was appalled by her behavior. She cannot leave this island. She does not know how to comport herself! Anabel would get herself into a world of trouble—"

"She's not stupid. She can take care of herself. You just don't want to be alone." I gripped the arms of my chair.

He paused. "Well, in that aspect you are correct. I don't want to lose my daughter, and I know that she would not be able to visit me once she left."

I stared at him, the room reeling. "Why?"

"Once she left she couldn't come back. The entire facility is Top Secret, and she does not possess a security clearance."

"I won't—I won't abandon her," I declared.

"No, you've decided she's some sort of crusade, I understand." Jonathan looked pensive. "But just consider what you're doing to her, Jared. Getting her hopes up isn't healthy for her. She needs to face facts. She is a problem—"

"She is NOT a problem!" I roared. "You don't appreciate what you have." I stood up, still gripping the back of the chair for balance. "Good-bye, Jonathan."

"Stay away from her, Jared," he warned. "Or you will live to regret it, this I do promise you."

Then I slammed the door and stumbled down the hall, focused on one goal: to find Anabel. I remember thinking that I would save her, that I wanted to tell her how much she meant to me. And she did mean something to me, I knew it. I had to tell her, my drunken state told me. I had to tell her what I wanted her to be to me, but even more, I wanted to tell her I would not let her crazy father entrap her here any longer.

But, I don't remember what happened after I got to her door. It's a black hole in my mind, and I think my brain won't let me remember it. What I do remember is waking up a few hours later, with a splitting headache and the taste of whiskey in my mouth, opening my eyes to see Anabel with her knees tucked under her chin, rocking on the floor. I remember realizing what I had done to her. I saw the look of betrayal on her face, which hardened the moment she realized I was looking at her. I heard her scream at me. I saw the bloodstain on the rug and on her nightgown and wondered how badly I had hurt her.

Then all I could see was her bedroom door. I skulked down the hall, for the first time in my life feeling like everyone had been right about me, after all. There was no recourse for what I had done. What would her brother say? He had trusted me with her, and I had traded our friendship for a night I didn't even remember. Anabel's screams as she had thrown me out of her bedroom still rang in my ears as I locked the door to my room behind me. I climbed into my bed and shut my eyes, praying for sleep that I knew would never come.

Chapter 22—Anabel

Jared did not protect me with what he said, which was good. The truth was the truth, and the one comfort I had was it couldn't hurt me anymore.

He told the council that my father had noticed him taking an interest in me—and played a mind game. They all nodded; there was no doubt that he was a manipulative man. When he got to the part about Jonathan drinking with him, several surreptitious glances were shot my way.

Somehow, though, an inner peace entered me, and I was calm and relaxed. What had happened wasn't pretty, but it had happened, and I just wanted to move on. I rested my hand on my belly and felt Emma squirming around in there. She was certainly an active child. Her presence comforted me and gave me the courage to listen to Jared's story about how my father just wanted to control me, about how he had thought he would rescue me, and about how wanting to save me had turned into something far more sinister. Jared did not once look my way, but I studied the back of his blonde head intently.

I could never look at him the same way again. Still, Jared off of the island was becoming a case study. There was a vulnerability to him that I had never noticed before. Of course that was probably because he had been putting on a front for me while we were together on Caereon. Jared did not like to let people in, and that was his primary problem with me on the island. I had such a powerful desire to be loved, to be liked, to be a part of someone else's life.

In retrospect, I had come on very strong.

I knew what Jared had done to me was not my fault. However, it had become more than just an act of violence. It had been an outright betrayal. He said he did not know how it happened, and that really was not a good enough excuse for me. I had other things to consider. Emma was going to be here in less than four months. While there was this big part of me that wanted to take our little girl and run far away from him, I knew that would be unfair to her. Having grown up with only one parent, I did not want the cycle to repeat itself.

Really, then, what I needed to ask myself was, could I trust Jared? After that night I had looked him up on the internet, I had read plenty more about him—especially when I came to the United States. Shortly after our arrival in DC he had informed my brother that he would be taking an extended vacation, which Sam understood. After all, he had witnessed a murder. Then he had called in his resignation, which puzzled Sam—until he started to guess that something had happened between the two of us—and the media had started to speculate. So there had been one morning where Sam, Alexis, and I were having our usual awkward breakfast at Blair House, before I knew I was pregnant. Alexis was reading the paper and she scoffed at Sam.

"Look," she noted, "it's your former golden boy, stirring up problems again."

Shooting a reproving glance at me, he took it from her.

"What does it say?" I implored.

"Nothing, don't worry about it."

"Sam, I want to read the paper."

He glared at Alexis, but handed it over to me. The story contained images of Jared, but also one of me from when I first arrived at Andrews Air Force Base, looking rather wan and pale. Never having been on a plane before, I had gotten violently sick during the tortuous trip. The article went on to detail how Jared, known for his popularity with women, had been carrying on with me at Caereon. I shoved my waffles away. "I've suddenly lost my appetite." Taking the paper, I made for my room.

In the comfort of my bed I reread the article, which implied that Jared would go after anything that had two legs and a vagina—and it seemed to make its case by publishing the rather unflattering picture of me. "How President Sallinger ever trusted this man is a total mystery," I read. If they only knew, I thought. I had fallen under his spell; I had no desire to ever see him again.

Then a week later, I realized it had been awhile since I had my period. That was when I realized that not seeing Jared would be an absolute impossibility.

Looking at him now, however, caused some mixed emotions. I loved our baby, but could I ever get past my anger toward Jared? Could I ever feel for him again what I felt before? Honestly, I wasn't really sure what exactly I had felt. I guess it was a girlish infatuation; it could not have been love. I knew that now.

What was really getting at me, I reflected, was this newfound sense of nobility in him. I mean, to go from partying with actresses and models to wanting to do the right thing by me—it just didn't make sense. It did not fit in with my picture of him, and it was throwing me off. He had offered to marry me. My sense of principle rejected this idea; I could not possibly marry someone I did not love and did not respect. I especially could not marry someone who did not love me.

Unless he did.

I sighed, and bit my lower lip. Maybe Jared just felt pity for me, and that was why he was acting the way he was. Still, I considered, he had made an effort to talk to me before he even knew I was pregnant. He had wanted to take me out to dinner, have a conversation with me. If he had wanted to cast me aside entirely, he would not have done that, right?

But now I was justifying him. He had hurt me, and I needed to remember that. If I did not do that, I might descend into some dangerous territory.

I wanted Jared. I wanted him so badly. It was sick, really. It was disgusting to me, but at the same time I was drawn to him. I wanted him to be the good guy in this piece. I mean, my life was based on books, right? Sometimes the hero screwed up, but he always came out alright in the end.

Right?

Tugging at my hair, I had to face facts. Our whole affair was an awful mess, but the new elements to it made me pause. It was clear from the gift of the BlackBerry that he was at least paying attention to what I was saying. Maybe he just wasn't as soulless as everyone said. I was growing discomposed. I could not rationalize the situation. I felt sweaty, and I put my hand on Sam's arm. "I need some water," I whispered.

He grabbed the pitcher, filled a glass, and passed it my way. I drank deeply from it, realizing I was close to hyperventilating. So much for inner peace.

"You okay?" Sam whispered back.

I shook my head. "I hope we get a break soon."

His eyes filled with concern. "Are you in pain?"

"No, just a bit cranky."

"I wish you would come home, you know."

"I wish Alexis didn't hate me so much."

"Maybe if you came home with us, we could sort this whole mess out, Annie."

"I don't want to talk about this now, Sam," I whispered. "Besides, I don't have a home."

"I've done my best, you know, Anabel." He sounded sad.

I sighed. "I know you have. I'm sorry; I'm a hormonal mess today. We'll talk after this, okay?"

He nodded, and we refocused on Jared, who was now detailing how the next day he tried to find me, but I was nowhere to be found.

And that was when they called on me to speak.

I was sobbing into my pillow. I could not think, I could not feel, I could barely breathe. Finally, I stopped crying and the numbness set in. I felt cold, empty, and very, very alone. I slowly slid out of bed, feeling sore, feeling broken. Then claustrophobia set in. The room felt too small. I needed to go somewhere—but where? Now more than ever, the truth hit me: there was absolutely nowhere to go. Unsteadily, I stepped over the bloodstain on my rug and stood in front of the mirror.

Two very dull, very bloodshot blue eyes stared back at me. My beautiful nightgown was ruined. I yanked it off and stared at myself, naked in front of the mirror. I took a moment to appraise my bruised arms, the bloodstains on my thighs, and the swollen state of my face. I felt a deep sense of shame consume me. I could barely look at myself in the mirror, and I raced to my bathroom and turned on the shower.

The water was extremely hot, and I turned it up to the point where I could hardly stand it. I wanted to scald the feeling of Jared off of me. Time slipped away as I sat in the bottom of my shower, letting the hot water run through my hair, down my back. At points I remembered to scrub myself. My muscles started to relax a bit, and I watched the blood swirl down the drain, removing the evidence. I shuddered at that thought.

Why would he do this? As the tears began to flow again, I struggled to make sense of everything. Sure, I had not bothered to hide my interest in Jared. But he had gone out of his way to let me know that he wanted nothing to do with me. I reached my hand into my hair and began to yank on it. He hadn't wanted me. That had been evident.

"So," I murmured through the water, "he drank himself to the point where he did?"

And that was the very ugly truth. None of this would have happened if he hadn't been drunk.

"And whose fault was that?" I wondered aloud, the unforgiving, unrelenting reality setting in. Ah, but life was ironic. I shut off the faucet and sat there for a moment, feeling the water cool upon my skin. I wondered how Jonathan would feel knowing he had launched the chain of events that lead to my deflowering. I shut my eyes and pulled my knees to myself, and buried my head in my arms. Then, from the pit of my stomach, a cry erupted and I began to shake again. My body was racked with sobs. I cried for myself, for my father, and for everything I had lost.

I was shivering when I got out of the shower, and everything just felt so numb as I went through the motions of combing my hair, brushing my teeth, applying lotion. I slowly walked to my wardrobe and stared at everything in it. I started yanking at my hair again. Then, without thinking, I reached in and started pulling everything off of its hangers. I threw my clothes all over my room, onto my bed, and on the floor, covering my rug. Dresses, skirts, sweaters—all lay in a pile all over the floor. Gasping, I surveyed what I had done. Still pulling my hair, I opened the bottom drawer and gingerly slid into a pair of sweatpants. I yanked a tank top on, and pulling on my sneakers, I set out to find Jonathan.

I sidled down the hall, lost in my thoughts. Everything seemed surreal as I wound my way out of the building. My quarters were located in the so-called "safe zone." It takes a long time to get down there, and a series of combinations prevents anyone out of the small group of us from being in that particular area of the fortress. Of course, I reflected, we had given Jared the passwords.

Pushing the heavy doors open, I found myself in the blaring sun. Squinting, I shaded my eyes with my hand and looked around. There were guards, but not as many as usual. I saw Major Briggs, our Head of Security, and approached him. "Major," I greeted him.

"Anabel," he acknowledged me. "Are you out here by yourself?"

"Yes, I'm looking for my father."

He nodded. "He's finishing up in the prison, would you like me to escort you?"

I almost smiled. "You know, it would probably be a good idea."

He offered me his arm, and we started across the piazza.

"The mood is funny today, Anabel," he remarked.

"What do you mean?"

"A lot of the guards have suddenly come down with an illness, and so we're short staffed. The ones who are out here seem uneasy."

"I see," I noted. "Well, maybe Jonathan yelled at them? He's been in a foul mood ever since Jared arrived on the island."

"Speaking of Jared Sorensen—"

"If it's all the same to you, Major," I cut him off, "I'd rather not."

"Just stay away from him. He's bad news. He has a reputation back in the US, and I just want to warn you, Anabel."

"I appreciate it," I got out, trying not to lose my composure. "I can assure you, I want nothing to do with him."

As we approached the prison, Jonathan emerged. He looked harried, but stopped when he saw me walking with the Major. "Briggs?" he asked.

"Your daughter was looking for you, sir." He saluted me and was off.

Jonathan turned to me. "You look like a train hit you. What's wrong?"

I ignored the insult. "I need to talk with you, alone," I told him, my voice dry.

"I'm very busy. Can it wait?"

"No, it can't."

"Well, what is it then?" He was studying his clipboard.

"Daddy," I said.

"What, Anabel? I really—"

"Daddy, I need to go somewhere private and talk to you," I pleaded, my voice breaking.

"I have things to do, Anabel."

"For once in your life, can you act like my father and just be there for me when I need you?" Tears were welling in my eyes yet again.

And then Jonathan really looked at me, taking in my bloodshot eyes, my messy hair, and my tears of desperation. "There is no need to cause a scene," he told me, his voice cold. "We'll go to my office."

Sniffling, I followed him as he moved across the piazza, into our building, and down the hall to his office. I followed him in, shutting the door behind us. He went to sit behind his desk as I lowered myself into a chair.

"Well?" he queried.

I started to cry.

He sighed. "I think I know what this is about."

"Oh, I don't," I muttered.

"I am assuming from your behavior that Mr. Sorensen has told you what he told me last night, about his recommendation to Sam," he continued.

Oh. I had forgotten about that.

"There has been a great deal of question regarding your emotional stability, child. I have talked to Mr. Sorensen extensively about this, and we have both agreed that the best course of action for now is to keep you here so I can support you as you go through this...transition period in your life."

"Transition period?" Was the man insane?

"You appear to be going through…some things," Jonathan went on to say. "We may need to get a counselor for you, but I want to make sure your needs are adequately met."

I stared at my father. "You want my needs to be adequately met, huh? Isn't that the same phrase you used when you took Kevin away?"

Jonathan stared at me, his gaze never wavering. "You seem to have a habit of attracting the worst sort of men, Anabel. I think it would only get worse for you if you were to leave here, to be unsupervised."

I began choking on my own rage. "You are so clueless, you really have no idea what is going on." I stood up. "Allow me to spell it out for you, Daddy. Last night, after you drank Jared under the table, he did show up at my bedroom door. But it wasn't to talk to me about any little bosom conversations that the two of you had."

His eyebrows shot up, and I continued. "Look at me, Jonathan. Just look at me. When is the last time I wore sweatpants?"

"What are you getting at?"

I rolled my eyes. "I normally care enough about my appearance to wear a dress, or a nice pair of slacks. I normally style my hair. I only wear sneakers on the treadmill." I was pacing now. "Also, I know that if you caught me like this under other circumstances, you would force me to change. Well, I look like this because right now, I don't care what I look like. Because last night, thanks to you, Jared Sorensen burst into my bedroom and had his way with me."

The words took a moment to sink in, and then my father's tone became low and dangerous. "So you seduced him then?"

I stared at him. "Are you serious?"

He glared back at me.

Disbelieving, I asked, "You really are determined to believe the worst of me, aren't you?"

"Your behavior of late indicates exactly what type of woman you are, Anabel. You clearly have become the worst sort of harlot. Surely you invited Mr. Sorensen in."

I was at a loss for what to say. Then, something inside of me snapped. "Yup. That's it. You have completely revealed my character, Daddy. So good work. However," I raised my voice a bit, "I think you should see this." Without a word, I held out my arms to him, so he could see the ugly bruises that had formed on them. "In case you were wondering, these bruises exist because he was holding me down while he forced himself into me. I have some similar ones on my leg, from being shoved to the ground. You know, I really thought that I could come to you with this, and that you would step down from your high horse and for once, be a parent, and defend my honor, or something." I reached inside my bag and pulled out the bloodstained nightgown. "This," I snarled, throwing it onto his desk, "is what that man did to me last night, and to be honest, I don't hold him half as responsible for it as I do you."

"Don't be ridiculous, Anabel!" he shouted.

"I most certainly am not being ridiculous!" I screeched back. "You were the one who got him so drunk he didn't even know what he was doing! And you know, at this moment, I can honestly say that I despise you. You have never once cared about me, or put me first. It's always been you, and your needs, and your sick, twisted desire to have control over my life."

"How dare you disrespect me," he seethed.

I scoffed. "Please. The only thing plaguing you right now is not any concern for my well-being, but a wonder if you might be able to use this for your own gain." I started to head for the front door. Then I turned back. "You were all I had, you know. You took Marilyn away, and I so desperately wanted some sign of affection from you." Tears pricked at my eyes. "But now I know that all of that was wasted on you. I now know that you are impossible to love—and you don't deserve my affections one bit. Do not come after me."

That, of course, was the last time I saw him.

Chapter 23—Anabel

I sat back in my chair. Sam looked at me with concern, and I attempted a half smile at him. I did not bother looking Jared's way; I figured he was going through enough as it was.

"Thank you, Miss Martin," the Congresswoman said. "I think we shall adjourn for lunch. We will reconvene at 1 p.m."

Sam sighed. "Well, at least that part's over."

"It is," I agreed. "Listen, I need to go find Mr. Holbrook, he said he wanted to discuss Jonathan's will with me."

Sam frowned. "Isn't there usually a will reading for that?"

"Well, I am his only heir," I pointed out.

"I want to come with you."

"Me, too." Jared had materialized.

I shrugged. "That's fine with me." Mr. Holbrook was approaching us.

"Miss Martin, Mr. President," he said, nodding to Sam. He ignored Jared. The act made me want to giggle, but I refrained.

"My brother and Mr. Sorensen will be accompanying us, Mr. Holbrook," I announced.

Mr. Holbrook did not look too happy with this, and it seemed like he was literally biting his tongue. "I see. Well, I will send my assistant for lunch. We can meet in a room that I have arranged."

So we followed him, and headed to a room with a large oval table. Jana, his assistant, came in about five minutes later with warm sandwiches. As I bit into mine, Mr. Holbrook handed me a packet of documents. "These are your personal copies," he said. "I assumed, Miss Martin, that you would want to have them for your reference."

"That is very good of you, thank you," I said, around my sandwich.

He put on his glasses. "Now then," he continued, "You are Jonathan's sole heir, so everything—his bank accounts, his estate, and his life insurance policy—those all go directly to you. I have taken the liberty of changing everything into your name, I just need some signatures."

I frowned. "What exactly does his estate entail?"

He took off his glasses. "Miss Martin, you are aware that your father owned two properties?"

"Mr. Holbrook," I returned, "my father did not trust me with the most mundane of details, this is not the sort of thing that he would volunteer to me."

"Very well. One of the properties is actually in Mclean, Virginia. I spoke to the caretaker and it is ready for you if you should decide to move in."

"Wow," was all I could say.

"If you will look in the file, Miss Martin, you will find that your father left you extremely well taken care of, and as soon as the inquest is over, you will be awarded his 1 million dollar life insurance policy."

I stared at him. "Are you serious?"

"Quite," he returned. "In the meantime, I have procured for you bank cards with your name on them, so that you have access to your funds."

I stared at the account balances. "Are these right?"

"As I mentioned," he went on, "your father provided handsomely for you. He has also provided me with an extensive retainer, so I am yours at any time."

I felt overwhelmed. I showed Sam the paper. "This is a lot of money, right?"

"Wow," he whistled. "Well, it makes sense. His housing and all of his expenses on the island were provided, and I'm sure he got a fair amount of Cassidy's fortune during the divorce." He grinned at me. "You're a very wealthy lady, Missy."

"Your documents, Miss Martin," Mr. Holbrook continued. "Your passport, birth certificate, credit cards—"

"Credit cards?"

"I had specific instructions as to what to provide for you should a situation such as this ever occur." He leaned forward. "I know this must be a bit overwhelming for you, and I apologize if I seem curt, it is just we have a great deal to get through in such a short time." He glanced at his watch.

"No, thank you," I managed. I glanced over at Jared. He had been silent throughout the presentation. I offered him a small smile. "See, I told you I would pay you back."

"It was a gift, Anabel," he stated.

"Alright then," I said, looking to Sam. He rolled his eyes.

Jared stood up. "It is 12:45, we should head back." And he did, without a backwards glance at either of us.

Sam and I exchanged a glance. "And I thought I was the one with all the hormones." I grinned at my brother. "So, do you want to check out my new house with me tonight?"

"Unfortunately, I have a speaking engagement at American University."

"Well, maybe Jared will get his temper under control and come with me," I suggested.

Sam frowned. "You shouldn't spend time with him outside of these proceedings, Anabel. It doesn't send a good message."

"You keep saying that, but I don't know how much more my reputation could suffer." I stood up and shook Mr. Holbrook's hand, and Sam helped me get all of my paperwork and new house keys into my bag.

The hearing room was buzzing, and I walked over to Jared and put my hand on his shoulder. "Hey."

He did not glance up. "What?"

"I was thinking I would go check out this house that Jonathan left me." I shifted on my feet. "I would like it if you came with me."

"I'll think about it." And with that, I was dismissed.

I walked over to Sam and slumped down next to him. "Sit up straight, Anabel," he admonished.

I groaned and put my head down on the table. Thankfully, they called Marilyn for questioning, so I did not have to say anything for the remainder of the day.

Five o'clock rolled around and Sam shot me a sad smile. "So I take it you won't be coming home tonight?"

"I don't think so," I admitted. "I'm sorry, Sam."

He nodded. "Well, I've already taken some precautionary measures." He turned to a man standing in the back and gestured him over.

This man caught my attention immediately. He was tall and extremely good-looking. He was dressed in khakis and a button down shirt, but he carried himself with an erect posture that exuded confidence. His dark brown hair was almost the same color as his eyes, which seemed kind, but guarded. For the first time in a long time, I felt conscious of my appearance.

It was, of course, Matt.

"You may remember Matt Moore. I've hired him to be your bodyguard."

"What?" I wasn't paying attention. Sam let out a frustrated sigh.

"Anabel! I'm paying Matt to look after you until this is resolved."

"Hi," I managed, feeling shy.

Matt barely acknowledged me. "Hey. Now Sam, where are we setting up shop?"

"Well, Anabel found out today that she has inherited a house from Jonathan. It's in Mclean, so that is probably the best place for the two of you."

My eyes narrowed a bit. "So you are going to be staying with me?"

"That is the point of a bodyguard." He sounded amused, and even gave me a small smile. My insides melted a little.

I looked at Sam. "I don't even know where this place is."

"Do you have the address?" Matt stepped a little closer to me.

"Yes."

"We'll be fine then. Anabel, you will be riding with me over there. Sam has already given me a lot of your clothing so you should be set for at least a few days."

I shot Sam a questioning glance, and he nodded. "I knew you weren't going to come back."

I hugged him. Then he stood up. "Well, I need to head out. Annie, you're in good hands." He walked out, his Secret Service detail following him.

I looked at Matt and smiled. "So it's just you and me, then?"

"Am I no longer invited?"

Oh, right. I had forgotten about Jared.

"Jared, this is Matt, my new bodyguard. Matt, this is Jared, who—"

"I know who he is," Matt cut me off.

I was surprised. "Do you two know each other?"

"We've met," stated Matt, before Jared could open his mouth. He turned back to me. "So, you and I will go to Mclean, I want to scope out the area. Sorensen," he turned to Jared, "I think it would be best if you met us there in an hour or so."

That was an order. I looked at Jared, who appeared to be struggling with an inner conflict. Finally he nodded. He wrote down the address, kissed me on the cheek, and walked out of the room.

I turned to Matt, my eyebrows raised. "What was that all about?"

"Nothing I want to go into," he replied. He held out his hand. "Shall we?"

I accepted and he helped me up. "You realize you are going to tell me what is going on between the two of you."

"That will not be happening, Anabel."

I smirked. "We'll see."

Chapter 24—Jared

I ran down the hallway, and caught Sam just as he was getting into his town car. "Matt Moore? That's a low blow, even for you."

What seemed like a thousand reporters heard me say this, and they immediately turned their cameras towards us. Sam barked, "In the car. Now."

I hopped in next to him, and he was glaring at me. "You have no right," he began.

"He hates me more than you do."

"With good reason." Sam was cool. "I realize you think this is some sort of personal attack, and I can understand that. But there is no one else in the world that I would trust with the overseeing of my sister than Matt, and you know he did a great job with my kids."

"I would watch out for her," I argued.

"Yes, but she changes her mind on an hourly basis as to whether or not she wants to see you," Sam seemed to be enjoying himself. "Look, she needs more stability than you can provide. She's also not going to take your mood swings either. I saw how you were when you heard about her money." He looked at me hard. "I know you don't like it, you've never liked people with more money than you. She's had enough stress, and the pregnancy has really done a number on her, with the bleeding, and—"

"What bleeding?" I asked.

Sam groaned. "She didn't tell you. Great. Long story short, right about when she hit nine weeks was when we found out she was pregnant, and then when she hit ten weeks she had what's called sub-chorionic bleeding." I stared at him, so he continued. "Sometimes when the placenta implants into the uterus it forms a little pool of blood. Most of the time the body just absorbs it, but Annie had some spotting, and she flipped her lid." He sighed. "I'm serious, Jared. She was in hysterics. I shudder to think about what would have happened if she had lost the baby. Thank God Kevin came when he did, and told her what it was."

"But nothing's wrong, right?"

"No," he sighed. "Her body absorbed the hematoma, and she hasn't had problems of that nature since. She has had multiple urinary infections, however, which stresses her out because she's worried about antibiotics hurting the baby. This is why she needs someone who will be a steady influence. And I can't count on you, based on your past behavior, even if I wanted to. If I give her Matt, he'll watch her and not put up with her absurdity."

"If you give her Matt," I scoffed. "Don't think I don't know what you're doing, Sam."

"You know how I feel about what you did to her."

"You used to be my best friend," I pointed out.

"And where did that get me?"

"I love her," I said.

He looked like he would punch me. "Never say that again," he ordered. "I don't believe you. I don't even think she believes you."

"Look, I told you I never wanted this to happen. Even Anabel admitted as much today. I would never have touched her if I hadn't been impaired."

Sam sighed. "I warned you about Jonathan. You saw firsthand what he was doing to her."

"I can't argue with you anymore," I groaned. "But I'm not going to let you deliver her into Moore's waiting hands. He'll use her to get back at me, and do you really want to do that to your own sister?"

"He likes saving things," Sam pointed out. "And you prevented him from saving his sister."

"It wasn't like that! You know it!" The image of Natasha Moore from that morning in the park flashed through my mind again. It was a face I saw a lot, as she still haunted my dreams.

"You should have left her alone."

"She was the one who made a point to make sure I noticed her. She was always around the corner, or waiting for me outside your office. She made a concerted effort to make sure I paid attention to her."

"So did Anabel." Sam sounded strained.

"I know you don't believe me, but I do care about Anabel. It was different before. Natasha knew what she was getting into with me." I looked ahead. "Look, since you invited me on your ride here, can you drop me off in Northwest? I'm going to see Meghan."

"So you're saying you were upfront with Natasha? She knew that you never cared for her?" Sam leaned forward. "That's a change for you."

"I told her I was still hung up on Jessica. How could she not believe me?" Before Natasha Moore, I had dated an actress. "I did care about her. I just never thought we'd be anything more than what we were. She had a different opinion."

"Well, we've got a car ride, Jared. Tell me what really happened."

I looked at him sharply. "You told me you didn't want to know before."

"Well, now I do. So go ahead."

In fact, Natasha and Anabel shared a lot of similarities. They were both young (although Natasha was twenty-one), very bright, and nothing like the sort of women I usually dated. Natasha had been working as a White House Intern when I met her. She was a pretty little thing, very athletic and petite, so I had noticed her, but hadn't thought much of it. She hung around the oval office a fair amount, and one day I ran into her carrying a bunch of papers and accidentally knocked them from her hand.

"Wow, I'm sorry." I bent over to pick them up.

Kneeling, she giggled. "Oh well. I was just standing here, attempting to look like I was doing something." She leaned in close and whispered, "I'm hung over and my boss just handed me this stack of papers—and I have no idea what I'm supposed to be doing with them!"

"Your honesty is refreshing. Jared Sorensen."

"Natasha Moore." She flashed very white teeth at me. "So how are you going to make this up to me, Jared?"

"Excuse me?" I was late for a meeting with the vice president, and this intern was harassing me?

"Well, you did make a mess of my paperwork," she pointed out.

"So now I owe you something?"

"Why yes, Mr. Sorensen," she purred, standing up and reaching to straighten my tie. "You do."

I took the bait. "I could buy you a drink?"

"That's more like it," she said with a smile. She turned on her heel, and walked away. Then she called over her shoulder, "Meet me back here when you're done for the day."

As with most women I dated, drinks turned into sex, and Nat and I were inseparable. She was fun and vivacious, and extremely smart—but for me, it was just supposed to be fun. I had just gotten out of a semi-serious relationship; I wasn't looking for anything but a good time. And I told her that.

Still, I don't think she believed me. She would joke about me leaving her for the next supermodel that came to town, but as time went by, the jokes became accusations. While I never cheated on her, I never went out of my way to assuage any fears in her mind. It was twisted, what I did to her, and I regret it more than I can say. But the fact was, I didn't want a needy woman, and that's exactly what she was. It had gotten old, and while I didn't see any reason to break up with her, my interest was definitely waning the last night we were together.

She and I were on a run in Rock Creek Park. I always enjoyed the park; the deer were prominent, and that early autumn evening felt crisp and cool as we jogged. One thing we had in common was exercise, and Natasha was fanatical about it.

"I've been meaning to talk to you about something," Nat mentioned, her sleek ponytail bouncing as we made our way down the path.

"What's up?" I was enjoying nature so much that I missed the note of foreboding in her voice.

"The lease on my apartment runs out soon." She took care to keep her voice light.

"Oh? Can you not renew?" I squinted into the fading sunlight. "Or do you want some help looking for a new place?"

"Well, I thought I would move in with you," she said bluntly.

I stopped dead in my tracks and stared at her.

"Well, I mean, I'm over there all the time anyway, and it would help me financially..." she trailed off, and looked into my eyes. Her face spelled out her disappointment. "You don't like the idea."

"Nat, I don't think we're ready for this."

"Why? I'm your girlfriend, after all." She stood with her hands on her hips, glaring at me.

"Yeah, you're my girlfriend. There's nothing beyond that."

Natasha's face blanched. "So what? I've been wasting my time with you?" Her voice raised an octave.

"Nat, baby," I appealed, "it's been a lot of fun. I wouldn't call it a waste of time. But you and me...I don't see us going anywhere beyond where we already are."

She didn't cry. I'll give her that. Her face contorted with rage, and she hurled a great deal of nastiness at me, and finished with, "My brother was right about you!" and then took off in the opposite direction. I called out to her, but she kept running...and running...and then, she was gone. Frustrated, I turned and ran in the opposite direction back to my place, figuring I would call her in the morning and try and smooth things over.

However, I never saw Natasha after that. She was murdered in the park that night by a man named Carlos Ruiz Mercado.

I had been a suspect, but I was cleared when they caught Mercado. Still, it had damaged my reputation, and that was when Sam had started to distance himself from me. He had my back, but I knew our relationship wasn't quite the same. Also, I had more than one ugly encounter with Matt—Nat's brother—who wholeheartedly believes that his sister's death is my fault.

This is why I did not want to leave him alone with the woman carrying my child.

Chapter 25—Anabel

"Sooo," I drew it out, "why don't you like Jared?"

"I think a better question is why do you?" Matt stared straight ahead. He had maybe said two words to me since we got into his truck, and I could hardly stand it. I was excited about his presence, but it also left me a bit confused. Matt was throwing me for a loop. If I was the star, and Jared was the hero, where did Matt fit into the mix? I decided he was the variable in the story.

So I considered. "I wouldn't say that I like Jared." I looked over at Matt. "He's not really a likeable guy."

"You got that right," he muttered. "Look, Anabel, there are some ground rules, okay? I don't want you to have the wrong perception of things."

"Okay," I grinned.

"Rule number one, stop asking me annoying questions."

"Ouch," I said, affronted. "What else?"

"Rule number two, you're not going to get anywhere with that little act you've got going on. None of this damsel in distress crap. Just because those big blue eyes work on everyone else does not mean they will work on me."

I pretended to be hurt. "I'm sure I do not know what you are talking about, Mr. Moore."

"Matt." He stared at the road. "Rule three, call me Matt."

"Matt," I made myself the picture of sweetness, "why are you being so harsh with me? Don't you know? Everyone else treats me like I'll shatter into a million tiny pieces at any given moment."

"You're not breakable," he answered. "You proved that in those hearings."

"Ah yes, the hearings. So how long have you been following me around?"

"A while." His eyes were on the road.

I shifted in my seat. "So when you told me you worked for my brother—"

He was nodding. "I'm an independent contractor. Your brother and I go way back, and he expressed an interest in hiring me for your protection. So, we made an arrangement that suits the both of us."

"Do you think I need to be protected?" I asked.

He shot me a sidelong glance. "Anabel, I'm one of the few people who actually knows what you went through after Jonathan was murdered. I've watched the security tapes. I do believe that you are at risk."

I slumped in my seat. "Um, I need to pee."

"You went right before we left."

"The baby likes to make a game of kicking my bladder all day."

He chuckled a bit. "We're almost there. Can you hold it five minutes?"

"I suppose," I replied. We lapsed into silence again. My natural instinct was to like him, which, I reflected, was how it went with me. I mean, after all, my relationship with Jared proved that I was a poor judge of character. But Matt seemed different...but also discomfiting. I especially hated that he had known that I was pregnant, and whatever it was that was going on with him and Jared also made me wary.

"So do I have to deal with Sorensen later?"

"I did invite him," I admitted. "I thought maybe we could get together. For dinner. To which I guess you will be coming." Since when was my speaking ability so impaired?

"Okay, if we go up to Tysons Corner there are a lot of restaurants." He paused. "I can probably help you pick something."

"Thanks." I felt shy again, and stared out the window. "I'm so glad you know where you're going."

"So what's with your name?"

"Excuse me?"

"Well, it's spelled funny."

"I don't want to talk to you about my name," I stammered.

"Why?" he asked, smiling at me, showing a little warmth. "I'm just curious."

"I'm named for a literary character," I managed. Why was he discomposing me so?

"Which one?"

"Annabel Lee. It's a poem." I should not be embarrassed about this. But having Matt put me on the spot made me flustered and uncomfortable.

"Didn't she meet a terrible end?" He made another sharp turn.

"I think my mom just liked the way it sounded," I told him. "Anyway, she really liked the name, and then she saw a reference to it in another book—" here I winced, and hoped he didn't notice—"so she decided it was perfect for me. She wanted to put a weird spin on it and name me Aniyabel, but my dad said absolutely not, and stripped it of extra vowels and letters, so it was simply, 'Anabel.' My father wasn't one for...superfluousness." Was that even a word?

"I see," he said.

"I'm kind of impressed you know the poem," I commented. "Do you like Poe?"

He grunted, and I wasn't quite sure what that meant. So I tried again. "I mean, most people don't know 'Annabel Lee,' much less the content of it."

His eyes stayed on the road. The silence persisted again, but now Matt was slowing down, and so I eagerly awaited my new place.

Then, he turned into a driveway. "So this is it, I guess."

I stared. "This is mine?"

"It matches the address you gave me."

"Wow," I breathed. It was gorgeous. The house was a red-brick, two story number, with a sweet little garden in front. In fact, it was exactly what a house should be, in my opinion. It looked so quaint and charming that I couldn't believe it was mine. I stared at it, wide-eyed, until a cough shook me from my awed state.

"I believe," Matt added, "this is where Jonathan and Cassidy lived prior to their divorce."

I stared at him for a moment, and then burst into tears.

He sighed. “Anabel, I’m sorry.”

“N-no,” I sniffled. “I’m glad you told me.”

He parked the car and I just sat there, wiping tears away and sniffling. Matt was kind enough to look away until I got myself together. “Shall we?”

I nodded.

“I wonder where the caretakers are,” I pondered as we walked up the path.

Matt was looking around, not even noticing me. This again irritated me, and I felt a vexation at him start to grow. Everyone noticed me. Who did he think he was?

“Should we ring the doorbell? In case the caretakers are in?”

“I suppose so.” I pushed the button.

A moment later, a balding, middle-aged man answered. “Yes?”

“Hi!” I beamed. “I’m Anabel Martin, this is my house!” Matt rolled his eyes.

This turned out to be the wrong thing to say. His face literally fell. “Oh, Miss Martin,” came his halfhearted greeting.

“It’s nice to meet you. I’m so sorry, but I don’t know your name.” What had I done to cause this poor man pain?

“Phil Albertson,” he introduced himself. “You should come in.”

“Oh right,” I agreed, giving him my best smile. “This is Matt, my new best friend.” Matt raised his eyebrows at me. I smiled back.

So we walked in and I was admiring the neat hallway that led into the sitting room when Phil said, “Miss Martin, because of the short notice from Mr. Holbrook, while we are packing right now, we haven’t found a new place yet.”

“Wait, what?” Pulled from my appreciation for my beautiful surroundings, I was confused.

“Well, my wife and daughter and I, we have been living here, and I imagine you’ll want us to leave.”

“Why would I want that?” I asked.

He stared at me, disbelieving.

I shrugged. "Well this is your home. And I was hoping you'd stay on, I don't know how much time I'm going to be spending here."

Phil's face relaxed a bit. "Well thank you, Miss Martin, we're much obliged."

"My name is Anabel, you can call me that," I offered.

"Anabel," he beamed, "let me give you the grand tour."

So he showed me around the kitchen, the living room, the family room with the cute fireplace, a quick peek at the library (the room caused a reappearance of the tears and Matt yanked me out of there), and then the upstairs, which was divided. There were four bedrooms and an office—Phil's family was located on the right half, and he showed me the left, which had the master suite with the adjoining office, and a bedroom across the hall.

"Oh, how sweet!" I admired, looking at the smaller bedroom. "That will be perfect for Emma's nursery."

"Anabel is expecting," Matt told Phil.

"Well congratulations! We did know, but it's hard to keep up with all of those hearings," Phil said, smiling at me. "And are you the father?"

Matt looked a little green. Quickly, I corrected, "No, Phil, that would be Jared, who is going to drop by later."

"Will he be moving in, Anabel?" Phil asked me.

"I don't know at this point," I answered, shaking my head. "I doubt it though. I apologize for disrupting your lives."

"No, no, no," Phil reassured me. "Now, I expect you'll want to unpack. My wife, Charlotte, and our daughter, Carrie are out at the market. Will you be joining us for dinner?"

"I wish, because that sounds lovely," I said. "But Matt and I have a dinner engagement. How about tomorrow? That way we can get to know each other a little better."

"I'll tell Charlotte," Phil beamed. "Now, you should get settled. Is there anything else in the truck?"

"Yes," said Matt.

"Well, I'll go get it!" And he took off.

I grinned at Matt. "He is precious!"

He was staring at me, unsure. "Are you for real?"

"What?"

"Anabel, this guy is your caretaker, not your family. You're just going to let some strange man and his wife and kid live in a house with you? You don't even know them!"

I stared at him blankly.

"It's also a nightmare for me. I haven't even done background checks on these people. You're not allowed to be with them alone until I give the say so, okay? You need to consult me on matters of your security," he admonished.

"Oh," I said. "I hadn't thought about it like that. What was I supposed to do? Kick them out of their home? That hardly seems fair."

"Well it's not really their home, kid."

"Well, I don't feel like it's mine." I sat down on my new bed. It was gorgeous, a four-posted number. "You can go sleep in Emma's nursery, there's a bed in there. Is that okay?" I smiled at him. "I don't think it would be a good idea if you slept in here."

"You're forgetting rule number two." As he walked out to check out the room across the hall, I chastised myself. Stop attempting to chat up your bodyguard, Anabel.

He stuck his head back in. "I'm going to walk around the house and just scope it out, okay? Please stay here."

"Will do," I promised. I lay back on my incredibly soft bed. I could do with a rest, as it had been a long day and now this man was hurling brutal verbal assaults my way. It really bothered me that Matt, who had seemed so nice the first couple times I met him, was suddenly cold and distant, and didn't really seem to want to have anything to do with me. I closed my eyes and hoped that traffic was bad, and Jared would be delayed. With all of this going on, I didn't want to deal with him right now.

Then what seemed like moments later, Matt was shaking me awake. "Jared just called your phone. He will be here in ten minutes."

"I didn't hear it ring."

"I took it out of the room so you could rest."

"But I just fell asleep," I whined, flustered by this abrupt awakening.

"You've been passed out for an hour, Anabel. And," he added, grimacing, "you might want to mouthwash."

"You really go out of your way to make me feel self-conscious, don't you?" I blurted out.

"And you say whatever pops into your head without thinking about it," he returned. "So here we are."

I furrowed my brow. "Why don't you like me?"

"Who says I don't?"

"I can tell."

He smiled wryly. "You're funny, Anabel." Then he left, and I rummaged through my bag for my mouthwash, perturbed.

In a very desultory state of mind, I met him downstairs, smoothing my blue dress as I walked to the front entryway. He quickly glanced at me and then looked away, and I bit my lower lip a little, thinking of the borderline lewd glances Jared always shot my way. "We're meeting him in Tyson's Corner," he announced. "Does Italian food sound okay to you?"

"Mm," I said, looking at him. He looked freshly showered, and I liked the way his blue shirt complemented his dark brown eyes.

Matt noticed me appraising him. He looked like he might say something, but he didn't. So I called good-night to Phil and followed him to his truck.

We rode in silence, and this began to drive me crazy again. So, in my most mature fashion, I shot him mistrustful glances and sighed to show my annoyance. But that didn't matter to Matt. He just stared at the road, ignoring me. Finally, I couldn't take it anymore. "Why do they call it Tysons Corner?"

"I have no idea," he replied.

"Fat lot of good you are," I muttered.

"What now?"

"Nothing," I snapped. I stared out the window.

He sighed. "I need you with me on this, Anabel," he told me.

"What?" I was startled.

"I know you think I'm not being nice to you—"

"I know you're not being nice to me," I put in.

"I just want to protect you."

"Of course you do." I was exasperated. "That's what you're being paid for."

"I also want to protect you from Jared."

"Oh, Matt," I almost laughed, "no one has been able to do that thus far."

He looked at me. "That doesn't mean I can't be the one to do it."

But then I frowned, recollecting something. "Wait a minute. I thought you said he was meeting us at the house."

"Yes," said Matt, and I caught a gleam in his eye, "that."

We turned into the parking lot of the restaurant. He jumped out and went to open my door. "I think you should know something," he said.

"Oh?"

"Jared called to say that something came up and he would have to reschedule. He wasn't thrilled that I told him you were asleep. So, you and I are getting dinner alone."

"Why, Matt Moore," I raised my eyebrows, "I underestimated you."

He cracked a grin. "Come on, Anabel. It's time we got to know each other."

So he made me laugh, he did. It turned out that we had a fair amount in common, similar tastes in food (he had hit the mark with the Italian), favorite movies (we both adored Cary Grant), and were both strongly opposed to James Joyce. What caught me off guard about Matt, though, was his self-assurance and complete disregard for propriety. It was like one moment I was drawn to him, and then the next, repelled by a snappy insult.

"So, I'm pretty pregnant," I commented.

"Yeah, you look it," he replied.

"And I'm the one who says whatever pops into her head," I shot back, taking an angry bite out of a breadstick.

"Well, you do," he acknowledged. "I told you I knew the moment I saw you. Besides, I've been watching you in these hearings, Anabel. Not to mention your little stunt when you revealed your pregnancy to Jared."

I looked up at him. "I was angry."

"Yeah, and not thinking." He took a spoonful of soup. "You like attention and seem to go out of your way to get it."

"I don't have to," I pointed out. "The press follows me around like...like..."

"Well, you're a sideshow." He met my eyes. "They never know what you're going to do or say. Plus, your brother kept you hidden for almost five months after they smuggled you back into the country. You never came to church or any other function with him and Alexis."

"I've never been to church," I admitted. "On Sundays Marilyn read the Bible to me and that's really it. So I don't know how to behave in church. That was Alexis' rationale, anyway. I think it was just another excuse to not let me be around Sam. She hates how much he cares about me."

"Yeah, she really doesn't like you," he agreed. "Every time she's interviewed she sneers a bit when your name comes up. And earlier today at the hearing there was blatant dislike in her face."

"I know," I agreed, feeling glum. "I don't understand why she hates me so much."

"It's because she's insecure as a person, and she hates the fact that your brother loves you." He said it so matter-of-factly that I dropped my breadstick.

"That's probably the first honest assessment I've heard of her."

"I've known Alexis for a long time. I've worked for your brother for a long time."

"So is that how you know Jared?" I picked up my breadstick again.

"Our paths never actually crossed, in spite of the fact that our families know each other. I worked privately for Sam as a bodyguard for his children. Now that they're in Martha's Vineyard with Alexis' sister, he wanted to keep me here to keep an eye on you and the hearings. I've been watching you for a while." He offered me a smile, and it was again warm and friendly. "And you know, buying you smoothies."

I was thoughtful. "So are you going to tell me how you know Jared, or are we going to keep playing this game?"

"If you really must know, it was a very sad circumstance that brought us together."

"I'm sorry to hear that. So when did you meet him?"

"After my sister died last fall." He stared into his soup.

I frowned. "I'm so sorry." I paused, not knowing what to say.

He looked away. "Go on, I know you want to ask me."

"How did she die, and what connection does that have to Jared?"

"She was murdered in Rock Creek Park. She was on a run with her boyfriend at the time, and they had a fight and he let her run off, alone. A man murdered her and left her body in the park. It was days before anyone found her."

My eyes widened. "Are you saying what I think you are?"

"She was with Sorensen, yes. She was very much in love with him and he broke her heart." He looked at me. "He's not a good guy, Anabel."

"I think I know that better than anybody," I replied.

He leaned forward. "Then tell me this: why are you letting yourself fall in love with him?"

"Oh, no," I groaned, putting my face in my hands. "Is it really that obvious?"

"Yes. Which is why I wanted to talk to you tonight, alone. I saw firsthand what he did to Nat. She cried a fair amount throughout the relationship—was always convinced he was cheating on her. She never felt like she was good enough for him."

"Did you talk to him after it happened?"

He sighed. "Yes, and his response was that she knew what she was getting into. To be fair, she had told me as much. I think she just felt like she could turn him around."

"I don't know what woman could do that," I commented. That prospect sounded exhausting.

"Well now, see here's the problem," he continued, growing serious. "What's his deal with you?"

"What do you mean?"

"Jared wants you."

I snorted. "What do you mean, he wants me?"

"I've been watching him. He doesn't like not being in control of you. He doesn't like it when you push him away. So he wants you."

"Or he cares about me?" I suggested.

"Well, that could be a possibility."

"Well if it is that, then I worry it's just out of guilt." I sat back in my chair.

"You know that he doesn't have the best track record with women. I just think for the sake of your daughter you need to be careful what choices you make with regards to him."

"I feel so dirty," I muttered. "By all accounts, I should hate his guts, right?"

"You're emotional," he reminded me. "I mean, you have what, five million hormones coursing through your body at any given moment? Isn't that what you said to Sam to justify your behavior?"

I laughed. "Yes. Yes, that's exactly right."

"And," he continued, his voice gentle, "you are so uncertain right now, you don't quite know what to do. Somehow, in your sense of right and wrong, it seems right to you to maybe pull a family together—you, Jared, your little girl. After all, you never had a family, isn't this what you always wanted?"

I started blinking back tears. "You know me better than I know myself."

"I doubt that."

"No really, I think you're the first person who has managed to figure out what I'm feeling." I shook my head. "But I still feel ashamed of who I am at this point."

"No, no," he soothed, taking my hand. "The only person who should have any shame for their behavior is Jared." His eyes were compassionate, and I decided to push down any barriers I had put up between us.

"If I stayed with him I could never trust him," I declared. "But how unfair is it to Emma, to keep her away from her father?"

"You wouldn't do that," he replied.

"You don't know me that well, Matt."

"I think I know you well enough, Anabel. You're tough. Most people would think twice if their baby was threatening their life."

I was startled. "What?"

"Don't pretend like you don't know what I'm talking about."

I looked down. "I haven't told Jared."

"Of course you haven't," he responded. "You know he would try and talk you out of it otherwise. What exactly is wrong?"

"Well, it started with the bleeding."

"The bleeding?"

I nodded. "When I was nine weeks we determined I was pregnant. When I hit ten weeks, I had what's called sub-chorionic bleeding, where a hematoma forms where the placenta implants. Mine was very, very small, so it wasn't an issue, but from then on I've been worried every time I go to the bathroom that I'm going to see something." Tears formed in my eyes just thinking about this. "Kevin assures me I don't have anything to worry about, but I can't help it."

"That's not the only thing that's going on though, is it?" he persisted.

I sighed. "I'm at risk for a fair amount of labor complications. We discovered around week fourteen that I was developing blood clots. So I had to take blood thinners, and it seems to have helped, but we have to be careful of that given my condition. I'm more than likely going to have to have a C-section, and Kevin has suggested to me more than once that this could have dire consequences. I could have massive blood loss once

I deliver."

"And the baby?"

"Should be fine," I told him. "It's just me."

"And you're not going to tell him?"

I looked away. "I will, at some point. Just not now. Believe me, I don't like lying to him, and neither does Sam. Kevin was fine with it though." I gave a harsh laugh. "Sam seems to think that if we lie to him it makes us just as bad as he is, but I disagree."

"Are you scared?" he asked quietly.

I shook my head. "No. I have no intention of dying." I glanced at my watch. "If it's all the same to you, I'd rather talk about something else."

We were interrupted by the waiter bringing us our food. I stuck my fork into my pasta and twirled it, lost in thought.

"You should actually eat the food, you know," Matt said.

I took a bite, slowly chewing the fettuccine. "Well, Matt, you seem to have all the answers. What should I do?"

He gave me an appraising stare. "I'm not going to tell you what to do, Anabel."

"I wish somebody would."

"You'll figure it out. You're a bright girl," he replied, taking a bite of steak.

"You're very confusing." I leaned forward again. "I mean, on one hand, you keep telling me what an attention whore I'm being."

"I never called you an attention whore."

"Okay, you didn't use that phrase, but you accused me of needing to be in the spotlight." I felt my temperature rise. This guy had a serious talent for driving me crazy.

He smiled at me, that slow, infuriating smile. "Like I said, I've been watching you, Anabel. I know you pretty well."

I was unnerved. "What does that mean?"

"It means I know you're still that little book-loving girl on the island. But

I also know you're really starting to figure out who you are, and I think that as time goes on, you'll become a force to be reckoned with." He glanced at his watch. "We should get you home soon. I'm sure you need your rest for another day of fun in the hearings tomorrow."

But I was staring at him. "Who are you?"

"I'm your best friend. You said so yourself." He looked self-satisfied.

I shook my head. "Alright then. I guess I will just have to accept that my life just gets weirder every day."

As we walked back to his truck I had a surprising thought. I was having fun. I was out somewhere with a person who almost counted as a friend, having dinner, not having the eyes of the world scrutinizing me. The thought buoyed my spirits.

Phil and Charlotte had waited up for us with tea and biscuits. Even though I was overstuffed, I gratefully accepted mine, and Matt made an effort to appear almost cordial as he thanked Charlotte, who beamed at him. They were adorable, the two of them. Charlotte's red hair was almost as messy as mine, and the way that she and Phil looked at each other made me wistful. Clearly, these two were very much in love. Phil sat close to his wife, holding her hand, looking at her like she was the most beautiful woman in the world. She kept shooting him these adoring glances that melted my heart.

For the first time I realized that I wanted that. I wanted someone to think that I was beautiful while I was wearing sweatpants and an old t-shirt. I wanted stability. I wanted a relationship.

Which wasn't what I had wanted with Jared.

With Jared it had been about wanting sex. I may as well be honest with myself. My attraction to Jared was based on what amounted to an animalistic lust. I had fallen into these feelings without any thought of the consequences, and had attached myself to him—but I had known full well what kind of a man he was, and my expectations had been realistic. I had never expected the two of us to live happily ever after— and I hadn't wanted that with him. But studying Charlotte and Phil made me wonder. I already adored them, and I enjoyed pleasant banter with them until Matt reminded me, none too gently, that I might want to consider getting some sleep.

"Oh right," I sighed. "Silly hearings tomorrow. Well, goodnight then, it was wonderful to meet the both of you!"

Matt followed me up the stairs and into my room. At the door, I turned around and stared at him. "Um," I began, giving him a coquettish look.

"I need to check your room," he demanded. Matt really was immune to my charms.

"Paranoid much?"

"Someone has to be." He lifted the bed skirt and checked under my bed. I sat down and crossed my arms, amused as he ducked into the closet and the bathroom. He looked at me. "Okay."

"Okay?"

"I think we're in the clear." He rubbed his eyes, looking tired. "What time do you have to be in the District tomorrow?"

"Um, the hearings start at 9:30, but I like to get there early."

"How long does it take you to get ready?"

"I showered today, so I don't need to tomorrow, so fifteen minutes, plus eating breakfast."

"What do you mean, you don't need to tomorrow?" He looked repulsed.

"My hair...if I wash it every day it gets really dry. There's nothing wrong with that. And saving water, you know."

"Yes, save the planet. I'd forgotten who I was talking to," he said with a touch of sarcasm.

"Oh I forgot, you can't be nice for too long," I snapped at him. "What are you all up in arms about now?"

"Well, your brother was big on climate change reform—"

"So what, that makes me president of Greenpeace? Please," I spat. I grabbed one of my bags and opened it for him, showing him my vast collection of electronic hair styling implements as well as aerosol sprays. "I think this alone disqualifies me."

He was trying not to grin. I could tell.

"So if you have all that, why is your hair always a mess?"

I stared at him, unsure of what to say.

"Alright, Anabel," he announced. "I'll make sure you're awake in the morning."

"Okay," I agreed, feeling confused. "Goodnight, Matt."

Then he walked out without another look, and left me standing there like a fool. As I closed the door, I was biting my lip and couldn't help but wonder why I wanted him to come back.

Chapter 26—Anabel

The next morning he was shaking me again. "Hey. Get up."

"You know, you could sing a song, or something," I mumbled. I was never at my best when I first awoke, and this was not my preferred method of being wrested from my precious slumber.

"You really want me to sing you a song?" I blinked up at him, and could see he looked amused. He also appeared to have been up for much longer than me.

"It's better than having you shake me like this," I grumbled. As he walked back toward the door I contemplated throwing my copy of The Bonfire of the Vanities at him. "What time is it, anyway?"

"Seven. Get dressed and meet me downstairs, ASAP." He was gone again.

Great. Another infuriating man in my life. First Jared, then my brother, and now the man that was being paid to watch over me was nothing but a pushy, overbearing...I collected myself. He might be pushy, but, for some reason, I did trust him. I had poured my heart out to him last night and let him see me at my most vulnerable...and telling him about my health complications was definitely my most vulnerable. I shoved that out of my mind; I didn't want to think about that. What I needed to concentrate on now was how to deal with Matt. The problem, I reasoned, sitting up in my bed, was that I had let too many men into my life. The solution I saw in front of me was simple: I clearly needed a female friend. Maybe Charlotte? I should call Meghan tonight, and I grabbed my phone and made a note reminding me to do so.

I washed my face and decided that I would attempt brushing my teeth if I managed to get some breakfast down. Checking myself in the mirror, I was pleased to see that well-rested Anabel didn't look half bad. Pulling on a modest purple dress, I wandered downstairs.

Matt was eating a delicious-looking pile of waffles. "Miss Anabel!" cried Charlotte, bouncing around her kitchen. "Here, dear, I just finished your waffles."

"Oh, thank you." I took my plate and my seat. Matt did not bother to glance up from his food. So I decided to eat in silence, as well.

By the time he and I got in the car together, my animosity was blatant and I made no attempt to make conversation with him. We were listening to some oldies station, and I was running my hands through my hair, yanking on it.

"You're going to go bald if you keep doing that."

"It's how I deal with my life."

"That's silly, Anabel. I don't think your life is that bad." His tone was light, which made me even more irritated.

"Nobody asked you," I snapped.

"I mean, you went through some tough stuff, but it's all coming together for you now, right?"

"Mm," I grunted, noncommittal.

We stopped at a light and he looked my way, frowning. "Why are you angry with me?" He seemed genuinely surprised.

"I don't know. I just am." I looked out the window, hoping he would not point out how preposterous I was being.

"Look, I don't think you're used to someone like me. There are different types of people in the world, that's all."

"Will you at least tell me why don't you like me?" I asked, again.

"It's not that I don't like you. It's just how I am." He didn't meet my eyes.

"You were nice enough last night."

"Well, I wanted to get to know you. I don't have anything against you, you know."

"What is that supposed to mean? You don't have anything against me? And you wanted to get to know me? So now that you've gotten what you need, you're done with me? Great. I feel used and degraded." I was back to pulling at my hair. Then I felt a hand stop mine.

"Please, Anabel. You need to be calm and relaxed for today." The voice was almost tender.

"I don't understand you." I shook my head and closed my eyes, willing him to no longer be there.

But he still was. “It's for your own good, okay?”

“Oh yes,” I said, heavy on the sarcasm. “Everything is for my own good, haven't you heard?” I tried to turn away from him, but my ever-growing stomach was hindering my movement. I slumped in my seat, hoping he hadn't noticed.

He had.

“Don't be so childish,” he reprimanded.

I looked at him. “Excuse me?”

“If you want to talk about it, just do it. There's no need to sit and sulk over there.” He sounded smug.

“Ugh, and I thought Jared was the most self-satisfied human being on the planet.”

“Don't class us together.” He didn't sound mad, but I mentally chastised myself for comparing him to the man who caused his sister's death. So, taking a deep breath, I reconsidered.

“I'm sorry. I'm just used to everyone treating me like I'm fragile and special and fawning all over me and you...well, you aren't paying me any attention!” I breathed a bit. “I just don't know what to do with that, Matt. What kind of a bodyguard ignores the person he's supposed to be protecting?”

At the next traffic light he stopped and stared at me for a moment. “Listen to me. I already told you, I think you're made of stronger stuff than anyone else gives you credit for. So no, I'm not going to treat you like you'll shatter at any second.” He paused. “But you are very special. It takes some real strength of character, some real intestinal fortitude, to go through everything that you have and still remain true to yourself, and you've done it.” He lowered his voice. “But don't think for a moment that I will ever let you out of my sight. Ever again.”

“Is that a promise?” I whispered, intoxicated by his words.

“Absolutely.” He then turned back to the road, but I was smiling. I opened my mouth, and then closed it, and then looked at him again. Then I looked down at my hands, biting my lip, suppressing my grin. Then I let out a giggle, and caught his eye. He sighed. “Go ahead, I know you want to."

"Intestinal fortitude? Really?"

"Shut up, Anabel."

Chapter 27—Jared

I had barely seen her at the hearing.

I hadn't talked to her in three days.

Anabel, Anabel, Anabel.

She must've talked to Matt about it by now. A large part of me did not blame him for hating me. The other part was mentally punishing myself for getting involved with Nat in the first place. This whole thing could have been avoided if I had just left well enough alone.

I was home, trying to watch TV but getting nowhere with that. Then I picked up a book. Then I tried to do laundry. It was no use. Every time I closed my eyes, I could see her.

I couldn't take it anymore. So I called her.

Anabel answered on the third ring. "Hey," came her voice, heavy with sleep.

"Oh, baby, did I wake you up?"

"It's okay," she mumbled. "I was just taking a nap. What's up?"

"Is it too cheesy to tell you I was thinking about you?"

She started to giggle. "I've been thinking about you a lot as well."

"Oh yeah? What kind of thoughts?" I asked, lowering my voice.

"Why do you make everything dirty?"

"Why do you make it so easy to make everything dirty?"

She groaned. "Jared, you're...I don't even know what you are, I almost feel like I need to make up a word to describe you."

"I look forward to hearing it."

"Don't worry, it won't be any worse than what Alexis has been saying about me," she promised.

"Yeah, I don't quite know what's going on there. Whatever did you do to get so high on her hit list? You might be above me."

"You never did tell me why she hates you so much," said Anabel, accusing.

"Maybe I'll tell you next time we see each other. How's that?" I evaded.

That made her testy. "Why did you wake me up?"

"Why have you been ignoring me?" I shot back.

"I haven't been ignoring you," she denied, but her voice was uneasy.

"Don't lie to me. I don't like it." I didn't want to make her mad, but I didn't want to let her get away with this garbage either.

"Jared," she sighed, "I just need some time to think, okay?"

"What's there to think about? We're having a baby. You want to be with me, I want to be with you..." It was clear as day to me. "Has something changed?"

"You're making a lot of presumptions."

"Has something changed?" I repeated.

"Nothing's changed, I just don't know how to fix this," she replied.

"What do you want from me, Anabel?" I asked her, exasperated.

She fell silent for a moment, and then, "I don't want anything from you, Jared. I mean, I really and truly do want you to fit into my life somehow. I just don't know where."

"I want to see you," I told her.

"Well you're coming to my party on Thursday, right?"

"Right, you hit the big 2-0," I said with a derisive grin. Charlotte and Phil, the caretakers at her house, had insisted on throwing her a party when they found out her birthday was soon. I still hadn't made it over there, so I was looking forward to it as well. I was also relieved that her birthday was so close. At least now my sister could stop referring to Anabel as my "teenage girlfriend."

"Yes!" she proclaimed, and almost mirroring my thoughts: "I'm excited; I'll no longer be referred to as an unwed teenage mother."

"We can fix that, you know."

"Jared..."

"I'm serious, Anabel." I really was. Anabel was quite possibly insane, but so was I. Somehow I adored and hated her at the same time. It also angered me that she was rebuffing me at every turn. Here I was, offering a way to get rid of the complications, and she had the nerve to reject me?

And she was being stubborn again. "I don't want to talk about that," she declared. "Is there anything else you want to say?"

I could've told her that I loved her. I could have told her that I wanted to make this work and that I couldn't picture my life without her inane little self in it. But the words failed me, so I lied to her. "No. There isn't."

"I'll see you on Thursday then."

I hung up my phone and stared at it. Then I threw it across the room. I was sick of her turning me down. More than that, though, I was worried. If neither of us made an effort, this would all fall apart. She had no interest in making things easy for me, and every time I tried to talk to her logically, I made her mad. Where exactly did that leave us?

Chapter 28—Anabel

And a few days later, I woke up and it was my birthday.

I turned and glanced at the clock. 3:02. Too early to get up, too late to do anything. I rolled back on my back and sighed. I really missed sleeping on my stomach.

Today was October 12. My twentieth birthday. Of all the places that I could possibly be on this date, I had never thought it would be here. Sleeping in my parents' old bedroom, in the home that they had briefly shared before my father took me away and I never saw my mother again. I was in my 23rd week of pregnancy. I had been carrying Emma for almost six months. The same amount of time that my father had been dead.

My father was dead.

He was dead, and he was never coming back.

And with that, I burst into tears. I cried like I never had before. For the first time, I allowed myself to grieve for him. I hadn't been able to do it when we first came back, especially since we hadn't had a real funeral for him, just a quiet memorial. Being around Sam and Alexis, and then being in the hearings—everyone had been treating me like I was about to fall apart, and I couldn't stand that sort of coddling. So I had been putting on a front. I didn't want their pity. I didn't want them to feel sorry for me. But now, alone in my bedroom, I was weeping convulsively, almost retching. I clung to the bedpost as my body shook with sobs. How could this happen? How could he be dead? "Daddy," I cried, "Daddy why aren't you here? Oh Daddy, I really need you." I hiccupped violently. "I can't-do-this. I can't do it without—you." My sobs and wails were getting louder, and I couldn't control myself.

That was when Matt burst through my door. "Anabel? What's going on?"

"Matt," I bawled, "Matt, my Daddy is dead, Matt, and he's never, never coming back."

So Matt came and sat down on my bed, and wordlessly pulled me close to him. He let me cry it all out until I was a sniffling mess with my head buried on his shoulder. It crossed my mind how gross he must find me; he wasn't wearing a shirt and I was getting snot all over his bare chest. He bore it very well though; through my tears, I was impressed.

"Hey now," he said, running his fingers through my hair. "Anabel. Sweetheart. How long have you been keeping that in?"

"A really, really long time," I sniveled, reaching for the Kleenex box and blowing my nose rather loudly. "I'm so sorry I woke you up. You can go back to bed."

"No I can't." He was incredulous. "You can't think I'd leave you like this." He paused. "Do you want to talk about it?"

I contemplated him in the semi-darkness, unsure.

"You don't have to," he continued. "But if you need me to listen, I'm here for you."

That did it. So I told him. I told him how much I had loved my father, and how I had never felt I measured up to his expectations. I told him how awful I had been, and how I had gone out of my way to say the most atrocious things to him that I could in the days leading up to his death. I got quiet when I relayed how it had cut me to my very soul when Jonathan accused me of seducing Jared. "He could never see any good in me," I lamented.

"I think you're exaggerating, Anabel. He definitely saw the good in you." He reached his finger under my chin and pushed it so I was looking into his eyes. The moonlight shone in them, and they were sincere. "If he didn't, he wouldn't have wasted his time, buying you all those books. He knew what you loved and provided it for you. I think that was his way of showing you he loved you."

I sniffled. "Why could he never tell me?"

"Perhaps his heart was too ponderous for his tongue." He was studying me, and I averted my eyes and smiled.

"I know that one," I acknowledged. "It's from another messed up father and daughter story. That's King Lear."

"I knew you would." He was stroking my back, and I realized that I didn't want him to stop. I think he realized it, too, because his hand stopped, but didn't move away. "I think he'd be proud of you, Anabel. He really would."

My mouth felt dry. "It's getting really late; we should probably go to bed."

But he was smiling at me. "I want to make sure you fall asleep. You need your rest. Now then," he said, suddenly businesslike, "what can I read you off with?" He flipped on my bedside lamp.

Blinking furiously in the new light, I shoved A Treasury of Best Loved Poems at him. "Wow me," I taunted.

He cracked it open, and began, "I once met a traveler from an antique land..."

"Oh no. No. Do not read me Percy Shelley!"

"And what do you have against Shelley?"

"Just that he broke his first wife's heart. He marries her and tells her that he loves her, but then he meets Mary and goes, 'Hey, you're still great, but can we live like brother and sister from now on?'"

"Okay," reasoned Matt, "but without Mr. Shelley's connections, and that night when Percy, Mary, and Lord Byron got together and had a writing competition, we would not have Frankenstein."

"And I thought I was the only person who knew all this esoteric crap. Seriously, are you as much of a nerd as I am?"

"My mother is a professor of English Literature. These are the stories I grew up on."

"Really?" I sat up. "That is so fantastic!"

"Yes, and if it makes you feel any better, I'm also a disappointment to my mother. Between her and my father, who is Headmaster of one of the prep academies here, the fact that I chose to not go into an academic field upset the both of them."

I was biting my lip again. "I don't think it makes me feel better, but I appreciate the effort."

"I did have to try." He wasn't looking at me, but I was warming to him.

"How many brothers and sisters did you have?"

"Well I'm the oldest, and then I told you about Nat. I also have a brother named Scott, who is four years younger than me."

"How old are you?"

"I'm twenty-nine, Anabel." His hand still remained on my back, and I silently willed him to not let go of me.

"When's your birthday?"

"It was a couple months ago, in August."

"Are you close with your brother?"

"Not really. He lives in California, and works for a software company. Nat and I were, though. I could never see her as anything but my baby sister, and I was always trying to protect her. But you understand that," he commented. "It's the way Sam views you."

I let out a yawn. "I do indeed know all about that. I want to meet your mom. Maybe that will make it easier for me to figure you out. Can I?"

"Yes, but you need to go to sleep now. I can read to you or we can sit here in silence until you drift off, it's your choice."

That was when it hit me. Matt had dropped everything and ran and comforted me when I needed him. He had probably been enjoying some respite from the craziness of our daily lives, and when he heard me in distress, he had gotten here without even putting on a shirt. The fact that he was sitting next to me in his boxers made me a little bashful. That thought caused me to think about the other night when Jared had just sat there while I sobbed and then left. He had just abandoned me, left me to cry on his sister's shoulder. That night, as I relived everything that had happened between us, I had really, really needed him.

And all he had done was leave.

But Matt was there for me, and he didn't need to be. All his job required him to do was to make sure I was alive. He could have easily ignored my sobs and wails. But he hadn't. He had come running, and was now treating me like...like...

Matt was treating me like I mattered to him.

"You know," I commented, settling back in bed, "I think I'm ready to go to sleep now. You don't need to read to me anymore, I'll see you in the morning."

"Are you sure?"

"Yes," I affirmed, a bit shy. "Thank you, Matt."

"You're very welcome." He walked to the door and then paused. "And Anabel?"

"Yes?"

"Happy birthday. We'll do something to celebrate today."

I fell back asleep with a smile on my face, and my dreams were sweet.

Chapter 29—Jared

"Well if it isn't the most notorious bachelor in town." Carly Waterstreet bent over and gave me a lingering kiss on the mouth. "Sorry I'm late, I had a meeting with my buyer, and that girl is such an idiot. I think I'm going to have to fire her."

"How long has this one lasted?"

"Three weeks." Her smile was vicious. "Her name is Sandi with an 'i.' I shouldn't have even considered her based on that stupid spelling alone, and the fact that she dots her i's with a heart!" She sat down on my lap, and whispered in my ear, "Needless to say, I definitely need to...relax...tonight."

"Well, you've come to the right place," I grinned broadly, resting my hand on her thigh.

Carly was probably one of the smartest women in DC. We had been in the same class at Georgetown. During our graduation ceremony she had leaned over and whispered to me that she had decided she didn't want to be a lawyer anymore.

I had scoffed, but she was serious. She was a brilliant law student, and turned out to be an equally brilliant businesswoman. She used all of her persuasive skills to talk her way into a bank loan to open a boutique in Georgetown where she sold high end fashion and served all the best clientele that DC had to offer. She often frequented the pages of Washingtonian Magazine—and I always enjoyed the times that she had me with her.

"Well," she said, her voice seductive, "I guess I can't spend the entirety of our meal on your lap." She stood up and I caught her arm.

"Are you sure?"

She smiled. "Poor Jared. Life's been rough, huh?"

"Yes." I sat back in my chair. "By the way, thank you for prying yourself away from work for an evening."

"I had to. I couldn't let you mope over some silly girl." She sat down and adjusted herself. All of herself, an act clearly done for my benefit. "I can't believe it. You finally found someone who doesn't want you."

"No, she wants me, Carly. She wants me very much."

"Are you just saying that because you don't want to look pathetic? Honey, I've seen you puking your guts out into my bathtub, you can't sink much lower."

"I seem to recall you weren't too turned off by that."

"Well, what can I say, love?" she purred. "You and I always had something special."

"We did. What happened to it?"

She considered. Then she broke into a smile. "What does it matter? We can try and rediscover it tonight." I felt her foot against mine. "And don't worry, Jared. You won't get me pregnant. You've got enough trouble with what's-her-name. The fat one."

"That's low." I glanced down at my phone. The screen had lit up, and I saw it was a Virginia number. Probably Anabel's house. "She's having a baby."

"Well, pregnant or not, I seriously doubt she'd be able to fit into anything in my store," Carly snapped.

"What's with you?"

She didn't answer. Instead, she reached across and covered the screen of my BlackBerry with her hand. "Hey now," she sounded angry. "What's more interesting, me or that thing?"

"You, of course," I lied.

"Good," she warned. "I won't tolerate anything but the best."

"And you'll get it," I promised her. But from that point on, I was distracted.

My phone kept ringing.

First, Anabel called.

Then Matt called.

Then Anabel called again.

It was getting really difficult to ignore her.

I didn't know what to do with her. I was also irritated she had Matt calling me—if he hadn't told her that day when we last spoke, I was sure he had filled her in by now about what had happened with me and his sister. I still hadn't gotten over how she had behaved on the phone the other day. She had been such a brat, and I didn't want to deal with her at the moment, not when there were much more pleasant prospects in front of me.

"I'm sorry," I said, smiling at the beautiful woman across the table.

Losing Sam's friendship had been hard on me, so I had been spending way more time with Carly—up until Anabel's big revelation that she was having a baby. And this made Carly angry—she didn't like having to share me. Even though we had never had an official relationship, I knew that she considered me hers. And most of the time, that was fine with me. After Sam, she was my best friend.

She just also happened to be a friend that I had sex with, and I hadn't done that since I found out Anabel was pregnant.

"Your phone keeps ringing," she noted, throwing her head back a little.

"I'm a popular guy."

"I see that," she concurred with a cold smile. "Is the little girl calling you?"

"Yes, Anabel has called," I was annoyed. "Can we not discuss her, please?"

But this was where Carly rose to the task. Like she had done several times during mock trials, she started circling, getting ready to go in for the kill. "What did you see in her anyway? Oh that's right," she said cattily, "you didn't."

That was once. "I asked you to not talk about her."

"I just don't understand why you would get involved with someone like her. I saw those pictures of her in the paper, Jared. She was a mess. She still is."

Twice. "Carly, lay off of her."

"You might just want to reconsider your priorities. That's all I'm saying." She took a bite of her salad.

And three times. "That's enough," I warned. "Don't forget, she is having my baby."

"Alright then, honey," she teased with a flirtatious smile. "I won't tease you about the cranky little teenager any more. As long as it doesn't take away from the...rest of our evening?"

This was bad. I wondered if I should try and get out of this situation, but I was having a really hard time keeping my eyes off of her. My conscience was nagging at me though: it wasn't fair to either Carly or Anabel to be jerked around by me. But one of these women had very little interest in me at the moment, while the other was offering herself to me on a silver platter. Being with her was a lot easier than being with Anabel, and it was a welcome change of pace. Besides, Carly was right about one thing: it wasn't like Anabel had been nice to me lately. I decided to ignore any further calls from her, and focus on having a good evening.

But then my sister called. Twice. Three times. "Excuse me," I apologized to my dinner companion. "What?" I barked into my phone.

"Where are you?"

"What are you talking about?"

"Have you forgotten," my sister whispered, "what today is?"

"Thursday?"

"Jared, it's the Princess' birthday," she hissed. "She told me not to call you, but I snuck away and, oh, is she ever mad."

"What? No, that can't be right, her birthday is..." I swallowed. "Thursday. Today."

Carly sniffed, and made a show of adjusting the strap on her dress. I had to force myself to focus on my phone conversation. "Should I come over there?"

Meghan sighed. "I would call first." And then she hung up on me.

Wonderful.

I tried to smile at Carly. "Will you excuse me for a second?"

She sniffed again.

So I dialed Anabel's phone. She answered on the second ring. "Yes?"

"Hey, baby," I said.

There was silence.

"I screwed up, huh?"

"Why couldn't you at least answer when I called?" She sounded very calm, very cold, and very, very angry.

"I'm sorry, Anabel, time got away from me, and—"

Carly made a point of yawning loudly and saying, "Jared, I do wish you would get back to me..."

"Who is that?" came Anabel's voice in my ear.

"I'm having dinner with a friend, honey, I—"

"So what you're telling me," she started to shout, "is that you met some girl and you're having dinner with her instead of coming to my party! You said you would be here, and you're off getting...well, you know what you're getting. I can't believe you, Jared! I was worried! I thought you were dead!"

"Honey—"

"No," she cut me off. "Just no. You know, it makes it really hard for me to defend you when you go out of your way to make yourself into a villain!" For the second time that night, I was hung up on.

Great.

Carly raised an eyebrow at me. "I take it you and I won't be spending the rest of the evening together?"

"As much as I would like to, I have a very upset birthday girl I need to see." It was too bad, she was a gorgeous woman. "Rain check?"

She smiled an icy smile, and I knew I had blown it with her. We wouldn't see each other again for a very long time. I walked out shaking my head, wondering how long it would take for Carly to forgive me. Getting into my car, the thought did cross my mind that her reaction was probably nothing compared to what awaited me in Mclean.

I slammed the steering wheel as I pulled out. How did I forget Anabel's birthday?

There was no doubt about it. I was screwed.

Chapter 30—Anabel

So, this was my first real birthday party, and I wasn't having any fun.

I mean, don't get me wrong, I wasn't ungrateful for the effort. Meghan had come, and I was pleased to see that she and Kevin were deep in conversation. Sam and Matt were chatting and they kept pretending not to look at me, but I knew they were. Charlotte and Phil were being gracious hosts, keeping everyone's drink filled, serving all sorts of food, and even Alexis was making an attempt to be civil by talking with Charlie—although whatever it was they were talking about seemed to make them both unhappy.

But Jared wasn't there.

So I sat on my couch, pulling at my hair and thinking. It's not like I had been shy about the fact that my birthday was approaching; I had mentioned it to him at least three times, and I had even called and left a message for him yesterday. My heart was hurting, because I had wanted him to be there.

I guess I had just thought that it would be a chance to see what we could be like as a couple. I wanted to see what it would be like to be together because we wanted to be, not because a hearing or a death had caused us to be in the same room together. Part of me wanted to pretend that we could be together for a reason other than the fact that there was a baby on the way. Not only that, but I had resolved to tell him tonight about my health issues. After spending the day with Matt, weighing the pros and cons, we had agreed that Jared had a right to know there was a possibility he'd be raising the baby by himself. On top of it all, I was irked because I had spent nearly an hour straightening my massive pile of hair and had even made an attempt to apply makeup. Matt came and sat down next to me, avoiding making eye contact. "I don't want to hear it," I told him.

"I wasn't going to say anything," he replied. "I just thought you could use a friend right about now."

I stared at him.

"I mean, this is your party, and you're just sitting here and moping."

I shrugged. "Everyone else is busy talking to someone. They don't seem to need me."

"Maybe none of them know what to say."

"Or maybe," I said darkly, "you're all just afraid that I'll go off on you."

"Well, the thought did cross our minds, and I was the lucky one who got selected to talk to you."

"I'm so sorry they sent you into the lion's den." Was he flirting with me? It was hard to tell, but there was a definite twinkle in his eye.

"Don't be. I'm lying; I just couldn't stand to watch you sit around like this anymore."

I looked at him then, and realized that I was developing a problem, and that problem's name was Matt Moore. I rubbed my belly.

"The baby's not giving you trouble, is she? Because I can have a little chat with her." He put his head near my bulging stomach.

"Nah, I think she's asleep." I leaned back into the couch.

"How do Alexis and Charlie know each other?"

"I thought they just met tonight."

"Really?" He was frowning.

I punched his arm. "Forget them. I want all of your pity focused on me. Do you know what it's like to be at your own birthday party and feel like you're the least attractive person there?"

Matt looked around. "Oh, I don't know. I'd say you're the best looking brunette in the room."

I glanced at the two redheads and the blonde who were my rivals for this honor, and started to laugh. "I guess it's a good thing that you aren't comparing me to the men in here, I'd have some stiff competition from you," I teased him.

He grinned at me then, the color rising in his cheeks a little. "I don't know about that, Anabel."

"Are you blushing? Because that's seriously adorable." I leaned in and touched his face.

He eluded my grasp. "So are you going to sit here and feel sorry for yourself all night? It's unfair to yourself, you know, to just waste the opportunity to have a good time."

"I had fun with you earlier." Indeed I had. Matt had taken me for a picnic in the park, and then we had seen my first movie in a theater. We had also spent a fair amount of time finding ways to throw popcorn down each other's shirts. "Doesn't that count?"

"Yes, but I think you might want to allow yourself to have a little fun now," he pointed out.

I groaned. When he was right, he was right. "Okay, I'll pull myself out of this funk. Now help me up."

Just then, the doorbell rang. "I'll get it!" called Meghan, and I took the two hands that Matt extended to me. As he pulled me up, I lost my footing a little and fell a bit into his arms. He caught me, and steadied me. "Are you okay?"

I nodded, holding tight to him. "Just lost my balance." I stared into his eyes, and for a moment, I thought, I should kiss him. Then I checked myself. What was I doing? Still, gazing into his eyes, I had to fight back the urge to do it.

Impulsive Anabel, however, was restrained by the sound of Jared clearing his throat. As I turned to look at him, I felt Matt stiffen. I caught his eye and nodded at him, and then I turned to Jared. "So glad you could make it," I didn't bother to hide my scowl. I turned and smiled at my guests, and said, "Excuse me." Then I took Jared's arm and marched him outside.

It was cool, and I instantly regretted not having my sweater, so I crossed my arms and glared at him. "Do you have anything to say for yourself?"

He swallowed and looked down. "No."

I studied him for a moment. I'd never seen him so shamefaced. But I had learned that Jared was proud, and wouldn't own up to any wrongdoing unless I prodded him. So I turned away. "So that's it? No apology? No explanation? Nothing?"

"Would it matter if I did apologize?" He came up behind me, and I felt his breath on my neck, and that was when I realized that Jared really did know me too well.

So I started to cry. "No," I sniffled. "It wouldn't."

"I am sorry, Anabel." Now his arms were around me.

"That doesn't change the fact that you're insensitive and self-centered." I should pull away, I should go back into the safety of my home, and I should get as far away from him as I could.

"You knew what I was when you met me," he pointed out.

"You're right about that one," I sighed. Then I turned to look at him. "But I also saw what you could be, and I'm extremely disappointed that you won't even try to be that man." I started to step away, but he held me firmly in his grasp.

"It's hard to change, baby. Even for you."

"Like you even want to."

"I do, Anabel." His grip on me tightened, and I could feel myself relenting, but I tried to hold fast to my resentment.

So I sighed. "I just don't know, Jared."

"Let me make it up to you," he pleaded in my ear.

I shook my head. "I don't see any way you can do that. I only have one birthday. The next one won't be around for another year." I extricated myself from his arms. "I can't believe you couldn't at least do this one thing for me."

"Will you at least let me try to fix this?"

"How?" I scowled at him.

"We could go on a date," he offered.

"A date?" That threw me for a loop.

"You. Me. Alone," he intoned, coming closer to me again. "I could take you anywhere you wanted, Anabel. It would be fun."

I stared helplessly up at him. The fact was, I wanted to tell him to go away and just come back when his daughter was born, but I couldn't. I also knew I shouldn't be with him. But there I was, and it was crystal clear to me what the problem was. Stupid Jared with his stupid good looks and his stupid charming smile and...why was I not running away? But I was glued to the spot, and he was close enough to kiss me. I wouldn't let him, I thought, I wouldn't let him hurt me again...

But he was smiling, in that smug way, indicating to me that he knew he had won. Because Jared knew I would forgive him, and he knew all he had to do was smile at me and I would let go of my animosity. One look from him was enough to send my very confused insides into frenzy, and he knew that too. He knew he had a hold over me. So he also knew very well that I would agree to go out on a date with him.

Jerk.

Chapter 31—Jared

A few days later I was in Georgetown with Meghan, who had agreed to take the afternoon off and help me find a gift for Anabel. "Of all the idiot things to do, how could you forget her birthday, Jared?"

"I don't know," I grimaced, gritting my teeth.

"The poor child, you should have seen her. Everyone tried to talk to her but she just sat on the couch, moping. The only one who could get through to her was that Matt Moore…" She trailed off.

"Not you, too."

"I can't help it. He's a beautiful man, Jared." She gave me a mischievous smile. "Alas, he wants nothing to do with me. I think I have some guilt by association by being related to you. He's only got eyes for her."

I looked at her, alarmed. "Are you serious?"

She nodded. "I wouldn't worry about it. She's a bit oblivious. I don't get her, she's a smart little thing, but then she does things like not notice when men fall in love with her."

"Meghan," I said, pained.

"I do think he has a thing for her. The way he watches her..." She shivered a bit. "I know what you're going to say, that it's some sort of revenge tactic, but you couldn't be more wrong. He's a good guy." She patted my arm. "Look, it's clear that she's still very hung up on you. She did sulk for a long time before you showed up."

"I guess I should be relieved. Now what should I get for her?"

Meghan considered. "I have no idea. I got her a gift card for Barnes and Noble. She was fascinated by the concept. I sometimes forget she lived on a desert island."

"It wasn't exactly a desert." We walked into a jewelry store.

"Um, she's an October baby, so you should get her opals if you're going to get her jewelry. She'll be impressed you knew that."

"Or suspect I had help." I raised an eyebrow at my sister. "So does this mean that you like her?"

"I love your little pregnant princess," she conceded, frowning as she considered the items on the counter. "She's something else. I find myself wanting to hang out with her just to hear the absurdities that pop out of her mouth. I was telling Crystal about it the other day, and she can't wait to meet her."

"Is Crys coming home sometime soon? I haven't talked to her in over a month."

Meghan shook her head. "I think she's having some torrid affair with her dissertation advisor over there. I'm the only one of us who doesn't feel the need to be constantly embroiled in a scandal."

"You need to be more adventurous."

She grimaced. "Not like that. Sometimes I feel like I'm not even related to you two."

"If it wasn't for the fact that you and Crystal are mirror images, I'd agree with you," I told her.

She ignored me. "About Anabel, though...well. Just don't break her heart again, Jared. I'm pretty sure this was strike two." Then she opened her mouth as if to say something, and then closed it again.

"What? Meg-a-han, tell me what you're thinking." I poked at her arm.

"Don't call me Meg-a-han, I hate that." She turned away. "It just keeps coming back to this for me: how has she forgiven you? If I were her, I would've slapped you with a restraining order so fast your head would've spun. But from what I understand, she tried to protect you from Sam? And now she has all these convictions about having this baby and having you in its life? It doesn't make any sense to me."

I shrugged and shook my head. This was something that bothered me too. "Maybe it's because she's a better person than the both of us?"

"I'll say," she grunted, pausing to look at some bracelets. "That one. You should get that one for her."

I glanced at the price tag. "You have expensive taste, sis."

"Is she not worth it?" Meghan challenged.

"She's worth it," I responded. "I just doubt she thinks that I am."

When Meghan didn't say anything, I tried to cover. "Thanks for your unwavering support."

"Jared, it doesn't really matter what I think, it just matters what she thinks. And right now she thinks that you don't have your priorities in line when it comes to her. Especially after you went out with Carly Waterstreet last night. And let me just say that when I found that out, I wanted to beat you. She's disgusting."

"She's a very well-respected businesswoman," I snapped back.

"Why are you even bothering with her? That woman only wants you for one thing, as much as that grosses me out to say." My sister shuddered. "Now that you don't have the political connections anymore, how often has she called you? Except when she wanted—well. You know."

Meghan had a point. I looked away from her.

"Now don't get me wrong," she said, "I love you, and I know Anabel loves you, because she's said as much."

"Has she come out and said it?" I asked.

"Well, no," she admitted, looking uncomfortable. "But if she didn't want to at least give you a chance, she would have told you so, right?"

"Well, I would hardly expect her to spare my feelings." I nodded at the guy behind the counter. "I'll take that one."

"Good call," Meghan approved. "Next time we can look at rings."

"I've asked her twice, she's avoided it each time."

"Yeah, about that. Jared, let me ask you a question. Have you asked her in person, or just over the phone?"

I frowned at her. "On the phone, and I'm guessing she told you."

"Okay. You need to consider who you're dealing with. This is a girl who has read all of those romantic sappy claptrap books. Do you honestly think going, 'hey, we should get married' will work with that one?"

She did have a point. "Well, what do you think I should do?"

"Give her some time to get her head together, she's a cosmic mess. And then ask her the right way. Barring her falling in love with someone else, I think you'll be fine." Meghan smiled.

"What about Matt?"

"I think he's too professional to go after her. Besides, she is having your baby. After what happened to Natasha, he probably doesn't want anything connected to you."

"How do you think she feels about him?" I didn't want to hear the answer, but I knew I needed to.

Meghan pursed her lips. "It's hard to say. Anabel seems to love everyone she comes in contact with. I think she definitely respects Matt. But she hasn't confided any romantic attachments to me."

"What did she say when he told her?"

"What do you mean?"

"Meghan, I'm sure he's told her by now."

Meghan looked guarded. "Here's the thing. He may have told her, but I don't think Anabel's connected the dots yet. I don't think she's figured out that Matt's sister and Natasha from the night you...well anyway, I don't think she's associated the two yet."

"Wonderful. So there's still a chance that when she figures it out, she'll never talk to me again."

The look on Meghan's face wasn't comforting.

Chapter 32—Anabel

"I don't like this at all," came Matt's voice from my doorway.

"I know you don't," I muttered, pulling on my boots. They were a gift from Alexis and Sam, and had come at a very opportune moment. It was sixty degrees outside, and to me, that was really stinking cold. "I told him I'd give him a shot, that's what I'm going to do."

"He forgot your birthday," Matt stressed.

"Look, we're going out to dinner, it's not like I'm going to sleep with him." I zipped up my boot and smiled at him from my bed.

Something flashed across Matt's face then, something that looked an awful lot like relief. He nodded. "I still wish you would let me come with you."

"It's not much of a date if I bring another guy along with me."

"I'm not just some guy. I'm your bodyguard."

"Don't worry, I won't tell Sam," I grinned at him.

"That's not why, Anabel."

I turned to him then, and it dawned on me that Matt was worried about me. "Oh, Matt," I said, walking over to him and putting my arms around him, "it's okay. If he tries anything with me, I'll just call you and have you come beat the tar out of him. I know that's what you really want to do," I said in his ear.

"You have no idea what I really want to do," he muttered.

I pulled back, grinning. "I won't be gone too long. I'm sure we'll run out of things to talk about at a point, and then I'll come home to you."

He cocked his head, and I turned away again, confused. I hadn't forgotten about wanting to kiss him the other night, and the thought flitted through my head again. Bad Anabel, I scolded myself. Keep it together. You're about to go on a date with another man—you know, the one whose baby you're having? Still, the knowledge that I was coming home to Matt was calming.

There was a moment of supreme awkwardness. We stood there, and it seemed that neither of us knew what to do or say. But Matt seemed to get it together when the doorbell rang. "Alright," he said. "I'm going to have a word with him."

I started to laugh. "Oh good, and then challenge him to a duel to defend my honor? You're being silly."

He ignored me and walked out of the room. Sighing, I took a deep breath.

So this was it. Jared and Anabel: Part II.

Or Part III, if you counted the whole hearings fiasco.

Would it work this time?

I gave myself one final look in the mirror, and then I walked downstairs in time to hear Matt say, "If she's not home by eleven, I'm coming after you."

"That's cute, Matt, but if she wants to stay over, it'll be her doing, not mine."

I cleared my throat. "Jared, knock it off. I'll be home before eleven, Matt." I smiled at him and breezed through the front door.

Somehow, I wasn't surprised to see that Jared drove a Corvette. He opened the door for me, and I gingerly lowered myself in. As he got into the car, I shot him a sideways glance. As annoyed at him as I had been, I had to admit, he looked good. Really good.

"Before you say anything," he began, "Meghan pointed out that I am going to need a new car."

"Why?"

He gestured. "No room for the baby."

"Good call. Seeing as how you're the only one of us who can drive at the moment, it would probably be a good idea to get something that at least has a backseat."

He grinned at the road. "Yeah. Wait, you can't drive?"

I shook my head.

"We'll have to fix that. And then get you a Mom car," he suggested.

"Not funny. I'm not driving a minivan." I leaned against the cool window.

"Minivans are hot," he teased.

I bit back a laugh.

We drove in silence, me staring at the floor, him looking at me out of the corner of his eye until he finally spoke.

"Do you remember that dress?"

I feigned innocence. "What dress?"

"You know what dress. The white one."

"Oh yes, the one that began my debauchery with you."

He ignored that. "You looked great in that dress."

"Yeah?" I smiled a little.

"Oh yeah." Then he chuckled. "I was so mad at you that day."

"Well I can't really say I blame you," I replied, embarrassed. "I'm ashamed of my behavior."

He shot me a glance. "You certainly made an impression."

"Yes, I've gotten very good at doing that." I looked out the window. "Are we there yet? I'm starving."

"Yeah, we're almost there."

"Where are we, anyway? I thought we were going into the District." I leaned forward and looked at the unfamiliar terrain.

"No, this is Arlington. Bailey's Crossroads, actually. I figured you might want to go somewhere quiet."

I sent him an appraising glance. "That's very thoughtful of you, Jared."

He didn't say anything, and we turned into a parking lot. It looked a bit seedy. I bit my lower lip. "Um, you didn't bring me here to murder me, did you?"

He laughed. "I know how it looks, but this place has the best Middle Eastern food in town."

I looked at him dubiously. "Okay, whatever you say." We got out of the car and walked toward the Jerusalem Café with trepidation. Or at least I did. Jared was as composed as ever.

It turned out he was right, the food was excellent, but it wasn't long before we ran out of conversation topics. It was just so different than it had been when we were on Caereon together. I had been fascinated by Jared, but now that I knew who he was—and what he was—I was a bit turned off. Plus, his daughter, who was getting bigger and bigger by the day, was starting to feel like the only thing that was connecting us. What if I did decide to try and make it work with Jared? Was this how it was going to be? Were we going to have awkward nights like this all the time?

Plus, there was the unspoken matter at hand. Part of me didn't want to bring it up. A larger part of me did. While I wrestled with how to ask it, my temper started to flare a bit. And then something very bad took hold of my brain, and possessed me to go down that road. "So," I asked him, "do you want to tell me who that girl was?"

Jared looked startled. "What girl?"

"You know what girl." I attempted to stifle my anger by taking another bite of my chicken schwarma.

"Oh, that girl," he smiled at me, trying to be charming. "She was just a girl."

"Jared, I wasn't born yesterday."

He looked at me, and there was sincerity in his eyes. "Anabel, your brother is no longer my best friend. While I understand that, it makes it hard because I used to talk to him about everything, personal and professional. So now, I've had to turn to my friend Carly for confidences."

"Did you turn to her for anything else?" The tone of my voice was harsh, and I could see Jared's temper rise.

"No, your phone call interrupted that."

That stung. "I'm ever so sorry I ruined your sexual conquest."

"That's right, baby, a few more minutes and I would've sealed that deal." He was mad, probably as much as I was, but I swallowed hard and continued to provoke him.

"But you didn't answer when I called. You only did when Meghan called." That recollection only caused me to get angrier. "So what you're telling me is that if we hadn't gotten ahold of you, you would have...I mean, you and this Carly..."

"Be fair, we go back a ways," he admonished me.

"Have you slept with her before?"

"Excuse me?"

"It's a simple question," I stated, low and dangerous. "Have you slept with her before?"

He stared down at his food, and I started to cry.

Jared looked alarmed. "Anabel, it's not like that. I just needed some company, and she was there for me."

"I bet she was," I sniffled.

He groaned. "Don't ruin this. Why are you acting like this, baby? We were having a great time."

"So let's say," I managed through my tears, "that you get mad at me one night, and you go to this...woman...for comfort, and get it in both senses of the word?"

"Don't be crass, Anabel."

"You can't deny it's a possibility." I looked down. This was hurting. It was hurting a lot.

"Look, if I'm with you, I'm with you. Nobody else. Okay?"

"Would you stop being friends with her?"

"Now you're being unreasonable."

"No," I defended myself. "I don't think I am. If I asked you to stop being friends with her, for the sake of our tenuous relationship, would you do that for me, Jared?"

"Only if you got rid of Matt." It was like he had thrown down the gauntlet, and I lost it.

"He's my bodyguard! He's protecting me! That's completely different from what you were doing."

"Look, I know this is all probably because of Natasha, but you need to get over it. Matt knows that wasn't my fault."

"What?" I stared at him, uncertain. "I don't understand."

Jared scoffed at me. "Don't play dumb with me. I know Matt's told you about his sister by now."

"Natasha?" I asked, frowning. Then my eyes widened. "He called her Nat, I never made the connection."

We sat for a moment, him staring at his plate, me lost in thought. He broke the silence with, "I never meant to hurt her, Anabel."

A life lesson from one of my favorite childhood books flitted through my head, so I looked at him sadly and said, "Yes Jared, but people like you never mean, it's what you do."

"You're unfair."

"Why did you call me her name after you did what you did?" I asked, point blank.

"Don't dance around it, babe. Say what you want to say," he taunted me.

But I held it together. "Answer the question, Jared."

"Look, I barely remember that night. Maybe I thought you were her, I don't know."

"Maybe you thought I was her?" I gasped. "So what, you would've done that to her, too?"

"I need you to stop this," he warned me. "I can't handle much more of it."

"Fine, let's get back to you kicking your lover to the curb."

"Do that with Matt, and we'll call it even." He crossed his arms.

But I was now done with him. "I don't have a choice where Matt is concerned, you know that."

"Well, you seem to feel threatened by Carly, so I think it's fair that you give up something similar."

"Oh, no," I retorted. "Matt's there for my safety, Jared. I'm so sorry if this offends your sensitive ego, but he's there for a reason. Carly is only there for you to get some. So no. This conversation is done."

And it was. I didn't say a word to him while he paid the bill. When we got into the car I stared stonily ahead as he drove me back to my place. A couple times I turned my head and let the tears fall. When we arrived at my house, he tried to say something, but I jumped out of the car and ran to my front door and let myself in.

When I walked in, Matt was sitting on the couch, waiting for me. He took in my teary eyes and red face and immediately started for the door, but I stepped in front of him. "Move," he barked.

"No," I refused. "Let it alone. Everything's fine, I'm just a bit emotional."

He looked frustrated. "Anabel, I'm supposed to protect you."

On impulse, I stood on my toes and kissed him on the cheek. "Matt," I told him, "you are everything I need you to be." Then I started up the stairs.

"Wait," he called. I turned and gave him a tired smile. He started to follow me. "Do you mean that?"

"With all my heart," I assured him, continuing up to my room. "Goodnight."

But he caught my arm and I turned back toward him. "Anabel," he said.

"Yes?"

He gave me a swift, searching look, and then came, "I need to double check your room."

I smiled at him. "Alright."

I grabbed my pajamas and went to my bathroom to change, and then when I came out Matt was standing next to my bed. "I figured you would have left," I commented, sliding under my covers.

"I wanted to make sure you were okay," he told me.

"I am," I assured him. "Some things just need to be resolved, and I think I know where to go from here."

He looked like he wanted to ask me, and I wanted to tell him, but instead he nodded. "Goodnight, Anabel."

"Goodnight," I wished him, and when he closed the door I was alone with my thoughts, and I lay awake for a very long time that night.

Chapter 33—Anabel

The next day I was moping in my bedroom when suddenly Matt burst in and threw a suitcase on my bed. "Do you ever knock?" I snapped.

He ignored that. "We're going away for the weekend."

"But Mr. Moore," I pretended to protest, "we've only just met. Shouldn't we wait to start planning holidays together?"

He ignored that. "Look, there are photographers camped out all around your property, and I'm tired of Jared calling here. So we're going away."

I brushed a stray hair out of my eyes. "Where?"

"To meet my parents," he announced.

"Meeting your parents?" I echoed.

"You said you wanted to."

"Well, yes, but hardly like this," I told him, pulling myself off of the bed. "I mean, look at me." I gestured at my belly.

"I do all the time," he replied.

I stared at him.

"It's my job, Anabel," he sighed, frustrated. "Now pack." He turned to leave, and then paused at the door. "I would bring some of your nicer stuff."

"Why, are we going out?" I asked, eying my closet.

"My parents insist on dressing for dinner."

I looked puzzled. "Don't most people dress for dinner?"

He gave me a wry smile. "Yes, but my parents insist on nice attire."

"Oh. Well then. I'll be ready soon."

"Call Jared so he doesn't have a coronary," he called over his shoulder as he exited the room.

As much as I didn't relish the idea of meeting new people, I was excited about going away for the weekend with Matt. In spite of the fact that I felt like he didn't particularly care for me, he did seem to be warming a bit, and I hoped that spending time away from the circus that was my life would maybe make our business relationship easier. I would try and ease up on the flirting and teasing...but it was just the way I was with him. I didn't really know why he brought out that side of me. It wasn't like it was with Jared on the island, where I couldn't keep my hormones in check. It was just...

...I liked Matt.

I liked him a lot, and I wanted him to like me as a person. That was all, I told myself. I just couldn't stand the idea that he may not like me, and I wanted to rectify that. I straightened and began packing while dialing Jared's number on my BlackBerry.

He answered on the second ring. "Hey, Anabel."

"Hey, Matt's kidnapping me," I sang. "He says we need to get out of town for the weekend so I can avoid the paparazzi. So I won't be around."

Dead silence.

"Jared?"

"Oh, I'm here, babe," he told me, his voice cold.

"Don't be like that," I chastised. "It's for my own good, if I say one more idiot thing to the press, Alexis will have my head chopped off."

He chuckled. "Well, there's a point. I just don't like the idea of you leaving town."

"I'll be back soon enough," I promised.

Jared switched on the charm. "Next time we get together I'll make it well worth your while, Anabel."

"Good-bye, Jared," I replied, and I hung up.

Matt reappeared just as I was zipping up my bag. "Hey, are you ready to go?"

I nodded, pushing away hair. "Do I look presentable enough?"

He gave me a once-over, and I found myself feeling self-conscious. "You'll do," he pronounced. "It doesn't matter, Anabel. My mom isn't going to like you." He grabbed my bag. "Let's go."

I chased him as best I could down the stairs and out to his truck. "What do you mean? What did I ever do to her?"

He sighed and turned on the truck. "Buckle yourself in and I'll explain."

I did so, glowering. "You're so bossy."

"So are you," he returned. "Look," he said, pulling out of my driveway, "you said on your birthday you wanted to meet my parents, so we're going to do that. But as charming as you are, I don't think my mother is going to care for you, and you really shouldn't let it get to you."

I was a bit stung. "Okay," I managed.

"Anabel," he sounded much warmer now, "it's just one of those things." He focused on the road. "It's my fault, actually."

"What do you mean?"

"Right before I took the job for Sam, watching you," he explained, "I was going to take a job teaching, working for my father."

"Oh." I was at a loss for words.

"You know," he said, and I almost caught a sneer, "an acceptable profession. But then Sam asked me to take care of you, and I couldn't say no."

"Why not?"

"After I met you, I felt I couldn't." He stared at the road. "But she blames you."

"I see," I commented, biting my lip and trying not to smile. "So I guess I can expect an equally frosty reception from your father?"

"My dad thinks you're funny," he admitted.

"Oh yeah?"

"He thought it was hilarious how you explained to your brother in front of the press why his economic policies didn't work."

My cheeks reddened. "I'm slightly ashamed of that."

"Well, my father is a staunch Republican, Anabel. He thinks you're golden." Matt was smiling. "He thought it was genius how you revealed your pregnancy and informed me that nothing pleased him more than the look of abject horror on Jared Sorensen's face."

"Well at least somebody's getting enjoyment out of this," I muttered, slumping in my seat.

Matt's arm reached toward me and he began rubbing my shoulder. "I know it's hard, kid," he consoled me. "But you're doing a good job, okay? I just wanted to warn you about my mom, she'll come around."

I nodded, trying to ignore the sinking feeling in my stomach.

"Don't be upset about this," he attempted to reassure me.

"I shouldn't be," I muttered. "But I guess for some reason, I wanted her to like me."

"Not everyone is going to like you."

"I wanted Alexis to like me, too."

"She's an idiot," he pronounced.

"Maybe she's right."

Matt stopped the car. "Anabel. Look at me."

So I did.

"You know the only reason why she's like that is she's jealous of you," he said. "If she could get over herself, she'd realize you're pretty great and Sam couldn't ask for a better sister."

"All I ever do is make things worse for Sam," I sighed.

"You could probably watch what you say more, but nobody doubts how much you love him," he continued. "You okay?"

I nodded.

"We're almost there."

"Where are we, anyway?" I asked, adjusting in my seat. "This doesn't seem like Virginia."

"That's because we're in Maryland."

"I thought it smelled funny."

"What, you hate Maryland now?"

"Don't you?"

He considered. "You got me there. But we're almost to Potomac Prep."

"Your parents live at a prep school?"

He shot me a sidelong glance. "My father is the Headmaster, Anabel."

"Oh." I slumped as far down in my seat as my pregnant belly would allow. "Right."

We continued the rest of the trip in silence, and as I looked out the window I noticed that we were in a nice area, perhaps almost as nice as Mclean. The grass was green, the people looked friendly, and I was just starting to think that this might be okay...

...And then I saw the school.

Potomac Preparatory Academy was absolutely formidable. The stone walls that encompassed the property reminded me of a prison. The dormitories that Matt pointed out to me were severe, and the young men walking across the campus all looked the same, dressed in uniforms that looked crisp and stern. I felt self-conscious of my messy hair and my dress that had begun to wrinkle. A few of the boys turned to eye Matt's truck, causing me to look down and stare at my feet.

Matt made a sharp turn, and then we went up a pathway and then I saw it.

"The Headmaster's House," he announced.

"More like the Headmaster's castle," I gawked. "Did you grow up here?"

Matt gave a curt nod.

"Wow," I managed, at a loss. This beautiful building put my sweet little house to shame. It really was almost a castle, built in the same stone style as the rest of the campus. It even had a couple turrets. I turned to Matt, wide-eyed. "Where's the drawbridge?"

"It's not like that," he defended, and I detected a hint of embarrassment.

I slid my arm through his. "Oh come now, Matt. I grew up on a bloody island. You needn't be like this around me."

"I needn't?" he grinned.

"No," I returned his smile, and then it hit me again that I really, really liked him. I felt a faint blush creep into my cheeks, and I looked away as he led me to the front door.

"Anabel?" He rang the doorbell.

"Yes?"

"You may want to tone it down a little," he suggested.

"Or I may as well accept the fact that your mother is determined to hate me."

He nodded. "I guess there's no point in pretending otherwise."

I grinned. "Don't worry, Matt. I know how to play the game."

And so I did. When I first set eyes on Clara Moore it only took me half a second to ascertain that she did indeed despise me and there was nothing that I could do about it. So I sucked it up, smiled as widely as I could, and caught her off guard by giving her a warm embrace. "Thank you so much for inviting me into your home, Mrs. Moore."

She was stiff in my arms. "Dr. Moore."

"Dr. Moore! How silly of me," I admonished myself. I turned to Matt's father. "And you must be the other Dr. Moore?"

There was a mischievous twinkle in his eyes. I think he saw right through my little charade. "I'm Geoff, Miss Martin."

"Anabel."

"Anabel," he pronounced, offering me his arm. "You are everything I hoped you'd be."

"And how's that?" I asked, lowering my voice.

"Let's just say I am now certain that this will be a highly entertaining evening."

I shot Matt a backwards glance. I couldn't quite read the expression on his face, but it looked like he was somewhat torn between mortification and amusement. So I winked at him and then smiled benevolently at his mother. "Such a beautiful home, Dr. Moore."

"Thank you." She nearly choked on the words. Geoff bit back a laugh. I might have some fun this weekend after all.

Clara showed me to my room, and I hurriedly unpacked, as she had informed me (in a very cold voice) that dinner would be in half an hour. I unzipped the garment bag and pulled out the blue sparkly dress that Charlotte had assured me would be fine. I liked it because it didn't look like a typical maternity dress and it matched my eyes. Shimmying into it,

I paused in front of the gorgeous antique mirror and laughed at myself. So silly, Anabel, I thought. I pulled a comb out of my bag and quickly ran it through my tresses and pulled some of it away from my face with a clip. Not bad, not bad. I turned sideways to admire my baby bump, and that was when Emma took the opportunity to nail me with a swift kick to the spine. "Ooof!" I gasped, bracing myself against the dresser.

Matt suddenly barged in. "Anabel? Are you okay?"

"I'm fine," I muttered, rubbing my back. "I'm just being castigated for my vanity."

He raised an eyebrow, so I went on to say, "I was admiring myself in the mirror and Emma decided to punish me for it."

He laughed a little. "You look nice."

"Yeah?" I couldn't contain the hope in my voice.

"Yeah," he reaffirmed. "One thing though..."

"Stop flirting with your dad?" I grinned.

"Yes, that would be good," he said, brushing some hair out of my face. "He's already quite enamored, and Mom is already not thrilled with you."

I laughed. "I'm glad he gets such a kick out of me."

"There's something else," he added, and hesitated for a moment.

"I'm pretty sure he knows I'm not seriously interested in him. I won't break his heart," I teased.

"No, not that, although that is good to know," he continued, and then hesitated again.

"What?"

"Well, Scott is here."

"Your brother? I thought he lived in California." I began digging through my bag looking for chapstick.

"He was visiting this weekend. I hadn't realized. Look, the point is, my brother hates Jared Sorensen even more than I do," he explained. "I can't pretend like he won't try something with you to get back at Jared."

"Try something with me?"

"He might...hit on you. Or worse." Matt's brow was furrowed.

I started to giggle. "Are you serious?"

"I'm always serious, Anabel."

I rolled my eyes. "Look, your sister was gorgeous, right? While that was what attracted Jared to her, it's not really how it was with me. I just happened to be the only female on Caereon who was under thirty. So while maybe that was Scott's original plan, I'm pretty sure that once he gets an eyeful of me he'll drop that. Or maybe even run away screaming at the sight."

"Oh knock it off. Being pregnant doesn't alter the fact that you're beautiful, either," he said, and my heart did a flip-flop. "What? Don't act so shocked. Your mother was gorgeous, and you look a lot like her."

I looked at the floor. "That was the last thing I expected you to say."

"I'm not blind, Anabel. It's a fact," he continued. "Don't you ever read what the papers say about you? Everyone thinks you're beautiful. Including my mom, which is part of why she doesn't like you."

"She doesn't like me because she thinks I'm pretty?"

He sighed. "My mom's a bit narcissistic. She was prom queen at her high school and hates making way for someone who is younger, prettier, and more attractive to my father."

"That last one is just silly," I pointed out.

"That may be, but my mother is territorial. So play a little closer to the chest, okay?"

I nodded. "What's for dinner?"

"Chicken and a million side dishes," he said, turning. I trailed after him and he paused at the doorway. "Come on," he said. "I can't have you getting lost."

"Okay," I said, following him out. "I can't believe you grew up here! This place is amazing. Sort of like a Jane Austen novel combined with Hogwarts."

He chuckled at that. "No ghosts here, alas."

"What about a three-headed dog?"

He looked solemn. "Don't go in the basement."

"Oh, Matt, I had no idea you had a sense of humor." I lowered my voice to imitate him. "I'm always serious, Anabel. Stop being such a slut."

"You're not a slut," he stated.

"No," I mused. "No, I'm not. But I could behave myself better."

"Where would the fun be in that?"

We sat down to dinner and I was seated between Geoff and Matt, which was a good thing, considering that the other two members of our dinner party were less than enthralled with me.

Matt's brother Scott was, as far as I could tell, his complete antithesis. He was blond and blue-eyed and rather brash. There was something downright sleazy about him, as he eyed me with speculative interest. I flicked my eyes over to Matt, and he shot me a look which made me decide that it might be best if I held my tongue.

As we dug in, Clara made some cool remarks about the weather, and asked Scott several questions about his trip down. It started to dawn on me with the pointed questions that she was asking Scott, she meant to snub us, and I started to feel a bit protective toward my bodyguard. My irritation grew as she then turned the conversation to Scott's work.

"So how is the new software coming?"

"Fine," replied Scott, taking a rather large bite of chicken.

Clara finally deigned to notice me. "Scott has been working on a project for a defense contractor. Once he finishes it, it will do a lot to protect national security."

"Indeed," I said, stabbing my carrots with my fork. "Is this project top secret?"

"But of course," replied Clara. "Scott does important work."

"Well, it can't be that important," I said. "Or you couldn't have mentioned it to me. And if it's that vital to national security, he shouldn't have told you about it, now should he?"

Geoff snickered.

Clara bristled. "Perhaps you would know more about this sort of thing, Anabel, if you actually had a security clearance."

"Well that could very well be, Dr. Moore," I agreed. "But your oldest son has a security clearance, and he knows how it works. Besides, I think I'm the only person in this room who actually was a piece of Top Secret information, and based on that experience I know how vital it is to keep your mouth shut about that sort of sensitive material. I mean," and I paused to shove another bite in my mouth, "my very existence brought down my brother's presidency. What exactly do you think would happen if the information that you just shared with me got out?"

"Are you planning on leaking it to the press?" She was getting angry.

"Oh heavens no," I replied. "The press and I share a common interest, which is me, so I think I'll ride that puppy as long as they'll let me." Geoff was shaking with laughter, as I gave her my most benign smile. "Besides, Matt won't let me do anything destructive."

Clara scoffed. "You clearly have a high opinion of yourself."

"Somebody around here needs to," I retorted. "I realize you don't particularly care for me, Dr. Moore, and I've tried to be as nice as I can, but I'm not going to sit here and watch you praise your sulky little golden child over there and ignore your other son who is an amazing human being." I felt Matt's eyes on me, but I continued to maintain my glare at Clara.

"All you've ever seen him do is watch you, which only takes half a brain."

"Oh be fair, I get myself into all sorts of trouble without trying. Matt's ability to keep me alive is unparalleled."

"Matt's talents are wasted in babysitting for a spoiled little girl," Clara snapped.

"That's enough, Mother." Matt was calm.

"No it's not enough! You could have done so many things, and here you are, playing nanny to a Sallinger!"

"I'm not technically a Sallinger," I remarked.

She ignored me and turned to her son. "You just let your skills waste away."

"This isn't the time or the place," he said.

"Well I hope she's worth it," Clara huffed. "Because once these hearings blow over, Sallinger will drop you."

"Well then I'll retain him," I declared. "Matt's been invaluable to me."

"Why? So you can try to get in his pants, since you've already been in—"

"MOTHER!" And now Matt was on his feet. "That's enough," he said, his tone heated.

I shook my head. "Everyone really does think I'm a slut." I let out a dramatic sigh and stretched. "Well, I hate to miss dessert, but I think I'll give you all some family time now." And with that, I stood up, and stomped out of the room.

"She even makes a dramatic exit," I heard Geoff say.

"She's sassy," came Scott's snide remark.

"Stay away from her," Matt retorted, and then I heard him chasing me, which only strengthened my resolve to make it to my room before he could see the fact that—

"You're crying," he noticed, catching my arm.

"No I'm not," I denied, wiping away tears. "It's just an allergy attack."

"You are a terrible liar," he muttered. "I'm so sorry, Anabel. I thought it would be slightly awkward, but I had no idea that this would happen."

"I probably should've kept my mouth shut," I admitted.

He put his arm around my shoulders. "You know, no one has ever done that before."

"Done what?"

"Stood up to her. Defended me."

"Not even your dad?"

Matt sighed. "He doesn't like to get involved. He doesn't love her, but he lets her run his affairs."

"Well that's sad," I assessed. "It would be terrible to be married to someone you didn't love. I mean, that's why..."

"Why you can't marry him?" he asked. "I know that's what he wants."

I nodded. "I guess I love Jared in a way, but I'm not really in love with him."

"After what he did to you, you still have feelings for him?" I felt his grip on me tighten as we walked into my room.

"It's complicated."

"Sam says you have Stockholm syndrome."

"Are you serious?" I started to laugh. "I don't sympathize with Jared, if that's what you're getting at. It's just messy," I lamented.

"I see that," he said, letting go of me and checking under the bed.

"We're in your parents' house. Do you really think—?"

"It's my job to check," he cut me off. "You know, I'm done with you telling me how to do my job."

I was taken aback. "I'm sorry," I stammered.

"What?" He sounded surprised.

"I'm sorry. I don't mean to be critical of you. I think you're wonderful." It all came out in a rush. "At taking care of me," I added, feeling the blood rush to my cheeks.

Matt studied me for a minute and then cracked a grin. "You know, if anyone else ever criticizes you, you immediately get defensive. I get angry with you for a second and—"

"—I beg your forgiveness." I came to stand before him. "It's because I don't care about what anybody else thinks of me. Only you."

"Only me, huh?" He was softening.

"I really value your opinion," I told him.

His face relaxed. "Alright, well I think I'm going to stay in here tonight."

"With me?" That came out at a much higher pitch than I had anticipated.

"Yeah, I think given the circumstances—my brother eying you like you were that chocolate cake you turned down—"

"It was chocolate? I am clearly an idiot."

He ignored that. "And the nagging feeling I have that my mother would smother you with a pillow if the opportunity presents itself solidifies that decision."

"There's only one bed," I pointed out.

"I'll sleep on the floor."

"That's stupid. This is your house."

"Fine, I'll sleep with you," he decided.

I felt my eyes widen. "Oh."

"Unless you don't want me to," he said quickly.

"No...that's...fine," I managed.

"It's not like I haven't seen—"

"I know," I interjected.

His face grew concerned. "Anabel, surely you don't think I would—"

"NO!" I said, a little too loudly. "No, that's not it. It just caught me off guard, is all." I offered what I hoped was a convincing smile. "I'm going to put on my pajamas now."

"I need a few things from my room, anyway," he told me. "I'll be back in ten minutes. Try not to kill yourself in the interim."

I nodded, and watched him leave. Then I quickly dug into my bag, rummaging for my pajamas. I sighed at the sight. I had brought an oversized T-shirt that had belonged to my brother and some oh-so-sexy maternity pajama bottoms. With haste I disrobed and slid them on, and grabbed a brush and ran it through my unruly hair, pulling it into a low ponytail. After brushing my teeth, I noticed that Matt had left the door cracked. As I went to close it, I heard voices.

"You could do a lot worse," I heard Geoff say.

"This is not open for debate," came Matt's voice.

"She likes you."

"And you think I'm not aware of that? Anabel's about as subtle as a thunderstorm." I colored and tried not to giggle.

"I like her a lot," Geoff commented. "She's feisty. I wouldn't mind seeing you happy, either. There's the matter of that baby, but I think you have enough character to deal with that."

"That baby is a Sorensen." He was firm.

"What happened to Nat—look, it's not Jared's fault, Matt. You've got to let that go," said Geoff.

"What if I can't?"

"Then it probably wouldn't work with Anabel, and you're wise to keep your distance," he replied.

"You think she would make me happy?" Matt sounded thoughtful here.

"She's not the only one who's easy to read." Geoff chuckled. "You should've seen the look on your face when she took your mother to task."

"I was just impressed. She doesn't usually stick up for herself, let alone somebody else." Matt's tone was guarded.

"Well, let me ask you this. Why did you bring her here?"

"She wanted to meet you all."

"I don't think that's the only reason." Geoff paused. "I'll just say that I like her, and we'll leave it at that."

"This was her own doing." Now Matt sounded defensive.

"Whatever you say, son. Goodnight."

"Night," I heard Matt say, and I hurried to make my way back over to the bed, my heart pounding. I smiled up at him when he came in. "Do you want the right or the left side?"

"The left. I'm guessing you want the side closer to the bathroom."

"Good call." I slid under the covers, pulling a pillow between my legs and turning on my side, looking at the wall. I felt Matt climb into the bed and I started to giggle.

"What's so funny?"

"I haven't shared a bed with anyone in a long time," I admitted.

"Besides Emma, you mean."

"Yes, besides Emma." I rubbed my belly. She kicked where my hand was. Such a clever child.

"Are you okay for the night? Do you need any water or anything?"

"I had the foresight to bring some bottled water. It's on the nightstand." I turned and looked at him. "You really do take such good care of me."

"It's my job," he told me.

"Well, you're the best friend money can buy, Matt."

He laughed at that. "Thanks. You're not so bad yourself."

I maneuvered myself over to look at him. "Do you mean that?"

"Anabel, why do you think that I hate you?"

"I guess I just...I'm trying to figure out where I stand with you."

He stared at the ceiling. "Where you stand?"

I shifted, trying to get comfortable, which was proving to be a challenge. "Well, sometimes I think that we're becoming friends—like, real friends—and then other times I think that you regret taking this job."

He turned to look at me. "I've never regretted taking this job. Not once."

More butterflies. I swallowed. "Even though I'm a spoiled princess?"

"You aren't what everybody thinks you are. Do you need some help?" He had noticed that I was readjusting myself.

"I can't find a position," I gasped, pushing up on my arms, "where I don't feel like I'm squished."

"Come here," he ordered. He sat up and gently helped me over to him. I rested my head on his chest and felt his arm go around me. "How's that?"

I couldn't deny it. "Perfect."

"Good. So, I was thinking maybe we should leave a little earlier than I anticipated."

"So your mom doesn't get a chance to poison me?" I smiled into his chest.

"I hadn't thought of poison. That's a good call. No, I think we'll stay through lunchtime though. If you want I'll test your food."

"Sounds like a plan," I agreed. "And then go home for dinner?"

"No, let's go out," he suggested. "There's a restaurant down the street I want to take you to. I know the owner."

I want to take you to. More flutters. "That sounds great."

"I figure that if I'm going to make you suffer through my childhood memories you may as well get some really good food out of it."

"So why don't you and Scott get along?" I asked.

"You picked up on that, huh?" I felt him stroke my hair. "You're too perceptive."

"I'm guessing your mother tries to pit you against each other."

"Scott is, as you put it, the golden child. He could never do any wrong, unlike Nat and me. She got a free pass because she was the girl, though."

"So you were the scapegoat," I concluded.

"Pretty much," he replied. "It used to bother me. But I was always my father's favorite, so that helped."

"I like your dad."

"He thinks you're great as well," he assured me, and I could hear a smile in his voice. "Now Anabel?"

"I'll shut up now."

"Goodnight, sweetheart."

"Goodnight," I bade him, and I fell asleep with a smile on my face.

Chapter 34—Jared

Meghan flung a sugar packet at me. "Why am I here, Jared?"

"To keep me company?" I asked half-heartedly.

She snorted. "You've been staring at the menu in silence for a good ten minutes now. Our waitress is afraid to come over here, and I'm hungry!"

"I'm sorry," I muttered. "I'm ready."

"Good," she said. "WAITRESS!"

"Is it really necessary to draw so much attention to yourself?"

"You seemed to miss the part where I'm starving. I haven't eaten since breakfast."

"That's not good, Meg. You need to eat."

"I know," she concurred. "Instead I spend all my time taking care of my mopey brother. I had a date tonight, you know."

"You should've gone on that. I'm not very good company."

She sighed. "Look, why don't we just talk about Annie and get it over with?"

My laugh was bitter. "She's away somewhere with her bodyguard."

"Is that what this is all about?" Meghan shook her head. "I got news for ya, buddy. She's always somewhere with her bodyguard."

"They took a trip. Together."

"Maybe she just needed out of here. I wouldn't blame her. This place is suffocating," Meghan smiled at our waitress. "We need bread. Now."

After we placed our food orders, Meghan turned to me again. "Look. Anabel has every right to be mad at you. I think it was downright compassionate of her to call you and say she was going out of town. Give it a rest, okay?"

"Okay," I agreed. "Let's talk about you."

"I'm dating Kevin Miller," she announced.

"Seriously?"

She nodded. "He asked me to go get coffee after Anabel's fiasco birthday party. We've been seeing each other since."

I rubbed my forehead. "I wasn't expecting that."

"He's over her. She's too much of a mess for him, he's acknowledged as much."

"She's also not interested," I pointed out.

"Well, she's never been," noted Meghan. "Which is why it doesn't bother me."

"Anabel's a lot to deal with," I admitted.

"Yes, she is," she agreed, taking a sip of water. "Kevin says the baby's doing really well," my sister continued. "As long as Annie sticks to her regimen there shouldn't be a problem with her making it through the birth. It looks a lot better now than it did in the beginning."

"What are you talking about?"

Meghan looked nervous. "You mean she didn't tell you? I thought for sure she had..." She trailed off. "She must have decided not to after you forgot about her birthday."

"Meghan," I reiterated, "what are you talking about?"

"I really shouldn't be the one to tell you," she protested.

"Well you're going to. Right now."

She looked uneasy. "Can you call her first?"

"Now, Meghan," I demanded.

She sighed. "Okay. Anabel has blood clots and she's on this heparin regimen to keep her blood thin so that they don't get stuck in her brain or her lungs. However, once it gets closer to the birth, Kevin is saying she has to not take the heparin anymore, and that can cause complications."

"What kind of complications?"

Meghan swallowed. "She could die, Jared."

I was stunned. "Why didn't she tell me?"

My sister touched my arm. "You know why."

And I did know why. Because, like my sister, I knew that Anabel would not listen to any suggestion that she didn't put the baby's needs above her own. I also knew that my neglecting her had made her decide that I didn't need to know about this.

Meghan was staring at me, concerned. "I really shouldn't have told you. That was Anabel's place, not mine."

"Does everyone else know?" I asked.

"Um, I think just me and Matt. And Sam, of course."

"Of course Matt knows," I scoffed.

"I think Sam told him." Meghan glanced at her phone. "Princess' ears must've been ringing. She just texted me."

"What's it say?"

"Am back earlier than expected. Matt's mom hates me. Hope your mom doesn't feel the same." Meghan got wide-eyed. "Interesting. I guess she spent time with the Moores." She shook her head. "Poor Anabel. That can't feel good."

I picked up my phone.

"I wouldn't call her," she began.

"No, I won't do that," I replied, typing in a message.

Can I see you tomorrow? I want to give you something.

A moment later I got this reply:

Is it a pony? My response depends on this answer.

I grinned and wrote back: *Absolutely.*

Liar. Come by my house in the afternoon.

At two o'clock the next afternoon, a very tired-looking Anabel answered the front door. "Hey!" she greeted me, but her expression was guarded.

"Hey yourself. Not sleeping?"

She groaned. "Baby doesn't seem to get that we sleep at night." She smiled. "Would you like to come in?"

"Yes," I said, and she stepped aside. "Anyone else here?"

"Um, Matt is somewhere, but I asked him to give us some space," she told me. "Charlotte, Phil, and their daughter went to a movie. So it's just us."

"And Matt."

"And Matt," she agreed. "But I don't know where he is. So where's my pony?"

"That was a ploy to get you to see me," I smiled at her.

"I knew it! Well is the big pink squareish bag for me?" She started to take it from me.

I drew back. "It's too heavy for you, honey."

Anabel sighed. "I'm not allowed to lift anything anymore. So what is it?"

"It's for your room. Can we go up there?"

She hesitated. "Okay."

We walked up the steps, and I saw Anabel biting her lip. "You okay?"

"This feels weird," she admitted, looking down. "I'm still kind of peeved at you."

"I know," I told her. "Like I said, I won't be long. I just wanted to give this to you."

She grinned. "Well I'm guessing it's for the baby, with the pink and white polka dots."

"No, it's actually for Matt. Too bad he's not around."

She laughed and smacked my arm.

We walked into her room, and she immediately froze. I knew she was thinking about the last time she and I had been in her room, alone together. I tried to lighten the mood. "I realize this probably isn't the time to tell you this, but I need you to close your eyes."

Her eyes widened. "Are you for real?"

"It takes me about five minutes to set this up. I practiced earlier and timed myself. But you have to trust me, Anabel. Can you do that?"

She looked like she was about to bolt, but she nodded, climbed onto her bed, and sat cross-legged with her eyes shut. "I better not regret this,

Jared."

"You won't," I promised her.

She sighed. "So what did you do this weekend?"

"I had dinner with Meghan last night."

"So if I call Meghan she'll verify that?"

"Ouch. Yes." I grunted, snapping a lock into place.

"Don't hurt yourself, whatever you're doing," she murmured.

"How was your trip?" I asked.

She groaned. "A total disaster. I don't want to talk about it."

I paused and stared at her. She'd gained some more baby weight, but as I watched her sit there, rubbing her belly, I really couldn't help but think that I did truly love her.

I think she knew I was staring at her, because she inquired, "Is it done?"

"Almost." I locked the top bar into place. "Open your eyes."

She did, and they grew very wide. "Oh my goodness."

"It's a cosleeper," I explained. "Meghan told me that you wanted to keep Emma in your room with you, so what this does is it attaches to the bed, and you can have her right there."

"It's beautiful," she whispered. "Oh Jared, thank you." She got herself off the bed—no small feat—and gave me a hug.

"You're welcome," I replied.

"And it's pink," she breathed.

"Yes, so that doctor of yours better not have screwed up. If that kid comes out with a penis, I am not putting him in that thing."

She laughed. "It's perfect." She kept her arm around my waist as we admired my handiwork.

"You probably want to wash the sheet before she comes, you know. Do you have baby detergent?"

Anabel made a face. "No, not yet. But Meghan told me to hold off until after the baby shower she's apparently throwing me."

"She told me about that. Sounds like the exact sort of thing you love."

"You got me there." She was starting to warm up to me again. "Meghan's been wonderful, but it does seem a little much. She invited Alexis, after all"

"What about Clara Moore? Did she invite her?"

Anabel's jaw dropped. "I'm guessing your sister told you."

"What did you do to her, Anabel?"

"You know, I don't even know, but she seemed determined to not like me." She dropped onto the bed. "She accused me of trying to get into Matt's pants. Like I'm trying to get into anybody's pants like this."

I shook my head. "I've only met her a handful of times. She doesn't care for me either, but she has a reason to despise me."

Anabel nodded, looking at her bedspread.

"I hate myself for what happened to Nat," I confided, coming to sit next to her. "I didn't...I liked her and everything, but she wanted way more out of the relationship than I did." I looked into her eyes. "I swear, Anabel, I never wanted to hurt her."

"I believe you," she whispered.

I changed the subject. "What did you think of Geoff?"

"Absolutely adored him," she grinned.

"I imagine he enjoyed you as well."

"I made him laugh," she admitted.

"He's the only one who doesn't blame me," I shared.

"Well he seems to be the only rational one in the bunch," she commented. "Scott's awful, too."

"You met Scott, huh?"

Her mouth moved into a tight smile. "He thinks I'm sassy." She stretched her legs. "He seems to hate you more than—"

"Than Matt does? I know." I looked at her. "Look, we don't exactly get along, but I don't think Matt blames me. He just hates what I did to her."

Anabel nodded. "Yeah, I don't think he blames you either."

We sat there for a few moments in silence, me watching her while she studied her bedspread. Finally she turned to me. "I sort of miss you."

"I sort of miss you, too."

"But I don't know what to say to you anymore." She leaned against me. "Remember when it used to be easy?"

"Was it ever?" I asked her.

"There used to not be consequences."

"There were always consequences with you and me, baby." I put my arm around her. "It was just which ones we were getting ourselves into."

Anabel nodded. "If it wasn't hurting my father or my brother, it was—"

"—hurting each other," I finished.

"Yeah," she said. "We've hurt each other a lot, haven't we?"

"Me more so than you," I acknowledged.

"Still, I haven't exactly made things easy," she admitted. "But I haven't wanted to."

"Yeah, but now there are consequences—very fitting word—that you hadn't foreseen," I sneered.

She picked up on my tone. "How's that?"

"There's the issue of your bodyguard." I didn't want it to be true, but somehow I knew it was.

She frowned. "Stop trying to bring Matt into this."

"Why did he bring you to his parents' house?" I needed to control my temper, and now I was standing up, facing her.

She shrugged, not meeting my eyes. "I needed out of here. It was somewhere not too far away, and I just about invited myself. I wanted to meet his family."

"Don't you find that a little odd? Wanting to meet your bodyguard's family?" I was getting angry at her again. "You haven't even met mine yet."

"I know Meghan," she was defensive. "I guess I thought that it might be nice to talk to Matt's mom since we have similar interests. She's a professor of English Lit."

"Is that all?"

She nodded miserably. "Yes, and it turns out she despises me. So that's lovely. Matt's one of the few friends I have, Jared, and I don't really expect him to hang out with me too much if his family hates me. And you, for that matter, seeing as how the baby is yours."

I felt sorry for her. She really looked upset. "Hey, baby, I'm sorry," I apologized. "I didn't realize it meant that much to you."

"I really like and respect Matt," she declared. "He's the only one out of you who doesn't treat me like a crazy person."

"And that's all?"

Her eyes narrowed. "What are you getting at, Jared? I mean, he's not the one who stares at me like I'm a piece of meat."

"Are you saying I do?" I moved closer.

She took another step back. "I'm not about to play this game with you again."

"I'm just curious what you think about me," I kept my voice light. "That's all."

I was getting to her. Anabel gulped. "I think we should stay on opposite sides of the room for the moment," she whispered.

"You keep fighting it," I stepped closer.

She didn't step away this time, but looked down. "I have to," she stated. "I can't keep it up."

"Why?" I asked her.

"I can't," Anabel faltered. "I just can't, okay? I care about you a lot. Isn't that enough?"

"Not really, no," I replied.

"What do you want from me?" she demanded.

I studied the face that looked pretty close to tears. She looked desperate, and I think at that moment she would've said whatever I wanted to hear.

Except for the fact that Matt walked in right then. "You alright, Anabel?"

She nodded. "You should go, Jared."

Without a word I left the room, and I made it almost to the top of the stairs before I heard her burst into tears. Fantastic way to end things. Just great.

Chapter 35—Jared

A week later, I was standing outside of the Capitol Building with my sister. "So let me get this straight. You've just left her alone? With Matt? For an entire week?"

"I think she needed some time away from me."

"I'm sure," she noted, and then pursed her lips. "From what little she's told me, you did a number on her the other night. Matt probably looks really good right about now."

I grimaced. "I am well aware of how perilous the situation is now."

My sister took a sip of her latte and grinned. "I just tell it like it is. So anyway, Mom and I were thinking Cheesecake Factory. I think you'll score points with Princess, as she said to me the other day that she loves fresh guacamole. Apparently she never had it on the island and now she can't get enough of it."

"Great. I'll meet you there." Meghan and I were standing just outside the hearing room. I had wanted to wait outside for Anabel, as we had been avoiding each other. She hadn't been returning my calls or text messages, and on the rare occasion that she did communicate with me, she indicated that "now wasn't a good time." I also suspected that Matt may have had a hand in that. So here I was, lurking, even though Meghan had more than once commented that I looked "like a total stalker."

"Yeah, I'm not exactly thrilled about driving all the way out to Tyson's, but whatever." She scanned the crowd. "Mom really wants to see her house. I'd like to see it again as well. I wonder what kind of property taxes that little beauty racks up."

"Okay," I told her. "I can't deal with this anymore. I need you to be normal, okay?"

"I need you to stop behaving like a pedophile."

"I am not—"

"I'm just saying, you don't have to stick around. She's not making you."

"I love her," I said.

"Then behave like it! Sweep her off her feet. Do something to make her realize you love her, because if I was Anabel, I would think you didn't care about me at all." Meghan looked serious. "If you had any sense whatsoever, you would throw yourself on her mercy and make her realize that despite everything, she wants to be with you and only you."

"I don't know who you are. This isn't like you. Since when have you become such a sappy romantic?"

Meghan considered. "I guess it's just her. I've never liked anyone you've been with, and I would love to see the two of you happy together." She kissed me on the cheek. "I have a meeting. I love you." And with a twist on her heel, my sister was clicking down the hall. I was left alone to wait.

As if on cue, Anabel showed up walking with Matt and smiling. When she saw me her eyes got bigger. "Hey!" she called. "I am so sorry I haven't been in touch, we've been busy. Matt's trying to get me to not make a complete idiot of myself. We'll see if he's succeeded."

I laughed mirthlessly.

"Was that your sister, Sorensen?" Matt asked.

"Yeah, that was Meghan."

"Oh, I missed Meghan!" Anabel looked disappointed. "Is she coming with us tonight?"

"Yeah, we were thinking Cheesecake Factory in Tyson's, 7 o'clock?"

Anabel looked at Matt, and he nodded. "We'll meet you there."

"My mom actually wants to see Anabel's house," I hinted in what I hoped was a casual tone.

"Well why don't you all come by around 6? We can all head over there together then." She looked earnest.

"Sounds good," I agreed. Matt's face remained unperturbed, but I suspected he didn't like that idea.

"We should go in," he suggested to Anabel.

She nodded. "See you inside."

They walked in together, and I realized Meghan was right. I definitely needed to do something about them.

It was a rather painless day for both Anabel and me, to the point where I caught her falling asleep on her brother's shoulder. They were interrogating Major Briggs for his take on the day Jonathan was murdered. Charlie was also there, and he would probably be testifying tomorrow. And while I did not turn around, I often felt Matt's eyes boring into the back of my skull. As Anabel let out a small sigh in her sleep, I wondered if he was staring at her as often as he was me.

"Of course, Charlie was there since we couldn't get ahold of Jonathan. Before we were aware of his murder. We later discovered that Sorensen had discovered Jonathan Martin's death and took Anabel out of the building before any harm could befall her," continued the Major.

Sam gently shook Anabel awake. "Mm? What?" She sat up, blinking rapidly.

"So good of you to join us, Miss Martin," Ms. Fischer said to her. There was a murmur of laughter around the room.

"I'm so sorry," she exclaimed. "I haven't been sleeping. Were we talking about me?"

More laughter.

As the hearing closed for the day, I walked over to her, but I was thwarted when I bumped into Charlie.

"Hello, Jared," he said.

"Charlie, how are you? I'm sorry we haven't gotten a chance to talk," I replied, internally groaning.

"Well, you've been busy, I'm sure," he acknowledged, nodding at Anabel. For some reason, I didn't like the way he was staring at her. "How has she been?"

"Anabel? She's fine, I guess, she just keeps having more nightmares."

"What do you mean?" He sounded curious.

"She's been having nightmares about the night her father was murdered." I glanced at her; she was deep in conversation with her brother.

"Really?" He seemed interested in this. "Does she remember something?"

"No, it's all fuzzy in her mind. I don't really know, Charlie, I haven't talked to her all that much."

"Right," he nodded. He looked at Marilyn. "Well, I'm sure I'll see you later."

I inclined my head and made my way over to where Anabel and Sam were seated.

"We miss you, you know," I heard him say.

"Maybe you do," she smiled. "I doubt Alexis does."

"Perhaps we should change the subject." Sam was always the diplomat. "I really like your house. Do you?"

"Yes!" she proclaimed. "I barely know what to do with it. Not that I've spent much waking time there, Matt and I went out to dinner again last night and it seems like the caretakers are doing an excellent job—Jared," she interjected, noticing me. "How are you?"

"Fine, thank you," I returned, noting that Matt was already taking her out to dinner. More than once. "Are we still on for tonight?"

"Yes!" She looked at Matt, who had materialized at her side. "We should probably go. I want to look nice for your mother." She smiled at me again, and then they were gone.

I stared after her, and then I looked at Sam. He looked smug.

"I don't care," I told him. "We have a child together, and that's a bond you can't break."

"I can't, no," he agreed. "She, however, is another story."

"You know, I can't believe you would do this to your own sister," I retorted. "Don't you care about her happiness at all?"

"I believe," he commented, not bothering to look at me, "she would be much happier without you."

"He doesn't even care about her. So you want her to fall in love with someone who doesn't love her?"

"It already happened once, and now she's having a baby in a little over three months." I started to protest, but Sam continued. "Besides, Jared, who's to say that he doesn't care about her? Matt's not the type to string a girl along."

That was the ugly truth that I wanted to put from my mind. Staring at the door that they had just gone through, I vowed not to let that happen.

Chapter 36—Anabel

My belly was getting huge. I stood sideways and looked in the mirror, thankful that there was not a scale in sight. I pulled my dress over my head and sighed. It was nice, blue and demure, and did a good job minimizing my stomach. A white pearly sweater complemented it well, and my freshly washed curls were frizz-free. It was the best I could do.

There was a knock at my door. "Come in," I called.

Charlotte stepped in. "Oh Miss Anabel, you look so lovely," she gushed. We had become good friends in the weeks I had been at the house, and she was borderline maternal with me. I kept trying to get her to not call me "Miss Anabel," but it didn't seem to be working.

"Thanks. I'm trying to make a good first impression."

"You'll do fine, don't you worry," she admonished me. "I just wanted to check on you, you have a lot going on. Especially with that very nice young man across the hall from you," she commented, and I caught her meaning.

"He's my bodyguard. He's being paid for that." I bit my lip.

"Of course. I'll see you later." Charlotte left, and I smiled at myself in the mirror.

Okay, so being with Matt for the past month was enough time for me to realize that he was everything that Jared wasn't, and I was falling for him, hard. I know. I know. This was ridiculous on more levels than I could even contemplate. I had flirted shamelessly with Jared back on the island, and now that he was interested in doing the right thing by me and helping raise our child, all I wanted to do was stare adoringly at my bodyguard who was only paying attention to me because my brother was paying him. Yes, I was aware of this new level of insanity that I had reached.

I had thought Jared was the hero of my story. But Matt was the one who took me for a picnic on my birthday. Matt was the one who burst into my room during my breakdown. He had made sure to set ground rules with Jared for my safety and security during our nightmarish date. He did a million little things for me every day—bringing me a glass of water, helping me prop my swollen feet up with a pillow, reading to me at night. Perhaps, I reflected, Jared was just a red herring.

There was, however, a big part of me that felt like I should make an effort to attempt to have something with Jared. There was another part that felt like I had tried enough.

What it really boiled down to was the same thing that had bothered me from the beginning. Matt had called me out on my feelings for Jared our first night together, and for the first time, I was really facing them. Was I attracted to him? Oh, sure, you cannot look at a man like Jared without feeling something. But did I love him? He told me he thought I did. Matt had asked me why I was allowing myself to fall for him—but I wasn't, really. I cared about him, sure, and on some level I loved him, but I was not in love with him. Furthermore, how could I even contemplate the idea of being with Jared if I couldn't trust him? The episode with Carly (who Meghan had informed me had a terrible reputation) had really opened my eyes to his true character. It was as if he was trying to blow his chances with me on purpose. I definitely didn't trust Jared now. And, as I stared into the mirror, I knew that the sad truth was I never could. I could forgive him, sure; I had done that already. But trust was something else.

Yet here I was, immediately trusting Matt, feeling like he was someone I could lean on, someone who could support me. "And I need all the support I can get," I murmured aloud.

"Talking to yourself again?"

I turned and glared at Matt. "Don't you ever knock?"

"You shouldn't leave your door open. You never know who will walk in."

"I see the dire consequences of that. You're right, as always," I smiled at him. "You look nice." He had gotten rid of his khakis for some nice dress slacks and a green shirt that complemented his eyes. I hopelessly adored Matt, but I was not insensible of how unappealing I was at this point. After all, I was carrying the child whose father was his sworn enemy. The baby weight probably didn't help either.

"Thanks. We need to talk before your guests arrive."

"Okay," I acquiesced, sliding into my silver flats. "What's up?"

"Shouldn't you wear your boots? It's going to be cold."

"I'll be fine," I smoothed out my skirt. "Now what did you want to ask me?"

"How many people are coming tonight?"

"Well, Jared, obviously, and his mom, and Meghan."

"You didn't invite anyone else?"

"No, I don't know if you've noticed, but I don't have any friends." I couldn't help myself, I was grinning at him again.

He nodded. "Okay, so if anyone else comes up, I am going to assume that they're hostile, and you will do what I say at that point."

I rolled my eyes and looked away. "You're a bit ridiculous."

"And you need to take me seriously, Anabel," he lectured.

I faced him then, trying not to be defiant. "I do take you seriously, Matt. I take you so seriously that I have followed everything you have told me to do to the letter. I haven't been alone with anyone outside of this house. I have not contacted Jared, despite the fact that I have received ten million text messages from him. I finally have a BlackBerry," I cracked, "and I do not use it because you told me not to. So, I think you could give me a little credit." I sat down on my bed and stared at my feet.

He dropped down on the bed next to me. "Look, I realize you've gotten used to a certain degree of autonomy since you left Caereon, and I understand that imposing all of these rules on you might seem a little harsh, but it's—"

"—for your own good," I chorused with him. "Oh yes, I'm very used to everyone telling me what's for my own good."

"Don't be mad at me over this," he sighed, sounding weary.

"Oh good, another command." Why was he sitting so close to me? His arm was mere inches away from my own, and I could feel the heat from his body. I swallowed. "What else can I do for you?"

"I'm here to take care of you, Anabel, not the other way around," he intoned, his voice low. "I just need to know that, if the time ever comes, you'll follow my directions to the letter."

I gave him what I hoped was a patronizing stare. "Matt, you do a better job parenting me than my father ever did. Of course I will do exactly what you say. I care much more about my daughter than I do myself, and I would never do anything to cause her harm." I rested my hand on my belly, and felt pleased when Emma moved. "See? She agrees with me."

"Is she kicking?"

"Yeah, do you want to feel?" But I didn't let him answer. I took his hand and placed it on my belly.

And Emma went crazy! She started kicking and moving around at a rate I had never felt before. "She likes you," I smiled at Matt. "She doesn't do that for anyone else." I wondered if my daughter could tell that my heart was aflutter.

"That's incredible," he commented, sounding awed.

"I'm pretty excited about her," I said.

"Even though this wasn't your decision? I'm sure you've heard this from more than one person, but I'm a bit surprised at your choice. Most rape victims don't keep unintended pregnancies." His hand was still on my stomach. I decided to do everything in my power to keep it there.

"Well, when I first found out I was pregnant I was scared. And angry as well. Alexis and Sam both told me I should get an abortion. It was more like they pressured me, to be honest. But then I thought, my mother got pregnant young and unintended, and she kept my brother. And look at Sam! So I knew then that I couldn't do it. Every part of my body was resistant to that idea. And then I thought about how hard it was for me when I was growing up, and how I had desperately wanted real parents. Then I thought, I could be a real parent to my child, and that was when I fell in love." I smiled at him. "Alexis and Sam think that I'm crazy, but I don't care, because this is truly what I want. I talk to her all the time and I tell her how happy I am that she is coming, and how we are going to have so much fun once she is born."

"Even though she is Jared's child?"

"Even though she is Jared's child," I acknowledged. "He's a different story."

"Well, you cannot avoid the fact that half of Emma is Jared."

"No, you are right about that," I admitted. "But she is my daughter and I am not going to let the fact that she has him as a father change how I feel about her."

"So, what, you're not in love with him anymore?"

"I was never in love with him in the first place. I realize that, now that I have a basis for comparison," I admitted, looking at him.

Of course, doorbell rang right then. We stared at each other for a moment, and then I managed, "Matt."

"I shouldn't have asked. Forgive me." He got up and walked out, and I had to fight back tears. The fact of the matter was, I wasn't good enough for Matt, and he and I both knew it. I wanted to call Sam right then, but instead I plastered a fake smile on my face and went down to meet Jared's mother.

She was not at all what I expected. Jared and Meghan were both tall and lithe, but Aurelia Sorensen was five feet two and looked so round and comforting that I immediately hugged her with no introduction.

She held me at arm's length. "Remarkable. You really do look just like your mother."

"Um, thank you," I stammered.

She turned to her son. "You used to have a huge thing for Cassidy, didn't you?" She looked at me with a conspiratorial smile. "He watched that one movie where she played the princess over and over again when he was about ten."

Jared flushed, and I couldn't help but laugh. He put his arm around Aurelia. "What is it about mothers that they always try to embarrass you?"

Meghan kissed my cheek. "I don't think I told you this last time, but I have to say, this is a pretty swank pad, Annie. I really like it."

"Yes, this is where my father and mother lived before they divorced. "I haven't spent much time in any room except for my bedroom. It's a bit hard for me to think about the two of them making memories here." Oh good. I had made everyone feel awkward. "So! We're going to the Cheesecake Factory? That sounds promising."

"We should go," said Matt, out of the shadows. "I called ahead."

"Oh, thank you for taking care of that," I smiled at him.

His expression did not change. "I needed to make sure they would give us a table which would be strategically placed."

"Well then," Jared stepped in. "Should we head out?"

"Anabel and I will follow you," Matt announced.

Jared looked like he was going to protest, but I shook my head at him. "It's pointless to argue with him, Jared," I explained. "I have tried, and somehow I keep losing. This past week when we didn't have hearings I begged him to take me sightseeing, but he just slammed doors in my face."

Meghan laughed and linked her arm through her brother's. "It's just as well. We can't all fit in my Prius. I have too many boxes in the backseat."

I gave her a grateful smile. I knew she was doing her best to diffuse a difficult situation, and I admired her for it.

We got into Matt's truck, and I shot him a sideways glance. "Please don't make this difficult. I know that you don't like him, but—"

"I don't like him?" he repeated. "Did you really just suggest to me that I don't like him?"

"Matt, come on," I implored. "I told him I would meet his mother. This is not by any stretch of the imagination easy for me. You told me you needed me in on this with you, and, well right now I really need you in on this with me. Whether you like it or not, we're a team. At least until this whole 'who murdered my father' thing gets resolved."

His eyes searched mine, and he nodded. "I'm sorry. I sometimes forget that this is just as hard on you as it is on me." He then turned up the radio, and I knew our conversation was done. But it left me biting my lip, smiling.

So we got to the Cheesecake Factory, and I was happy to learn that they made guacamole to order. "This," I mentioned to Meghan, "is something I could get used to."

"Don't end a sentence in a preposition," came Matt's voice in my ear.

"My bodyguard is bossy," I confided to Aurelia.

"It's the DC area, dear. It makes them all think that they're in charge." I really liked Jared's mother.

I grinned at Matt and looked back at her. "I suppose so."

She turned to Matt. "How's Geoffrey doing?"

"He's fine," he responded, sounding surprised. "I didn't realize you knew him that well."

"We go back a bit," she shared, with a wink at me. Definitely liked Jared's mother. Especially since Matt looked thrown off; I had not been aware that that could happen.

Aurelia smiled at me. "So tell me a little bit about yourself, Anabel."

"I don't know if there is anything about me that is still sacred, given the fact that it seems I have read and reread my life's story in all of the papers," I professed. Still, as we munched on appetizers I chatted with her about my childhood on Caereon, my beloved governess, and my love of books.

"Whatever happened to your books, Anabel?" asked Jared.

I felt tears prick at my eyes again. "I fear I am going to have to replace almost all of them. As long as the investigation is going on, they remain on the island, since it is still a crime scene. And of course, I'm not allowed to go back, and I cannot imagine someone going all the way out there just to pack up and ship my books. I cannot even begin to fathom how much time, and expense..." I trailed off. "I'm just afraid that they're going to close the facility and just destroy them." This thought really disturbed me. "The only book I was able to save was my copy of Emma that had the map in it from when we escaped."

"How did you escape?" asked Meghan. "You haven't touched on it in the hearings yet."

"Well Jared saved me, of course," I said, my voice growing quiet.

He was devastatingly handsome, which was really throwing me off tonight. The low lights in the restaurant accented everything I had adored about his visage. The perfectly tousled hair, the alluring eyes, the sexy smile—all of it did nothing for my self-resolve. I looked down at my food, willing myself to be strong.

"You keep saying he saved you," Matt broke the silence. "But how?"

I considered Jared. "You know, I don't even know how it happened. We didn't really get a chance to talk once you convinced me my life was in danger. Why did you come rescue me?"

He looked at me, and I detected a trace of sadness in his eyes. "I had no alternative. I couldn't let anything else happen to you, not after—"

"Why don't you tell them, then?" I cut him off. "You know better than I."

Chapter 37—Jared

I slept off my hangover and managed to pull myself out of bed in the early afternoon. My head was fuzzy and there was a distinct ringing in my ears, and I got into the shower to try and wash away my sins from the previous night. Bits and pieces were swirling in my mind, and the fact was, I was embarrassed that I had gotten so drunk. Seeing Jonathan Martin was definitely something I was not looking forward to. I was not due to meet him until six, so I let the water slowly massage me awake.

I didn't feel right, though. Something was nagging at the back of my brain, and I thought about the glasses upon glasses of whiskey that I had consumed the night before, about Jonathan's snide remarks, my anger…

And then I remembered Anabel.

"Oh, no," I said, as images of the previous evening flashed in my head. Her screaming. The look of betrayal on her face. And blood. There had been a lot of blood. What had I done to that poor girl?

I knew I had to tell her father. Her relationship with him wasn't exactly cordial, and she wouldn't think that she could go to him. But after that mess I left her in, even though I knew full well he might try and kill me; I had to think about her. She shouldn't have bled that much. I cringed at that thought. She might need medical attention, and I doubted she would own up to Jonathan what had happened.

So I quickly dressed and walked down the hall to his office. What was I going to say, exactly? I don't know. "Mr. Martin, I'm sorry, I got drunk and raped your daughter, and she may need a doctor?" I was so screwed, it wasn't even funny.

As I approached Jonathan's office, I noticed that something seemed amiss. The hall was deserted. Getting closer, I noticed that the door was slightly ajar. When I pushed it open, my jaw dropped.

Jonathan Martin was lying on the floor, with no fewer than four gunshot wounds along his spinal column.

I raced over to him and flipped him onto his back, frantically feeling for a pulse. I then realized there was nothing I could do. His eyes were glazed over, and my guess was he had been dead for at least half an hour.

It had been apparent from Charlie's warning that Jonathan had enemies on Caereon, but I had no idea that someone was considering killing him. I wondered that I hadn't heard gunshots, but then I remembered someone commenting that the office was soundproof.

I punched the wall, having no idea what to do. You didn't exactly call 911 on a Top Secret island.

That was when my thoughts went to Anabel. If someone had killed her father, they might be after her. Swallowing hard, I got to my feet and sprinted out of the room.

I ran down the long hall to her room, and my heart stopped when I saw the door was open. I took a moment to pray to God that she was okay, and when I pushed open the door...she wasn't there.

The room was a mess though. Her clothes—all of them—had been thrown onto the floor. The bloody rug, a sordid reminder from last night, was covered in bed linens. Books were thrown all over her library. Either Anabel had had the mother of all temper tantrums, which I doubted because I don't think she would've thrown her books around like that, or (and this was what I didn't want to even consider) someone had already been here.

I had to find Anabel. I had to know she was okay. I wandered down the corridor for a long time, looking in rooms, but I didn't encounter anyone. About half an hour went by and with each passing step I grew more and more hopeless and concerned about encountering the most-certainly armed murderer. Finally, I hit a dead end, a spiral staircase that looked like it went up to the attic. I kicked the wall in frustration. Sighing, I turned away to go back, but then I thought better of it and quietly walked up the stairs.

By some miracle, she was there, asleep on top of an old couch. It was, I guessed, the most tranquil moment she had gotten since last night. So I hesitated. At the same time I knew it wasn't safe for us to be here, so I walked over to her and gently touched her arm. "Anabel, hey Anabel," I whispered.

Her eyes fluttered open, and she looked confused. "Jared?"

"Listen, something bad has happened—"

That was when recognition spread across her face, and her eyes hardened. She sat up and pushed away from me. "You!" She stood up and made for the staircase. "You get away from me. I want nothing to do with you."

"I know," I said, catching her arm, "and in any other circumstances, I would respect your wishes, but Anabel, something terrible has happened."

She tried to yank herself away, but I was too strong. "Let go, Jared," she demanded.

"No, I need you to listen to me." I had to be calm; I had to hold it together for her.

"I don't care about anything you have to say to me. If you don't let go of me, I'll scream!"

That was when I pulled her close and covered her mouth with my hand. She continued to resist, but she couldn't break apart from me, a fact that flooded me with shame. "Listen to me," I ordered her. "We need to be silent, Anabel, because your father is dead, and whoever killed him might come after you, too!"

I don't think it registered with her at first. Her breathing stopped, and I loosened my grip on her. She wouldn't run away from me now. She slowly moved out of my grasp and looked me in the eyes, horrified. "What did you say?"

"Baby, I'm so sorry—"

"He's dead?" She collapsed on the couch.

"Look, I know I'm the last person you want to be with right now. But I owe it to you and your brother to get you out of here. Is there somewhere we can go? That nobody else on the island knows about?"

She sat there, not moving. I didn't want to prod her, but I didn't know how long we had before someone would come looking for her again. Then she nodded. "We have to go to my room and get something."

"That was the first place I looked for you."

She stared at me blankly. "Did you see anybody there?"

"No," I said, relieved that she had finally responded.

"Okay," she whispered. "Okay."

I sat down next to her. "Anabel," I began.

"Please don't say anything." Her voice was emotionless, and again, all I could feel was remorse.

"Okay." I couldn't deny her that.

She got to her feet, and I followed her down the stairs. We walked in silence, not seeing anyone in the hall. She stopped about ten feet from her door. She beckoned me close and when I leaned my head in she whispered in my ear, "We're going to have to be very quick. I need one book, and then there's a way out. Nod if you understand."

I complied.

So she walked into her room and gasped, taking in the absolute mess. Then she pulled herself together and walked to her bookshelf and grabbed a copy of *Emma*. "Okay," she whispered. She motioned for me to follow her, and she led me back to a room that looked like an AV room with monitors. There were TVs, microphones, and what looked like a recorder. I barely had time to take that in when she entered a code and banged open a door in the back.

I blinked in the light. We stepped out into the jungle, and Anabel closed the door behind her. "We should have a decent start. Jonathan and I were the only ones that knew that password."

"Where are we going?"

"My father called it 'The Safe House.' It's basically a bomb shelter." She opened the book to the back page, and slowly slid out a piece of paper from the back cover.

"What's that?"

"A map. I've never been there, so this is the only way we're going to find out where it is."

"Anabel?"

She looked at me.

"I'm sorry."

"I think this will be a lot easier if we don't talk." She turned her back on me and began to make her way through the jungle.

"So," I revealed to everyone at the table, "I wouldn't say I saved her, I just got her out of there."

"Yes, well I would have died if you hadn't. I'm so very thankful that nobody thought to look for me in the attic." Anabel leaned forward. "I'll always be grateful to you for that, Jared."

"I don't deserve your gratitude." I muttered.

"Well Jared," said Meghan in earnest, "it was rather heroic."

I stood up. "None of you get it, do you?" I turned around and stormed outside.

The air was cool, and I took a few deep breaths. Thinking about the whole thing made me angry at myself all over again. I hated reliving hurting Anabel.

"Hey!"

I turned and looked at her. She had followed me, and was shivering. "I need to ask you something," she announced, her voice light.

"What's that?"

"Why didn't you get me anything for my birthday?" She came close to me.

I laughed. "I had no idea you were such a materialist."

"Emma's bed doesn't count, either. I refuse to have baby gifts for my birthday." She shivered again. "I should've listened to Matt and worn my boots."

I decided to ignore that. "I did get you something. I just haven't given it to you because every time I try we get into a verbal battle."

"That does sound like us," she conceded. "Why did you run out like that?"

"I can't deal with myself sometimes. I can't deal with what I did to you."

"Jared," she crooned my name, touching my arm. "I let it go. You need to as well."

"Why?"

"Why what?"

"Why did you forgive me? How can you possibly let it go?"

She considered. "I don't want to be like my father, letting my anger consume me all the time. Besides, there's another reason."

"What?"

She wordlessly pointed to her belly.

I took that in, and shook my head a few times. "So that's it. That's all there is between us. The baby."

"That and raw animal magnetism."

I looked at her; her eyes were mischievous. "Oh yeah?"

"That's probably also why we repel so much." She stepped away from me. It was almost like a dance with her: one step forward, but always two steps back.

"We could make it work, you know," I told her.

"Jared," she sighed, "it's not like you've been trying all that hard. You forget my birthday. You go out with other women—"

"I told you I was sorry about the birthday thing."

"I was sorry too. It let me know where we stand." She took another step away, and I knew I had to take drastic action.

"Anabel, I love you."

She looked startled. "What?"

"I love you. There. I said it. Are you happy now?"

"No!" she snapped. "I don't want you to tell me you love me when we're in the middle of a fight! All we do is fight!"

I groaned. "Well, that's not all my fault."

"It's not all of mine either."

"What are you getting at?"

"Being with you scares me," she admitted. "Look, I have strong emotions toward you, Jared. But I don't know what they are. I get so angry at you sometimes, angrier than I've ever been at anyone, even Jonathan."

I walked up to her. "But we've had some good times too."

"Have we?"

"Just because I can't think of any at the moment..." I smiled at her.

"Every time I'm with you, I have the same thought."

"What's that?"

"I should run away from you right now." She looked down.

"You don't want to," I pulled her close. "Because you know that nobody loves you like I do. Nobody gets you like I do."

She laughed, and it sounded strangled. "That's a bit disheartening."

"You love me."

"You broke my heart. And the rest of me, for that matter." Anabel met my eyes defiantly. "Can you commit to me, Jared? Could I really be first in your life? Or would I always be looking over my shoulder, wondering about the other women?"

"There wouldn't be any. Only you."

"Somehow I have a hard time believing that," she rolled her eyes.

I ignored this. "Stop going in circles. You and I both know what it comes down to. Can you honestly tell me you don't love me?"

She hesitated.

"You can't," I said, triumphant.

"No," she admitted. "But I don't think I love you the way you want me to."

We looked at each other, and Anabel re-crossed her arms in front of her and smiled, but her eyes were hardening again. "You and me, we do this, and it's all a game to you, isn't it?"

"Not this again, Anabel."

She sighed. "It's the same cycle every time. We do this thing where we're sort of civil, and then we scream at each other, and then we kiss, and I wind up confused."

"We're not screaming at each other this time," I pointed out. "So why don't we just get on with the kissing?"

"It is all a game to you!" She was getting mad.

I pulled her close.

She met my eyes again, but this time hers were fearful. "Don't do this, Jared."

"Do what?" I murmured, staring back down at her.

"Tell me you love me," she whispered. "I want to hear you say it."

"I love you," I told her, and I meant it.

I could see tears forming in her eyes. "It's not enough," she said. "It's not enough for me."

"It could be if you'd let it." I kissed a tear away.

"I think you should let me go," she begged.

"I can't do that, Anabel."

"Please, Jared," she pleaded, sounding scared, her lower lip trembling. What was she scared of, I wondered. Her feelings for me? Another flare-up of both of our tempers? But I couldn't let the moment pass. I couldn't lose this last chance with her. I had to do the one thing that I knew she didn't want me to do, but I did it anyway because I knew it was my only chance at winning her back.

I kissed her.

Chapter 38—Anabel

He kissed me.

But for the first time, I didn't kiss him back. My eyes opened and I studied what I could of his face, and a pang hit me. It dawned on me then that this was it. If I couldn't kiss him, I couldn't tell him I loved him, then I needed to deal with the matter at hand. I didn't want to hurt Jared, but I had to face facts.

It wasn't Jared. It had never been, and I knew it. Listening to him tell me he loved me made me realize how much I had longed to hear those words spoken aloud—from someone else. I was in love, but not with him. Jared wasn't the one for me, he had never been. I knew then and there that it was Matt.

I heard someone clearing their throat. Oh, no. I broke away from Jared, but I knew the damage had been done. I turned to face him, hoping it wasn't too late, or that maybe it was Meghan who had come out to find us.

But I had no such luck. Matt was staring at the ground. "I'll meet you when you're done," he said to me, and then turned and walked away.

Jared barked a laugh. "He's finally left us alone."

"Who says that's what I want?"

"I think you just made it pretty clear what you wanted, Anabel," he replied, pulling me back toward him.

But by that point, I was done with Jared. I yanked myself away from him. "You've really done it this time."

"Anabel, you need to face facts. He and Sam have some scheme to make you think that he likes you, so that you'll leave me." His tone was almost pleading.

I paused. Maybe Jared was right. Maybe it was a ploy. Still, I needed to know—and that didn't change my feelings for Matt one bit. "I was never with you in the first place," I declared. "Give my apologies to your mom and Meghan." I walked away from him then, as quickly as I could, and caught up to Matt at the front door. He didn't look at me, but led the way to the parking lot.

We got in the car in silence. I kept shooting him furtive glances, but his eyes were on the road.

"Matt?" I ventured.

"Not now."

His harsh tone made me feel like I had been slapped. "You don't understand-"

"Look, Anabel, maybe you're a lost cause." He stared straight ahead.

"I'm a lost cause? Nice, real nice. He kissed me, you know. I did not expect that." I wanted to cry, but my growing frustration with Matt Moore was taking over and now I was just plain mad.

"He was staring at you like a dog in heat all night." Matt made a sharp turn and I fell against the side of the car.

"Ouch!" I rubbed my arm. "I'm pregnant, you know."

"Oh yes, Anabel, you remind all of us of that on an hourly basis," he snapped, his voice heavy with sarcasm.

"What is that supposed to mean?"

"It's just your way of getting attention, from him, from me, from anyone else." He wasn't bothering to suppress his rage.

"I don't want his attention," I retorted.

"Then explain to me why you spent two full hours this afternoon getting ready to see him, and then proceeded to flirt with him during dinner. You also practically chased him outside when he left."

"He seemed really upset. I just wanted to make sure that he was okay." Why was Matt doing this?

"It didn't seem to me that you were doing a great deal of discussing matters."

"I didn't get dressed up for him, Matt."

"Oh? And who exactly did you get dressed up for?"

"Who do you think?" I spat.

"I think," he said, his eyes fixated on the road, "that you are as fixated on him as ever."

"It's not him, you know!" I cried, frustrated. "It's you. How can you not see this? I've spent every moment I possibly can with you. I ignored Jared because you told me to. Do you not realize that I don't follow orders? You're the reason I tried to look pretty today, and I know that it's impossible for me to do that when I'm ballooning up like a whale and all. And I know," I continued, "that there is no way that you return my feelings, but I need you to understand this, Matt. It was you from the moment I met you, and no matter how badly you treat me, I'm in love with you, so just deal with it!"

He turned the car into a deserted parking lot and stared at me.

"I can't help what happened between me and Jared. It will always be there. But you have to believe me, when he kissed me tonight, I did not kiss him back." I touched his arm. "Look, I realize that you probably think I am insane, just like everyone else, and I realize that I am a lot to handle. I was a lot to deal with before I was even pregnant, so I cannot imagine what is going through your head right now. I know I'm impulsive, but I also know that I'm always sure of my feelings and right now it is killing me to have you look at me with such disgust. Maybe I ruined everything that ever could have been between us, and that's my own fault, but I'm going to at least tell you that for the first time in my life, I'm in love with someone."

He continued to stare at me. "Oh please, please spare me from all the verbal diarrhea that I am going to continue to spew until you say something," I implored him.

"'I'm in love with you, so just deal with it?'" he repeated, raising his eyebrows.

I managed a small smile and looked down. "Okay, I realize that's not the most romantic thing I could have said, but it is how I feel. You yourself told me I always say what comes into my head without thinking of the consequences."

"I did say that," he admitted.

I couldn't look at him. "Look, I don't expect anything in return from you, and I realize this is a bit of an awkward position for me to put you in, for which I am sorry," I continued. "And you're so...so nice. You're wonderful, really. You wouldn't want to hurt me, I know that. I can't pretend to be insensible of how my saying this might affect you. I never wanted to cause you any sort of pain, but I can't keep this to myself, and—"

Matt shut me up by kissing me. For a long time.

Kissing Matt was completely different than kissing Jared. Jared's kisses were always borderline animalistic: they were intense, hard, and wet. Matt's kisses were slow, sexy, and seductive.

And they left me reeling.

"Was it everything you dreamed of?" he asked when we broke apart.

"Everything and more. You do have a high opinion of yourself," I teased, still trying to recover from what had just transpired. "Well. Here we are."

"Yeah, Anabel, this is not something we can let anyone get hold of at the moment." He rubbed his eyes.

"This?" My heart was light for the first time in a long time.

"You know darn well I love you too," he growled. "I'm not totally heartless. When I told you I had been watching you for a long time, it wasn't just because Sam was paying me. You caught my attention like no one else ever has, and I really didn't want to take the bodyguard job, because I knew this was going to happen."

"What was going to happen?"

"It was going to be harder to restrain myself when we were alone together."

"So what are you saying? You fell for me the moment you met me?" I asked.

"What can I say?" He shot me a lazy smile. "I haven't been able to think about anyone but you."

I beamed at him.

"You can't do that in public," he warned.

"Do what?" I asked innocently.

"You know. Do that thing where you glow at me. You do it all the time." His hand pushed a stray tendril out of my face.

"I'm not really one for hiding my emotions," I pointed out.

"Yes, well, I don't think we should tell anyone. Not your brother, certainly not Jared, and so help me if the press gets wind of it."

"Yes, sir!" I gave a mock salute.

"Anabel," he warned.

"Oh Matt, I'll do my best. But can't you just let me be happy for a moment?"

"I guess I can allow that," he said, leaning in for another kiss.

We sat there a bit longer, me staring at him and him staring at me. Then I felt playful. "So for how long, exactly, were you going to pretend that you didn't care about me?"

He sighed. "I would have done that until I had convinced myself that I didn't."

"When did you really fall for me?" I asked him. "I looked horrible that first day of the hearings, be honest."

He frowned. "I don't recall you ever looking horrible, kid. I did honestly feel something for you then. But I realized that my feelings for you were a problem the other night."

"What other night?"

"Don't you remember our encounter in the kitchen?" He kissed my cheek, very close to my ear, and whispered, "The one where I got a glimpse of your very naughty underwear?"

I gasped at him.

About four or five nights ago, I was awake at 1 a.m. I was restless. Emma had decided that I had no need of sleep and was doing acrobatics in my stomach. I was hot. So I sat up and stripped naked and laid back down, willing myself to be asleep.

Around 2 a.m. I realized that this wasn't happening. So I got it in my head that I should do something useful.

I pulled a tank top on, the kind with the support bra to give some sort of relief to my enlarged bosom, and fished out a pair of panties from the bottom of my drawer. To my dismay, they were the lacy ones, which barely fit anymore, but all of my practical ones were either dirty or not unpacked yet. Making a mental note to get my act together, or at least have Charlotte do my laundry, I yanked them on and slowly headed downstairs.

I meandered into the kitchen, looking for something to do. Anything. My eyes settled on the stainless steel dishwasher. Perfect! I thought. I could put away dishes. That's easy enough, right?

Well, it would've been if, prior to that evening, I had spent more than five minutes in the kitchen. It was an effort to go through all of the cabinets (did I really need so many?) and figure out which plate went where. Then I had to figure out where the cups went, because they apparently had a different home than the nice glasses. It also took me a fair amount of time to discern where all the silverware was housed. I was on a step stool, hanging the copper pots on the hanger, when I became conscious of someone staring at me from the stairs. I gasped and lost my balance, and in a flash Matt was there, catching me before I fell.

"You startled me," I gasped.

"You idiot girl," he said, with a calm rage that unnerved me. He set me down and put his hands on my shoulders, staring hard into my eyes. "What on earth were you thinking?"

"What do you mean? I—"

"That's right," he went on, ignoring me. "You weren't. How do you think I felt, Anabel, when I woke up and realized you weren't in your bed? Don't you think it might've been a good idea to check in with me before you decided to go on a midnight romp in your underwear?"

"I wasn't romping." My cheeks were pink. "You know, this is my house. I can do what I want in it."

"What if you had fallen, Anabel? What then? What if you had fallen and hurt yourself—or hurt the baby?"

I looked at him, stricken.

"You don't think," he continued. "You really don't. Why are you awake right now, anyway?"

"I couldn't sleep." I stared at the floor, feeling miserable. "It's the baby, she won't chill out." I swallowed. "I would never do anything to hurt her."

"Hey," he said, reaching to push my chin up so I would look at him. I allowed him to do this, but I wouldn't meet his gaze. "Look at me."

So I did. His eyes were compassionate. "I'm sorry, I overreacted. It just freaked me out when you weren't in your bed."

I nodded, and my cheeks were still red—but for a different reason this time. Matt's proximity to me, the fact that we were both barely dressed (Matt was wearing his trademark boxer shorts without a shirt), and my growing attraction to him all combined to make my mouth go dry. "I'm sorry, too," I whispered.

He shook his head and grinned at me. "What am I going to do with you?"

There was no denying it. I felt saucy. "Perhaps you should punish me," I suggested. "For being such a bad girl."

He raised his eyebrows at me, and I expected some sort of lecture, but instead Matt gave me an appraising stare. "Oh, Anabel," he sighed. "You're something else, you know that? But you know what?" he whispered in my ear.

"What?" I breathed, feeling my skin tingle.

He pulled back and became businesslike once more. "You need to go back to bed. Now."

My jaw dropped, but I refused to let him bring me down. "Whatever. You and I both know you're thinking about how you'd like to punish me right now."

"To bed, Anabel," he ordered. He took me by the shoulders again and spun me around.

I giggled at him as he hurried me up the stairs. "I'm just saying, if you think I deserve a good spanking, I quite agree with you."

He slammed his door in my face.

"So that was when you knew I was the only one for you?" I asked, grinning at him.

"It was a bit much to come down and find you in your underwear," he recalled, shaking his head. "I was having trouble controlling myself around you. Besides," he commented, "there's nothing more attractive than a woman in love with you."

I blushed, glad it was dark. "It was that easy to tell, huh?"

"It was pretty adorable when you tried to hide it. It was even better when you didn't."

"Oh, Matt," I reproached him.

"Oh, Anabel," he teased back.

"So," I wheedled, "can we do something tomorrow? I mean, I'm going to need to practice being out in public with you and pretending like I'm not infatuated."

He sat up a bit. "What did you have in mind?"

"Could we go to a museum?" I begged.

He looked thoughtful, and then nodded. "If you can get your brother to send a car for us, yes, we can go see the Smithsonian. But I want you dressed as unlike yourself as possible, and no drawing attention to yourself in any way. You're going to have to wear pants."

I looked at him in mock horror. "Oh no, not pants!"

"You always wear dresses," he explained. "Pants, sunglasses, the whole deal. Got it?"

"It's a deal," I agreed.

When we got back to the house I fairly floated up to my room. Matt did his now-routine thing where he looked under my bed and checked out my shower, but all I could do was sit on my bed and beam at him.

"Well, everything looks fine. Shall I wake you up around nine then?" He looked tired.

"Nine sounds fine." I gave him an expectant smile.

"I told you before; those eyes do not work on me. Goodnight." And he left.

Oh, but I did not care. I undressed and slid under the covers. I was in love and life was finally good.

Chapter 39—Anabel

Until suddenly I was screaming.

Jonathan stared blankly at me, and then he fell forward. "Daddy!" I shrieked, and stepped forward, but then I stopped when I saw the gun level at me. "You," I said, disbelieving. "How could it be you?"

I don't know how long I screamed, but the next thing I knew, Matt was in my room. "Anabel? What's wrong? Are you hurt? Is something wrong with the baby?" he asked, his voice full of concern as he approached my bed.

"Matt? What's going on? He killed Jonathan! He tried to kill me," I whimpered, tears running down my face.

He sat on the bed with me and held me, and I began to regain control of myself. For several minutes I didn't speak. It had seemed so real. I had really thought I was in my father's office, watching Jonathan's eyes as the life slowly faded from them. I shivered, taking a deep breath and leaned into Matt. "I'm so sorry," I apologized. "You can go back to bed now."

"Out of the question. You're shaking, Anabel, come on and lie down with me."

"Don't let go of me," I implored.

"Wouldn't dream of it." He slid under the covers next to me and held me until I stopped sniffling and steadied my breathing.

"I haven't had the nightmares in a couple weeks," I confided. "I had them when I first came to the States, and then I had a few back when I was living at Blair House, and then one at Meghan's."

"That was a pretty bloodcurdling scream," he replied. "I was afraid something had happened to you. What was that about, honey?" He stroked my head.

I sighed, snuggling next to him, even though I was hindered by my belly. "It's the same as before, just more vivid this time. You see, I'd been having these dreams, where I run down the hall, I push open the door, and then my father," and here my voice caught again, "falls to the ground. His shooter points a gun at me and then—" I paused and gulped for air. "And then I wake up. Sweating and crying."

"You dreamed about your father's murder? Did you see who did it?"

"No, but it was weird, because the person felt familiar, but I could not see his face." I sighed. "I talked to him in this version, I said something like, 'I can't believe it's you.' Look, I used to have these all the time, it is probably a residual."

"Anabel, you don't really remember too much before Jared found you, right? Sam told me that you don't really know how you got to the attic in the first place."

"I may have just gone up there to hide."

"But you don't know what you were doing up there." He was really persistent.

So I played along. "No, I was sleeping, or something—"

"What if," he cut me off, "what if you actually saw it happen and your brain repressed it? And now you are having nightmares because your subconscious is trying to reassert itself?" Matt seemed excited.

"That would explain why someone was trying to kill me," I admitted. "In the dream, I was convinced I was about to die."

"I think we need to take you to a psychologist," he suggested. "I will make arrangements for that in the morning."

"Look, I know this is silly, but will you stay with me until I fall asleep?"

"I wouldn't dream of leaving. Now go to sleep, Anabel." He kissed my forehead, and comforted by his presence, I fell back into a lazy slumber.

I was rather startled when I awoke the next morning to find he was staring at me. "Oh," I stammered.

He grinned. "I couldn't leave you by yourself. I was afraid you'd wake up, and we'd have to repeat the whole cycle, so I just decided to stay. Besides," he added, stretching, "this bed is incredibly comfortable."

"I KNOW!" I said. He winced. "Sorry," I lowered my voice. "Sometimes when I get excited, I—"

"Anabel, stop apologizing for yourself all the time. It's getting really old."

"Alright then," I smiled at him.

"You know, I was thinking, while I was watching you sleep."

"Oh, that's not creepy," I commented.

"You know who's going to figure this out really quickly is—"

"Charlotte," I finished for him. "I know, I thought about that. She's been dropping hints pretty much ever since we moved in. Meghan made some comment to me as well. And Jared's been freaking out every time you're around. And even my brother wanted us to get together."

"I suppose I should be honored. You should hear the way Sam talks about you. I think he thinks you're his kid."

"I'm not surprised," I smiled. "He's always felt like my parent. He certainly talks to me like I'm a child."

"Well, you know, he only saw you about once a year, and watching you grow up couldn't have been easy for him."

I propped myself up on my elbow. "I know. So I suppose it's a good thing he likes you, for all he despises Jared." I buried my face into his chest. "Oh, Jared. He's going to flip."

He got serious. "I thought about what we said last night, but I don't know if you can hide it from him. You probably should tell him."

"I'm glad we're of the same opinion on that one," I sighed. "I'm just not looking forward to it, is all."

"I would do it sooner rather than later, Anabel. He'll be hurt."

"Why do I feel bad about hurting Jared?" I wondered aloud.

"Because," Matt murmured in my ear, "if you didn't, you wouldn't be you."

Alas, our idyll was interrupted. Just then there was a knock at the door and Matt sprang out of my bed. It opened and suddenly Jared was there.

"Hey, I'm sorry, I know it's early, but—" he stopped and took in Matt in his boxers and my horrified face. "Wasting no time on this one, I see."

"This really is not what it looks like," I told him. "I had another nightmare last night and Matt heard me screaming and he came in and fell asleep when I did. Or maybe it is just what it looks like, I don't know." I decided to omit our professions of love to each other.

Jared stared hard at me, and I returned his gaze without blinking. He looked conflicted, and he walked over to Matt. "I know why you're doing this," he growled.

"Yes, I am paid to be here," Matt was calm.

"You still blame me for—"

"—something that is your fault, yes," interrupted Matt. "It doesn't have anything to do with Anabel."

"It has everything to do with her, and you know it!"

"I'm not doing this with you, Sorensen. It'll only upset Anabel."

"No, we're doing this now."

I cleared my throat. "Um, guys, I am sorry to disturb you, but—"

"Stay out of this," they both said.

"No seriously—"

"What, Anabel?" asked Jared, exasperated.

"No, but um...I'm...bleeding." Horrified, I saw the stain on the bed.

Matt snapped into action. "Jared, call 911 for me. Sweetheart," he said to me, "I need you to lie still, okay? Relax as much as you can"

I nodded, my eyes fearful.

"It will be okay, Anabel," he said to me. "I promise you. Do you trust me?"

I managed to shake my head yes.

"Okay, thanks." Jared hung up his phone and turned to me. "They're sending an ambulance. They said not to move her."

"Good," Matt said.

My sense of right and wrong was weighing heavily inside of me. "Matt, can you give Jared and me a minute alone?"

He nodded. "I'll go downstairs and wait for the ambulance."

He left and we looked at each other. "I'm scared," I whispered, my voice shaking.

"Oh Anabel," he began, coming to sit by me, taking my hand. "It'll be okay."

"I can't lose her, Jared, I just can't," I choked out.

"You know these things happen, it could be nothing," he tried to comfort me.

I nodded, staring at my quilt.

"I'm sorry about last night."

"It doesn't matter now," I replied.

"But it does, Anabel." He looked away. "I can't believe I'm saying this, but I'm afraid I'm going to lose you to Matt."

"There wasn't really much to lose, Jared." I was annoyed that once again, he turned all of this around to be about him.

"I hate when you do that. I'm sick of you always cutting yourself down." He ran his fingers through his hair.

"Why do you want me in the first place?" I asked him. "Seriously, Jared. Can you give me a good reason, besides the fact that you got me pregnant?"

He stared at me, dumbfounded. "I love you, Anabel."

"Why?"

"I…just…do," he managed.

"See, that's just not good enough for me. I need a reason why. And believe me it pains me to say this, I think the only reason you want me right now is because you don't know if you can have me. I'm no longer throwing myself at you, so suddenly I'm more alluring. And you always want what you can't have, and that's me at the moment."

He looked stunned. "Is that what you really think?"

I nodded. "Look, I do think you care about me, I do. But you don't love me, Jared. And if I were to succumb to you, I'm so afraid that you would lose interest in me once you had me." I ran my fingers through my hair. "I need to be the center of someone's life, and I would always worry that I wasn't the center of yours."

"Is there nothing I can say to you?" he asked.

I shook my head. "I'm sorry."

He stood up. "Well then, I see that Sam has won."

"Jared, no," I began.

"I will see you at the hospital." He gave me a hard stare, and then he left, and I sat there alone, fighting tears until the paramedics came.

Chapter 40—Jared

Matt and I were sitting outside her room, not saying much. We'd been there for over an hour and the doctor had kicked us out of the room so he could examine Anabel. When he finally came out and nodded at us, Matt and I both sprang to our feet.

"How is she?" I asked.

"She's fine," he told us. "Baby's fine, too. She had some breakthrough bleeding, but her cervix is still closed and the baby's heart rate is fine. She just needs some bed rest for the next week or two."

I glanced at Matt, and his face mirrored my relief. "So when can we take her home?"

"Well, she's dehydrated, which may have contributed to the bleeding, so she's going to have to stay here overnight. We'll pump her up with some fluids and I'm going to have the nurse give her a very mild sedative—won't hurt the baby," he assured. "The best thing for her is to just get some sleep, and we can monitor her here and you won't have to worry." He glanced at his watch. "You can go see her now, but once she gets that sedative she won't be too lucid."

We watched him walk off, and then Matt turned to me.

"I suggest we watch her in shifts. Do you want to go first or second?"

"Aren't you her bodyguard? I don't really think she's my responsibility right now," I snapped.

"Maybe you should've thought of that before you impregnated her," he replied coldly. "Look, I have to sleep at some point, and don't pretend like you don't care about her, because I know you do."

"Okay," I agreed.

"The thing is, you cannot—we cannot—leave her alone," he continued. "I'm still not convinced that whoever got her dad isn't going to come after her, and this is the perfect place for that to happen."

"I get it. I'll do first shift." I looked down at my phone and saw Sam was calling me. "Oh great. With everything that happened I completely forgot that she and I are supposed to be in a hearing right now. Hi Sam,"

I said into the phone.

"Where are you? Where is my sister? Did you do something to her?"

"Good morning to you too, Mr. President." I didn't bother holding back the sarcasm. "Look, we should've called you, but I forgot about the hearing." Matt smacked his forehead. "So here's the deal: Matt, Anabel, and I are all at the hospital. Your sister had some bleeding this morning and they rushed her here."

Sam sucked in his breath. "Is she okay? Is the baby okay?"

"She's fine and so is the baby, but I will not be making it there today and neither will she. Apparently she's dehydrated, so they're giving her some fluids and making her rest." A nurse breezed into Anabel's room, and Matt followed her. Anabel's eyes lit up as Matt sat next to her and as he took her hand, my heart sank.

I was jarred back to reality by Sam's voice. "I will be there as soon as I can," he told me.

"There isn't anything you can do at this point. They're giving her something to make her sleep and that is probably what she's going to do for the next few hours. I'm going to stay here so Matt can recharge, and then he'll be back with her. You may as well wait until the hearing is over."

Sam paused, and I knew he knew I was right. "Okay. I will come after all this is done. Thanks Jared." And he hung up the phone. I noted that it was the most cordial conversation we'd had in a long time.

So I went into the room, where Anabel was glaring at the nurse. "You're sure," she asked in an accusatory voice, "that this won't hurt the baby?"

"No, Miss Martin." The nurse sounded exasperated.

I intervened. "You should just take it, Anabel. The doctor said that rest was the best thing for the baby."

She looked at me and hesitated, but then she nodded and accepted the pills and a cup of water. Then she lay back against the pillows.

"Your brother called," I told her, watching Matt hold her hand.

"Oh?" She didn't seem to care too much.

"We were supposed to be at a hearing today."

Anabel groaned. "I completely forgot. I didn't think we had anymore until next week." She turned to Matt. "I guess that would've ruined our sightseeing plans."

"You should rest, Anabel," he admonished her.

Her eyelids were beginning to droop. "Alright then," she whispered, adjusting herself onto her side.

"I'll come back later," he told her.

"Is Jared going to stay with me?"

"Yes, Anabel," I said. "I'll be here."

"Don't leave," she murmured.

"Wouldn't dream of it," I promised.

She smiled then, and she was asleep.

So Matt left, and I was alone with my thoughts and the sleeping Anabel. Her mass of hair was spread across the pillow and she shifted around a couple times, but mostly she lay there quietly. I sat there for hours, thinking about her, thinking about the baby, thinking about the sorry state of affairs this had all boiled down to. It was hard to be mad at her while watching her sleep.

Then I realized she was staring at me. "Jared?"

"How are you feeling?"

"I'm okay. Wh—wh—what's going on?" she asked between yawns. "What time is it?"

"It's about 3 p.m. You gave us quite a scare."

She blinked, confused. "We're at the hospital, aren't we?"

"Yeah, they wanted to keep you for observation and make sure your fluids were okay. You haven't been drinking enough water, according to the doctor."

She frowned. "That doesn't make any sense. I drink all sorts of water." Her hand rested on her stomach. "So Emma's going to be okay?"

"Yes, but no strenuous activity, and you need to keep your temper under control. I think the doctor suggested bed rest for a week or two."

Anabel laughed. "I'll sign up for anger management right away." She snuggled back down under her blankets. "So what, are you on babysitting duty?"

"Yes, Matt should be here soon to relieve me." I tried to keep my voice light, but she stretched out her hand to me. I took it, and then I asked her the question that I needed to know. "So what's going on with you and Matt?"

She hesitated.

"Something changed with you two last night, didn't it?" I asked her.

"Jared," she sighed. "I don't want to hurt you in all of this, truly I don't."

"You aren't really the one with motives here, Anabel. Matt and your brother are."

She looked affronted. "So what, you think this is all an act? Keep Anabel away from Jared?"

"You need to relax," I soothed. "While I think that's your brother's motivation, I do believe that Matt cares about you. That doesn't make it any easier for me, is all."

"I am sorry," she stated. "I never mean for these things to happen."

"You meant for you and me to happen," I pointed out, half expecting an angry retort.

But she looked thoughtful. "Yes, I suppose I did. I just wanted things to be different." She bit her lip. "Just so you know, Sam keeps insisting that the only reason I still talk to you is I have some case of Stockholm Syndrome, but that's not it at all." Then came her sad smile. "But you're right; I wanted something to happen with us. So I suppose you could say I got my way."

"Did he go after you?" I had to know.

"No," she admitted, "he treated me like you did, but worse. I've never met anyone who was less interested in me. I guess I just cannot stand the lack of concern—although you at least seemed like you cared about my plight. Matt seems to feel like I got myself this far..." She trailed off.

"So what happened?"

She looked away from me. "I realized last night that I'm in love with him. So I told him."

I exhaled. "And what did he say?"

"He told me he felt the same. And I believe him," she added.

"If he told you that, I'm sure it's the truth," I said, defeated.

Her eyes filled with compassion. "I am sorry, Jared. I really tried, I just couldn't help it." She shook her head. "This is ridiculous. At some point I need to start taking responsibility for my actions. I can't keep saying I couldn't help it, because I guess I could. I just didn't want to."

I gave her an empty smile. "I don't fault you."

"But you fault him. Really, Jared, he's spent so much time criticizing me, I can assure you, he wasn't making an effort to sweep me off my feet."

"And that did it for you, huh?" I tried to joke.

Her eyes fastened on me. "Oh Jared, I've never been in love before now," she explained. "Quite honestly, he is right. I have spent far too much time whining and complaining and getting everyone else to do everything for me. Everyone has walked around me as if on eggshells, and Matt is the first person to treat me like a normal human being." She shifted onto her side. "I know you can't possibly understand, but it feels so refreshing to have someone wholly unconnected to this whole business with my father."

"I think I do understand," I told her.

She nodded, looking serious. "So as to where this leaves you and me, well."

"There never was a you and me," I finished for her.

"I still care a great deal about you," she reassured me. "I just think maybe it might be good for me to be with Matt." She sighed. "You know, I don't even know what's going on right now, the moment I have Emma he might run away from me."

"Yes, but you're following your own advice," I pointed out. "You told me not to wait for you because you didn't know when you'd be able to handle anything between us, and you told me that if I saw fit to see someone else I should."

"I did not expect to be the one seeing people." Anabel stretched, looking groggy. "I think I ought to go back to sleep."

I smiled at her. "I'll watch you."

"Won't take your eyes off of me?" she teased.

"There's no one else I would rather look at."

She beamed at me then. "I'm sorry I'm not much company. I guess I really do need the rest."

"I will see you on my next shift then. I'll bring Meghan, if you like."

"Oh, yes please," she murmured, but her eyes were closed and in a few moments she was out again. I pushed a few hairs out of her sleeping face and thought. At least she did not say everything was over between us.

Chapter 41—Anabel

When I awoke again he was there. I knew it before I even opened my eyes. I wondered how I should play this.

Of course he beat me to the punch. "I know you're awake."

I opened my eyes and smiled. "What time is it?"

"About six," Matt replied. "Jared left not that long ago, and they've agreed to let me sleep in your room tonight." He gestured toward a cot that had materialized.

"I think I'm hungry."

"I figured as much. You haven't eaten all day. I got you something from the restaurant down the street, I wasn't about to let you have what I saw some poor unfortunate soul getting earlier." He gestured to some heat wrapped plates, which I dug into greedily.

"So what are the doctors saying?" I asked, after I demolished everything.

"They are talking with Sam now. I think they will probably be in here in a couple minutes to check on you."

"He's here?"

"One of your many visitors. The local news got wind that you're here," he grimaced.

I groaned. "Great. You'd better bring my hair and makeup people, I'm sure I look a fright."

"Do you even wear makeup?"

"No, Jonathan didn't care for it, and now I'm just too lazy to bother," I admitted, sitting back on my pillows.

"You don't need it," he commented. This caused me to grin ear to ear and I was positively radiant when my brother, Kevin, and some other people I did not know walked in.

"Hi Sam! Hi Kevin!" I was very happy to see them.

"Annie!" My brother enveloped me in a hug.

"Miss Martin, I'm Dr. Corddry, I've been overseeing you today," said one of the men in a white coat. "I think we can probably release you tomorrow evening, but I want to keep you overnight and the morning for observation. The baby is fine, and you should be able to resume your normal activities. If you start spotting again, however, we'll more than likely have to put you on bed rest." He glanced at his clipboard. "Also, you need to do whatever you can to remain calm, and keep any emotional outbursts under control."

"Why, Dr. Corddry, you've been watching me on the news," I grinned.

He didn't seem amused. "Mr. Moore has been granted permission to stay the night in a cot here, and I just need you to sign a few forms."

After I finished that, Kevin sat down next to me. "You should've called me first, you know."

I sighed. "I'm sorry. I was scared and I wasn't thinking."

He nodded. "It's not easy, Annie, but you're okay. Keep resting, but you'll have to keep doing exercises to keep your blood flowing, okay?"

I nodded. "I figured as much. I've been stretching and everything in between naps."

"Good girl," he approved. "I'll come help them discharge you tomorrow, and get you home, and we'll work on a care plan for you." He got up to leave.

"Oh Kevin?" I called. "Give my love to Meghan."

His face reddened. "I don't know what you're talking about," he grinned.

"How silly of me." I smiled back, glad to see that he seemed happy. He walked out.

"What was that all about?" my brother asked.

"Kevin and Meghan are an item," I told him. "I have this matchmaking business going on."

Sam rolled his eyes at me. "This is what you do with your time? I should never have let you move out."

I scoffed, and he patted my arm. "You scared me, Anabelly."

I blushed. "Don't call me that." I glanced at Matt, who looked amused.

"Why? It's just me and Matt here. It's not like you're trying to impress Jared anymore."

"Yes, Anabelly," Matt agreed. "It's just us."

"I'm not trying to impress Jared," I muttered, making a mental note to beat Matt the moment Sam left.

"I really think that you have—"

"I do not have Stockholm Syndrome!" I cut him off.

"It's just, honey, I can't figure out any other reason that you would want anything to do with Jared."

"I just want him to be Emma's dad. That's it," I hoped I was making myself clear.

Sam looked surprised. "So you're not—"

I rolled my eyes heavenward. "It just wasn't him, okay?"

Then he looked suspicious. He looked at Matt, and then at me. Then he smiled a knowing smile. "I see."

"You don't see anything," I snapped.

"Of course not, Annie." He turned to Matt. "So you know I'll kill you if you hurt her, right?"

"Yeah, I know," replied Matt. "So I won't."

I buried my head into the pillow. "This isn't happening," I groaned.

"Because I like you," Sam continued. "But I have people..."

I threw my pillow at him. "Aren't visiting hours over?"

"I should go," Sam admitted. "But I like this. This is good, Anabel." He kissed me on the cheek. "Goodnight."

"'Night," I muttered.

"So that went better than expected," commented Matt, after Sam shut the door.

"I'm fairly mortified," I replied.

"I figured he'd lose it at me," Matt admitted.

"Whatever. He totally wanted me to be with you," I noted with a smile.

"So what now?"

"You need to get some sleep," he ordered.

I groaned. "Matt, all I've been doing is sleeping. Can't we at least talk, or something?"

He sat down next to me. "Alright, scoot over." I made room for him on my hospital bed. He stroked my head and I leaned into him, grateful for his presence. He smelled nice.

"Did you shower?"

"Yes, the rest of us like to shower, Anabel," he cracked.

I ignored that. "So are you going to take me out of here tomorrow?"

"Yes. I despise hospitals. I think Jared will be here too, so we'll get you out of here and back home as soon as possible. I think it will do you good to have the weekend to rest."

Oh, right. Tomorrow was Friday. "I keep losing time," I mused.

"Yes, I've never met anyone with as much of a predilection for calamity as you."

"You got that one right," I muttered. "Maybe at some point my life will slow down and be normal."

"So what are you going to do when all of this is over?"

"You mean the hearings?"

"The hearings, the baby..." He stopped.

"Yes, the baby." Now was as good a time as any. "We probably should talk about the baby."

"What about her?" he asked, putting his hand on my stomach. "Aside from the fact that your back will be very grateful when she's out."

"Well, that's just it, she's coming out at some point. Matt, I'm about to give birth to another man's child, you must have some opinion about that."

"Hey, there is something I need to tell you." He sounded serious. "Let's say, Anabel, down the road, we decide to stay together."

"Okay," I played along. I could go for this idea.

"Well, there's something I didn't tell you about my brother. He has hemophilia." He took my hand. "While the disease isn't fatal, it's awful, and part of why Scott resents me so much."

"Because he has it and you don't?" I mulled that one over.

Matt sighed. "It was rough for him, growing up. Thankfully he escaped his blood transfusions without getting a horrible disease, which wasn't the case with a lot of boys from his generation."

"So you don't want kids?" I asked. "Is that the point of this?"

"It's not that I don't, but there are a lot of genetic diseases that run in my family. I have to consider that."

I touched his arm. "Things are easier nowadays. It's not ideal, but people with these diseases can live their lives."

"I know," he said. "But for right now, Anabel, I don't want to even think about it. But it doesn't really matter. The point that I'm trying to make is, if you did decide, down the road, that you wanted to stay with me, at least I know that you did get the chance to have a child."

I kissed him. "I love you."

"So now you know all my deep dark secrets." His arm tightened around me.

I leaned against him. "And you know all of mine."

"Except one," he noted. "I need you to tell me something."

"What's that?"

"I want you to tell me what happened the night your father died."

"Oh, that," I sighed. "Really?"

"I need to know, Anabel."

I knew what he meant. "You want to know if anything else happened with Jared. I can assure you it did not."

He paused. "Wow, I need to be careful, or everyone will be in the know on how I feel."

I laughed a little.

"Alright, well he told you how we got out of the building, before he and

I got all mad at each other."

"And he kissed you," Matt reminded me.

"Yes, and he kissed me." I closed my eyes, and then I was back in the jungle.

Being around Jared was painful. I couldn't bear to look at his face, but every step he took toward me caused me to involuntarily shudder. I kept quickening my pace, but my body and soul both ached. The knowledge that Jonathan was dead—well, I couldn't even begin to think about that. I knew that, like it or not, Jared had come and made sure I got out of the building; I had to take us the rest of the way.

I clutched my copy of *Emma*. "We can't be far."

"That's pretty genius of your father, to have the map in a book where no one would think to look," came Jared's attempt to make conversation.

"Yup," I acknowledged, refusing to look at him. I didn't think I owed my rapist any small talk.

"Anabel," he began.

"Let's not talk unless necessary, okay?" I lifted up a palm frond. "We don't know if there is anyone out here, and I don't want to jeopardize anyone else's life. Even if it is yours."

He fell silent after that, and I was grateful for it. I did not know how to feel. The numbness that had seeped into my bones had been untouched by the news that my father was dead, but I was confused by Jared rescuing me. God only knows what would have happened to me if someone else had come upon me. I looked skyward and silently asked why, oh why, was this my lot in life?

Of course looking skyward caused me to miss an upended tree root, which caused me to fall and twist my ankle and emit a cry. "Oh no," I moaned. I had heard a sickening crack when I landed—that couldn't be good.

Jared was at my side. "Let me help you."

"NO!" I shrank away from him. "No, don't touchhhh," I groaned as I pulled myself up against the tree. "I think it's broken." I did my best to blink back the tears that were forming, but he noticed them anyway.

He nodded. "Look, I understand you don't trust me right now, and that's understandable, but we've got to get you somewhere safe. Will you allow me to carry you?"

"Like I have a choice," I spat venomously.

Without a word he scooped me up. Oh, how awkward was this? Craning my neck and making an extraordinary effort to make sure as little of my body was touching him as possible, I consulted the map. "Alright, the river is coming up; it should be on the opposite side behind that piling of rocks."

"We'll have to wade through the water," he told me.

I attempted to ignore my pain and focus. "It's only a couple feet deep here, we should be okay. If you need me to I can walk if you support me."

"I'll be fine," he declared. "Don't you worry."

"That is all I do when I'm around you," I muttered. He stiffened, but to his credit, did not give in to my belligerence and made it deftly through the lake. He carried me to the pilings and supported me while I entered the passcode. One of them moved aside and, supporting myself, I made it in. I looked up at Jared. "So, this is The Safe House."

He shook his head "Jonathan never left anything to chance, did he?"

"No," I heard my voice say. "No, he did not."

"Why were you in the attic? I found you by pure chance."

"I don't remember," I admitted. "Jonathan and I had an argument, and I went to my room, but other than that, I don't know." I was still reeling. "I told him about, um, last night."

Jared looked shocked. "Really?"

"Don't worry. He didn't blame you." I tasted the bitterness in my mouth.

Jared looked torn, and seemed to struggle for something to say. "Thank God you weren't in your bedroom," he muttered finally. "We would have lost you, too."

I decided to ignore this, and I hobbled into the room.

It wasn't much, but it wasn't supposed to be. It was a collection of three small rooms, a bathroom, a refrigerator, and some canned food. Jared pushed the button to close it behind us and I limped over to the couch and elevated my foot. "Jared, there is ice in the freezer, I hope, so if you could make a compress for my foot that would be great."

"Of course," he leapt into action. There was a silence as I sat on the couch, staring at my poor broken foot (which was already sustaining substantial bruising). Concentrate on this, Annie, I told myself. If you focus on this you will easily forget the more pressing matters of your situation, such as the fact that your father is dead, you yourself were almost killed, and (and this is the worst part, really) the person who saved you from an almost certain death is the last person in the world who you want anywhere near you at the moment. To make matters worse, you had to go and be absolutely clumsy and fall to the ground and break your foot, and let him rescue you again.

"Why?" I spat.

"What?" he asked, putting the compress on my foot.

"Ohhh," I moaned. My eyes watered again. "Why did you come find me? They probably would have killed you, too."

"I didn't think about that," he admitted.

"How did it happen?" I asked.

"What?" he asked.

"You know what." I was impatient. "Don't try and spare my feelings. Just tell me how it happened."

He sighed. "I don't know, Anabel. I walked into his office because I wanted to tell him about what I had done to you, and I saw him on the floor, with blood spilling out underneath. He had been shot."

"I see." Tears were forming again.

He looked at me with pity in his eyes. "I'm so sorry."

I shook my head. "So he was...he was..." I felt so helpless. "He was alone."

He nodded, still looking at me with concerned eyes.

All I could do was stare at the floor. My father was dead. I could not feel a thing. I should feel sadness, but I did not. I should be scared, but I was not. I was empty. This emptiness, this loneliness—it gave me the courage to look Jared squarely in the eyes and say, "Here is what is going to happen."

He looked at me. "There is a satellite phone in the bottom drawer of the desk. I don't know if it has battery, we may have to charge it. I need you to get that for me."

He sprang up and found the sat phone, but grimaced and said, "It's out of battery. I'll plug it in."

I nodded. "It will take at least an hour to charge. Plug it in and then come back over here."

He did, watching me with unease. "Thank you for saving my life," I said.

"Oh Anabel, I am so sorry about everything, I really, truly am." He knelt next to me, the picture of contrition.

"Jared, I don't care." There was no point in lying.

"I don't blame you." I caught a trace of bitterness.

"Good. I do not want to talk to you. In an hour we will try my brother. In the meantime, I am going to read my book," I held up *Emma*, "and I would appreciate it if you would leave me alone."

He looked at me, about to protest, but then I think he saw the seriousness in my eyes. "Alright then." And he stared at the wall, and I read.

Maybe that seems cold, I don't know. But something kicked in with me that day. I had to do something normal. I knew that if I did not read my book I would go down that dangerous road of thinking about things, and having Jared in the room was too much for me. Being in his presence shook me to my very core, and I told myself that I would ignore him.

But then I couldn't concentrate. He was there, pacing about the room, shifting his feet, looking nervous, letting out little sighs. You couldn't ignore Jared, especially if he didn't want you to. This whole act that he was putting on was clearly to get my attention, and it was working. I threw my book down in frustration. "Will you knock it off already?"

"I'm sorry, Anabel. I just can't handle this as calmly as you."

"I'm not calm. I'm just practical. There's nothing to be done until I talk to my brother."

"Right, then all of our problems will be solved," he shot back.

So that's what this was all about. "Look, you don't have to worry; I'm not going to tell Sam. You'll still...have a job," I finished.

He shook his head. "I'm resigning."

I narrowed my eyes. "I just told you that you don't have to. I don't see any reason to tell my brother. He's going to be stressed out enough as it is."

"That is far more than I deserve," he told me. "I don't have an excuse for what I did. All I can tell you is that I am so sorry."

"Stop. Just stop," I demanded. "We are not going to talk about that, understand me?"

He hesitated. "Have you stopped bleeding?"

I stared at him, incredulous. "As far as I know."

"Okay, good." He sounded relieved. He stopped again. "You should get that checked out when we get out of here."

Was he serious? "If it's all the same to you, I think I'll keep this to myself. I don't need the world finding out that I'm the latest notch on Jared Sorensen's bedpost."

"It wasn't like that," he protested.

I steeled myself. "I can't talk about this with you."

"I never wanted to hurt you," he said.

"Oh, for crying out loud." I was disgusted. "Let it go. Let's just move on, okay?"

"But Anabel, I want to make this right, somehow."

"You can't, you just can't." I looked down, searching for something to say. "This isn't something you can fix. It just doesn't work that way."

"Come on, there must be something I can do." He was pleading with me now, and way too close to me.

"Please move away from me!" My heart was racing and I could feel a panic attack coming on.

He moved and sat in one of the chairs. "Well, can we at least talk?"

"I cannot think of anything we could possibly chat about, but if you want to make an effort, go ahead," I informed him.

"I did come rescue you," he pointed out.

"Yes, and I thanked you. Forgive me if I did not immediately throw myself into your arms and tell you how you were my hero. It's not really my deal." My foot was in serious pain, and my temper was very thin.

He frowned. "This isn't like you."

"Maybe you forgot this, Jared, but I did just lose my closest family member. Hours ago. I am not quite myself, so please excuse me." Wincing, I readjusted myself on the couch. "Look, I haven't eaten all day and am starving. There should be some sort of canned something in that cupboard and I think there is some aspirin in the medicine cabinet, could you please get that for me? With a glass of water?"

Jared nodded and found some canned peaches for me to eat, but no pain relief, which made me even crankier. I gently turned over my beautiful, leather bound edition of *Emma*. It had been a gift for my sixteenth birthday, a second edition. Wistfully, I thought of a rare happy moment for me and my father, when he had presented me with it. "It is gorgeous!" I had proclaimed. "A second edition! Daddy, how did you find it?"

"I have my ways," he had smiled at me. "If you love a book, you should have a beautiful copy of it."

Later, when we were in private, he showed me the back cover. It had a pocket where you could store documents, and in my book, he had included a map of how to get to where I was currently hiding with Jared. "You never know, Anabel," he instructed, "you always must be prepared."

I turned to the inscription. "To my Anabel, on her sixteenth birthday. May you always have the good fortune and happiness of Emma Woodhouse, with a bit more sense." Then I remembered our last exchange, and tears burned in my eyes.

"Anabel?"

"Please, please, I cannot talk about this right now," I begged, my voice quavering. "I really—I just—I can't," I finished lamely.

"I'll try the phone," he announced. "Who should I call first?"

"Sam. I need my brother now."

He called Sam's direct line and my brother answered, worried sick about me. He had been trying to call me for hours with no response. When Jared handed me the phone I told him that in no uncertain terms that I would not disclose my location to anyone but him and that he was going to have to come and get me.

So Jared and I waited the whole night together, eating canned food and not really talking too much. I feigned sleep, but kept my eyes on him at all times. I didn't trust him, and even though he sounded repentant, I wasn't about to let my guard down. For his part, Jared spent the majority of the time fiddling with the radio, flipping through old magazines, and attempting to make me talk to him. He was not successful on that last part.

"When Sam arrived on the island, I gave him directions and he personally carried me out of there," I explained to Matt. "He's a good man, my brother."

"Yes he is. Married to that horrible shrew of a woman, but still," he replied.

"Why do you hate Alexis?" I was starting to feel drowsy again.

"She has it out for you," he remarked. "Also, I suspect she's cheated on your brother."

I was awake now. "Are you serious?"

"I just need to get the guy to admit it." I didn't like his tone of voice, and I knew who he was thinking of.

"But Jared hates Alexis, and she him," I commented. I began to imitate her. "I cannot stand that man, Anabel, what on earth were you thinking?"

He laughed. "Stranger things have happened in this town."

"I can't believe that of Jared. Although..." I sighed. "I know what Jared is capable of, and whether he wants to admit it or not, he has done some rather despicable things."

"When I think of him with his hands on you, it makes me want to kill him," Matt said, with an intensity that startled me.

"Look, I don't have fond memories of the night Emma was conceived, after all."

"It's hard for me, Anabel."

"I understand that," I told him.

"I love you," he kissed me.

"I love you, too," I smiled. "Will you read me to sleep?"

He pulled out The Bonfire of the Vanities. "Oh good," I said, "will you do voices?"

Chapter 42—Jared

When I got to the hospital the next morning, she was already awake and smiling. "Hi Jared!"

"Hey, Anabel." I nodded at Matt, who didn't look like he had slept very much.

"I'm going back to your house," he told her.

"Okay," she said. He gave her a terse kiss goodbye, which managed to leave her radiant after he left. Then she turned to me. "How's it going?"

"Good." I sat down. "How did you sleep?"

"Ugh, fine. All I do is sleep," she replied. She sat back in the bed. "Look, I have to tell you, I told Matt last night about the rest of the night when my father died."

I stared at her, unsure of what to say. She shrugged. "Look, we were going to have to hash it out anyway, and he asked me, so I told him."

"I see," I pulled the chair closer to her.

"I know you haven't been pleased with me, Jared, and I understand that, but we have to put this past us. You and I...we've been through a lot, you know? I really want us to be friends." She sounded earnest.

Now I looked at her with disbelief. "I don't know where you come up with this stuff."

"What do you mean?"

"Let's review your activities recently, shall we? One minute, you're kissing me in your brother's living room, then you're flirting with your bodyguard, then you're kissing me again—"

"You kissed me, that last time," she pointed out. "I did not kiss you back."

I quickly reviewed the moment in my mind, and...she was right. She hadn't kissed me back. I sat back in my chair, shaking my head.

She sighed. "I'm sorry."

"I think it's best if we don't talk," I muttered.

She gave me a sad little smile. "I remember saying the very same thing to you."

And I was reminded yet again of what I had done to her, and I was shamed into silence.

"I need you to not be mad at me," she pleaded.

"It's hard to be mad at you when you're all pitiful in your hospital bed," I offered.

"There's the Jared I know! Much better." Anabel leaned forward. "Look, it's just..." She searched for words. "I guess a lot of people around me, I view in black and white, you know?"

"What do you mean?"

"Well," she continued, "it's like, who's good and bad, you know? Like I see Sam as a good person, Matt as a good person, your sister as a good person." She stopped.

"Alexis not so much?"

She laughed a little. "She really hates me, doesn't she?"

"I don't see why," I said.

"You know what the weird thing is? We were actually quasi-getting along for a little bit there, before I started telling everyone about the baby." She paused. "Maybe that's it. Maybe it's the embarrassment I caused. But anyway, the point is everyone else I see in black and white. But not you."

"And how do you see me?"

"You're like me," she smiled. "You're somewhere in the gray. And like I can deal with all of my faults and failings, I can deal with yours."

"So you see me like you see yourself? That's hardly a fair comparison," I protested.

"Maybe so. But I think maybe being with Matt...someone who's not in the gray...might make me a little less...dark," she explained.

"So we're too alike?"

"In certain ways, yes," she agreed.

"Wow." And once again, she had me at a loss.

She looked thoughtful. "It's rather a breakthrough for me, to admit that. Isn't that exciting? I think I'm making some progress."

"It would be exciting if the mother of my child wanted to raise my daughter with me," I retorted.

She sighed. "What do you want me to do, Jared? What do you want me to say? I can't just make my feelings magically change."

"No, but you could give us a chance," I argued.

"Why?" Now she was wide-eyed. "Give me a good reason, Jared, one that does not involve Emma, and I will consider it. But you have to give me a darn good reason, and telling me you love me just does not cut it."

"You are different, Anabel, just so different from any other woman I've ever been with. I care about you so much. I was scared out of my wits when I thought you might be dead. I spent months trying to contact you, and now that we are actually talking, I am afraid to leave you because I worry that you won't be here when I come back."

She smiled at me. "Oh Jared, you gave me a cell phone, remember? You can always contact me now."

"Matt hates me. It's only a matter of time before he sways you to his side."

"Matt goes out of his way to be respectful of the fact that you and I are having a baby," she pronounced. "Also, I do not know if you have noticed this, but I have a tendency to have my own opinions, no matter how much they differ from those closest to me. Since you've known me, I totally defied my father, I haven't listened at all to my brother—the man who was once the leader of the free world— and in spite of the fact that my bodyguard does not like your presence, I still keep you around." She grinned at me and I felt the knot in my stomach unclenching.

"You still keep me around, huh?" As usual, it was hard to be mad at her.

"Now look," she lowered her voice, "I need you to do me a favor."

"What's that?"

"Look at this food." She pointed to her untouched breakfast tray. "It's disgusting, and there is no way I can eat it. This is where you come in."

"I'm not supposed to leave you, Anabel—"

She waved a hand. "Oh please, has anything happened to me? I just want you to run down to the Burger King in the cafeteria and please bring me a Croissanwich."

"That sounds just about as disgusting as your tray of food looks," I told her.

"No, they're delightful," she sighed. "Please, Jared?" And she shot me the big blue eyes.

"Alright," I groaned, getting up.

Anabel clapped her hands. "Thank you so much."

"Just do me a favor, okay? Don't tell Matt about this," I warned her. "He'll kill me."

Anabel was the picture of innocence. "Of course not. I'd like some hash browns as well. Oh, and a glass of orange juice."

"I take it you're over your morning sickness."

"Jared, I'm so hungry," she wailed.

So against my better judgment, against Matt's warning, I left her.

Chapter 43—Anabel

It was way too easy to manipulate Jared. I shook my head at the thought. I sat up in my bed and started to pull my hair into a braid. It was greasy, and I briefly contemplated how much I desperately needed a shower.

After Jared had been gone for about ten minutes the door swung open, and I was about to greet the nurse when I realized that it wasn't her at all. It was someone whose presence made me very uneasy. She closed the door, and then I was face to face with Alexis. She quietly entered the room and came to stand next to me. "Hello, Anabel."

"Hi, Alexis," I stammered. "I have to say, you were the last person that I expected to come visit me."

She cocked her beautiful head, and glanced around the room. "This isn't a social call. It's a business one." I did not like her tone at all.

"What do you mean?" I felt a slight adrenaline rush, and I wanted to be anywhere but here. Alone with Alexis.

"You understand why I'm here, don't you, Anabel?" She eyed me speculatively. "You and I have never gotten along, so I'm not going to play at pleasantries with you. Besides, we don't have a lot of time."

"Time? For what?" I squeaked.

"You've ruined my life, you know" she went on, slipping on a pair of gloves. "I didn't think that it was possible that someone so…inconsequential…could do something like that. I've spent so many years worried about my enemies here, but you…in a matter of weeks you have destroyed everything." Her tone was so matter of fact; she could have been talking about the weather. "You've turned my husband against me. You've taken my children away from me. Sam and I are probably going to get a divorce."

I was shocked. "I had no idea."

"Mm," she said. It was so unnerving, she was completely emotionless. But I felt my heartbeat racing and I started to wonder if it might be a good idea to yank out my IV and run for it.

"But you know, Anabel," she continued, edging closer to me, "that's not what got me. What bothered me the most is the fact that you have taken away from me the only person who I ever truly loved."

"Alexis, I'm sorry about Sam, I—"

"Sam?" she stopped, and then laughed. A high, cruel laugh. "No, it was never Sam. I just used him to get to where I wanted to go. And then you destroyed all that we built."

"I don't understand."

"You don't have to," she returned. "He'll be back soon, won't he? He won't leave his precious Anabel alone for long." The disdain dripped from her voice, and it was then that I fully understood the depths of her hatred for me.

So I began to panic. "No, Jared will be right back."

"We haven't much time then." She gave me another icy smile. "You know, I've never done anything like this before, but to tell you the truth, I think I'm going to enjoy it, Anabel." And then she shoved me against the bed, hard.

"Alexis!" I gasped. She was pressing right on my chest. "Alexis, the baby—"

"Shh, Anabel," she whispered, taking a pillow and pressing it against my face. "It'll all be over soon."

So this was it. I was going to die. Well, I wasn't going to go without a fight. I kicked her, managing to knock Alexis away from me and against the wall, and I attempted to get myself extricated from all the medical equipment that was binding me to the bed, but I knew she was coming, and—

"Lexie," I heard a low voice say.

I looked up as she turned. "Jared?" she asked. The hatred was gone from her voice; it was now soft and gentle.

He stood in the doorway, but this wasn't a Jared I had ever seen before. His eyes, normally so cool, were full of feeling—and even compassion. "Lexie," he crooned again, in a voice that was almost a caress. "What are you doing?"

She trembled, and it dawned on me then that Alexis' biggest problem wasn't what I had done to my brother. It wasn't even that I had made a mockery of everything they stood for. Even now as she stood inches away from me, wanting to kill me, it suddenly hit me that while she had never been all that great to me, she hadn't turned nasty until that night at Blair House when she had heard Jared admit that he might be in love with me.

Because at the heart of it, while she missed the power and her status, nothing had blown Alexis away more than the fact that Jared could feel that way about me. Me. Not her.

I swallowed. That's what all of this was about. For the first time, I saw how she stared at him, her expression raw. I could feel it and, probably more than anyone else had ever been able to, I understood it.

Alexis was in love with Jared. Every emotion that manifested itself on her beautiful face betrayed that. I had never seen her like this—so weak, so tremulous and fragile. So needy.

My eyes went to Jared, and I saw he wasn't any better off than she was. His face was pained, and again, in that voice that was almost sweet, he said, "Lexie, why are you doing this?"

"She's nothing, Jared," she told him, and her voice almost broke. "She's nothing. So why her? Why her and not..." But she couldn't finish.

So Jared did it for her. "Why her and not you?" He came closer to her. "You know why. I couldn't do it to Sam."

"He hates you," she whispered, touching his arm. "He hates you, because of her. So what does it matter anymore?"

It was gut-wrenching, watching this. I watched him touch her face. "Once upon a time you loved him, you know."

"She ruined everything," she declared, and her voice hardened.

"No, it was before Anabel." Now his arm gently went to her waist. "Look, I was flattered, but I never took it seriously, and I thought you never did either. But I had to back away after that night in Vermont."

"Why?" Now she sounded like a child. Her tone was soft and pleading. "I wanted it, Jared. And you did, too."

"Of course I did," he murmured, slipping his other arm around her. "But what did you want from me? No good would have come from it."

"If you leave her," she began, reaching up to him. "If you leave her, I won't hurt her. But Charlie will. He knows she knows too much."

Charlie. Oh my gosh, Charlie had killed my dad. I gripped the rails of my bed, reeling from this knowledge.

But it didn't look like it had even registered with Jared. "Alright then, Lexie," he agreed. "I'll leave with you, right now. And I won't look back."

"Oh, Jared," she breathed and then kissed him.

Now when I kissed Jared, I was always a bit hesitant, but Alexis kissed him with complete abandon. It was all I could do to just watch and feel the electricity that passed between them. It shook me to my very core. How could I have missed it before? The chemistry between those two...

But then suddenly Jared broke apart from her, and in a flash pinned her against the wall. "Anabel," he barked. "Call security."

But I couldn't. I just stared at Alexis' face, pressed against the wall, and I saw the hurt, anger, and betrayal that overwhelmed her as she realized Jared had used her to protect me. Then I watched as everything drained out of her and she deflated, and all of the hope left her.

I know she would've killed me without a thought. But I couldn't help but feel extreme pity for her.

"Anabel!" he snapped. "Push the call button, if nothing else!"

So I did. I sat there in silence and watched the scene unfold: the nurse immediately came to my room and when she saw Alexis and Jared, called security. I watched as two police men handcuffed Alexis and led her away. I watched Jared call my brother and tell him what had happened, and I saw the pain that flashed across Jared's face at Sam's angry response.

And then we were alone, and I think Jared realized I hadn't said anything to him. "You okay?" he asked, taking a seat next to me.

"What happened in Vermont?" I whispered.

He sighed. "Your brother was in Vermont when he found out he was to assume office. He and Alexis and I celebrated, and Alexis especially drank too much." He paused.

I kept my eyes on the floor. "Okay."

"She kissed me and then apologized in front of Sam," he continued. "And then as I was leaving to go to my hotel room, she insisted on walking me out, and kissed me again." He swallowed. "I just laughed it off, especially since we had never really gotten along. I figured it was just because she was high on the alcohol."

"Jared, that sort of thing doesn't erupt from two previous kisses. Get to the point."

"After I went to bed, she came into my room." He stopped again. "Do you really want to hear this?"

I nodded mutely.

"She climbed into my bed, but—" he stopped. "But we didn't. I could never betray Sam."

"Was that the only time?" My voice was small.

"Lexie was persistent," he admitted.

"See? You even have a nickname for her." I attempted to swallow the lump that was forming in my throat.

"We never—" and he searched for a word—"consummated it, if that's what you mean." He shook his head. "Look, Anabel, I know what you've heard and what you probably think of me, but I couldn't do that to your brother. I've never slept with Alexis. And what happened between you and me stopped her from chasing me around anymore. She put me on her hate list the moment you arrived here."

"You should have told me," I whispered.

"Why? And make you think even worse of me? I didn't want to press my luck," he persisted.

"Did you love her?" I asked. "And do you still?"

"Anabel, no," he denied, trying to hold me, but I pulled away.

"Then explain to me what I just saw." Now I sat up. "I've never seen anything like that. There's something between you two."

"There's nothing between us because I would never let there be," he stated.

"But you love her."

"I've never loved anyone like I love you," he told me.

"That doesn't mean you don't love her." I met his eyes. "Jared, that—whatever that was—makes what you and I had look like nothing."

"You can't be mad at me over this. You're in love with Matt."

"Well there's a point." I swallowed again. "I can't do this."

"What can't you do?"

But I couldn't explain it to him. It all hit me at once: Jonathan was dead. I was pregnant, and my baby's father had some sort of twisted thing going on with my brother's wife. The one who wanted to kill me. Plus, Charlie had killed Jonathan. Charlie, who had claimed to love me as his own child, had murdered him in cold blood, and would've gotten me too if—

—and then I remembered everything.

After my dramatic exit from Jonathan's office, I stalked into my bedroom. I haven't done anything wrong, I thought. This wasn't my fault. It was Jared's fault. I don't deserve this, I told myself. Coming to my father, and begging him to help me, only to have him accuse me of seducing Jared—well. I was angry. More than angry, I was livid. I was sick and tired of everyone on the island. None of them cared about me. None of them loved me, not even my father.

This is no longer my home, I thought. Homes are supposed to be safe and welcoming, and there was nothing left for me here. Jonathan's rejection of me, his accusations—I realized then and there that I would never trust my father again to be there for me.

I had rarely come to Jonathan for comfort or for advice; growing up, I had always had Marilyn and my father's interest in me waxed and waned. As a child this was bewildering: one moment Daddy wanted nothing more than to spend an afternoon doing puzzles with me, and then the next day if I fell in the courtyard and scraped my knee he wouldn't come over to pick me up and kiss me and tell me that it was okay. He could never console me, I thought grimly, pacing harder. Jonathan didn't like to be around his crying daughter, he left those situations for someone else to clean up.

I had thought that Jared had broken my heart the night before, but I was wrong. He couldn't have broken it because my father had done that a long time ago. The truth was I had tried to pull it back together for Jared.

I had wanted Jared to be the one that reunited the fractured pieces of my heart, but instead he had shredded them even further.

I couldn't change the situation with Jared. But my father was my father, and I deserved better from him.

Well, so be it. I was going to give Jonathan a piece of my mind.

I had come back down the hallway toward my father's office, my thoughts turbulent. I kept asking myself the same questions over and over. How could he not defend me? For once in my life, I was going to stand up to him. He had treated me like a child for far too long, and I wanted to hurt him with my words as much as he had hurt me. Approaching the office, I hesitated a little, but then I steeled myself and approached the door. My hand was resting on the doorknob when I heard six gunshots, in rapid succession.

I gasped, and the door cracked open, and there was my father, face down on the ground, with a masked Charlie standing over him, clutching the still-smoking gun. I was frozen to the spot. "What have you done?" I whispered.

He quietly said, "I'm sorry Annie—I didn't want it to be this way." I gasped in horror, and as he slowly raised the revolver, but no shots came as my body launched into fight-or-flight mode. I ran down the hallway, toward my bedroom, but then hesitated at the door. Something told me not to go there, and instead I continued down the hallway for a long, long time, and then I raced up the coil of stairs that led to the attic and I hid, paralyzed by my fear, and I fell into practically a catatonic state until Jared came upon me.

"Anabel, say something," he pleaded, bringing me back to reality. But I couldn't do it. I was spiraling out of control, because as I looked at him, Charlie was still pointing a gun at me, and my father was dead. I had been raped. My baby's father loved somebody else, and I loved someone who would quite possibly leave me the moment she was born.

So I fell into myself.

Chapter 44—Jared

Kevin shut her bedroom door, where we were all anxiously waiting. "Let's go downstairs," he suggested.

As we sat around Anabel's living room, Kevin cleared his throat and said, "Physically, she's fine. But she's refusing to speak."

"What do you mean?" asked Matt.

He pulled out a sheet of paper that was covered in Anabel's neat handwriting. "I asked her why she wouldn't talk to me and this is what she wrote: 'I don't want to fall apart.'" He sighed. "I think Anabel's memories and what happened at the hospital are too much for her at the moment." He handed the paper to Meghan, and she and I pored over it. "You can see what she says."

I don't want to fall apart.

I don't want to see anybody.

That's not true, I have been eating. Charlotte can attest that I clean my trays.

I gave a written statement. I don't have to testify.

That's good news.

"What's good news?" Meghan asked.

"Oh, I cleared her for vaginal delivery," he announced. We all looked surprised, and he went on to say, "The heparin worked, she's not having pain anymore and she wants to do it naturally, which explains this comment." He pointed to the line that read, I guess I'll have to find someone to go to childbirth class with me.

"I'll go with her," I muttered.

Kevin pointed to the line that read, *I don't want to see him.*

"She didn't write a reason," I scanned the page.

"Does she need one?" Meghan asked. Matt looked like he agreed.

"Did you say anything to her?" Kevin asked. "Something that might have pushed her over the edge?" Charlotte, Meghan, and Matt were all looking at me, and I hesitated at Carrie's presence.

"Go upstairs, Carrie," said Phil.

She sighed and exited the room, so I said, "I told her about what happened with Alexis and me."

"You told her about Vermont?" gasped Meghan. "Why?"

"What happened in Vermont?" Charlotte asked.

"Alexis attempted to sleep with him," explained Meghan.

Matt looked at me sharply. "But didn't succeed?"

"I never slept with her," I replied. "Look, Sam was my best friend, okay? I would never have done that to him."

"Messing around with his sister fell under your code of ethics, however," he snapped.

"Oh for crying out loud, Matt, shut up," Meghan said, irritated. "You're not going to get her out of that room by provoking a fight with Jared." She folded her hands underneath her chin. "Let's focus on what we know. What exactly is running through Anabel's head right now?"

"She thinks I'm in love with Alexis." I sighed. "I don't blame her, Sam thought it too." Things had changed with us after Vermont, even though he had said he believed me that I didn't want anything to do with his wife. Our business relationship had been fine, but our personal one had become tense, and had only gotten worse after Natasha's death. I had viewed my assignment to see Anabel as a way to repair that, but I had screwed that up, too.

"Are you in love with Alexis?" Matt asked.

"No, he's not, but the two of them should never be allowed near each other," Meghan scoffed.

"Thanks for answering for me," I retorted. "Do I even need to be present for this conversation?"

"Alexis has always had a thing for my brother," she continued, ignoring me. "And Jared—whether he wants to admit it or not—plays into it. It was even before their little fiasco in Vermont. One time I watched them at a press conference and I seriously thought they were going to rip each other's clothes off right then and there."

"And this bothered Anabel?" Matt asked quietly.

"I don't think it was just that," I assessed. "I think it shook her pretty bad that Alexis was about to kill her, and then I came in and started kissing her—"

"—so it broke Annie's trust," commented Meghan thoughtfully.

"And then the poor girl remembered watching her father die," put in Charlotte.

"So it's all too much for her," finished Kevin. He turned to Matt. "Plus, there's this." He pointed to a line that read, Why? He'll probably leave. I'm not good enough for him.

"Is that really what she thinks?" He shook his head.

"She's always thought that," I replied. "She told me as much."

"Did she?" he asked, and I heard the anger in his voice.

"It was a passing comment, Matt. In the same breath she informed me that I had no chance with her while you were around." I looked at Kevin. "So what should we do?"

"Give her some space," he suggested. "Let her sort this out. She'd never do anything to cause the baby harm, and what she's been through is a lot for any person to stomach." He turned to Matt. "You can try with her, she might respond to you."

He hesitated. "I don't know. She wouldn't even answer the door earlier."

"Get creative," Charlotte urged.

"Maybe she just needs some space," suggested Phil. "Like Kevin said. She has been through a lot."

But it was killing Matt; I saw it on his face. At that moment, I had to admit to myself that this definitely was not an act— he really did love her. I watched as he stared at me, at Meghan, at Phil, and then he just nodded and slowly walked up the stairs, and we heard his door close.

Charlotte and Phil exchanged a glance, and then Charlotte said, "I made some spaghetti."

"That sounds excellent," announced Meghan. She grabbed my arm. "Come on, let's go spoon up some spaghetti for everybody."

"I'm not hungry, Meg."

"Do I look like I care?" she snapped. Then she pulled herself together. "Come on, Jared. You need to eat."

I followed her into the kitchen, and she got to the point. "What do you think you're doing?"

"What are you talking about?"

"Stop trying to ruin everything for Matt and Anabel," she ordered. "They love each other. Deal with it."

"I just told him she said there's no us with him around."

"Yeah, and that's quite charitable of you, but you also need to remember he's wondering right now about what's going on in her head after watching your little display with Alexis." Meghan sighed. "Matt's wondering if Anabel's having second thoughts, and the fact that she won't talk to him isn't helping things."

"I shoved her over the edge," I lamented.

"It was bound to happen sooner or later."

"Thank God they caught Charlie," I commented. Once news of Alexis' arrest had been leaked to the press, he had tried to make a run for it, but they caught him trying to catch a flight out of Dulles. A K9 unit had brought him down, and it had been all over the news. In confidence, Charlotte had told me that Marilyn was devastated and had called, begging to talk to Anabel, but Anabel had shoved a note under her door that read, Forget it.

"I can't believe he and Alexis were working together," remarked Meghan.

"I know," I replied. Once certain that I really had betrayed her, a broken Alexis had confessed the whole thing: Charlie had contacted her a few weeks after Anabel's arrival to the States and explained how he had murdered Jonathan—and why he thought Alexis was the person to assist him in finishing off his daughter. Alexis agreed the best way to salvage Sam's political career and keep Anabel and I apart was to get rid of her, but the chance hadn't presented itself until I had left her alone at the hospital.

And if I hadn't gotten back when I did, Anabel and Emma would both be dead. And it would have been my fault. Once Sam had gotten over the fact that Alexis had made an attempt on his sister's life, he felt the need to remind me of this fact over and over again. At least Matt had the decency to not say that right to my face.

"Did she say why he killed Jonathan in the first place?" Meghan asked.

"He thought it was the only way off the island," I told her. "He thought that if everything came out, about Caereon's existence, he could get off and be with Marilyn. But then Anabel saw what happened, and so he'd been biding his time with her. When he found out that she had been having nightmares—and I, of course, was the one who told him that," I continued, shaking my head in disgust, "he realized there wasn't much time left before she remembered."

"And Alexis offered to do it," she whispered.

"I had no idea she felt that much for me," I replied.

"I did, but I didn't factor in the dose of crazy that accompanied it," Meghan shook her head. "What a mess, Jared. Well, look at it this way. At some point Princess will run out of paper."

"I'm pretty sure it's over now," I stated. "Whatever chance I did have. She's been holed up in her room for three days. She won't talk to me."

"Or Matt," Meghan pointed out. "What do you think that means?"

"I don't know for him, but I know what it means for me," I said.

Strike three.

Chapter 45—Anabel

I couldn't talk, and nobody understood why.

I know that they didn't understand because they kept knocking at my door.

"Anabel, it's Charlotte, dear. I'm leaving your tray and some water outside. Make sure you take your vitamin."

And then: "Hi Annie! It's Meghan. Just wondered if you wanted to go for a walk."

A very pained voice said, "It's Jared." And then nothing.

A few times Matt knocked, and for those I actually went to the door. But even for him, I couldn't find the words.

Everything hurt too much.

So every day I took a shower and washed my hair. I would comb it and dry it, and then I would check Emma's kicks to make sure she was moving around properly. I would eat my breakfast and do some prenatal yoga.

Then I lay in my bed, lost in thought, getting up every hour to stretch my legs and do my exercises. Occasionally someone would knock and ask something that required a response, so I would write them a note and shove it under the door.

Twice Kevin had showed up and I permitted him to come into the room and check me out, listen to Emma's heartbeat, and ask me questions, the answers to which I wrote down for him. Most of the time I would write down the answers to questions I knew he was going to ask me in advance, and I would hand the paper to him and his visits were short.

I was being selfish. I knew this. But I didn't want to see any of them. I didn't want to see Jared, because I couldn't get the image of him kissing Alexis out of my mind. I didn't want to see my brother, because I knew he must be devastated. I didn't want to see Meghan's caring eyes, or Charlotte's compassionate smile.

However, I desperately wanted to see Matt, but I couldn't summon the courage.

It was November, and I was ridiculously pregnant. I was now so round that I couldn't stand myself. I felt puffy and swollen and as much as I loved my little girl, I was not a happy camper.

On the seventh day of my self-imposed exile, I heard a knock at the door. I heard Charlotte's voice call, "Breakfast, Anabel." I waited about a minute, and then I opened the door and came face to face with Matt.

"Hi, sweetheart," he greeted me.

I bit my lip and stared at him, shaking my head.

He bent over and picked up my tray. "Listen, I know you don't feel like talking right now."

I nodded cautiously.

"But I thought maybe, if it was okay with you, I could read to you. Would that be alright?"

I wanted to say no, I really did. I wanted to tell him to get far away from me because I would ruin his life. I wasn't what he deserved—he deserved someone who was at least somewhat sane.

But my feelings for him overwhelmed me, and I nodded and stepped back.

He carried my tray into my room, and I almost smiled when I saw what he had brought. It was a beautiful leather-bound version—just like one I had had on Caereon—of *Alice in Wonderland* and *Through the Looking Glass*. The book's presence made me think of a conversation we had once had.

We were headed to a hearing and had been riding in silence when I got annoyed. "Why won't you talk to me?" I had asked.

"On what particular subject would you like to converse?" he had asked lazily, taking a turn in the truck. "Shoes and ships and sealing wax?"

"No," I had rejoined with a smile. "Cabbages and kings."

"Excellent. Then we can discuss next why the sea is boiling hot."

"And whether pigs have wings," I had finished. Then I had spontaneously kissed him on the cheek. "You're fun sometimes. When you're not being a total jerk."

His hand flew to his face, and then he grinned at me. "You're fun sometimes, too."

It was that memory that gave me the courage to drop onto my bed and eat my pancakes and cantaloupe while Matt sat down in the armchair and read to me for two hours. Then he closed the book and asked, "Is it alright if I come back tomorrow?"

I had nodded, and he stood up. "Is there anything I can get you?"

I shook my head.

"Tomorrow at breakfast, then," he promised, and showed himself out.

This continued for several days. We finished *Alice* and then moved on to *Harry Potter*, and he read to me for increasingly longer periods of time. When he got to the part about the three-headed dog, I thought I caught a twinkle in his eye, but then it went away and we finished *Sorcerer's Stone*.

The following day I wondered what book he would bring next, and he carried my breakfast tray in along with a small binder. "I thought we'd do something different today," he announced.

I looked at him.

"You haven't said a word to me in over two weeks, Anabel," he commented. "That hurts more than I can say."

I scrambled for a pen, but he placed his hand over mine. "Let me finish."

I nodded again and sat back on the bed.

"I thought about what I wanted to say to you, how I could comfort you, but I know that nothing I say will make you feel any less than what you currently do," he continued. "I wish you would let me be there for you, but since you won't, I need to find out something."

I pursed my lips together and tugged on my hair. "Don't do that, sweetheart," he implored again. So I took a deep breath and met his eyes, and he went on, "Just let me read to you, okay? And if you can't say anything to this, then I doubt you'll have anything to say to me ever again, and I'll leave you alone."

So I sat there, and a smile spread across my face when he read Buttercup's speech to Westley, proclaiming her love for him. When he finished with the door slamming in Buttercup's face I looked at him, my eyes full of meaning, but he then launched into Shakespeare's *116th Sonnet*. Then he read to me the discourse between Emma and Mr.

Knightley as the two of them realized they were in love with each other. And just when I thought he had outdone himself, he launched into this:

"I can listen no longer in silence. I must speak to you by such means as are within my reach. You pierce my soul. I am half agony, half hope. Tell me not that I am too late, that such precious feelings are gone forever. I offer myself to you again with a heart even more your own than when you almost broke it, eight years and a half ago. Dare not say that man forgets sooner than woman, that his love has an earlier death. I have loved none but you. Unjust I may have been, weak and resentful I have been, but never inconstant. You alone have brought me to Bath. For you alone, I think and plan. Have you not seen this? Can you fail to have understood my wishes? I had not waited even these ten days, could I have read your feelings, as I think you must have penetrated mine. I can hardly write. I am every instant hearing something which overpowers me. You sink your voice, but I can distinguish the tones of that voice when they would be lost on others. Too good, too excellent creature! You do us justice, indeed. You do believe that there is true attachment and constancy among men."

Then he stopped and looked at me, begging me with his eyes to speak. I opened my mouth, and willed myself to be strong. Taking a deep breath, I managed, "Have you even read *Persuasion*?"

"My mom made me," he admitted, sitting next to me. "In case I ever needed to bring out the big guns with a girl."

"Matt," I began.

"It's good to hear your voice," he cut me off. "It sounds a bit out of tune."

"I suppose it would."

"Why won't you talk to me?"

"Because I love you," I told him. "But I don't know if we can make this work."

"Why?"

"Well, for starters, I'm having a baby in eight weeks," I pointed out. "One that isn't yours." I stretched my legs out.

"That doesn't bother me," he replied.

I looked into his eyes, probing. "You sure about that?"

"It did at first," he admitted. "But Emma's a part of you. And I love all of you."

Why was he so good? I looked away. "There's another big problem."

"What, honey? Tell me, and we'll fix it." He sounded sincere.

"I can't have sex with you." I flushed and looked down.

Now he put his arm around me. "Never?"

"Well, no, not never. "But I don't know when I'll be ready." I sighed. "If I'll be ready."

"So you think that's a problem?" he asked.

I met his eyes. "I'm not stupid, Matt. I know it's probably a deal breaker."

He nodded, and we sat there in silence. Then he finally said, "Not all of us are like Jared, you know."

"You aren't like him at all," I responded. "But that's not it." Then I paused. "I have to tell you, I'm starting to wonder if there are any women in the DC area he hasn't slept with."

"He didn't sleep with Alexis."

"You should have seen them," I shuddered. "I felt like I was intruding."

"So you think he loves her? Is that it?" I couldn't read Matt, but I figured I may as well be honest.

"No," I admitted. "But she loves him. I know it, because she kissed him the same way I kiss you." I started to wring my hands. "That's what killed me, Matt. And I think that's what would happen if Jared and I were ever together. It would always be one-sided." I searched for words to try and explain. "He was completely convincing with her. So how do I know that it wasn't all an act with me, you know?"

"He's devastated that you won't see him," he confided. "I haven't had the heart to tell him I've been spending time with you, even though you wouldn't say anything to me."

"He just doesn't get it." Now I started chewing on my nails. "Here's my problem. We had this conversation where even though I told him I loved you, I got the impression he still had feelings for me, and then I saw him with her. And it just took everything out of me, because that just twisted me up inside. Why did it have to be Alexis?" I moaned.

"What are you saying, Anabel?"

"I'm saying that's why it's so hard for me," I explained. "Facing him, it's too much. I know why he did it, but they have something, Matt. Something real. Like what you and I have."

He rubbed my arm. "I know, honey. I know."

"I know how much you love me," I told him. "I really do. But I also know that I can't give you what you deserve." I sighed. "It will take me a really long time to get to a place where I can do that, and it's not fair for me to ask that of you."

"Anabel," he said. "Sweetheart, I've never had any expectations from you in that regard."

I looked at him sharply. "You haven't?"

"No, honey," he soothed, stroking my face. "Look, you are right in that it is a deal breaker, but not now, not any time close to now. Down the road sometime. But you need to recover emotionally before we even try to go there." He pulled me to him. "Is that really what all of this was about?"

"Just with you," I almost laughed. "I can't talk to my brother because his life is in shambles because of me. I can't talk to Charlotte because she'll ask me a million questions. And I can't talk to Jared because he broke me again."

He pulled away from me then, and put his hands on my shoulders. "Look at me, Anabel." As I met his eyes, he sighed. "Let's not stray from the subject, okay?"

I nodded again.

"I haven't forgotten that you're almost ten years younger than me, you know. And unlike Jared, I haven't been with half the population of DC, and I would never push you into anything that you didn't want—and weren't ready—to do."

"What if it takes a long time?" I asked in a small voice.

"Then I'll wait." He smiled at me.

"I'm afraid of losing a part of me. Even worse, I'm afraid that I already lost part of me, and I can't get it back and give it to you." I now bit my lip so hard that I drew blood. "You shouldn't be with me."

"Anabel, I'm going to tell you something that I don't like to share, okay?" I nodded, and he went on. "You know I used to be Secret Service."

"Yes, but you left." I didn't see what this had to do with anything.

He leaned in. "Well, don't you want to know why?"

I frowned. "I guess."

"I was in a relationship with my boss for six years." He looked away from me.

"Wow," I commented. "That's a long time."

"It's a very long time to be in a dead end relationship." He grimaced. "This isn't something I'm proud of, Anabel. She was separated from her husband, but she and I both knew that in the end she would go back to him."

I nodded, digesting this. "So why did you stay with her?"

He shrugged. "I loved her, I guess. I thought she and I were meant for each other, but we weren't. In the end, it was always him for her." He looked at me sideways. "But she's the only person I've been with."

"When did it end?" I asked.

"Two years ago."

"Who ended it?"

"She did," he said. "So when it was over I had to quit my job. Sam had always liked me, so he kept me around."

"So wait, you haven't slept with anyone in two years?" I was shocked. "Wow."

"It hurt me a lot," he admitted. "So I stayed away from women. I didn't think there was anything for me beyond my relationship with Rachel." He smiled. "I didn't think I'd meet someone like you."

"Why do you love me?" I asked. If he could answer that, then we might have a shot.

He considered. "Because I can't stand the idea of living without you."

Wow. "That was good."

"I've waited two years for you, Anabel."

"So I guess that's proof you can hold out a little," I mused.

"Do you believe me now? Do you think this can work?"

I considered. "You aren't going to run away when I have the baby?"

"I promise I won't," he said, the picture of sincerity.

"Then I guess there's nothing left to do but this," I said, and kissed him.

He grinned when we broke apart. "Ready to face the world?"

"No," I admitted. "No. Just stay with me?" I pleaded.

"Always, if you want me to," he responded, pulling me into his arms. We lay back against the pillows, neither of us speaking, but both of us knowing we'd have to exit our haven at some point.

Later we emerged from my bedroom and walked down the stairs, my arm around his waist and his around my shoulders. "Is anybody here?" I called.

"Anabel?" I heard a girlish voice say. Carrie popped around the corner. "Oh my gosh, it is you!"

"Hi sweetie," I greeted her. "Is anyone else here?"

"Let me get my mom," she said, and then Charlotte came racing toward me and enveloped me in a hug.

"Anabel dear!" She proclaimed. "It's so good to see you!"

"Thanks," I said, hugging her back. "I'm sorry it took me so long. Thank you for all of the food you made for me."

"It was my pleasure," she beamed.

I turned to Matt. "I guess I should let everyone know I'm not a mute anymore, huh?"

"Are you ready for that?" He looked anxious.

I kissed him on the cheek, and grinned as Charlotte squealed. "As long as you're with me," I said.

He handed me my phone, and as I called Jared I heard Charlotte say in a none-too-quiet whisper, "You're back together, aren't you?"

"Charlotte," said Matt, "you ask too many questions."

I giggled, and then suddenly heard, "Anabel?"

"Hey Jared," I tried to sound relaxed. "I've decided being a mime was too hard."

He ignored my attempt at humor. "Are you okay?"

"I am, I'm much better now," I assured him. "Can you come over?"

"I'm on my way."

I managed to collect him, Meghan, and my brother. Meghan arrived first and practically assaulted me. "Oh Anabel!" she cried, wiping away tears.

"Meghan," I said, astounded at her display of emotion, "what are you doing?"

"I'm so happy to see you!" she said, taking me in. "My goodness, you're pregnant."

"She's coming early," I said absently. "I won't have to endure this for too much longer."

"So are you done with your breakdown?" she asked, linking her arm through mine.

"I think so," I responded. "How's Kevin?"

Meghan's face lit up. "He's good. He'll be thrilled you're talking again."

We sat down on the couch and she took my hands. "Jared's been taking this really hard."

"I'm sure." I looked down. "I'm sorry. I just couldn't deal with everything."

"Princess, no one blames you, okay? But I'm glad you're talking now, because your baby shower is next week, and I didn't think the whole silent thing was going to go over well."

"Oh no, are we still doing that?" I looked at Matt. "We should've just stayed in my room until it was over."

Meghan's eyes narrowed. "What do you mean—ooh," she gasped. Then she smiled knowingly at the two of us. "I get it."

"You get nothing," I protested, but was cut off by the arrival of my brother.

He looked like he had aged a great deal in the past two weeks. I could swear that his hair had taken on more gray strands. He stood in the entryway and quietly said, "I'm so sorry, Annie."

"It's okay," I smiled at him. "But look, I need you to come over and hug me, because it's gotten much harder for me to move myself around."

Meghan left the couch and Sam came to me and drew me into a tight embrace. "I'm so glad you're okay," he said in my ear.

"I'm sorry about what happened with Alexis," I whispered.

He laughed bitterly. "She's not. She maintains she would've killed you if she could have."

"Well, at least I won't have to send her a Christmas card this year."

"I can't believe you're taking this so lightly," he began.

"I'm not," I said in a more serious tone. "But I'm trying to make you feel a little better." I kissed him on the cheek. "I love you, you know."

"I love you, too," he said. "I'm glad you're talking again."

"You know what I'm glad about? We don't have to go to those wretched hearings anymore," I commented, sending Matt a smile.

My brother kissed the top of my head and stood up. "I can't stay, Annie, I'm sorry," he apologized. "I have to get home to my kids."

"Oh, are they here?"

"Yes, we flew them down last week." He frowned. "They needed me."

"Well of course they did," I replied. "Go be with them. We'll talk later."

He turned to leave, and then looked at Matt. "Anything I should know about?"

I groaned. "You are so annoying. Mind your own business."

And then my brother gave me a smile, a real smile. "I know what that means. Good. Bye."

"Goodbye," I muttered, meeting Matt's eyes.

Meghan came back over and sat down with me. "You've really kind of exploded, haven't you?"

"Thank you, Meghan," I tried to maintain politeness.

"Well, it's just before, you sort of looked pregnant, but now there's really no question, and—"

"I said thank you, Meghan," I raised my voice a little.

She patted my arm. "Well, you still look lovely," she began.

"No, I think the term 'exploded' sums it up." I frowned. "Where is Jared?"

"He just pulled up," noted Matt. "That car is ridiculous."

Meghan rolled her eyes. "Tell me about it."

"I think we should give them some space, Meghan," Matt suggested. "Will you come with me to the library?"

I frowned at him, but Meghan nodded and they quickly exited, leaving me alone to answer the doorbell.

I walked to the door and pulled it open, and found myself face to face with Jared.

"Hi," I managed, suddenly feeling a little shy.

"Anabel," he said. "Anabel." But he was struggling.

"I know," I attempted to keep my voice light. "As your sister so eloquently put it, I have exploded."

"You look beautiful," he returned.

I shook my head. "Don't lie. Come on in."

I stepped back and he walked in, and we walked back over to the couch and sat down. Oh, this was awkward. "I don't know what to say," I admitted.

"There's a first," he cracked, but there was no mirth in his eyes.

I touched his arm. "Jared. It's okay, you know."

"It's not okay," he spat, losing his cool. "Anabel, if I hadn't gotten back when I did, if I hadn't stopped Alexis, you and Emma would both be dead. How am I supposed to live with that?"

I raised my eyes to the ceiling, searching for answers. "I guess you just need to remember that you did get back in time and you rescued me once more. With your tongue, no less."

He was trying hard not to laugh at that one. "Baby, I feel horrible."

"I know you do. And I'm sorry it's taken me so long to talk to you," I told him. "But seeing you with Alexis really did a number on me. Plus remembering everything took a lot out of me, too."

"It was just a stupid attraction. I never let it get anywhere," he began.

"I know," I reassured him. "I know because I watched her face once you pulled away from her. But watching that really made me realize that you and I are best off as friends."

He was silent for a moment, and then said, "I guess I should be grateful that you still want to be friends."

"Well, we have a baby to raise, and I don't have time to do it all myself," I informed him. "I was reading a baby book and apparently initial baby poop is disgusting, so I expect you to be the one who deals with that."

He laughed. "I guess that's fair."

I searched for words. "Jared…I guess I kind of love you." Then I hesitated.

"But not like you love him," he finished for me. "I know. I can see it in your eyes."

"You need to be with someone who wants you like Alexis does." I looked at him. "I was sort of afraid the two of you were going to go at it right then and there."

"I did what I had to," he began.

"I know," I told him. "But what you and I had never came close to that." I whispered in his ear, "That was hot, Jared."

He pulled me into a hug, and I leaned against him, taking in his smell, his strength, and I relaxed. It was easy for me to be close to him like this, I realized. For once, I felt comfortable with Jared.

And that was good.

Matt and Meghan decided to make their reappearance then, and Meghan's eyes were sparkling. "I know something you don't know," she taunted me, and then planted a kiss on her brother's cheek.

I looked at Jared. "What happened to your sister? I miss morose and serious Meghan."

Jared shook his head. "It's this being in love garbage. She's intolerable."

Matt and Meghan exchanged a look, and then she said, "Jared, we have to go, we're picking up Crystal from the airport in half an hour."

"Crystal's here?" I asked.

Meghan nodded. "Yeah, she decided that she wanted to come meet you. She was convinced that she was the one who could get you to talk."

"She hadn't counted on Matt," said Jared, almost masking the sourness. "Do you mind if I leave my car here? I'll come by tomorrow to check on you."

I nodded, and he kissed me on the cheek. Meghan hugged me again, and they left.

Matt sat down next to me, and I leaned against him. "I'm glad that's over with."

"Other people want to see you," he began.

"I can't see Marilyn, Matt. It hurts too much." The thought of dealing with her made me ill.

"She says she knew nothing."

"I know," I said. "I read the papers. But I'm not ready for that yet."

He nodded, and slid his arm around me. "My dad also wants to come visit you."

"That's fine." I felt pleased. "I kind of miss Geoff."

"We also will need to set up an interview with the press." I could hear the gears turning in his head, and I pulled his face to mine and kissed him. He pulled away. "What was that for?"

"I don't want to think about that stuff right now," I smiled at him. "I want to talk about more pleasant things."

"Like what?"

"Like what we're going to do for my first holidays off of Caereon."

"Well, you can come with me to Thanksgiving at my parents' house," he began. "I already agreed to come, so we're sort of stuck on that end."

I raised an eyebrow. "And how will Clara take that?"

"Probably about as well as can be expected," he admitted. "We can have Christmas here, as I'm guessing you won't want to move around too much at that point."

"I want you to stay here," I began.

"It's just as well. The lease on my apartment is up at the end of the month anyway."

"Well I guess that's settled, then." Then I smiled. "You know, I've been meaning to ask you, where did you get those books?"

"The ones I read to you?" A look darted across his face then, and I could've sworn Matt looked almost devious.

"The Alice one is almost exactly like one that I used to have."

"No it's not," he said, a little too lightly.

"Yes, it is. I think I know my own books, Matt," I stated, offended.

"Clearly you don't," he replied. "You didn't recognize your own copy."

I was stunned. "My own copy?"

"I managed to get a friend who owed me a favor to get some of your books sent over," he told me. "Come on."

He helped me up from the couch and led me into my library, where I saw a box laying in the center of the room. I could hardly believe it, and I squatted down and began sorting through. There they were: A Christmas Carol. Sense and Sensibility. The Complete Works of William Shakespeare. The Harry Potter series, and—

"Ah, Lolita," I said, gently running my fingers down the spine. "One of my favorites."

"I can't believe your dad let you read that one," he commented. "By the way, I figured it out. That's where your name came from."

I grinned. "You're too smart for your own good." I flipped it open. "I always felt sorry for Lolita. Humbert's agony is what we have to deal with, but I wonder what the story would have been like if it had been told from her perspective."

"What do you mean?"

"Well, especially now, I understand her. She put on a show, but at the heart of it, she was just a messed-up kid," I lamented, and I wasn't really sure who I was talking about at that point.

Matt of course picked up on that right away. "You're not messed up, honey. You've done well," he said, helping me up.

I leaned into him. "So what now?"

"I think," he said slowly, "we should go back upstairs and finish making up for lost time."

"Oh yeah?" I asked. "And how's that?"

"Well, I'll read to you some more, of course," he said, businesslike.

"Is that what they're calling it these days?" I asked innocently, as we made for the stairs.

"You're terrible," he said, fighting a grin.

"You adore me for it," I replied.

"That I do," he returned. "That I do, Anabel."

Chapter 46—Jared

On the day Emma was born, Anabel woke me up by poking my arm. I had been camped out on her couch for the past week, since she had been swearing up and down that Emma was coming early. It was two in the morning and she said, "Hey, so...my water broke."

Those words sunk in and I sprang to attention. "Are you serious?"

"Quite," she said. "Totally ruined that carpet." Anabel started to fidget.

"But you're early, isn't that bad?"

"I'm 37 weeks," she replied. "Would have been 38 tomorrow. Emma's full term, there's nothing to be done now." She grinned. "Told you she was coming early."

"So what do you want to do? Are you having contractions?"

"No," she sighed. "I'm not, which sucks. I called Kevin and he's on his way over, but I highly suspect we're going to have to go to the hospital."

"What does all of this mean?"

She grunted and sat down next to me. "Well, if I don't start contracting on my own soon, they're going to have to give me some medication to make me do it. And I'm not too thrilled with that idea." Anabel had decided she wanted an all-natural childbirth, and had forced me to attend classes with her. I had done it because she wanted me to, but I had my doubts about the whole thing.

I patted her arm. "It'll be okay, Anabel."

She nodded. "I think we're in for a long day, Jared." She smiled. "I'm going to go wake up Matt. He may as well join the party."

By the time Kevin and my sister arrived, Anabel had experienced exactly one contraction and was getting more frustrated. Matt, Charlotte, Phil, and Carrie were all staring at Anabel with a mixture of fascination and fear, and the moment Kevin showed up she began flipping out. "I don't want Pitocin," she warned him.

"Fine," agreed Kevin. "Then get your labor started in the next ten hours, and we won't use Pitocin."

"Ten hours?" she whispered.

"Look, this is the way it is. I'll give you twelve hours from the time your water breaks, but that's it. I'm sorry," he said brusquely, "but you have to let me do my job."

She then sighed and put her head in her hands. "Okay."

I stroked her back. "Hey."

"What?" she asked through her fingers.

"We're going to have this baby today, Anabel. It'll be good."

"There's something I should've told you..." she began.

"I know," I cut her off.

She looked surprised. "You know?"

I nodded. "I know why you didn't tell me. It's okay."

"Oh, Jared," she cried, beginning to tear up. Then she stopped. "That's another one," she said, grabbing her belly.

"Great," Kevin said. "That's two contractions in two hours. I need you to get them to at least five minutes apart by 2 p.m."

She glared at him. "We really need to work on your bedside manner."

That was when Sam arrived. "Hey," he said, coming and giving her a hug. "Are you okay?"

But Anabel was still glaring at Kevin. "How exactly do you propose we get this going?"

"Well, you could try walking around, go up and down the stairs..." he gestured. "Stay active, Anabel. Sitting around like this isn't doing you any good."

She got up and growled at Meghan, "I really don't know what you see in him," and flounced off.

Matt got up to follow her, but then stopped and walked over to Kevin. "Is she going to die?" he asked, point blank.

Kevin sighed. "I hope not. Chances are good that she won't. But it's not 100 percent, just like it isn't with any birth."

Matt nodded. "When do you think we should leave for the hospital?"

"Preferably, when her contractions hit five minutes. But if they don't, well..." He shook his head. "She's going to have to have Pitocin and she's going to be pissed about it. Her water broke, and there's nothing I can do about that—I have to get her labor going after twelve hours or she's at risk for infection."

"Pitocin does what exactly?"

"It's a synthetic hormone that will make her uterus contract. It's quite painful, especially if your water has broken." He paused. "Look, she can move around all she wants, and that might help her, but I don't think she's going to get anywhere fast." He hesitated. "When your water breaks, you want to be having contractions. The fact that she's not tells me that she's going to have a rough time getting the baby out. And since I told her she didn't have to have a Caesarean anymore, she's going to be stubborn about the whole thing."

Kevin was right on both counts. At two p.m. we arrived at Reston Hospital and they hooked Anabel up to a machine to give her the medication, and she was not happy. It also didn't help that the nurse had to stick her about six times to get the IV in. Her bruised arms did nothing to improve her mindset, leaving Anabel looking for someone to blame. She was shooting angry glares at everyone and finally said that she wanted everyone besides me and Matt to leave.

"Baby, you need to relax," I told her.

"How can I?" she spat. "I shouldn't be in bed. That's not a good thing. I'm trapped here, and if I want to freaking urinate I have to be unstrapped from all of this."

"Anabel, you made me attend almost twenty hours of those natural childbirth classes. The one thing they told you to do was relax. You've got to do that, or it's going to be even harder for you."

She looked surprised. "I had no idea you actually were paying attention."

"I was," I retorted. "Now, what do you want? Want me to sneak you some crackers?"

She smiled a little. "Jared, I'm scared," she admitted.

"I know." I took her hand. "I am, too. Matt hasn't said anything in the last hour, so I'm guessing he's in the same boat."

Matt looked up, and wordlessly nodded.

"But you can do this, Anabel. I know you can."

She took a deep breath. "Okay," she muttered. "Okay. Now unhook me from all this crap. I have to pee."

The Pitocin worked quickly, and Anabel's dilation went from three centimeters to nine in about two hours. Unfortunately, she was in a great deal of pain and there wasn't much we could do to help her. Matt and I assisted her all we could, helping her change positions, helping her to the bathroom, helping her move around. But nothing seemed to relieve her, and she was absolutely miserable—the baby was facing the wrong way, and Anabel was having back labor, so as the contractions got stronger, the amount of pain she experienced intensified. As did her language—I heard a lot of words come out of her mouth that I had never heard her say before, half of which I was surprised she even knew.

"Jared," she said, after a particularly hard contraction, "I hate you so much."

"I know, baby," I told her.

"If I survive this, I'm going to kill you," she proclaimed, and then groaned as the next one began.

"Good girl," I replied. "Save your brother and Matt the trouble."

She breathed through the contraction and when it was over started frantically grabbing at things. "What are you doing?" asked Matt.

"Looking for something to throw at him," she snapped. "Oh, for crying out loud," she moaned, staring at the printout which showed another one beginning. "They're right on top of each other. Where is my doctor?" she screamed at a nurse. The poor nurse went in search of Kevin, and Anabel braced herself for the next contraction.

"If I die," she begged Matt, "promise me you'll help raise Emma." She jerked a thumb toward me. "I can only imagine what she'll turn out like with just him."

"Of course, sweetheart, but you're not going to die," he reassured her, stroking her arm. He was interrupted by another slew of profanities as she pulled her arm back and gripped the bed rails.

"I want the epidural," she demanded.

"Anabel, you're so close," Matt pointed out. "By the time they give it to you, you could have the baby. This is what you wanted, remember?" He tried to take her hand but she snatched it away.

Kevin entered the room. "How are we doing?"

"I don't want a baby anymore," she wailed.

He laughed. "Oh, stop being such a drama queen. This will be over soon enough."

"You're so mean," she said. "Next time, I'm getting a woman doctor." Then she froze. "There's another one."

After it was over, Kevin checked her. "Annie, you're ten centimeters, and the baby's engaged...you managed to turn her, so good work."

"What does that mean?" Anabel was panting.

"Well, it's time to push."

"Are you kidding me?" she screamed.

"Calm down, Anabel," he soothed her. "Just give us a push. Next contraction. It might make your pain better."

"It's coming!" she cried, and then she started pushing. Everyone was counting and she managed to push five times per contraction.

"Don't you need to rest?" asked Matt, anxious.

"So help me, I'm getting this baby out," she gasped.

"She's crowning!" called the nurse. She turned to Anabel. "Do you want to touch the head?"

"NO!" she screamed. "I want her out, NOW!" Then she moaned. "I'm getting her out. This contraction. So help me." So she started pushing again. And pushing. And pushing...and I watched in absolute amazement as our little girl came out, screaming her head off.

Even covered in what Anabel had earlier referred to as "baby goop," she was the most beautiful creature I had ever seen. Kevin set her on Anabel's stomach and she reached forward to touch her. "Hey baby," she whispered. "Hey Emma."

"You did so well, Anabel," Kevin said, as the nurse suctioned Emma's nose as our baby girl screamed. "So well. I'm so proud of you."

"You really did, honey," Matt said, kissing her cheek.

Anabel beamed at Emma, stroking her face and letting the baby grasp her finger. "Jared?" she said.

"Yes, baby?" I whispered.

"She looks just like you," she smiled.

"She's gorgeous," I replied.

She looked at Matt. "See? Even now, he's such a narcissist—ohh," she said. Her face turned ghostly white, and the nurse picked up the baby as Kevin tensed. She looked like she was trying to say something, but she couldn't. And then Anabel's eyes rolled back in her head.

"Her uterus inverted," said Kevin. "Hang on, Anabel."

"Her heart rate is dropping," called a nurse.

"What's going on?" asked Matt.

"I need you two out. Now," ordered Kevin, and Matt and I found ourselves out in the hallway.

Sam and Meghan rushed over to us. "What's happening? Is the baby okay?"

I couldn't say anything, so Matt told him, "I think Emma's fine, but something's wrong with Anabel."

The nurse then wheeled Emma out on her warmer. "Do you want to hold her, Daddy?" she asked me. Meghan and Sam went to look at her, and the little girl stared at them, in a miniature imitation of Anabel's usual gaze.

"What's happening with Anabel?" I asked.

The nurse pursed her lips together. "I shouldn't be explaining this, but she has an inverted uterus, and it looks like the placenta tore part of it. She's bleeding a lot."

"What does that mean?" I asked helplessly.

"It means that Dr. Miller is doing all he can," she assured me.

"I can't hold her right now," I told her, sinking into the chair. Meghan clucked her tongue, but I couldn't do it.

The nurse nodded. "I'll put her in the nursery for now. You can come collect her when you're feeling up to it."

Kevin came out. "Matt?"

"Yeah?" He sprung to his feet.

"You might want to be with her." He sounded grave.

Matt went into the room, leaving Meghan, Sam, and I sitting there in absolute silence.

"This isn't happening," Meghan whispered.

Sam's face was white. "This is all your fault," he barked at me.

"I know," I retorted. Then I stood up and walked down the hall.

I walked and walked, up and down the halls of the maternity ward, unable to think. None of what the nurse had said had really registered with me, but I had learned one thing from childbirth class: what had happened to Anabel could easily be fatal.

I looked at my hospital band and tried to pull myself together. When she got through this (and I had to tell myself that she would), Anabel would be furious at me for leaving our little girl to fend for herself. So I made my way to the postpartum ward and the nursery and knocked on the door.

A surly looking nurse answered, and I held out my wristband. "I'm here for my daughter." That sounded weird.

She scanned it, and then nodded and wheeled out Emma. "You can go to room 16, that's the room reserved for Martin," she announced, looking at her clipboard. "I'll send someone in for you to explain how everything works."

I wheeled Emma in her little bassinet to room 16, which was small, but had plenty of room for us. I lifted the tiny girl out of her bassinet and watched as she slept on peacefully, which I hoped she would keep doing. It wasn't like her mother was there to comfort her.

"Anabel," I muttered, watching Emma's eyelids flutter. "You can't leave me alone with her. You just can't." What had I done to Anabel? First I raped her, then I screwed with her head, and then right when we got to a place where we were almost okay with each other, I went and kissed Alexis. To top it all off, thanks to me, she was now fighting to stay alive.

I shook my head, trying to be calm, and studied Emma. Anabel had been right: she did look a lot like me, although she had gotten her mother's nose. The chin and cheeks were mine, but on Emma they looked softer and sweeter. Her dark hair was tucked under her little pink hat, and her little mouth opened and let out a sigh now and then. Even though I hadn't been thrilled with the name, I had to admit, it suited her. I couldn't get over her, and I don't know how long I stared at her until I heard a voice say, "So here you are."

I looked up and saw Sam. The color had returned to his face, but he looked tired. "Sam," I began, searching for words. Not only had I ruined his marriage, but his sister's life was hanging in the balance.

So I was surprised to have him sit down next to me and say, "You okay?"

Incredible. "No, Sam, I'm not."

"Jared, I owe you an apology."

"What are you talking about?" I focused on Emma.

"No, I'm serious. Look at you, you're a mess. If nothing else, I know you love my sister. So I just wanted to tell you I'm sorry, I know you didn't hurt her on purpose."

I nodded. "Fat lot of good it does us now. She could die, Sam, and it would be all my fault."

"Oh no, she has assured me she's not going to die."

"Come again?"

Sam sighed. "She just woke up, Jared. The first words out of her mouth were, 'where's Jared,' and the second ones were, 'Look Sam, if you don't make up with him, I'm not going to let you see your niece.'"

"Are you serious?"

He nodded. "Bossy little thing, huh?"

I wasn't sure, but I had a feeling that we were friends again. Relieved, I asked, "Where is she now?"

"They're bringing her up here." He smiled at Emma. "So can I hold her?"

I handed him the baby, and a few minutes later the nurse wheeled her in, followed by Matt who was carrying all of her stuff. "Jared!"

I was immediately at her side. "You need to knock this off, Anabel."

"The whole trying to die thing? Yeah, I know." She beamed. "I want to hold my baby now, please."

"After we get you into your bed, Miss Martin." The nurse sounded exasperated.

Matt set her stuff down, and then helped her from the wheelchair into the bed. "The baby, Sam," she said, holding out her arms.

So Sam handed her Emma, and Emma opened her wide eyes and contemplated Anabel for a minute. "Hello, beautiful child," she crooned. "Hello, my Emma." She gently unwrapped Emma from the tight swaddle and pulled her close to her. "I'm sorry it took me so long to get to you, my only child," she murmured.

"Oh, you can always endure this torture again," I assured her, relieved she was alright.

She and Matt exchanged a look. "I can't, Jared," Anabel said.

"What do you mean?"

She gently guided Emma to try and nurse her. "Well, get this. I just found out that your baby destroyed my uterus."

I stared at her. "What?"

"When I started to bleed out, they had to do emergency surgery and I can no longer have kids."

"You seem awfully happy about this."

She laughed. "Part of it's the painkillers, but the other part is, Jared, I just gave birth. I have no interest in doing that ever again."

"You say that now..."

"Oh no," she affirmed. "I'm serious. I just want the one." She smiled up at me. "She's beautiful, isn't she?"

"Gorgeous. Best looking baby in the nursery. All the other ones are envious."

"As they should be," she smiled. "I'm glad to hear it."

"Come on, Sam," said Matt. He kissed Anabel on the cheek and the two of them left.

"And so it's just us," I said, sitting next to her.

"I guess we should let her have your last name. I like it better than mine," she said thoughtfully.

"I'm so sorry, Anabel. It seems like everything I do to you just—"

"Hey," she said. "It's okay, Jared. I'm okay, Emma's okay, and you and I are okay. Let's just bask in this "okayness," shall we?"

I took her hand, and she sighed. "I told you she was coming early. Why didn't anyone believe me?"

"I promise to listen better next time."

She grinned. "Well, there won't be a next time." She shook her head. "It's just as well. This child has both of our genes. She's probably going to be wreaking havoc before she can crawl." Emma sighed and had fallen asleep, and Anabel pulled the baby close to her.

It was clearly time for a change of subject. "I got you a push present," I told her.

Her face lit up. "And what's that?"

I handed her the keys. "It's not a minivan. It's an SUV. I figured that was a good compromise. The car seat's in it and everything."

She looked excited by this news. "So does this mean you'll teach me to drive?"

"Preferably without Emma in the car."

"You're already assuming I'm going to be a terrible driver?" she asked, pretending to be mad.

"I think you'll be as good at it as you are everything else." I kissed her hand. "You are amazing, Anabel."

"I know I said a lot of things while I was in labor," she began.

"Where did you learn how to talk like that?"

"Oh, shush," she smiled again. "Anyway I just wanted to let you know I'm not going to kill you. I need you to change diapers."

"You are truly generous," I told her. "Do you want me to go get Matt?"

"No," she said. "This is our moment. Let's share it, okay?"

And we did.

About the Author

AMANDA ROMINE LYNCH is a writer and blogger who grew up in Florida. After graduating with her degree in English from the University of Florida (Go Gators!), she and her husband moved to the "Great North" of Virginia, and they haven't looked back (except when it snows). She is the Eco-Friendly/Green Living Contributor at Prime Parents Club and blogs about her days raising two (soon to be three) kids and attempting to be friendly toward the environment in a world of disposable diapers over at her personal blog, The Semi-Organic Mom.

Made in the USA
Charleston, SC
13 February 2013